BOMBS AWEIGH

ON TO VIETNAM

WALTER F. CURRAN

This book is a work of fiction. Names, characters, places and incidents are the product of the author's imagination or are used fictitiously. Any resemblance to actual events, locales or persons, living or dead, is coincidental.

CONTENTS

PRAISE FOR *BOMBS AWEIGH-ON TO VIETNAM*

Set in the era of the Vietnam War, *Bombs Aweigh-On to Vietnam* is a rip-roaring sea-going adventure, whose surprises and pleasures come at you like unexpected waves.

William Connolly, a young sailor fresh out of the Merchant Marines academy, is hired as third mate on a cargo ship that's transporting bombs and weapons to Vietnam. But to his disgust and alarm, it turns out that the crew is loaded with drunks and druggies, as well as a couple of borderline psychotics. When chaos inevitably ensues, the ship's desperate captain must turn to the green, inexperienced William as one of the few he can trust to restore order. Confronting violent and unpredictable crew members at every turn, William is forced to assume greater responsibilities—and face greater consequences—than he ever imagined.

The novel is loaded with the sort of authentic shipboard detail only an experienced veteran of the Merchant Marines could supply. Author Walter Curran is a naturally gifted storyteller, and he turns that talent and his sailing experience to re-creating both the period and the colorful ambiance of daily life on a cargo vessel. Among the passages most vividly and palpably realized was his dramatic depiction of sailing through a raging typhoon. Curran also has an ear finely tuned for dialogue, and he portrayed his characters in deft, memorable strokes.

As much a coming-of-age chronicle as an exciting nautical adventure, Bombs Aweigh is a thoroughly engaging novel—the kind of tale Jack London wrote. Mr. Curran promises a sequel, and I eagerly await William Connolly's further exploits.

Robert Bidinotto - Author of *HUNTER,* #1 Bestselling Amazon Kindle Thriller

Walter Curran has presented us with the third installment of the coming of age story of William Connolly with Bombs Aweigh. Beginning with the clever double-entendre of the title, he lets us accompany our young hero on yet another voyage, first down the East Coast to take on cargo of bombs, bullets, and other necessities of the war in Vietnam, a stop on Florida to take on drunks and druggie crewmen who prove more deadly and dangerous than the cargo of weapons of war in the ship's hold. Curran holds our interest with considerable knowledge of the inner workings of a Merchant Marine vessel as it traverses the Panama Canal then the broad expanse of the Pacific. This is not a pleasure cruise, but a voyage of unparalleled danger with fights, murder and a hurricane. This is the best of the Mariner series and hopefully not the last we'll see of Mr. Connolly.

William J. Kennedy-author of *First Kill*, *Morally Gray* and *The Pentagon Years*

For those who do not know much about the Vietnam War and enjoy thrillers, Bombs Aweigh is a must read. It explores a little-known aspect of the war, the logistics of transporting weapons and support equipment from the U.S. to Vietnam. The book stresses the discipline the officers of the ship had to impose to control the often drunken and drug-crazed crew, during a period when Merchant Marine resources were strained. Highly recommended.

Frank Hopkins-award winning author of *Abandoned Homes: Vietnam Revenge Murders.*

It's the Vietnam War era and one would think being a merchant marine transporting arms to Vietnam would be safer than being a marine on the battlefield, but for William Connolly his life is at risk every day. Bombs Aweigh puts you in Connolly's shoes as he navigates through a cutthroat crew of boozers and druggies trying to keep fire axes and knives where they belong. But it's not all mayhem. Curran provides a rich experience of what it was like to man a cargo ship in the days before container ships. You can practically smell the salt air.

Jackson Coppley-Author of *The Code Hunter—A Nicholas Foxe Adventure*

Walter Curran's capstone to his Young Mariner trilogy, Bombs Aweigh, is as smooth and exhilarating a trip as the earlier books. Curran captures all your senses, including the one for adventure, as he takes us on a high-tension voyage filed with a lethal combination of drugs, booze, mutiny—and miles to go before landfall.

Rick Ollerman, author *Mad Dog Barked*

OTHER WORKS BY WALTER F. CURRAN

YOUNG MARINER SERIES

Young Mariner

On to Africa

SHORT STORIES

Non-Fiction

The Tribes of Port Baltimore-Maryland Writer's Association 2019 Anthology

The Long Weekend-Eastern Shore Writers Association, Bay to Ocean 2018

Fiction

Fated Course-ESWA, Bay to Ocean 2018 Anthology

Old Curbside-Rehoboth Beach Writer's Guild-2019 Anthology

The Window-Rehoboth Beach Writer's Guild, 2019 Anthology

A Conversation-ESWA, Bay to Ocean 2019 Anthology

POETRY

Slices of Life-Cerebral spasms of the soul

ACKNOWLEDGEMENTS

Bombs Aweigh-On to Vietnam is my third novel following the exploits of William Connolly, merchant mariner as he continues to explore new countries and encounter, interesting and dangerous people and delves deeper into his psyche and soul, discovering who he really is.

Once again, grateful thanks to my wife Marie who leaves me undisturbed for hours on end to pursue my writing and research, occasionally checking for a pulse.

Thanks to the many members of the Maryland Writer's Association and Eastern Shore Writer's Association who are supportive in my endeavors and a special thanks to the Rehoboth Beach Writers Group, led by the inestimable Marybeth Fischer for what they and she do to help writers of all levels.

The Gray Head Group (you know who you are) was invaluable in improving my work as we sat in our bi-weekly meetings gently crucifying each other.

Bombs Aweigh-On to Vietnam is a work of fiction but many of the elements of the book are taken from my experiences sailing as a deck officer.

Cover by Crystal Heidel.

It's all in your point of view. If you've never been outside your neighborhood, then the other side of town may as well be a different planet. Overcoming this stagnation, this alien outlook, and altering your point of view is the path to understanding in our world.

POINT OF VIEW

Often have I traveled, through lands both far and near

Each in turn an alien, fraught with angst and fear

Yet also each in turn have changed, as have my views of old

Once familiarity stamps its mark indelibly on mind and soul

As each has been revisited, in body or in mind

A mellowing occurs, dimming features, less defined

Once imminent images meld and fade, ne'er the same again

Yet somehow larger than before, more symbolic now than then

So be not quick to look and judge, or worse, not even see

The fullness of each sign and sight, as they were meant to be

For perchance, it might well be, true destiny of you and yours

By narrowed vision brushed aside, ne'er to regain rightful course.

*There are three sorts of people;
those who are alive, those who
are dead, and those who are at
sea.*

Anacharsis-6th Century BC

CHAPTER 1

It was the hearing to end all hearings, at least where my life is concerned. Monday, May 15, 1967, the day someone else would determine my future. Even though the crew had signed on in Jacksonville, Florida, the U.S. Coast Guard wanted to hear this one at its New York headquarters. Murder, suicide, stabbings, numerous fights, and one gunshot wound (my handiwork), guaranteed the hearing would be detailed, and for some, career-ending.

I hoped I wouldn't be one of the latter.

In the corridor outside the hearing room, six crew members of the *West Way III*, my ship, clustered at the far end of the first waiting area bench, two of them with legal representation. The captain and I sat at the far end of the second bench, together but separate, not talking. Outside, it was forty-five degrees and windy. All of us were wet from the rain squall that hit as we entered the building. The twenty-five miles per hour wind gust had inverted the cheap umbrella I held, so I'd left it in the gutter.

I sat waiting, head down, elbows on knees, and shivered, remembering the sight of the blood spreading over Joselito's shirt after I pulled the trigger—feeling the warm ooze of my own blood from my slashed arm. I remembered Smithfield appearing on the bridge, a fire ax in his hand, looking to bury it in someone's skull. I remembered the man standing on the railing trying to untangle the halyard, then, an instant later, gone.

Would someone have to pay for the violence, the chaos, the death? Would that someone be me? All this tore through my mind as we waited.

When the bailiff opened the door to the large hearing room, we entered. By deference or habit, the crew let the captain lead the way with me trailing him. They followed. Inside, the bailiff pointed to seats on the left side, behind the railing, and we sat—the captain and I in the front row, the others in two rows behind us.

There were possible criminal charges pending for at least three of us, but this was a civil procedure, solely for the purpose of determining whether we would retain our licenses and seamen's papers.

The presiding officer called the hearing to order and explained the process. He went on to state that it was rare to have a hearing with so many accused parties, but since all the charges were more or less related and all occurred on the same voyage, a general hearing would be held. If, after the opening session, the presiding officer decided it would be appropriate to split the proceedings into individual parts, that would be announced. He then read the list of charges against the individuals, including the captain and me.

The captain was called to the stand first. He gave his name, rank, and address, and the presiding officer recited the background of the voyage.

Thus, it began . . .

CHAPTER 2
Four months earlier

Monday, January 16, 1967, New York City

The sex was comforting. Strange thought for a twenty-two-year-old mariner after a three-day romp with Clara Simpson, a fifty-four-year-old, well-endowed, soon-to-be-divorced woman.

As I sat on the edge of the rumpled bed in the elegant room at the Warwick Hotel, I looked out the window at a bright, partly cloudy day, waiting for Clara to emerge from the bathroom.

I compared the smell and feel of Clara's middle-aged body with that of Meg—my young, lithe, sensuous, redheaded, incredibly sexy former lover. Former, because she chose South Africa over me. If Meg had chosen me, I would still be in New York, but alone, not with Clara or any other woman. I had resisted the advances of Clara and the captain's wife for most of the trip back from Africa, but the "Dear John" letter from Meg collapsed my paper-thin armor.

I thought back to the final week of my last trip on the *Mormacpride* and shuddered. I escaped from the *Mormacpride* by signing off. Captain Coltrain had killed his wife and thrown her overboard and gotten away with it. I'd left with a bag full of jewelry and gold coins with a dubious history, which I had stolen. They had been stolen from someone in Africa and put on board the 'Pride, entrusted to the captain, destined for delivery to Frankie, a local Mafia don in Brooklyn. The captain's wife took them from the captain's safe in a fit of petulance. I took them from her. If I hadn't taken them, she would have given them back to him and would probably still be alive.

For retribution against Captain Coltrain, and self-preservation, instead of keeping the jewels, I delivered them to Frankie, the self-same Mafia don, completing the circle of ownership. My relationship with Frankie is a long story. I told him how Captain Coltrain had screwed up the handling of the jewels and had murdered his wife. I was safe. The captain was dead. Frankie saw to that. The moral compass inside of me was spinning and true north wasn't to be found.

After seeing the hit-and-run body of Captain Coltrain in the gutter in Brooklyn, I felt comforting, therapeutic sex was exactly what the doctor ordered. The weekend with Clara calmed me down. Now, having showered and dressed before Clara awoke, and sitting on the edge of the bed in Clara's hotel room, I pondered my next step.

She emerged from the bathroom, hair still damp, smelling of Prell shampoo, bathrobe clinging to her ample curves She stretched, held a hand to her back, and smiled. "You wore me out William."

Smiling back, I said, "Just trying to help, ma'am."

"Oh, you did!" Stepping over, she leaned down and kissed my forehead, exuding overtones of hair spray, sex, and a tinge of Lady Manhattan, her favorite perfume.

"You really did." Sitting down next to me, she asked, "What are you going to do now?"

"Catch another ship. Jobs are easy to get now. As much as I like Moore-McCormack Lines, given what happened on the 'Pride, I think it's best I try another outfit to sail with."

"Will you be going back to Africa?" A not-so-subtle way to ask if I will try to retrieve my relationship with Meg.

"No. Meg made it clear in her letter she'll never leave South Africa, and I can't live in a country where apartheid is the law of the land. It's over."

"Too bad. I think you made a beautiful couple."

"So says the lady who tried to seduce me a week after Meg left the ship."

Laughing, she said, "You'll never understand women, William. We'll always try to reach out and comfort the lonely; it's part of our psyche. Besides, you didn't give in to my charms until after you received your 'Dear John' letter. That lets both of us off the hook."

Standing, Clara faced me, opened her robe and pirouetted. "Would you like a final farewell?" "Thank you, Clara, but I think it's time for me to leave." She smiled and nodded. "You're right. It's time."

Turning, she walked back into the bathroom, leaving me to grab my duffel and backpack and ease out the door. No "I'll call" or "See you later." A fitting end to a mutually beneficial short-term tryst.

CHAPTER 3

By 1100 hours, I was standing in the lobby of the Warwick Hotel. I lit a Marlboro, undecided whether to go to the Union Hall or check in at the Seamen's Church Institute. I opted for the SCI. The Warwick is on West Fifty-Fourth Street, midtown, and the SCI—a seedy, rundown, but cheap hotel for seagoing types—is at 25 South Street, down toward and east of The Battery. About five miles as the crow flies, a walkable distance; but since the crow didn't have to carry a duffel and backpack and I did, I took a cab.

The doorman called a cab then stood there stone-faced, looking for a tip. Normally, I was too cheap to pay someone a tip for just doing their job, especially when they looked like a third-world airline pilot with all gold stripes and gold-trimmed service cap. But, pay day was only three days ago, and I was feeling flush, so I gave him a dollar. After stowing my bags in the trunk and cursing after hitting my knee on the concrete raised planter at the edge of the curb, I settled into the back seat. Rubbing my knee, I opened the window, enjoying the unusually mild temperature—54 degrees, according to the thermometer beside the hotel entrance door.

The cab took off toward the Avenue of the Americas. Turning south onto the Avenue, he wove his way through traffic, the honk of horn and occasional glare being the parry and thrust of New York cabbies as they duel in the streets. Left on Forty-Sixth Street, right on Fifth Avenue, then left on Thirty-Fourth and he got on the FDR Drive south. The traffic wasn't too bad after the morning rush hour—in New York, always an oxymoron—and before the lunchtime sprawl of jaywalking pedestrians slowed the traffic. Fifteen minutes later, I stood on the sidewalk in front of the SCI and recalled my first visit here in June, prior to joining the *Mormacpride*.

No change. The same dingy, dusty walls, with well-cared-for religious artifacts. This was, after all, an establishment founded in faith and supported by several religious sects. The same gnomish bellhop led me to my room. The gnome carried the smaller backpack. Feeling sorry for him, I carried the larger duffel. The duffel was almost as big as he was. Passing the chapel, I noticed the six-foot-long and six-foot-high chalkboard, standing guard to everyone's conscience, and wafting chalk dust from the ledge at the bottom. It announced the same ad for Alcoholic Anonymous meetings as I'd seen before, this time with a little flair.

ALCOHOLIC ASSISTANCE BUREAU
Seamen's group of AA meeting Thursday nite. (Flatbush) group.
Give AA a fair trial for 90 days, and if you are not satisfied with the results we will reluctantly refund your misery.
THINK! AND DON'T DRINK!

They are serious about helping seamen stop drinking. The bar they have here is "boozeless." Every type of soft drink is available, but it's replete in every other aspect, including a brass foot rail. There's even a story about a young Irish lad who came in and asked for a beer. After four foaming ginger ales in mugs, the lad told the bartender, "No more now, it's off to bed for me or I won't get up in the morning," and he staggered out of the bar to the delight of all who watched.

They also have a post office where seafarers, the floating homeless, can set up a permanent mail address, and a luncheonette where they serve decent food for a fair price.

I gave the gnome a dollar. He was pleasant and did smile a lot, more than I can say for the Warwick doorman. Generosity was a trait I was acquiring, albeit reluctantly.

I lay down on the bed in my room, hardly more than a cell, four walls and a ceiling. One wall had a hole in it for a window, the opposite wall had a hole in it for a door. But for someone used to stingy shipboard accommodations, it was adequate, and more important, cheap. Listening to the symphony of clangs and groans coming from the radiator, I dared to replay in my head the events of the last trip.

As I pondered them, I wondered: Have I changed? Have events changed me, or have they rubbed away a veneer, exposing the real me? Who or what is the real me? Jewel thief? Accessory to murder or dumb city-kid still learning the ropes? Pensive for about forty minutes without coming to any conclusions, a sudden pang in my gut convinced me to change meditation positions, from the bed to the toilet bowl.

The door to the bathroom opened outwards because there was no room to open into the bathroom. Being alone, I left the door open, giving me freedom of posture. With a closed door, maintaining erect posture is critical when on the throne, since leaning forward put your forehead, or nose if yours is like mine, into dangerous proximity to the door.

With the pressing of the handle, my mental angst flushed away with the physical, lost in the sewage of Manhattan. Not a cure, a temporary cessation. There were many people adding more detritus than I to the sewer system, and I wondered if their success at dumping a load of their anxieties was as transient as mine.

The purging of bodily waste cleared the path for insight into my ideological wasteland, and I began to believe I hadn't changed so much as become aware of my innate self and moral limitations, inherent conflictions. A litany ran through my head.

I loved Meg and wanted to marry her, but not enough to live under apartheid. Not that the U.S. didn't have its own racial problems. In discussion with my past shipmate Greg, a black engineer from Baltimore, we had reached the same conclusion. The problems are real, the only difference being the U.S. government was trying to resolve them, whereas the South African government wanted to prolong the situation. Two tinderboxes, ready to catch fire.

I wanted to be true to the woman I loved, but raging hormones and the Dear John letter had won the battle.

I wanted to be law-abiding, but stole the jewels and subsequently cost Eunice her life.

I wanted to keep the jewels and get rich, but traded them off to exact revenge on the captain, partial payment for my culpability.

I want! I want! I want! Doesn't everybody? Sighing, I wondered if I should have kept half of the jewels. Would I have achieved the same outcome? Should I be despondent and miserable? I pondered before I papered. Is my moral compass the same as always or is it askew? Magnetic North versus true North. Unless you know the declination calibration, you end up a long way from where you want to be. Are things working out for me? If so, no harm, no foul.

A lot of questions but no answers.

I went down to the lobby, planning on calling home then checking in at the union hiring hall to see what was available. At the desk, I got a roll of quarters and walked to the payphone, wading through human flotsam, of which I was a part, representative of every country on earth. I waited in line behind four other seamen at the payphone. All four called overseas and had to be on tight budgets, because they talked fast.

I lent the last one three quarters as he fished in his pockets before he could finish the call. He spoke Norwegian, at least it sounded like Norwegian, so I assumed he called Norway. My limited exposure to the language started at Massachusetts Maritime Academy and expanded from meeting crews in bars throughout South America. The language has a distinctive sound.

In my upper-class year, our crew coach gave me a phrase to yell out at the start of the maritime day rowboat race. Besides all the other maritime schools, there was a crew from a Norwegian freighter. A good will type of thing. The coach said, "Just before the gun goes off, yell this out to the Norwegian crew. '*Du har en lasta bil av svenske henna muc!*'" This odd phrase stuck with me because of what ensued.

"What does it mean?" I asked, always suspicious and fearful of things I don't understand.

"It's a traditional way of saying good luck."

At the start line, we were right beside the Norwegian's. My timing was perfect. I finished the sentence as the gun went off and a roar went up from the Norwegians. We won. The Norwegians finished second. They weren't racing, they were chasing us. A rough translation of what I yelled; "Look at that boatload of Swedish chicken-shit." At the dock, our coach told their coach what he had done and offered to buy beer for the crew. All was forgiven.

I was next. Dropping in coins, I dialed home, and my sister Dotty answered. My oldest sister Betty lives with Ma, but Dotty was a rare visitor.

"Hey, kid," she said. Dotty never called me by name, always "kid." "How are you doing?"

"Hi, Dotty. I'm fine. What are you doing there? Shouldn't you be working?" Dotty had a good job as secretary to the general manager of the telephone company.

"My shift doesn't start for another hour," she replied.

"Shift? When did you start shift work? Aren't you a nine-to-fiver?"

"Not any more. I'm a lineman now, or rather line-woman. My boss even gave me a set of tools with pink handles when I passed the test." She laughed.

"That's great," I said, not knowing if it was or not, but happy that Dotty was happy. "Is Ma there?"

"Sure, hang on." She passed the phone to Ma.

"William, where are you calling from?" her cigarette-raspy voice always a treat for me. I pictured her sitting in her wingback chair by the front window of the apartment, spying on the world, Old Gold cigarette dangling from her lip.

"New York, Ma. I signed off the *'Pride* and I'm looking for a new ship."

"A new ship? Are you coming home at all?" Disappointment was clear in her tone. Behind her I heard Dotty talking. "Wait, wait a minute, Dotty wants to say something," and she handed the phone back to my sister.

"Hey, kid, I have a friend who works for a steamship company. I saw him last week, and he told me to have you call him if you're ever looking for work. You got a pen? I'll give you his name and number."

"Wait a minute," I pulled my pen out and wrote on the bottom of a page of the *Yellow Pages*, then tore it off and pocketed it. "Thanks, Dotty. How do you know this guy?"

She said, "It's a long story. I gotta go. Take care, kid." So much of Dotty's life was a mystery.

Ma came back on the line. We talked for a few more minutes, two quarter-dumps, then I said goodbye and hung up. No one was in line to call, so I phoned Dotty's friend, Jackson Palmer. She'd told me he was the Marine Superintendent for Westphalia Maritime Services Company, a tramp outfit that chartered old ships and re-chartered them to MSTS. MSTS is the acronym for Military Sealift Transportation Service, the arm of the government responsible for moving around the world weapons, cargo, and people, both military and civilian dependents.

"Westphalia," a strong, bass voice answered the phone.

"Hi, I'd like to talk to Jackson Palmer please."

"Who is calling?"

"My name is William Connolly. I'm calling about getting a berth as third mate on one of your ships."

"This is Jackson. Where did you get my name?"

"From Dotty Connolly."

A pause, then recognition, "Dotty, yeah. You're her kid brother, right?"

"Yes sir, I am."

"I got a ship going on charter to MSTS in New York in a few days. Can you get down here?"

"I'm already here, staying at the SCI."

"Great. Are you a member of the MM&P?"

"Yes, Local 88 here in New York."

"Even better. Go down to their hall this afternoon and bid on the third mate's job for the *SS West Way III*.

"Mr. Palmer, there's bound to be a lot of guys with more seniority than me at the hall."

"Don't worry. Just show up and bid when no one else takes the job."

This sounded strange, I thought, but said, "Okay, thank you," and hung up. Backing out of the telephone booth I bumped into someone.

"Sorry, pal, I—" and stopped. It was Greg Russell. Greg was one of the third engineers on the *'Pride*, a black man from Baltimore. We had become friends on the last trip and allies in our mutual dislike of the apartheid system.

"You trying to knock me over?" he said, grinning and reaching to shake hands.

"What are you doing here?" I asked.

"Just a minute, I have to hit the head. Watch my gear, will you? Be right back." And he jogged to the men's room, another monastic cell, hidden behind and past the check-in desk.

When he came out, we sat on one of the ancient settees in the lobby and talked.

"At the last minute, I decided to sign off," he said. "I didn't think I could stand another trip with Roy." Roy was the second engineer on the *'Pride*, a southern boy who failed to hide his racial prejudice behind ill-conceived attempts at humor.

"So, what are you doing?"

"Looking for a ship, like everybody else here," he said, waving his hand at the lobby.

I told him about my call to Jackson Palmer and the assurance from him I would get the job, regardless of my union seniority.

"Hey, it works the same in my union. Jobs are plentiful, so the senior guys wait for the good jobs. The companies are doing the union a favor, getting guys to fill in the less desirable berths. Do you know where the ship is heading?"

"No, but it's a military charter. The marine superintendent told me it was being chartered by the MSTS. Most likely, it's heading to the Pacific. Everything is going to Vietnam, it seems."

Greg stood. "I have to check in, then go to the union hall myself and see what's available. Good to see you, William." He paused. "Did you know Captain Coltrain was killed by a hit-and-run driver right outside the pier?"

"No," I said, distancing myself, "but given what we suspected of him and Eunice, maybe it's justice."

He looked at me oddly, then nodded. "Maybe it is," he said, and left.

Coming out of the SCI, I turned down South Street toward the Battery. At Whitehall Street, I turned right and continued into Broadway, past Bowling Green, and made a left on Morris Street. The usual New York morning crowd avoided eye contact, while my eyes roamed free of restraint, establishing me as an outsider. At Greenwich Street I turned back uptown, went past the Rector Street subway station, with its underground rumbling and occasional puffs of steam from the street-level vents, and turned left on Rector heading for the union hall.

Inside, the usual complement of old-timers sat off to the side playing cards, and a contingent of not-so-old-timers hung out, talking and smoking. They all eyed me when I walked in. It wasn't a friendly look. Was it New York "manners" or were they actually hostile? I couldn't tell. The hall had the faint odor of urine mixed in with body odors. The floor was littered with cigarette butts; ashtrays sat half empty on the table and ledges. I wondered when was the last time they cleaned the place.

I checked in with the dispatcher in the cage, lit a cigarette, and walked off to the corner, my back to the wall while I waited for the job call. I glared back at the occasional stare in my direction. Today, there were three off-shore jobs posted. When the dispatcher announced the calling of jobs, all the card-players lay down their cards, stood up, union cards in hand, and ambled to the front of the cage—Group A seniority. The first off-shore job posted, and no one took it. The same thing with the Group B seniority guys. They were all waiting for night mate jobs or coast-wise jobs. The other two off-shore jobs got the same treatment.

Five minutes before the window closed, I stepped up and took the third mate's job on the *SS West Way III*.

CHAPTER 4

Leaving the union hall, I walked back to the SCI, thrilled I had the job. Thinking of nothing but my next adventure, I was nearly clipped by a taxi while crossing Broadway at Morris Street. The blare of the horn and the glare of the driver harshly reminded me to pay attention. I was more alert the rest of the way. I walked into the crowded lobby and went straight to the payphone. Surprised there wasn't a line, with so many people there, I called Jackson Palmer to give him the news.

"What did I tell you, William? We're doing the union a favor getting them bodies to fill the slots. That's their job, and lately, they're not too good at it."

"I appreciate the opportunity, Mr. Palmer."

"Glad to have you. MMA grads have a good reputation in the industry. Here's an opportunity to continue the tradition."

"I'll do my best, sir."

"Okay. The ship is due at the Military Ocean Terminal in Bayonne on Wednesday. Check in before noon."

Hanging up, I took a deep breath, stepped back from the phone. and did it again, this time harder than before. I rammed into Greg Russell.

"Damn, William," he said. "This is becoming a habit, you trying to knock me over." Then he smiled.

"Sorry, Greg. My mind was elsewhere."

"Yeah, well, your elbow was here," he said, pointing to his ribs and rubbing them. "So, where was your mind? South Africa?" Another not-so-subtle reference to my recent love affair there.

"No. Not this time. I just landed a job."

"That's great. What ship?

"*The West Way III*. I have to meet her in Bayonne Military terminal tomorrow."

"Damn, William!" A big smile on his face. "That's the ship I picked up a job on."

Now it was my turn to smile. "Hey, fantastic, Greg." Then, for no apparent reason, I couldn't talk. It was a relief to know I would have a familiar and friendly face on a ship full of strangers.

He must have read my mind because he said, "At least we'll have each other to talk to. Ships running to Vietnam are having crewing problems. You never know what you'll get—hopefully not a shipload of Roys."

"Or a Captain Coltrain," I added.

Greg said, "How about we take a cab together Wednesday morning. Report-in time is noon."

"Sure. What time do you want to meet?"

"Let's meet at 0900. It'll take an hour to get there. That gives us a two-hour leeway."

"Okay. What are you doing for supper?" When he shrugged and didn't answer, I said, "How about here, around 1800 hours?"

"Sure, why not? See you in a while," and he worked his way through the lobby.

We perched at the counter in the luncheonette, opposite side of the lobby from the boozeless bar. The seat is a standard bar stool, but the padding had seen better days and my bony butt felt the frame. My supper that night consisted of two hot dogs, fortified by two bags of chips and a lemonade. Greg had a burger, slathered with mayo and ketchup, a colorful combination but not something I'd eat.

The bar was crowded and noisy, swathed in a thin cloud of cigarette, cigar, and pipe smoke, and a dozen different languages serenaded us. Everyone clamored continuously. Cheap prices are a great draw for seamen on low wages or between ships. One good paycheck doesn't wash away a lifetime of being stingy with money.

The three countermen serving, wearing khaki pants and white shirts, were short, trim, and efficient. Three lookalikes, except for the hair. Two wore reedy, plastered-down, mouse-brown hair resembling cheap wigs. The third sported a crown of pure white hair, belied by the smooth skin of his face, showing he was prematurely gray. Both brown-heads limited their conversation to "Whaddaya want?" or "Anything else?" The third, Mr. White-hair, tried to chat up everyone, his thick Brooklyn accent washing over the counter in waves. Holding the plate in his left hand, Mr. White-hair split and spread two rolls, dropped them on the plate, dabbed relish and a spray of brown mustard, then speared the dogs and dropped them in. Final flourish with a swish of mustard on top, and he delivered the plate. Less than a minute, start to finish.

Content to listen to the counterman's soliloquy while we ate, Greg and I didn't say much. I decided against dessert, settling for a cup of coffee. Greg ordered one piece each of apple and blueberry pie. While he chewed, I asked, "Do you know what really happened to Captain Coltrain, Greg?"

He swallowed, took a swig of water, and said, "Do I know?" He shook his head. "Uh-uh. But I can guess."

"Well?" I urged him.

"I think the good Captain Coltrain had too many Italian friends from the neighborhood, and he pissed one or more of them off. How many guys get killed by a hit-and-run on the corner of a street that doesn't have any through-traffic?" He stared at me and said, "That's what I think, William. What do you think? Was it justice?" Repeating what I had said to him earlier.

Edgy now, and defensive, I said, "Well, I said that because I think he threw his wife overboard and he got away with it."

"Maybe, but knocking off your wife at sea wouldn't be a reason for the Italians to take him out. There had to be something else." He looked at me, expecting a response, but I shrugged and sipped my coffee. "Anyway," he continued, "be careful picking your friends and acquaintances. You never know what a person is capable of, do you?"

Supper over, back in my room, I was bored. No television. No girlfriend. The thought of going out to a bar for a drink didn't appeal to me. I was a natural hermit until forced into being sociable. The radio reception was bad, so I reverted to my dictionary. When I was in grammar school, fourth grade, Sister Mary Beatta—the same nun I lost to in a fist fight—taught me how to improve my vocabulary.

"Young master William. If you read a word, spell it out loud, write it three times, and use it in a sentence; you will own that word forever."

She was right, and as much as I hated grammar school and high school, I loved to read, so I reached often for the dictionary. Initially, I would use it to learn a word I heard or read and didn't know the meaning of. The long, boring watches at sea are the perfect time to practice, so I started at "A" in the *Webster's Unabridged Dictionary* from Random House. Brown with gilt lettering and indented cut-out tabs, fourteen of them, it contained 15,000 entries, 2,256 pages and 2,400 illustrations. Dual purpose: It exercised my mind, and carrying it around exercised my body.

Whenever I reached a word I didn't know, I did my routine. I was well into the "E's" and tonight, started with "ecclesiology—the science or theory of church building and decoration." I found it ironic that I was in the Seamen's Church Institute when I learned what ecclesiology meant. By 2100 hours, my head was drooping, so I put away my worn Webster, brushed my teeth, took a leak, and crawled into bed.

Waking at 0730, I performed my morning ablutions, dressed, slung my winter parka over my shoulder, and went down to the lobby. The hallway was cold and the elevator colder. I put my parka on and stepped out to a frigid day and morning traffic sounds. The temperature was 27 degrees, wind from the north at fifteen miles per hour, and a clear sky. The wind blew any remaining morning cobwebs from my mind. Shivering, I turned back into the lobby, any thought of walking about now gone.

Heading into the luncheonette, I sat at the counter again, only ten people other than myself there. Mr. White-hair was serving and blathering on in his Brooklyn accent. I ordered coffee and a blueberry Danish, then looked around, wondering if I would see Greg today. We had become friends and supported each other. He, by being a patient and instructive tutor about race relations and the viewpoint of a black man; me, by being a shoulder to lean on when he got fed up with Roy's heckling and his patience drew thin.

Mr. White-hair derailed my train of thought by saying, "Good thing you got that winter coat. It's damn cold out."

"I know, I was going for a walk but decided against it. Anything interesting going on here today?"

He spread both arms wide, an infectious smile on his face. "Look around. People from all over the world come here. It's always interesting,"

"Well, I've seen the boozeless bar and the luncheonette. I've even checked out the post office, so I've covered all the tourist attractions here."

"I don't think so. You been up to the lighthouse yet?"

"What lighthouse?"

"On the roof. It's a memorial to the victims of the *Titanic*."

"Is it a real lighthouse or just a plaque?"

"It's real. Ya know, they laid the cornerstone of this building on April fifteen, 1912. During the ceremony, word reached port about the sinking of the *Titanic* earlier that morning, and right away they started a fund to build a memorial. They dedicated the lighthouse on April fifteen, 1913, a year to the day." It was obvious he had told this story many times and relished having an audience.

"Thanks," I said. "How do you get onto the roof?"

"Elevator to the top, then follow the arrows."

I paid my bill and left him a dollar tip, almost as much as the bill. As I left, I thought, I'm losing it with this generosity crap.

I stopped first at the men's room in the lobby, then took the elevator to the top floor. When I stepped out, there was a sign and an arrow pointing to a doorway which led up a long flight of stairs to the roof. Zipping up my parka, I stepped out into a blast of icy wind that pulled open the door, and I struggled to hold it, managing to get it closed behind me.

They built the lighthouse on a four-foot-high raised platform that had room for a circular walkway. A round, red-brick base about eight feet high sat in the middle of the platform and supported the glass-enclosed superstructure with another, smaller circular walkway around the light itself, which emitted a steady green beacon.

I stayed long enough to read the plaque and appreciate the irony of the quote published in *The Lookout* in the April 1912 edition: *And yet it seemed particularly appropriate that on this day, when heart and mind were turned toward the sea and the sailors who had gone down beneath the deep waters, there should be gathered a notable company of men and women to join in a service marking one of the final steps in the completion of a tremendous project solely for the benefit of seamen and their families.*

Descending from the roof and exiting the elevator, I decided to brave the cold and go for my walk rather than sit around and do nothing. For three hours I walked through downtown and midtown Manhattan, stopping only to get a cup of coffee and warm my hands at a deli on Broadway near Forty-Second Street. Returning, I bought a ham-and-cheese sandwich on rye with a lot of spicy mustard, along with another lemonade, and took them to my room to eat.

I spent the rest of the day reminiscing about Meg, and wondering if my sole chance at true love had come and gone.

CHAPTER 5

At 0900, I met Greg in the lobby. We left our gear at the SCI until after we checked in at the ship. We weren't sure when sign-off would be for the existing crew, so couldn't be sure we had a cabin ready to leave our stuff. Neither of us trusted to leave it on a ship where we didn't know anyone. We each grabbed a coffee to go from the luncheonette, then I followed him out to South Street, where a cab was unloading three people at the front door. It was a few degrees colder than yesterday but just as windy, so we buttoned up our coats.

"Hold it!" Greg called out to the cabbie, and we scooted into the back seat.

"Where to?" came from the driver.

Looking into the rearview mirror, I could see his smile, missing the two front teeth, but friendly.

"Military Ocean Terminal in Bayonne," Greg replied.

"That's gonna cost ya. We're only licensed for the five boroughs. If you wanna do a flat rate, I can stay off the meter and always go home for lunch after I drop youse off."

"How much?" I asked.

Pointing at the meter which read $.20 first ¼ mile and $.05 thereafter, he said, "On the meter until we enter the Holland Tunnel, then a flat rate of ten dollars plus the toll."

I looked at Greg. Shrugging, he said, "Okay, let's go," and the driver pulled out into traffic.

It was a bit of déjà vu for me, since Greg and I had taken a taxi together from the SCI the first time I caught the *Mormacpride* in Brooklyn. Unlike the first ride where, as uneasy strangers, we rode in silence, I peppered Greg with questions about the ship we were heading for.

"C3s are old, some older than you are, William. Most of them were built from 1939 through 1945, a few in 1946, I think. They're steam turbine driven, 8500 horsepower and they're slow. Top speed is probably sixteen knots. Nothing like the *'Pride*. She was a race horse compared to a C3."

"What kind of deck gear does she carry?"

Greg laughed. "Booms. All the old clunkers have booms. That's all I can tell you. I'm an engineer, remember? Better just hope they maintained everything well. I guarantee you there'll be more maintenance and breakdowns than what we had on the *'Pride*."

All I could think of was the winches back on the training ship at school. Ancient, needing constant maintenance. A regular pain in the ass.

We were going opposite the heavy traffic, most of which was inbound to downtown Manhattan and crawling along, so it only took thirty-five minutes to reach the main gate of the Military Ocean Terminal in Bayonne, New Jersey. The sign proclaimed that it was a U.S. Army facility, Headquarters-Eastern Area, and run by the Military Traffic Management Command, the Army's transportation command.

Knowing the MSTS is a Navy operation, supporting the movement of cargo and personnel around the world, and aware that the Military Ocean Terminal had been a U.S. Navy dry-docking and supply center, I was surprised to see the Army signboard.

There were four lanes inbound and three outbound. The two right-hand inbound lanes were truck traffic, and the two left-hand lanes for cars. The cab driver pulled up to the security guard in the left-hand lane.

There were two guards, one civilian, in his late fifties, the other one Army, a PFC who looked to be fifteen years old. The civilian guard asked for our IDs, and Greg and I showed him our "Z" cards, a mariner's standard identification document. He wrote our names on a list and noted beside them the medallion number of the taxi.

"Do you know where you're going?" he asked.

"We're joining the *West Way III*. It docked this morning," Greg replied.

After checking another clipboard list, he gave the driver directions to the berth.

"I thought this was a Navy installation," I said.

"Until two days ago, it was. Now it's Army. This young fellow"—hooking his thumb over his shoulder towards the soldier—"is keeping us safe and secure." At first, I felt he was trying to embarrass the soldier, but they both smiled so I ignored it.

In most piers, they won't allow taxis inside the facility. Here, it was almost a mile from the gate, so they let them in but restricted them to the marked roadways.

The driver pulled ahead and swung left, then right, where the truck lanes split from the car traffic. Moving at fifteen miles per hour, the posted speed limit, we cruised past acres of storage sheds, three rows of them leading from the gate area out to the graving dock at the end of the complex. I saw the ship docked to the right but told the driver to keep going to the end. The entire area alongside one shed, except for the doorways, was filled with Jeeps and Army ambulances. There were more ambulances, a somber sign.

At the end of the storage sheds, a three-story administration building blocked our way. Going left around it, a long, two-story, segmented building, faded yellow-brown exterior, guarded the graving dock which ended at the water's edge.

"Okay," I said to the driver, "back to the ship."

Making a U-turn, he wove his way through the sheds down to the berth, ignoring the roadway markers. There was no cargo activity, so I told him to pull up to the gangway. The ship had docked port side to the pier, facing out toward the channel.

Greg and I climbed out. He stretched while I paid the driver. When the cab drove off, I looked at the rust-patched side of the ship, looked at Greg and said, "You were right. It's old."

He laughed, slapped me on the shoulder, and said, "She's only a year or two older than you, William. It's all about maintenance, so you better keep on running those ladders or you'll look like this bucket of rust in no time. C'mon," he said, "it's cold. Let's get aboard." I followed him up the creaky, swaying gangway.

"Move your bony ass!" The words greeted us at the top of the gangway. A round man, maybe five-eight, two-eighty pounds, and cue-ball bald, shouted at a six-two skeleton of a man, no more than one-fifty pounds, standing at the sign-in desk—a make-shift plywood board no carpenter would be proud of.

The skeleton nodded and shuffled forward. Turning to Greg, the round man said, "Who are you?"

Looking somewhat hostile, Greg replied, "Greg Russell, the new third engineer." Tossing his head toward me he continued, "This is William Connolly, the new third mate."

The round man's attitude changed immediately, and he reached out to shake hands with both of us. "Sorry about the shouting." He pointed forward to where the skeleton walked. "Winkler there has to be told everything twice. He has to remind himself to breathe. Come on," he said, beckoning, "I'll take you to meet the captain and the chief engineer." Talking over his shoulder, he added, "I'm DeSantis, the first mate," and he opened the watertight door and stepped into the house.

A cold blast was cut off by the slamming of the watertight door behind us. Déjà vu. This time it sounded and felt like the slamming of a coffin lid. I shivered, nothing to do with the temperature. I had a momentary jolt of my déjà vu. Past episodes of déjà vu were unpleasant, even frightening. Was this a precursor to problems? Less than two minutes aboard ship and I was getting the heebie-jeebies.

With the WT door shut, the galley smells washed over us: boiled cabbage, onions, a hint of apple pie, all battling for the top spot with body odor, dirty laundry, and bunker oil.

We followed DeSantis up a deck. The interior was old, but unlike the rusty hull, the bulkheads and railings were painted and clean. Even the decks were relatively clean. Since the upkeep of the ship, other than the engine room, was the responsibility of the first mate, my respect for DeSantis rose.

He stopped at a door on the second deck forward, port side, and knocked. There was a slide-in bracket on the bulkhead to the right of the door and a hand-lettered cardboard sign inserted: "Chief Engineer."

"Come in," a voice called from within, and DeSantis opened the door.

"Hey, Chief, here's your replacement third engineer." He stepped aside and said, "Greg, meet Wesley Gibson, Chief Engineer." Greg stepped in to greet the chief.

"Catch you later," DeSantis said to Greg as he walked away and motioned me to follow him. We crossed the passageway and walked past the officers' salon on the forward end. As we entered the ladderway to go up yet another deck, he pointed to an office on the forward starboard side, directly opposite where the chief engineer's office was. "That's my place." There was another hand-lettered sign beside his door.

He continued up the ladder one more deck. The captain's office and cabin were on the forward end, in the center of the ship. Knocking on the jamb of the open door, DeSantis called out, "Captain, we got our replacement third mate." But he didn't step in until he heard, "Come in."

The captain sat behind a tiny wooden desk—gnarly oak, over-stained, pockmarked but glossy. It looked like a lap table and held a loose-leaf notebook. On one side it had two side tables abutting each other, end-on to the desk. A similar single side table abutted and paralleled the desk on the other side. All of them bore piles of document folders. Atop the papers on the right-hand table sat a Colt 1911 .45 caliber pistol.

As small as the desk was, the captain seemed shrunken behind it. Then he stood and offered his hand. Shaking it, I gawked. Towering over me, at least six-feet-six, he was all legs. His torso looked like it had been taken from another body and glued onto his hips. Thin, about one-eighty pounds, an Ichabod Crane lookalike, he looked to be in his mid-fifties, with a hint of grey at the temples of his light brown hair. He had a rummy's nose, red and veined, but looked sober.

"I'm Captain Johnston. What's your name, sonny?" Friendly enough, but since "Sonny" is what Captain Coltrain of the *'Pride* had called me, I felt goosebumps.

"William Connolly, Captain."

"Well, William, how long have you been sailing?"

"Half a year, sir." Not wanting to sound too green, I added, "I sailed on the *Mormacpride* right out of school until a week ago."

"And what school would that be?"

"Massachusetts Maritime, sir."

Nodding, he looked at DeSantis and said, "He'll do," and sat down.

DeSantis ushered me out of the office and we walked back to his room, where he offered me a cigarette—a Salem, mentholated—and a drink. Declining both, surprised at the drink offer this early in the day, I lit up my own Marlboro. He poured himself a shot of Dewar's White Label.

"We start loading tomorrow morning at 0800 hours. If you didn't notice, we're the only ship on berth, that's the only reason they didn't force us to start loading already. I've been here a half dozen times, and there were always at least three ships working."

"I didn't realize there was so much military cargo moving."

"There's a war on, William. It's getting to be unpopular, but it's still a war. A lot of our soldiers are getting their asses shot up. Like all wars, they need bullets, booze, food, and broads. We carry the bullets, booze, and food; the broads they find themselves."

"When are we—" I started, and he cut in.

"I'm still waiting for the loading plan. There's a military planner here who coordinates the loading of all the ships. The regular cargo, they give us lots of leeway, but the bombs and ammunition they're pretty strict about."

"They load bombs—" I began, and he cut me off again.

"We're part of a long delivery line, stretching from here to Vietnam." He paused. "What did you say?"

I realized he wasn't being rude, but his mind got on a roll and it took his mouth a while to catch up. I decided to simply wait a few seconds after he finished talking before I spoke.

"Do they load bombs here?"

"Hell no! All munitions are loaded at Sunny Point, North Carolina."

"When do you think we'll sail?"

Scratching his gleaming pate, he said, "Probably Saturday or Sunday. We'll be signing articles on Friday."

"I have to go back to the SCI and get my things. Greg left his stuff there, too. Is there an open cabin to store our stuff in?"

"Yeah. We've been missing a third mate since Hawaii, and the third engineer got off when we hit the Panama Canal. Their rooms are open."

"Great. We can get our stuff and come back tonight."

He nodded. "Okay. There's nothing going on right now. Let's get something to eat." Patting his belly, he smiled. "The chow is pretty good. When the chief cook is sober, he's great. The captain encourages him to stay sober."

"Encourages him? Why doesn't he demand it?"

"The captain belongs to Alcoholics Anonymous. He tries to help other drunks stay sober." Not realizing the irony of his statement while he sat with a glass of Scotch in his hand.

"And if they don't heed his encouragement?"

"They always do. Didn't you see the Colt .45 on his desk?"

CHAPTER 6

After lunch, Greg and I walked to the main gate, a cold hike, looking to catch a taxi back to the city. As we talked to the guard, we got lucky.

"I have to go into Manhattan to meet my wife," the guard said. "I'm off duty in twenty minutes. If you can hang around, I'll be glad to drop you guys off."

"Thank you, sir." Greg said. "That's really nice of you."

"No problem. Wait over there," and he pointed toward a small parking lot. "The green Chevy Impala."

Greg and I walked over to the lot and stood in the lee of a small shack, hiding from the wind. I lit up a Marlboro, and we stood talking until the guard approached.

"What do you think, Greg? The ship look okay?"

"The ship is fine, William. I'm always more concerned about the crew. Metal things that break can be fixed. Mental things—not so sure about."

"Anyone in particular?" I asked.

"Nah, just a feeling. We'll see."

I wondered if his "feeling" was akin to my déjà vu. Maybe we should think again about signing on.

The guard walked over to us. "Hi," he said, "I'm Jerry."

Greg and I introduced ourselves and shook hands.

He unlocked the car, and we climbed in, Greg in the shotgun seat, me in the back, behind him.

"We appreciate you doing this, Jerry," Greg said.

"Glad to help, guys. I've given a lot of Navy guys rides over the years. Merchant Marine guys help the cause, too, carrying all the stuff to Nam."

Nothing else was said until we cleared the Holland Tunnel. "How about I drop you off at Broadway and Liberty?"

"That would be great," we both said.

We looped out of the Holland Tunnel and headed south on West Side Highway, getting off at Chambers Street. A short run up Chambers to Broadway, right on Broadway to Liberty, and we hopped out, thanking him again. We walked the remaining six blocks to the SCI, the wind swirling from the funneling effect of the tall buildings.

"How about we meet here in the lobby in half an hour?" Greg said.

"Okay," I said, nodding, and went to my room to collect my things. I brushed my teeth, took a leak, washed my hands, took a final look around, then headed down to the lobby toting my duffel, backpack, and sextant case.

A sextant is used for taking celestial bearings to determine the ship's position. It can be sun, moon, or stars. My sextant is the most expensive thing I own. It costs four hundred dollars. Manufactured by C. Plath, Hamburg, Germany, it was brand new. The quality inspector dated and signed it on 12/8/66. I ordered it a month before graduation from Mass. Maritime and it only showed up at Ma's place last week. When I checked in with her by phone, I told her to ship it to me at the SCI.

When I got to the lobby, Greg was ahead of me, checking out. Ignoring the gnomish bellhop who appeared at our side, we lugged our bags outside and hailed a taxi, heading back to Bayonne. Two cabs refused to go to Bayonne that time of day, not wanting to fight the commuters leaving the city and losing out on multiple fares, because more people rode taxis when the cold wind blew. The third one agreed, but only after negotiating a flat twenty-dollar fare. We were in no position to argue.

This time, the traffic was going with us, heavy and slow. We didn't reach the terminal gate until 1800 hours. Paying off the taxi, we tramped up the gangway and went to our separate rooms. I dumped my gear and went looking for the first mate.

I knocked on his cabin door. "Hey mate, I'm back."

"William, come on in. I got a problem."

"What's the problem?"

"No second mate," DeSantis replied. "The union can't fill the job and the company doesn't have anyone. Your license is only for third mate, right?"

"That's right."

"How would you like to sail as second mate this trip?"

Stunned, I stood silent. I didn't even have a full year of sailing time, a necessary requirement before you can even sit for your second mate's exam. The look on my face must have said it all because he said, "The marine superintendent is applying to the Coast Guard for a waiver for you for this trip."

"The marine superintendent, you mean Mr. Palmer?"

"Yup. I told him you seemed like a good prospect but were still new at the game."

"What did he say?"

"He said you're an MMA grad. You should be able to roll with the punches."

"Wow."

"Not that big a deal, William. The Coast Guard issued a lot of waivers during the last year because of the shortage of mates and engineers. You'll do fine. In any case, get yourself over to the Coast Guard base in the morning and get the paperwork done. We're signing coastal articles on Friday. If, by chance, between Friday and the time we get to Jacksonville they find a second mate, your waiver will end. But I doubt if they'll find one."

"The timing is perfect. I just got my sextant." A new third mate could get away with using the ship's sextant for taking sunlines; a second mate was expected to have his own sextant. "Will they get a replacement third mate for me?"

"Not likely. We'll be sailing short-handed. I'll take the 8-to-12 watches until we reach Jacksonville."

"Thanks, mate. I appreciate your confidence in me. At least I'll have you to lean on."

"For a while. I'm only here as far as Jacksonville."

I went looking for Greg to tell him the news and found him in his cabin. "Damn, I'm not even unpacked, and I'm promoted to second mate."

"Hey, I'm happy for you William. The chief engineer just told me we have a similar problem. We're missing a third engineer, so I'm flying solo this trip."

Normally the two third engineers and the second engineer stand the watches, same as the mates.

He continued. "The first engineer will stand a watch while we're running the coast, but not at sea. That means a lot of long days."

"You said before you had a 'feeling.' Does being short-handed make that worse?" I asked.

He shook his head. "Not sure—but it's not all bad. Long days mean overtime. Moolah!"—and he smiled, rubbing his thumb and first two fingers together.

We shot the breeze for about an hour, reminiscing about South Africa. We both disliked the apartheid system. Greg, having to deal with bias all his life, was more pragmatic than me, recalling a story the British agent in Cape Town told him.

"'You know,' the agent said, 'the Brits here can be just as biased as the Dutch, but with the Brits, when pushed, they'll be practical. There's a long-running joke here about the Dutchman and the Brit being out in the jungle together for months without any women. One day, a woman appeared: Swahili—tall, elegant, graceful, beautiful, and black.

"'She approached the men and said, "I would make love to you, but you are South African and can't have a relationship with a black woman."

"'The Dutchman replied, with some reluctance, "That's right, no interracial mingling."

"'The Brit, however, said, "I'm philosophical. You've heard the expression; absence makes the heart grow fonder? Well, it also makes the dark grow blonder.'"

"We both laughed," Greg said. "It perfectly summed up the attitude of the British in South Africa."

"Well," I said, "You always tell me there's a moral to everything in life. What's the moral here?"

"Funny you should ask. The moral is, when pushed to extremes, always try and find the middle ground. You may even enjoy it."

I shook my head. "You set me up for that, didn't you?"

"Just trying to get you to look for alternative paths through life," and he laughed.

"I give up," I said. "I bow to the philosopher," and gave him a mock bow.

I went to my cabin and unpacked my duffel and backpack. Hanging up my uniform shirts and pants on the one closet bar under a single shelf on the bulkhead, I struggled to cram underwear, socks, handkerchiefs, running shorts, uniform shorts, and tee shirts into the two tiny drawers of the bureau. I stacked my high-pressure cap and my sneakers on the single shelf. This cabin, like my previous ones, was a monk's cell; but after living for three years on the training ship *Bay State*, stacked three high on pipe racks—a pipe frame with a piece of canvas laced to it for a bed—it was a palace. As second mate, at least I had this cabin to myself, and my own head. The two third mates had to share a cabin and use the common head at the end of the companionway. The bunk, similar to others, had a twelve-inch rail that could be raised and locked in place in heavy weather, a shorter version of a baby's crib rail.

I thought about the long hours ahead of me. Being paid overtime made the long hours tolerable, and less free time distracted me from memories of Megan. It was still early, but with nothing to do, I hit the rack. I hoped this trip would be different.

As it turned out, different, but not better. Worse—far worse.

The company had a taxi waiting for me at the head of the ship at 0700 hours. With my third mate's license and my "Z" card in hand, I headed for the Coast Guard station on Governor's Island. The taxi took me to downtown Manhattan, South Street, next to the SCI, where I caught the ferry. The driver gave me a card with the dispatcher's telephone number and said to call when I was boarding the ferry to return.

The processing for my waiver took forty-five minutes, incredibly fast for a bureaucracy. I called from the payphone at the ferry landing, and when I stepped ashore at South Street, the same taxi driver was waiting. I was back on the ship by 1030, with my waiver to sail as second mate.

The first mate congratulated me on my second mate waiver, then gave me a quick review of the loading plan and told me to go on deck and keep an eye on things. I bundled up and went on deck.

The *West Way III* had seen better days. It was a C3. The C3 had replaced the Victory ship of World War II, and the Victory ship had replaced the Liberty ship, each version a little bigger and faster. A general-purpose ship, the C3 has a length of 492 feet, beam of 69.5 feet, and a loaded draft of 28.5 feet. Steam-turbine driven, it can reach a top speed of 16.5 knots, with a range of 12,000 miles.

The government built 465 C3s, and they used them in government service from 1940 through 1947. Many were converted for the U.S. Navy as escort airplane carriers (CVEs), submarine tenders (AS), and attack transports (AKs), and were used during World War II. Most C3s were sold after the war to private steamship lines and used in the commercial carriage of goods. *West Way III* was one of those commercial carriers. There were five cargo hatches, three forward of the house and two aft, numbered #1 through #5 from forward to aft. All the hatches were serviced by cargo booms of five-ton capacity. On the 'Pride, it took less than five minutes to open any hatch cover. On the West Way III, it took about thirty minutes. The Mormacpride was also classified as a C3, but a much more modern version. The West Way III was a work horse, but a tired work horse, ridden hard and put away wet.

It was cold, dropping to thirteen degrees the previous night, and we didn't expect it to go above twenty-five degrees today. The sky was clear and the wind from the north at ten miles per hour. There were three longshoremen gangs working. The ship's crew had removed and stowed the hatch tarpaulins prior to the start of work.

One gang at #1 hatch was loading pallets of MCI-rations, which stands for Meal, Combat, Individual. Not much different from the MCI-rations of World War II, a case contained twelve individual packets. Each packet held four metal cans of wet food of some type and an accessory packet of coffee, chewing gum, sugar, salt, matches, cigarettes (only four and always stale), toilet paper (enough for one moderate crap), a plastic spoon, and a church key—the indispensable can opener. The flavors would vary per packet—beans with frankfurter chunks in tomato sauce, beef with spiced sauce, ham and eggs, etc. Many of them contained lima beans. I never met anyone who liked lima beans. The best that could be said of MCI-rations is, they are edible and will keep you from starving.

The troops in Vietnam didn't like them because the metal cans were heavy and they clanked together. In the jungle, on patrol, no soldier wants the extra weight or the noise.

The hatch openings on a C3 are similar but not identical. Hatch #2 through #5 were twenty-four feet wide, ranging from thirty to forty feet long. #1 hatch, due to the sheer of the ship at the bow, was narrower, twenty feet wide by thirty-six feet long.

The lower hold in #1 hatch tapered drastically in the forward end so the gang was breaking down pallets and, after laying dunnage—hardwood boards, to segregate and support the cargo—stowed the individual cartons in the irregular spaces at the sides of the ship, to effectively utilize space. It was slow going. When they reached the front edge of the hatch opening, they put a small forklift in the hatch and stowed full pallets through the remainder of the space.

Cargo space that is unutilized is called "broken stow:" Steel coils will use up the weight capacity of a particular hatch, but leave a lot of cubic space empty. Boxes of pillows will do just the opposite. Every first mate tries to balance the maximum amount of weight capacity and interior space as much as possible.

Stevedoring, the loading or discharging of cargo, is hard, dangerous work. The spaces are small and crowded. Large things are constantly swinging through the air above and beside you, any of which could maim or kill you. To a great degree, you depend on your coworker to watch out for you and you for him. Being careless can affect more than what happens to you.

Not paying attention isn't just careless. It could be, and often is, lethal. Living in this dynamic environment is part of the allure of this life. I never thought I'd have to be as wary of my fellow crew members as I would about the work environment. The trip on the 'Pride adjusted my attitude. Would this trip be cause for more adjusting?

A gang at #3 hatch worked with a shore-side truck crane. They were loading two types of armored vehicles: the M113 Armored Personnel Carrier (APC) in the lower hold, and the Cadillac Gage Commando in the lower tweendeck.

The Commandos were four-wheelers, eighteen-and-a-half feet long, seven-and-a-half feet wide, and six-and-a-half feet high, weighing 21,800 pounds. There were lifting rings at each corner, and they were easy to maneuver. The APCs were the aluminum models and weighed 27,000 pounds. They also had lifting rings at each corner. They had tracks and were borderline amphibious, in that the tracks could propel them through water. Looking at them, and as a mate, understanding the concept of displacement, I would not want to test their ability to float. In the ship, they were clumsy and difficult to maneuver. For the Commandos, I had to keep a sharp eye on the hatch covers so they didn't tear them up when maneuvering into stow. The longshoremen drove the Jeeps and ambulances, but Army drivers drove the Commandos and APCs. In most ports, the longshoremen are touchy about letting anyone do their work, but here, the longshoremen were friendly and kidded around with the Army drivers.

There was another gang at #4 hatch, working the forward gear. They were loading Jeeps and ambulances, the same ones we saw when we drove onto the terminal, using net slings at the wheels for lifting. Laying the slings on the dock, one forward and one back, they drove the vehicle onto the sling and lifted them. Spreader bars kept the slings from jamming in too tight against the sides of the vehicle. In the ship they reversed the process. The ambulances had lifting rings on the front and rear bumpers, but the gangs ignored those and used the nets to load them.

In addition, they loaded ten small, two-wheel trailers that were towed behind the Jeeps.

At lunch time, I came in and checked with the first mate.

"Let's eat," he said, and I followed him to the salon, where the aroma of fresh vegetable soup pervaded, the perfect meal for such a cold day.

The salon was stark. Dark green, wooden-top tables on steel legs, permanently fixed to the deck. The captain's table had chairs; the others had benches. The forward benches were fixed in place along the bulkhead. The after benches were free-standing. Both chairs and benches had fittings on the deck where you could pin the legs to prevent them from moving in rough weather. There were five small portholes on the forward bulkhead, stingy with light. Neon tubes lit the salon.

To the starboard side was the pantry and dumbwaiter leading down to the galley on the crew deck below. An old RCA television sat on an elevated brace on the port side. On the aft bulkhead stood a sideboard with dishes, cutlery, glasses, and cups.

At the table I met the other third mate. In his mid-fifties, he was bald on top with bushy gray side growth, and sported a scraggly, five-day-old beard. He had a lightning-bolt shaped scar on his right cheek.

"William," the first mate said, "meet Jeff Gillies. Jeff, this is William Connolly."

We shook hands, and he said, "I'm just here for the coastwise trip. Getting off in Jacksonville."

I thought this was a strange greeting, almost an omen. *Was everyone abandoning ship?*

CHAPTER 7

At 1300 hours, I got up to return on deck, but the first mate stopped me.

"Jeff will cover the cargo operations this afternoon. I want you to go over all the charts and make sure everything is up to date." Smiling, DeSantis said, "Remember, you're the second mate."

On merchant ships, the second mate is the navigation officer and stands the four-to-eight watches, enabling him to take star-sightings. "Is the bridge unlocked?" I asked.

Handing me a key ring, he said, "It will be when you unlock it. Bring the keys back when you're done."

The bridge was smaller than the 'Pride's. There were ten glass ports across the front, each two feet wide and three feet tall. A well-worn brass handrail ran the full width of the ports just below them. Sitting in the middle, four feet aft, was the helm, with the binnacle containing the magnetic compass in front of the wheel, and the newer, added-on gyrocompass ahead of but to the right of the wheel. Three feet to the right of the gyrocompass was the engine-order telegraph.

Directly behind the wheel, on the aft bulkhead, was the door to the chartroom. Both sides of the aft bulkhead had panels of warning lights. Smoke detectors on the starboard side, electric systems and the 1MC communication speaker on the port side.

The side doors led to the bridge wings. They were open.

Why did the first mate lock the inside bridge door and leave the wing-doors open? Was the third mate, Gillies, supposed to do it? Careless. It's the little things that cause big problems. Not a good start.

The walkway of the flying bridge acted as a roof and extended three quarters of the way to the side of the ship. There were windbreaks wrapping the deck, except for the aft segment nearest the house, which was open. Ladders there ran up to the flying bridge and down to the captain's deck. Not as tall as on the 'Pride, these windbreakers came only up to my sternum, which meant a wetter, windier watch outdoors.

There weren't any peloruses on the bridge wings, either. A pelorus is a compass stand that allows you to take readings on other objects to determine if the angle is opening or closing as they approach you. Opening angle means more room to pass. Closing angle means somebody better change course to avert a collision. Without the pelorus, we use the old-fashioned "eyeballing" method, utilizing the centerline of the ship and fixed points on the house and rigging as reference points. Either way, the goal is: Don't collide with another ship.

The chart room was tiny, barely enough room to pull out the chart drawers. I spent the next two hours verifying we had all the charts required to get down the East Coast to the Colon entrance of the Panama Canal. Exiting the

Panama City side, we would go to Subic Bay in the Philippines, Cam Ranh Bay in Vietnam, and Sattahip, Thailand, with a possible stop in Pearl Harbor, Hawaii. All the charts were there and reasonably up to date. I would have Notices to Mariners updates to make, but not many. I felt a little more relaxed, knowing I wouldn't have to make any wholesale chart requests.

At 1500 hours I went down to the salon for a coffee, but stopped by the first mate's cabin to check in with him. As I stepped up to the open door, a shadow loomed in it.

"Excuse me," I said, realizing I was blocking the exit.

"That you, William?" DeSantis's voice rang out from inside.

"Yes, sir."

The shadow stepped back into the cabin and became a six-four, two-hundred-and-forty-pound slab of beef.

"William," DeSantis said, "this is Billy Gaithers, our Bosun. Boats, this is William Connolly, our new third—I mean second, mate."

Boats—all bosuns were nick-named "Boats"— smiled, revealing two huge beaver teeth hovering over a three-tooth gap on the bottom, and reached out a hand the size of a small ham, engulfing mine. Thankfully, he didn't break my fingers, just bruised them.

"Welcome aboard, mate."

"Thanks, Boats," I said, trying hard not to grimace from the pain.

"That's all, Boats. I'll catch up with you later on the maintenance schedule," the first mate said, and Boats left.

"We've got two gangs working tonight until 2300 hours," DeSantis said. "We're supposed to get night mates, but I'm never sure of who the union sends, so I want you to work tonight. Okay?"

"Night mates" are relief mates who work at night and weekends when a ship is in port.

"Sure, mate," I answered.

"Good. They'll be working in #3 and #4 hatches. Make sure we've got enough cargo lights available. Boats keeps them in his foc'sle locker."

"Any particular problem you're worried about, mate?"

"Yeah. Keep an eye on the hatch covers in the tweendeck. The APCs are okay in the lower hold, they can't hurt anything there, but the Commando units might tear up the tarps or break a hatch board. By the way, call me DeSantis. Everyone does."

"Sure, mate...DeSantis."

He smiled and waved me out the door.

Sunset would be at 1704 hours, and by 1600 hours the sun was already low in the sky. High cirrus clouds provided a thin veil, and the occasional cumulus cloud scurried by. Wanting to get a head start on the cargo lights, I walked forward to the bosun's locker. The door was open. I called out, "Boats?" and a voice answered, "No, it's me."

It was Winkler, the AB that the first mate had been yelling at when I came aboard.

"Hello," I said. "You're Winkler, right?"

Hanging his head in a bashful manner, he mumbled, "Yeah, I'm Jason Winkler."

Just then Boats walked up and said, "Need any help, mate?"

"Hi, Boats. Just thought I'd break out the cargo lights early. Get a jump on things before it gets dark."

Boats nodded, whether in approval or from habit I don't know, then said, "I got Winkler on it. Told him to put one on each offshore corner."

"I'll give him a hand," I said and picked up two of the lights. They were a metal lampshade, two feet in diameter and a foot deep, with two, 100-watt lightbulbs and a fifty-foot cord. A hinged metal mesh covered the bottom to protect the bulbs from damage. There was a ten-foot sisal line attached, to tie off the light and let it hang.

"Thanks, Mate." Boats smiled that Bucky-Beaver smile and patted me on the back, practically shoving me out the door. I was pretty sure I'd made an ally of the bosun. I just had to make sure he didn't accidentally break any of my bones in the process.

The gangs usually stopped from 1700 to 1800 hours for a meal break, but the gangs that were staying for the night shift worked straight through. The gang in #1 hatch finished the lower hold and covered up. They had loaded a few drafts of MCI-rations into the lower tweendeck when the stevedore boss knocked them off at 1700 hours. They left, leaving the main hatch uncovered. With no rain forecast, the first mate said it was okay. It saves time in the morning if you don't have to wrestle with the tarps and pontoons.

The only surprise was that two gangs of carpenters, known as wood-butchers, came aboard at 1800 hours and started to secure the APCs in the lower hold of #3, and the Jeeps and ambulances in #4 hatch. Everything went along fine until the gang finished loading the APCs and wanted to shift to the lower tweendeck to load Commandos. In order to do that safely, they had to cover the hatch leading into the lower hold. There was a five-minute "discussion" between the longshoreman gang foreman and the carpenter foreman, while I stood and listened. It was a pissing contest and chest-thumper turf battle. There were a lot of "fucks" in that discussion, but the longshoreman foreman prevailed.

The carpenter foreman then asked me for three more cargo lights, so they could work with the hatch closed. The AB Winkler was nowhere in sight, so I dug out three more lights and gave them to the carpenters, showing them where they could plug them in.

When they finished covering the lower hold, I found the gang foreman and told him I wanted steel plates laid on the cover for landing the Commandos.

"Got it covered, mate. We put a tire through a hatch board a couple of ships ago and scared the shit out of everyone. Been using plates since then."

I stood at the offshore coaming and watched, attentive, as they lowered the first Commando into the tweendeck. There were two signalmen. One stood at the inshore, forward edge of the hatch coaming and watched them lower the Commando. He signaled to the second man standing at the railing, where the truck crane operator could see him. Coordination and timing are critical any time when loading cargo, but with two signalmen, even more so. They handled it well. No sudden lurches or swinging.

When they unhooked the Commando from the cargo fall, the engine started, and the Commando moved forward. That's when I realized the driver had ridden inside the vehicle while it was being lifted. That is a huge NO-NO! This business is dangerous enough without deliberately putting yourself at risk. I yelled to the signalman at the coaming and told him to stop, then walked inshore and leaned over the railing, looking down on the landing area on the pier.

"Where's the driver?" I shouted. Two longshoremen pointed at the turret of the Commando.

Shaking my head, I yelled, "No! No one rides the load."

The gang foreman, who had been sitting at the top of the gangway, walked up to me.

"Hey, mate. I told those guys this morning they shouldn't ride the load. They've been riding the APCs in and walking back ashore, but they're Army. I can't tell them what to do."

"Well, I can."

I looked down and saw the head of the Army driver sticking out of the hatch top.

"You drive it into position then get out. Your partner up here can park them."

The driver looked like he wanted to argue, but shrugged, clambered down, and walked back toward the waiting line of Commandos.

Turning to the gang foreman, I said, "If they try it again, let me know. You guys work with them all the time, so I'll be the bad guy and stop them."

"Thanks, mister mate," the foreman replied, smiling. "That does make it easier."

Returning to the hatch coaming, I saw the Army driver crawling out of the side hatch. There wasn't enough overhead clearance to open the top hatch. "Stay there," I told him. "No more riding the loads."

He looked like he wanted to say something, but he was Army, and my one stripe on a shoulder board out-ranked the PFC chevron on his sleeve. His insignia patch was Transportation.

The rest of the night went better. In #4 hatch, when they covered the lower hold and came up to the tweendeck, there was no "discussion." The carpenter foreman had asked me for four lights and I agreed. The AB, Winkler, was on deck at the time and fetched them from the Bosun's locker.

In addition to the Jeeps, they loaded about one hundred pallets of empty burlap bags, all across the forward and after ends of the lower tweendeck, and also loaded crated helicopter rotor blades, four to a bundle. They strung these fore and aft in the tweendeck wings. When the first mate told me about them, I asked, "What the hell do they need burlap bags for?"

"Sandbags for revetments."

"Why don't they ship it direct from India? That's where most burlap is made."

"Government contractors. Everybody gets their piece of the pie. The fact that it triples the price?" He shrugged his shoulders and shook his head. "It's the system, William, get used to it."

At 2245 hours, the longshoremen and carpenter gangs came up out of the hatches and filed down the gangway. We left these hatches uncovered. The last man going down the gangway was the Army PFC.

"Say, mister mate, I'd appreciate it if you didn't say anything to my sergeant about us riding the Commandos today."

I knew he had screwed up, he knew he had screwed up, so I figured, he's learned his lesson.

"No problem, private. We all make mistakes. Luckily, no one got hurt today."

He saluted, I returned it, and he walked down, off into the night.

I reported to the first mate, had a cup of coffee, and hit the rack.

Another cold morning. A few degrees warmer than yesterday, but still below freezing. The forecast said it would edge up to 36 degrees today. A gentle wind from the North, no more than five miles per hour, just enough to create a chill factor.

Sitting in the salon at 0700, hands warming around a hot mug of coffee, I awaited my ham, eggs, fried potatoes, and rye toast. The first mate, third mate, chief engineer, second engineer, a Swede named Ingvar Swenson who became a citizen ten years ago, and Greg were arrayed on the benches, busy eating, drinking, and smoking. No idle chatter. Greg had waved to me when I came in.

The captain tottered in. He didn't walk, his body was too gangly. Tottering is the best way I know to describe how he moved, like a man on stilts for the first time.

"Good morning, everyone," he greeted us, and a chorus of mumbled "Good morning, captains" returned fire.

DeSantis, the first mate, stood, stretched and sat down again. "They're pushing us to sail tonight, but I don't know if we can finish."

Gillies, the third mate, said nothing, so I asked, "Are there any changes to the loading plan from what you showed me yesterday?"

"Maybe in the upper tweendeck of #3, but nothing else," the first answered.

"What would go there?" I asked.

"More MCI-rations and crates of repair parts for the vehicles."

"Well, if they finish the Commandos, and we can cover up and let the carpenters work in the dark again, I don't see why we can't finish. They moved along at a good clip last night. When the carpenters came up, they had almost finished securing in the lower holds on both #3 and #4 hatch. Unless they add cargo, #1 should finish around 1500 hours today. There won't be much securing to do there."

"We'll see," DeSantis said.

"They can always double up and put two gangs in #3 to finish it. It's all small stuff, so they have room to work there."

"We'll see," he repeated.

They decided to add the extra cargo. By 1400 hours, the lower tweendeck of #3 hatch was covered, and they loaded crates of parts into the aft end and wings of the upper tweendeck, using the after gear. When the gang at #1 hatch finished, they shifted back to the forward end of #3 and loaded MCI-rations. It was tight, with two gangs working in the same hatch, but manageable.

The gang loading crated parts worked until the entire aft end was complete. When the aft gang ran out of space around 1600 hours, the forward gang knocked off. The union rules gave the gang that started in a hatch the "hatch rights" and they couldn't be bumped out. They take this stuff seriously.

I remember as a kid working in Boston as a Scalawag, an illegal replacement for a regular longshoreman, when they had a "hatch rights" issue. Four guys ended up in the hospital. I hid in the corner of the hatch during the fracas. Filing off the ship at the end of the day, the gang foreman followed me down the gangway. At the bottom, he grabbed me and said, "I didn't see you throwing any punches back there. You're either with us or against us. Ain't no other way. Remember that, if you ever want to work here again."

Now, nine years later and a different port, it was a union squabble. A lot of noise but no bloodshed.

The aft gang finished loading MCI-rations, filling the rest of the space. They knocked off at 1930. Only a few places required securing, since the pallets were tight against each other, and the carpenters were done by 2000 hours.

The first mate had called me on the walkie-talkie at 1500 hours and told me to come in and sign articles. As I walked into the salon, the signing of articles was under way, the same as on the last trip. Normally, the chief steward runs the show, with the captain overseeing things. We didn't yet have a chief steward, so the captain did the clerical work, with the Coast Guard ensign witnessing the signing of the crew.

A full crew totaled thirty-seven, but we were short-handed. The Deck Department comprised the officers—captain, first mate, second mate, two third mates (one of whom is called a junior third)—and unlicensed deck hands. They were bosun, maintenance man, six able-bodied seamen (AB), and three ordinary seamen (OS). We were missing a third mate.

The Engine Department comprised the officers—chief engineer, first assistant engineer, second assistant engineer, two third assistant engineers—like the third mate, one is often referred to as junior third—and the unlicensed hands. They were three oilers, three fireman water tenders (FWT), and one wiper. The oilers and firemen stood regular watches, like an AB and OS. The wiper was a day worker, like the bosun and deck maintenance man. We were missing a third engineer.

In addition, there was the radio officer, "Sparky," and the Stewards Department. Under the chief steward (who we didn't have yet) were the chief cook, baker, third cook, salon messman, salon pantryman (also missing), officers' bedroom steward (BR), steward utility (gopher for the chief steward), the crew messman, who served the unlicensed crew, and the galley utility, who did most of the menial jobs like peeling potatoes. No passengers, so the additional passenger utility and BR weren't needed. On a short trip, missing a few crew members is an inconvenience. On a long trip, it's a recipe for trouble.

Each crew member stepped up to the table and handed over his Z-card to the ensign, who examined it and handed it to the captain. A Z-card is a merchant mariner's standard ID card, issued by the U.S. Coast Guard. The captain told the men there wouldn't be any allotments set up, since this was coastwise articles. "Allotments" are arrangements made to have pay sent to a designated person at home. In Jacksonville, we would sign voyage articles, and any allotment forms necessary would be filled out at that time.

Each man signed the articles. It was all routine and ritualistic, but everyone knew they were signing a contract with the steamship company that controlled their lives for the duration of the voyage.

CHAPTER 8

Sailed from New York at 2100 hours. Clear, cold weather, twenty-seven degrees, low humidity, wind from the North at eight MPH. Choppy waters off the pilot station.

By the time the securing was complete, and the gangs and carpenters were ashore, it was 2000 hours. The bosun and the deck crew were busy battening down the hatches and trimming the cowls of the air vents aft, to minimize the amount of cold air going into the hatches. As we headed south, the temperature would rise. When it started to rise, we'd trim the cowls to face forward and circulate the warmer air through the hatch. By keeping the hatch temperature the same as the outside temperature, we'd minimize the condensation or "sweating" in the holds.

The Sandy Hook pilot was aboard. He arrived at 2000 and was relaxing in the captain's office. When the captain called the crew out for undocking, it was 2045. Although past my watch-standing time, I went to the bridge. The first mate, DeSantis, had the watch but was finishing up cargo details in his office. The third mate, Gillies, went to the fantail for undocking. Two ABs and an OS were with him. The first mate went to the bow with the bosun, two more ABs, an OS and the day man.

Every ship does it differently, depending on the captain's wishes. Sometimes the second mate will take the bow and the first mate does nothing. The third mate on watch stays on the bridge. Since there was no other third mate for this leg of the trip, there wasn't an option.

As the crew was breaking down the gangway, the pilot got a call on his walkie-talkie and told the captain they had a crew member making a pier-head jump. The captain leaned over the bridge wing and yelled to the crew on the gangway to stop and wait. They already had the gangway hanging from its bridle and had dropped one rail. Five minutes later, a car pulled up beside the gangway and a man got out. He pulled a suitcase and duffel bag out of the trunk. The AB grabbed the suitcase and preceded the man up the gangway, hanging precariously onto the remaining rail. I only got a glimpse of him when he ducked into the house at the top of the gangway.

The pilot—a tall, reedy man wearing an Irish Scally hat covering his mostly bald head, introduced himself as Timothy McHugh, and after asking the captain if he was ready, called to single up the lines. We had two tugboats tied alongside, one each at the bow and stern. The captain of the forward tug had come aboard and acted as the undocking pilot. In his absence, his mate ran the tug. The undocking pilot never acknowledged the presence of anyone other than the Sandy Hook pilot, McHugh. At a signal from McHugh, the undocking pilot spoke into his walkie-talkie and both tugs backed down, pulling the ship off the berth. When we were fifteen feet off, McHugh ordered slow ahead, and I rang down the order on the engine-order telegraph. I felt the vibration when the propeller bit into the water. As the ship gathered headway, the tugs came alongside, nudging and following, still tied to the ship but not pushing it.

After clearing the end of the terminal, the pilot thanked the undocking pilot and released both tugs. The undocking pilot went below and climbed down the Jacob's ladder, set at the forward end of the gangway, onto his tug. A Jacob's ladder is a portable, flexible ladder used to board and disembark ships. The name alludes to the biblical Jacob who dreamed he climbed the ladder to heaven. Originally, it was a network of lines leading up to the skysail on wooden sailing ships. It is difficult to climb. Watching the action from the bridge wing, the pilot ordered half ahead as soon as the tugboat cleared away from the side of the ship. The tempo and vibrations rose with the increased revolutions, and I felt a stir inside me. It felt good to be moving, heading out for new adventures.

He then altered course to the south, heading for the channel leading under the Verrazano Narrows Bridge and the Anchorage Channel. From there, we would proceed into the Ambrose Channel and to the Ambrose Pilot Station, where the pilot would disembark into the pilot boat.

Throughout the entire process, the captain stood in the forward, starboard corner of the bridge, near the door. He never said a word, fingers fidgeting and drumming on the glass port in front of him. Every few minutes, he glanced at the AB on the helm, as if to assure himself he was still there.

Five minutes after straightening up on the new course, DeSantis relieved me, and I headed below.

This ship was noisier than the *'Pride*. I always felt the engine vibrations, but aboard the *West Way III*, they were stronger. The rattle of loose things, a little louder. Hanging my jacket over the hook on the back of the door, I kicked off my shoes, undressed, and hung up my uniform on the short hanging bar. Still cool in the room, despite the radiator doing its best, I pulled on a sweatshirt, climbed into the bunk and conked out.

A subtle tapping on my cabin door, followed by a head inserting itself into the shaft of light stabbing the darkness, and stating, "It's 3:30, mate. Calling you out for the watch."

"Okay. Thanks," I replied, and the head disappeared along with the light. Yawning, I stretched, kicked off the covers, scratched my head and my balls, and got up. I took a leak, scrubbed my face in cold water at the sink, and got dressed, the same uniform. At sea, in cold weather and no sweating, I could wear the same uniform for three or four days before it even started to get ripe. In the tropics, one day was the limit, and in extreme heat two changes a day were called for; but with only guys around who stunk just as bad, I didn't bother.

Grabbing my jacket off the hook, I slung it over my shoulder and headed for the salon to check out the remnants of the midnight meal. A small, half-empty platter of cold cuts, an open loaf of white bread, and condiments sat on the sideboard. I slathered two slices of bread with yellow mustard, threw bologna, ham, and cheese on it, grabbed a mug of black coffee, sat down, and munched. A little dry, but edible. Wiping my mouth and hand where the mustard had dripped, I topped off the mug and went to the bridge.

At 0350 hours, ten minutes early—a long-standing tradition—I walked onto the bridge and greeted Jeff Gillies. "Morning, Jeff."

"Good morning, William," he answered, sounding cheerful. "We're on course doing fifteen knots, wind is out of the north. It's eased somewhat, down to six m.p.h. We've got three ships in sight. One passed to the east of us, heading to New York. One is ahead of us, about four miles and slightly inshore. She seems to be pulling away, but real slow. She's probably doing one knot faster than us. The third one is behind us about six miles, and holding a steady bearing."

"Thanks, Jeff. Anything else?"

"Standing orders are in the chart room. There are no night orders, but the captain wants a call if anything approaches within five miles. No need to report the inshore ship ahead of us, unless they change course enough to be a problem."

I peeked at the compass over the helmsman's shoulder to confirm the course, then said, "Okay Jeff, you're relieved."

As I spoke, the AB on my watch, Jason Winkler, relieved the helmsman, repeated the course aloud, and took over the helm.

"Good morning, Jason."

"Good morning, mate." His soft voice was barely audible.

Realizing I had forgotten to ask Jeff if we had a lookout posted, I asked Jason. "Is the ordinary on lookout, or in the crew's mess?

"I think he's in the crew mess. Don't know if anyone said to stand lookout."

Nodding, I went out on the starboard bridge wing and eyed the surrounding ships, verifying their positions. It was cold. The thermometer read 28 degrees, and the net effect of the ship's speed and the trailing light breeze was a nine miles per hour headwind. The wind-chill effect made it feel a few degrees colder. I had my own wind-chill factoring device. When my nose got numb, it was time to cover up or hide. Despite the cold, the tang of the salt air was a revival, a reawakening of my wanderlust. It felt good to be at sea again.

DeSantis, looking bleary-eyed and haggard, relieved me at 0800, ten minutes late, but he was the boss, so I said nothing. Walking past him, I could smell the stale stench of booze. He seemed oblivious to my stare. Below, in the salon, the captain, chief engineer, first engineer, and Greg were eating. Gillies passed me, leaving as I came in, nodding in greeting.

"Good morning, folks," I called out.

"Good morning, William," the captain replied. "Morning, William," Greg echoed. The others ignored me. I hadn't met the first engineer yet, but judging from his indifferent reception, I didn't try.

There was no pantryman, so I called down my breakfast order to the galley, stuck two pieces of bread in the toaster, and poured myself a mug of coffee. Sitting down at the table next to Greg's, I lit up a Marlboro. Typically, Greg would be reading something. He always had his head in a book or manual. Today, he sat hunkered over the leftovers of his meal—no book, no manual, no eye contact with anyone. My instinct told me something was wrong, but with others there, I didn't intrude, just sat smoking and drinking coffee.

A few minutes later, I heard the dumbwaiter bell ring in the pantry, and I retrieved my breakfast—scrambled eggs, bacon, and sausage. I buttered my toast, tossed it on top of the sausage, and returned to the table. Dousing the eggs with salt and pepper, I looked around for ketchup, my favorite condiment, but saw none on the sideboard, so I dug in, using my toast as a scoop against the fork. Old eating habits die hard.

I was on my last piece of bacon when the captain rose and left the salon, followed by the chief engineer and the first engineer two minutes later. As soon as they cleared the doorway, I asked Greg, "What's wrong?"

"Everything. The chief is a closet drunk, the first engineer doesn't speak to anyone, and most of the oilers and wipers are drug addicts. I haven't talked to the second engineer yet, so I can only hope he's normal. Signing on may have been a big mistake."

"I'm getting the same feeling," I said. "Last night the first mate was fine. This morning, he reeked of booze when he relieved me. He's getting off in Jacksonville. I don't know if that's good or bad. The third mate is getting off in Jacksonville, too. With a captain who is a recovering alcoholic and likes to keep a pistol on his desk, I hope he stays on the wagon. We only signed coastal articles, so if you are going to jump off in Jacksonville, I'll go with you."

Greg looked at me, then laughed. "Hard to believe you and I are the sober, conscientious ones on the ship." He shook his head. "We'll see how the next few days go. I don't like quitting on anything."

"Okay," I agreed, "but if the replacements in Jacksonville are assholes, I'm bailing out."

"Fair enough." Greg stood and left, patting my shoulder as he went by.

I should have listened to my own advice. The replacements were assholes.

CHAPTER 9

Leaving the salon, I went to my cabin wondering if I was in for another trip with a crazy captain. On the 'Pride, Captain Coltrain was a crook and a murderer, but he knew his stuff and was an excellent seafarer. I had no idea how good Captain Johnston would be at running a ship; but the fact he was an alcoholic, recovering or not, made me uneasy. There was nothing I could do about it other than jump ship, so I lay down on my bunk and dozed off.

The smell of frying onions woke me and made me think I was back on the 'Pride. Onions swept through the atmosphere there, like a tsunami. Here, it was only an aroma. A glance at my watch told me it was 1100 hours. Stretching, I thought about running the ladders for exercise, decided against it, and used the head. Rinsing my hands and face at the sink, I dried off, lit a Marlboro, and ambled to the salon.

The captain sat at his table with a stocky man, jet-black hair that seemed too dark to be real. He looked to be in his fifties, and he was clearly agitated. I went to the sideboard and poured a mug of coffee.

"William," the captain called. "Meet Andrew, our chief steward."

Leaving the coffee on the sideboard, I walked over. He stood, offering his hand. "Andrew Casano, nice to meet you." His grip was strong, but his hand soft.

"William Connolly, Andrew. Likewise." He was my height, give or take an inch, but outweighed me by at least twenty-five flabby pounds. "You were the pier-head jumper last night?"

"That's me," he replied, smiling.

"We're just finishing up here," the captain said.

Andrew glared at the captain. "You need to get rid of one or the other, Captain," he said. He nodded at me, gathered the papers, and left.

"Sit down, William. We have a minute before the others show up."

I sat, waiting for him to continue.

"You're young," he started, "on a temporary second's waiver, so you may feel a little intimidated."

He was wrong. I felt a lot intimidated.

"DeSantis is signing off in Jacksonville," he went on. "So is Mr. Gillies. No telling who will replace them. I hoped for a company regular for first mate, but the boys in the main office weren't making any promises. Since it's unlikely we'll get an additional third mate, it will be tight watch-standing. Most first mates don't like to stand a regular watch." He stopped and stared at me. Not knowing what to say, I remained silent.

After a pause he continued. "I'm a recovering alcoholic, and lately we've been getting a lot of drunks and druggies as crew. It's hard for the company and the union to fill the open berths, so we have to make do with what they send us. Do you have a drinking problem?"

Caught aback by the question, I paused before answering. Taking my pause to be an evasion, he repeated, "Do you have a drinking problem?"

"No sir, I do not. I like to have a drink when I go ashore, but can do without it." Staring directly into his eyes when I said it must have convinced him.

"Good. I have a feeling I'll have to rely on you a lot during this trip. Jacksonville has a bad reputation, insofar as crewing problems. Too many drunks, and worse, too many drug addicts."

"Don't do drugs, sir. Never have," I said quickly, thinking I should beat him to the punch on that question.

Looking at me for a few seconds, he said, "Good. Alcohol is a problem; drugs are Satan himself trying to take you down." He nodded at me, a sign of dismissal and I stood, retrieved my mug of coffee, and went to my seat at the mate's table.

The other officers drifted in for lunch. Gillies arrived first, then Greg, both preoccupied and only nodding hello. The chief engineer and first engineer arrived together, which surprised me because the first engineer was supposed to be on watch. He shouldn't leave the engine room until relieved, and Greg, his relief, had just ordered his lunch. Looking at Greg, I raised my eyebrows. Greg eye-browed me back and shrugged.

Calling down my lunch order to the galley—tomato soup, a grilled cheese sandwich, and a glass of milk—I stood in the pantry waiting for it. No one spoke. An eerie silence. A room full of people and no noise. I heard the dumbwaiter coming before the bell rang. When it arrived, it held my lunch and Greg's. Carrying mine to the table, I told Greg his was in the dumbwaiter. As Greg stood, the second engineer, Ingvar Swenson, walked in. Ingvar was noticeable. Standing six-foot-four and weighing around two hundred pounds, he had a hard body. The top of his head was bald, shiny bald, but thick tufts of blond hair stood at attention on the sides, intruding upon his ears. His lamb-chop-shaped sideburns ran all the way to the edge of his chin.

When Ingvar walked in, the captain looked up, appeared puzzled, then counted heads and called out, "Chief, can I speak to you a moment?"

The chief engineer looked up and replied, "Sure, Captain," and remained sitting there.

Tilting his head and giving a backward nod, the captain indicated the chief should come to him.

The chief got the message, stood, went to the captain's table and leaned over.

"Chief," the captain said in a taut voice, "just who the hell is on watch? All of your engineers are here."

The chief looked at the assemblage, then said, "Oh, yeah," walked over to the first engineer, and whispered something to him.

Throughout this, I sat, my eyes riveted on the interplay.

The first engineer, Frank Harrison, stood, gave Greg—who was passing him carrying his lunch—a dirty look, then left the salon.

Greg pretended to be unaware, but he saw the look. There was trouble brewing between him and the first engineer.

That trouble would extend to the whole crew before the trip ended.

The conversation had died when the captain called the chief engineer, and it remained dead—the clink of cutlery the only sounds heard above the rattle and vibrations of the ship. At 1145 hours, Greg stood, brought his dishes to the galley, then left to relieve the first engineer.

Gillies also left to relieve the first mate. As I swallowed my last bite of the sticky grilled cheese sandwich, DeSantis entered the salon and said hello to everyone. He looked better than when he had relieved me this morning.

I said hello in response. The captain grunted, and the chief engineer nodded. DeSantis ordered his food in the pantry, then came and sat across from me. At the same time, the chief engineer stood and, without a word to anyone, left the salon.

"What's going on?" the first mate asked in a low voice. "The captain looks pissed-off, and the chief engineer isn't talking."

Hesitant to say anything with the captain so close by, I looked over at him just as he stood, nodded in our direction and left the salon.

With the captain gone, I related what happened, and DeSantis said, "That's really dumb. No one in the engine room at sea. No wonder the captain was pissed." He paused. "So, how are you doing? Feel comfortable on the four-to-eight watch? No problems?"

"I'm fine, mate. There's not a lot of difference between the third and second mate's duties other than navigation, and I'm comfortable with that part."

"Good, good." Another pause. "Sorry about this morning," he said, catching me by surprise. I didn't understand what he was talking about, and it must have shown on my face because he continued. "I had a little too much to drink last night and was hurting a little this morning."

"Oh, that? No problem, mate."

"It wasn't, William, but it could have been. I shouldn't have drunk so much, and it won't happen again."

I brushed it off, but was glad he had brought it up and recognized it for what it was.

The first engineer never came back for lunch.

With nothing to do until my watch, since the bedroom steward (BR) cleans the room and makes the bed and will do my laundry, too, for a small tip, I went down to the engine room and found Greg at the control station. The engine room was older, noisier, and dirtier than that of the 'Pride, looked a lot like the training ship Bay State engine room, and it functioned the same way. The boilers provided steam to the turbines and got condensed back into water to start the cycle over.

"You must be bored," Greg shouted. Normal conversation was impossible with all the background noise.

It isn't normal for a deckie to spend time in the engine room, but my dad was an engineer during WW II and infected me with the machinery bug. I would have been an engineer if the engine room on the training ship hadn't been so damn hot.

"Yeah, I am. Curious, too," I shouted back. "Give me a tour of the plant."

We spent the next half-hour walking around with Greg pointing things out. I pulled out a cigarette and stuck it in my mouth and was reaching for my lighter when Greg's eyes widened. A hand, not Greg's, came over my shoulder and grabbed the cigarette out of my mouth, whacking my lip in the process. Instinct took over. I ducked, pivoted to my right, threw a left hook into the gut of the owner of the hand, and followed it up with an uppercut that had the power of my legs behind it, missed the chin but landed solid on the nose, knocking him backwards. He tripped over Greg's feet and sprawled face down on the deck plates.

The owner of the hand, gut, and nose was the first engineer.

Greg had one foot on the rail of the walkway to avoid stepping on Harrison. He tried hard not to laugh. Attempting to get up, the first's hand slipped on the deck plate, and he gave himself another shot to the nose when he landed a full face-plant. Greg grabbed his arm and helped him up. Blood pouring from his nose, he turned, and I waited, not sure if I needed to defend myself or help him. The adrenaline had kicked in and I was panting.

Holding up one hand in front of him, he said something, but I couldn't understand with all the noise, so I yelled, "What?"

He repeated it, I heard him, but couldn't understand, so I gave him the "what" gesture with my hands and pointed to my right ear.

Greg understood, and he put his hand on the forearm of the first and yelled, "He said, What the fuck did you punch me for?"

"You started it," I yelled back. "I just defended myself."

He blubbered something about "smoking." I knew there wasn't any prohibition against smoking in the engine room, and my confused look was obvious.

Greg yelled, "Just go, William," and waved me out, so I left and went to my cabin.

Alternately pacing four steps, then leaning with two hands against the bulkhead—a tension reliever—I stewed in my cabin for twenty minutes. Glad my reflexes worked but worried about the consequences, I decided to tell the first mate what happened, wanting to get in the first shot at my defense. DeSantis was in his cabin. Expecting to get my ass reamed, I explained and offered no excuse other than my instincts taking over. DeSantis surprised me when he laughed and said, "Fuck him. He's an anti-social prick. Maybe he'll learn to communicate better. Don't worry about it. I'll let the captain know, in case the guy tries to stir up some shit."

I thanked him, went back to my cabin, and got ready to go on watch.

CHAPTER 10

0615 hours on Sunday morning 1/22/67, sunrise. The trailing wind had died so the relative wind had increased to fifteen MPH. Calm seas under a partly cloudy sky. We would pick up the Cape Fear pilot at 0700 hours.

The weather was warming, expected to hit a high of fifty-six degrees, so the captain ordered the vent cowls uncovered and turned forward. This would push warmer air into the cargo holds in an attempt to maintain a constant temperature and steady humidity inside and outside the hull which, in turn, reduces condensation. Whenever transitioning from hot to cold or vice versa, we try to do it gradually.

As you arrive on the inbound sea lane, the pilot station lies the southwest quadrant of an imaginary circle surrounding the "A" buoy, which starts the approach channel to the Cape Fear River. Most of the channel is only five-hundred to six-hundred-feet wide. Starting at Baldhead Shoals, there are three reaches: a wide loop around Battery Island passing Southport to our port side, then a run of reaches—Lower Swash, Snow's Marsh, Horseshoe Shoal—and finally, Reaves Point. Just after entering Reaves Point channel, we turned left into the Sunny Point access channel. Staying straight would have brought us to the Port of Wilmington.

DeSantis relieved me at 0745 hours, and after stopping by my cabin, I went below to the salon. The first engineer, nose grotesquely swollen, passed me as I entered, giving me a shoulder bump in the doorway. Not wanting to get in any deeper with him, I said, "Excuse me," and stepped back. He kept going. I noticed it was already 0800 hours, so he was late relieving the watch.

There was a buzz of talk. Everyone else seemed relaxed. I was the only one feeling tension. Andrew, the chief steward, sat with the captain, more papers in front of him. Going to the pantry, I called down my food order—buttermilk pancakes and a side of bacon. As I finished, there was a loud commotion and shouting in the galley, which carried up the dumbwaiter shaft.

The chief steward rose, said to the captain, "They're at it again," and hustled out the door, brushing past me.

The captain said, "William, go with him. He might need help."

Having no idea what was going on, but orders are orders, I followed Andrew down to the galley.

In the galley, the chief cook—Joselito Bautista, a native Filipino—was screaming at the baker, Ruperto Andrada—another native Filipino—in Tagalog, the main language of the Philippines. Ruperto was screaming back. Screaming rather than shouting, because both men had high-pitched voices, the kind that claws at your eardrums like fingernails on a chalk board. The only problem was, each of them had a butcher knife in his hand.

Andrew walked right between them, not a prudent move but a ballsy one, and pointed at each of them.

"Enough!" he shouted. "Knock this shit off right now, or you're both fired."

Both started making excuses, blaming the other, and Andrew let it go on for ten seconds, then roared, "I…said…*enough!*"

While this was going on, I grabbed a large iron frying pan and came up behind the baker with it, prepared to whack him in the head if necessary. It wasn't, this time.

With Andrew's last roar, both men put the knives back in the rack. The baker left the galley, and the cook went back to cooking. Andrew turned, indicated I should follow him, and walked out. In the companionway he said, "Thank you for the back-up. I could see you were ready to take out Ruperto."

Giving a sheepish grin, I said, "Yeah, but only from behind. That took a lot of balls to step between two guys with knives."

"Oh, I knew they wouldn't come after me. They're no threat to anyone except each other."

"Why?"

"They're cousins. They've been squabbling since they were little kids. It's more serious now. I've sailed with them before. By themselves, they're fine. Together, they're gasoline and a lit match. The minute I saw them, I knew they'd be trouble. That's why I told the captain, one of them has to go."

"Jeez," was all I managed, and he said, "Let's go finish breakfast."

Entering the salon, everyone looked up at us. "Well?" the captain said.

"The cousins are at it again, Captain, this time with knives."

"Damn! Did anyone get hurt?"

"Not this time, but if we don't split them up, it's inevitable. They hate each other, and it gets worse every day."

"All right, I'll see if we can get a replacement. Which one will go?"

"Ruperto, the baker. Joselito was here first, and he's a better cook than Ruperto is a baker." Pausing, he added, "William helped. He was ready to take out Ruperto with a frying pan. He has good instincts."

Across the room, Greg snorted, and the captain and Andrew turned and stared.

The captain asked, "Is there something you find amusing, Mister Russell?"

"My apologies, Captain, it was the 'good instincts' remark."

"I fail to see anything humorous about that."

The chief engineer interjected, "It seems William's instincts are the reason for the condition of Stoney's nose."

"Stoney? Nose? What are you talking about?" the captain replied.

"Stoney is the nickname of the first engineer, Frank Harrison. He never talks, like a stone," the chief continued. "Apparently, William here mistook Stoney's attempt to remove a cigarette from his mouth as an assault on his person, and he instinctively"—he emphasized the word—"defended himself, splattering Stoney's nose in the process."

From the surprised look on the captain's face, it was evident that DeSantis hadn't told him the story, as he said he would. "I see," the captain said, then returned to his breakfast without further comment.

Reordering my breakfast—the first order being ignored during the fracas in the galley—I poured a fresh coffee and sat, nursing it while I waited. I fidgeted with the slider board on the table, the one designed to keep dishes and glasses from sliding off during heavy weather, clicking it in and out of position.

"That's annoying," whispered Greg from the adjoining table, smiling.

"So are you at times." I reluctantly smiled but stopped fidgeting. The dumbwaiter bell rang, and I retrieved my breakfast.

The captain stood and said, "William, after we dock, come and see me."

"Yes, sir," I replied.

At 0930 hours, the captain called for mooring stations, and I went to the bridge, my station during mooring operations. He was there. He had already sent the first mate to the bow, to his mooring station. The Cape Fear River pilot stood at the forward railing, calling orders over his walkie-talkie to the two tug boats coming alongside of us.

"Slow ahead," the pilot called out, and I rang down the slow ahead on the engine-order telegraph. He ordered both tugs to tie up on the port side, one forward and one aft. Half a mile later, he pivoted the ship in the channel, and the tugs pushed us alongside berth #3, starboard side to the pier.

By 1000 hours, we were secure at the berth, and the captain ordered finished-with-engines. The engine room shut down the main plant, and we were on auxiliary power for the rest of our stay here. Since we were traveling coastwise, there were no Customs and Immigration officials, only the U.S. Army security and our local agent.

After securing the bridge, I stopped at the captain's office and knocked on the door. The ship's agent was with him. "Excuse me, Captain, you said you wanted to see me. If you're busy, I can come back later."

"No, no," he said, waving me in. "I'll be with you in a minute."

I stood just inside the door for five minutes while he finished with the agent. When the agent left, the captain motioned me to the chair in front of his desk. "William, I've decided that you and I are going to be allies."

My confused stare encouraged him to continue.

"You don't know it yet, but I expect to have a lot of crew trouble on this trip. The history of taking on crews in Jacksonville is bad and getting worse. This will be no exception. You will be my enforcer."

CHAPTER 11

The surrounding area was known as Snow's Point. It started as a plantation run by former Province of North Carolina Governor George Burrington. In 1725, a rice planter named Robert Snow took over, hence the name. During the Civil War, a Confederate artillery battery was positioned there to protect the Cape Fear River. The actual site is located on the former Howe's Point Plantation, named after Major General Robert Howe, a Revolutionary War commander. In 1951, the Sunny Point military logistics center was built, and the facility opened in 1955.

Sunny Point is one of the largest military terminals in the world, serving as a transfer point between ship, truck, and rail for weapons, munitions, and military equipment. A few miles upstream of Fort Johnston and Southport, it is sandwiched on 8500 acres between the Cape Fear River and the town of Boiling Spring Lakes, North Carolina. An additional 2500 acres on Pleasure Island serves as a buffer zone between the things that go boom and the civilian world. Being a restricted area, no river traffic, boats, or ships may anchor in the vicinity of the terminal. It is transit only, and they watch as you go by.

The security is tighter than a gnat's ass. So are the fire-watch rules. On the way in, the pilot warned us an Army representative would come aboard when we docked and give us instructions about the fire precautions. He didn't tell us a sentry would be posted at the gangway, and no one was allowed aboard without prior written permission from the captain. In retrospect, that seemed logical—it was a military munitions depot. What surprised me is they allowed no one ashore in the terminal unescorted. Anyone going ashore had to have the sentry call security, and they would ride us to the main gate. The same process worked in reverse when returning to the ship. If you forgot your I.D., you didn't get back in.

Our cargo would be bombs, bullets, and artillery shells.

The bombs we'd be carrying were the Mark 81 general purpose bomb, weighing 250 pounds, and the Mark 82, a bigger version, weighing 500 pounds. These were destined for Sattahip, Thailand, in support of the ongoing "Operation Rolling Thunder." For safety reasons, fuzes weren't carried on the same ship as bombs. A bomb is designed to be inert and not be triggered by bumping or dropping without a fuze attached. The fact they were called "fuze" rather than "fuse" was never explained, either. It must be a military thing.

The ammo would include 5.56 caliber cartridges for the M-16 carbine, in wooden cases labeled "cartridges," plus twenty-round magazines. There were .30 caliber cartridges for the Browning M1919 medium machine gun, labeled "bandoleers." We'd also haul pallets of .45 caliber cartridges to fit the Colt 1911 semi-automatic pistol, the standard sidearm issue of the Army and Marines.

Finally, we'd be hauling 60 mm M2 mortar shells, plus 105 mm and 198 mm shells for towed howitzer cannons.

Earlier, when discussing the care required to handle these munitions, the first mate commented, "They all exist for one purpose, to kill people. Make sure none of us dies by accident."

The first mate sat in his office and called me when I walked by, after leaving the captain. With DeSantis was the stevedore boss. A wizened shadow of a man, his face was gaunt. What skin he had was drawn tight across his skull, giving the appearance of a Halloween mask. He looked sick.

"William," the first mate said, "This is Barney."

The guy offered his hand and I shook it, all bones and weak. I was afraid of hurting him.

"Yeah, I know," he said. "I look like shit. That's because I only got a few months to live. Cancer."

"Jesus, Barney, I'm sorry to hear that," I said, thinking, Now I feel bad about that "Halloween mask" image. Then I thought: Halloween is coincident with All Souls Day and honors the dead, so, what the hell. Short bout of conscience.

He shrugged. "That's the way the cards are dealt. I got no family except the guys on the waterfront, and the company said they'll let me stay on as long as I can move around."

DeSantis said, "I'm letting Barney use the missing third mate's room while they're working, so you know where you can find him."

I nodded my understanding.

"Okay, then, we'll have two gangs working. The gang at #2 hatch will load the 198 mm shells in the lower hold. Next, they'll load 105 mm shells in the lower tweendeck and upper tweendeck, after end. Finally, they'll load the M2 mortar shells in the upper tweendeck, forward end." He looked up to see if I was paying attention.

"The gang at #5 hatch will start with MK-82 bombs in the lower hold, MK-81 bombs in the lower tweendeck, and small arms ammunition in the upper tweendeck. They start work at 1300 hours today and will only work daylight hours, so we'll knock off at 1700 hours. I don't know if it's a safety issue or union issue, but they'll start again tomorrow morning at 0800." One more look and I nodded.

"William, these longshoremen are good at their job. They know their lives depend on handling things right. Let's make sure the crew is as alert. There are absolutely no matches, fires, or open lights allowed on deck or in the hatches at any time we're docked here. No one can even carry a lighter in their pocket on deck. Make sure the deck gang knows that."

"Will do, DeSantis."

"Okay, we've broken sea watches, and they're only working daytime, so I want you on one hatch and Gillies on the other during work hours. Both of you can stand your night watches in your rooms. There's a military sentry at the gangway in addition to our gangway watchman, so nothing will happen without everybody knowing it."

Gillies said he'd cover #2 hatch, so I took #5. It took a half hour to open the hatch all the way to the lower hold. The MK-82s came two to a pallet, strapped with metal bands, and the gang loaded two pallets at a time on a tray. They placed a small forklift capable of lifting 3000 pounds in the hold and would lift one pallet off the tray, set it aside, and lift the other pallet off so the tray could recycle. While the tray was moving out of the ship, the forklift driver stowed the pallet he had on his forks, then grabbed the other one and stowed it before the tray came back in with the next load. The driver was efficient but careful. Whenever he got a little behind, they would hold the load over the main deck until the forklift driver was clear of the hatch opening. Good, safe stevedoring practices.

The four hours passed quickly. Barney, the stevedore boss, came by once, then returned to his room. At the end of the shift, I saw one of the longshoremen helping him walk down the gangway. It was sad to see him in such bad shape, but nice to see the guys cared enough about him to watch over him.

Gillies took the watch from 1800 to 2400, and I took the rest of the night. He sat in the salon watching TV, and I slept in my room until 0500 hours without incident.

I had already drunk two cups of coffee and stood on deck by the gangway, talking to the Army sentry, PFC Alfred Czernicki. He was from Nashua, New Hampshire, and was grateful he wasn't in Vietnam.

"Man, I've heard horror stories from guys coming back, even the transportation guys," he said. "I'm hoping I stay lucky and hang in here."

As he finished, I heard shouting from inside and thought, It's the damn cousins going at it again. I said to Alfred, "I think that's a fight. Let me check," and I went inside.

In the galley, the chief cook had the baker by the throat and held a knife an inch from his right eye. "Joselito," I yelled, amazed I remembered his name, "back off right now and put that knife down." Remembering Andrew's comment, that they were no threat to anyone but themselves, I stepped up beside them, and Joselito cast a sideways glance at me.

"Back off, Joselito. It's not worth going to jail for."

"How you going to make me?" he yelled.

My anger flared, and I leaned in, my face six inches from his. Before I could respond, I was gently pushed aside. Alfred, the sentry, took my place and said, "Sir, this is how I'm going to make you drop that knife," and Alfred stuck his .45 Colt 1911 pistol in the right ear of Joselito.

That's all it took. Joselito dropped the knife on the deck and let go of Ruperto, who scooted away to safety.

Alfred took a step back and lowered his pistol.

"Thanks, Alfred," I said. "I'll take it from here. He's not going to give me any trouble," I said, glaring at Joselito. "Are you, Joselito?"

Joselito mumbled "No," and Alfred holstered his pistol and returned to the gangway.

All the time, I'm thinking, the captain wants me to be his enforcer. That's asking for trouble, when I've been trying to avoid trouble. But deep down, the nagging doubt persisted. *Was I?*

Marching Joselito to the chief steward, I told him what happened, and said, "He's all yours." Before I left, I stuck my right forefinger beside Joselito's ear and whispered, "The next time, motherfucker, it'll be my gun." Stressing the "my."

I found the first mate and related what happened. "I don't want the sentry to get in trouble," I said. "He got me out of a bad situation."

"Let's go talk to him," he suggested, and we walked down to the gangway. DeSantis introduced himself and said, "Thanks for helping out in the galley. You won't get into any trouble for helping us, will you?"

"I don't think so, sir. I'm here for security, and that man was a definite risk factor. Unless the sergeant's in a bad mood, I should be okay."

"Well, we won't report it if you won't," DeSantis offered.

"Thank you, sir, but I have to report any time I unholster my weapon. This will go in my log report."

"Okay, but we want you to know we appreciate your help."

"You're welcome, sir."

Afterwards, the two of us were sitting in the captain's cabin, where DeSantis had repeated the story. The captain said, "I guess I've chosen the right guy for my enforcer. No weapon, and you stood up to the cook."

"Captain," I said, "I stood up to him because the chief steward had convinced me he wasn't a threat to anyone but his cousin. The steward was wrong. That guy was ready to stick me, until the .45 got stuck in his ear."

"Well, William, maybe we need to get you a Colt .45."

CHAPTER 12

0800 hours, and the gangs were back at it. It's amazing how soon you adapt to heaving bombs and ammunition around. Yesterday afternoon, I was skittish every time a load would swing in mid-air, but the longshoremen were careful and I relaxed. On occasion, I would still hold my breath for a few seconds as the forklift teetered. The MK-82 is almost seven feet long, so the blades of the forklift must be fully inserted into the skid pockets, or the forklift becomes a see-saw.

By 1500 hours, the forklift had run out of maneuvering room, and they had lifted it out of the hatch. Now they had to land the pallets by hand in the hatch square, a much slower process. The lower hold was full by the time they knocked off for the day at 1700 hours. Carpenters were ordered to start at 1800 hours. The gang in #2 hatch had also completed loading the lower hold.

The first mate ordered the bosun to break out cargo lights for the carpenters. When they came aboard, the foreman inspected all the lights and rejected two for frayed electrical cords. Not taking any chances on an explosion while his guys were down there, he said, "We can outrun a fire but not an explosion."

Gillies again took the 1800 to midnight watch, so I was free to relax. While at Sunny Point, the salon is the only place aboard where we can smoke, so I sat there shooting the breeze with Greg and filling the room with smoke.

"Tell me the truth," he started. "Do you miss Megan?"

Pausing before answering, I pictured her: red hair, fantastic body, sparkling eyes, the sound of her voice, her sensuous walk—the love I left behind in South Africa. "Yeah, I do. Try to not think about her, but she keeps creeping back into my head."

"Horny seamen are bad enough to deal with," he smirked, "but love-sick horny seamen are hopeless."

Flashing him a rueful smile, I said, "As much as I wish I could refute your wise observation, I can't. The sex was fantastic but...I loved her...still do. Don't think I'll ever meet anyone like her."

"Well, it's been a few months since you saw her. Why don't you write a letter and see if she's changed her mind about never leaving South Africa?"

"No. She made that decision knowing full well it was the end of our relationship. Mother's influence is too strong. Who knows, maybe in a year? Right now, it's too soon." I waited until Greg looked me in the eye and said, "What about you? Got a girlfriend? Is there anyone out there waiting for you to come home?"

"Nah. Oh, I've had a few flings, but never been in love. I've had a serious case of lust now and then, but never love," and he laughed.

"Never even come close?"

His demeanor changed; a solemn look stilled the features of his face. "Once, but that was destined for failure."

"Why?"

"She was white. In Baltimore, black men didn't date white women. Not if they wanted to stay out of the hospital. We met working a part-time job at a downtown store. There were six whites and two blacks. She was the only one who talked to me, other than give orders. Even the other black guy wouldn't talk to me when he saw she was being friendly. Probably afraid of retaliation. Jobs were hard to come by, and he needed that job."

"So, what happened.?"

"On Saturdays she and I would close up the store at ten o'clock. One night, after locking up and shutting off the lights, as we stood by the back door, she grabbed me and kissed me. I was terrified and thrilled."

"And?"

"It got to be a regular thing. Every Saturday night, after the lights were out, before leaving we'd make out. Within three weeks, we were going at it on cushions on the floor."

"So? What next?"

"My dad asked me why I was getting home so late, and I told him about her. Jeanine. That's her name, Jeanine." Wistful and melancholy. "Didn't tell him about the sex, just the kissing and friends part. Man, did he get pissed off."

"What did he say?"

"He grabbed me by both arms, pushed me against the wall, and said, 'Son, I want you to find someone to love in your life the way I found your mother, but what you're doing is suicide! You'll ruin your life and hers. Her people won't tolerate her behavior, and they'll take it out on both of you—mostly you!'" Greg shook his head, remembering. "I argued with him, but I knew he was right. You couldn't survive being a black man in a white world back then unless you played the game. He talked me into quitting the job. Never even went back for my last pay envelope. I have no idea what happened to Jeanine, and still have mixed feelings about whether we should have taken on the world, but in the end, I was too scared to try."

"Jesus, Greg. I guess I shouldn't feel too bad about Megan after hearing your story."

"Yeah, William," he replied in a forlorn tone, "you should. Love is hard to find. You and I are peas in a pod. We both had great girls who loved us, and racial or family issues screwed it up."

We sat in silence for a minute, then Greg stood, patted my shoulder—a big-brother habit I had come to appreciate—and he walked out.

I hung around for another Marlboro, rethinking my flash of temper with Joselito. I've worked hard at controlling my temper, knowing how much trouble it got me into as a kid, and now dismayed at how quickly it came back. The provocation was real. What if it was me who held the gun instead of PFC Czernicki? Would the outcome have been the same, or worse? Crushing out my cigarette, I went to my cabin and lay down.

I had dozed off when Jeff Gillies knocked on my door. "William, you're up. All's quiet. Checked in with the Army sentry at the gangway. Nothing happening. The carpenters finished a few minutes ago."

"Okay, Jeff. I got it. You're relieved."

Jeff walked away but left the door ajar. I got up, looked out into the companionway. Nothing but emptiness, vent fan noise, and muted engine room sounds. Rinsing my face, I went to the salon, got a mug of hours-old coffee, and walked below to the gangway where I found the sentry and my AB, Jason Winkler.

"Hello, Jason," I said and nodded at the sentry, another PFC. He wore fatigues and his name tag read "Shields."

"Evening, Mr. Mate," PFC Shields said. Winkler bowed his head and said nothing.

"Good evening, Private Shields. How long will you be on watch here?"

"Until 0800, sir."

"Can I get you anything? Coffee?"

"Thanks. Not right now. Maybe later."

"Okay. Just ask Winkler here and he'll get you what you want." Turning to Winkler, I asked, "You alone or is someone else up with you?"

"Just me. I'll wake the other AB at 0400."

"What about your ordinary? What's his name?

Winkler smiled. "Roger Highstone."

"What's so funny?" I asked.

"That's his name and condition," and he smiled again, revealing a humorous side. "High and stoned."

I smiled, but the coldness must have shown. Winkler stopped smiling and bowed his head again.

"Mr. Highstone will be neither high nor stoned on my watch. You have my permission to let him know."

Leaning over the railing, I looked up and down the pier, then returned to the salon, refilled my mug, and lit up a Marlboro. Highstone, I thought—another problem looming on the horizon? I wandered the ship all night, restless. Nostalgic thoughts of Meg sparred with apprehensive thoughts of Joselito and Highstone, keeping me distracted.

0700 found me again in the salon, talking to DeSantis with Gillies listening in.

"Two gangs again," the first mate said. "#2 lower tweendeck is 105 mm shells, and #5 lower tweendeck is MK-81 bombs. Did the carpenters cover the hold last night?"

"No, they finished about 2330 hours and left," Gillies answered.

"Have you checked the securing?"

"Only from looking over the coaming. I didn't climb down the hold."

"How about you, William?"

"The same. I didn't climb down, either."

"Get out there, both of you, and check it before they cover up," he barked. "We've got enough explosives on board to blow us halfway back to New York, if it starts banging around.

We stood and walked out, Gillies to #2 hatch and me to #5 hatch.

The manhole cover was open and secured, a safety precaution. Don't lock it in the open position, and you're likely to have it come down on your head or hands when climbing in or out. I put on my gloves and lowered myself through the opening, a tight squeeze. The manhole covers in the upper tweendeck and lower tweendeck were also open, and secured in the upright position. Halfway down the lower hold ladder, I stepped off onto the stacked bombs and crisscrossed the hatch, checking the securing, comprising mainly 4' by 4' lumber. There was a break-out space in the center of the square, and they had created plywood walls in the space and spanned the gap with 4' by 4' posts.

By the time I had finished, the longshore gang had already positioned the hatch beams and were working on placing the hatch boards. Every time they banged a hatch beam against the fitting, I jumped. Only three feet over my head, everything echoed in the tight spaces. As I walked toward the ladder, a hatch board landed three feet in front of me, the narrow end slamming into a case of MK 81 bombs. I jumped back and stumbled, falling hard on my right hip and jamming my right wrist. I looked up and eight pairs of eyes were riveted on me.

"Jesus, mate, I'm sorry!" one longshoreman said. "You okay?"

Shaken, but getting more pissed-off by the second, I stood up, ready to scream at someone— then realized I shouldn't have been standing under the space where they worked. I wanted to yell at them, but I knew *they* knew I was equally at fault for being in the wrong place, so I did the next best thing. Craning my neck, I called up, "You got any toilet paper? I think I shit myself."

Everyone laughed. Situation handled.

The last thing I did on my way up was close the lower-hold manhole cover and dog it down. As I started up the next ladder, the guy who dropped the hatch board came over and again said, "Sorry, mate."

"It's okay," I replied, and climbed out of the hold. When I reached the main deck, the gang foreman greeted me, and he apologized. "We take safety serious here. That shouldn't have happened."

"No, it shouldn't, but I shouldn't have been standing underneath them, either. Lesson learned on both sides, okay?"

"Sure, mate," he answered, and shook my hand.

I reported to DeSantis that all was secure. I also told him about the near miss and the subsequent conversations.

He laughed, and said, "Go get some breakfast before going back on deck. You must be empty after shitting yourself."

Two gangs worked all day, finished loading the lower tweendecks, and moved into the upper tweendecks. The #2 UTD was filled with shells for the M2 mortars, and the #5 UTD they filled with cases of .30 caliber, .45 caliber, and 5.56 mm ammunition. We completed loading by 1800 hours and had everything secured by midnight. We went back on sea watches at midnight, set the sailing board for 0700 hours, and I hit the sack.

CHAPTER 13

A tapping on my door woke me. "Yeah?" I called.

The OS from the twelve-to-four watch answered, "Time for watch, Mr. Connolly."

"Okay, thanks." Kicking off the sheet and blanket, I swung my feet over the edge, stood and stretched. Now awake, I went right to the bridge, skipping coffee.

"Good morning, William," Gillies called out as I walked in.

"Morning, Jeff. Anything happening?"

"Not now, but that crazy cook and baker got into it again around 0200 hours. The captain had the Army sentry handcuff the baker, and hauled his ass off the ship."

The captain walked onto the bridge as Jeff finished. "The bastard's lucky I didn't shoot him, carrying a meat cleaver. When I called him out, he turned and started at me. Thought better of it when I showed him Mr. Colt's handiwork," he said, patting the.45 sitting in a holster on his right hip. "Good riddance. One less asshole to deal with."

"Did they arrest him, Captain?" I asked.

"No. Too much paperwork, and I would have to come back here for a hearing if I pressed charges. I had the ship's agent get him at the gate. We'll have someone pack his gear and send it ashore in Jacksonville."

The captain ordered us to mooring stations at 0630, and by 0700 we let the last line go. With only one tug assisting, in most cases it's easier to undock than dock. We slipped down the Cape Fear River under clear skies, temperature at 52 degrees, and a light, northerly breeze at eight miles per hour.

The coastal run to Jacksonville was smooth sailing. When I came off watch at 0800 and went in for breakfast, the captain told me to see him in his cabin after I ate. Not knowing the reason, I was nervous. I gulped down two slices of toast, washed them down with coffee, peed again, nerves more than bladder issues, and knocked on his open door.

"C'mon in, William."

When I stood in front of his desk, the .45 colt back in its perch on the side, he said, "Have a seat." I sat.

"How proficient with guns are you?" he asked.

Surprised, I didn't hesitate. "Pretty good with a rifle and pistol. So-so with a shotgun."

"Where did you learn to shoot?"

"In the Boy Scouts. The scoutmaster was a little different than most. He wouldn't let you become a First-Class scout until you could shoot over 90 out of 100 with a rifle, a .22 caliber, and 40 out of 50 with a pistol, also a .22." I chuckled, thinking back to the time I was a scout, and the captain asked, "What's funny?"

"We also had to learn to drive a 1945 Willy's Jeep. He kept it at the scout reservation camp grounds. It's a miracle no one ever got killed. We rolled that Jeep over at least a dozen times. There were different size wooden blocks he'd strap to the pedals, so the kids with short legs could reach them."

"Your scoutmaster sounds like an interesting guy."

"Interesting?" I repeated. "More like dangerous."

"How so?" the captain asked.

"He was queer."

The captain said nothing, so I continued. "When a new kid came into the troop, the older guys would warn him. Some kids understood, some didn't. In the cabin on the scout reservation, we had two tiers of bunks, and the scoutmaster slept in the middle, top bunk. He always assigned the new kids the bunks next to him." I paused, remembering, "He was a pedophile. I didn't know what that meant until my senior year in high school, long out of the scouts. Until then, he was just a queer who tried to hit on us."

The captain stared at me. "Weren't you a new kid at one time?"

I stared back. "Yeah, but I understood. When he tried to grab me, I yelled like I woke up from a nightmare. Woke everyone else up. He never tried again. Next time at the cabin, I had a different bunk assignment."

The captain scratched his head. "If everyone knew he was queer, why didn't they tell their parents?"

"We were kids. We did fun things in that troop no one else did. He paid for camping trips that most of us couldn't afford. We figured, no harm, no foul." I paused.

"There were probably a few kids who did tell their folks, but if so, nothing ever happened."

The captain shook his head. "Okay, you've convinced me even more that you can deal with dicey situations. I told you before, you'd be my enforcer, and I meant it. I don't want you going around beating the crew up, but I will have to rely on someone to intercede when altercations break out."

"Why are you so certain there will be 'altercations'?" I asked.

"Half of our crew are drunks and druggies. The sober ones are getting off in Jacksonville. Whoever replaces them will be a drunk or druggie. Trust me, I know. Our biggest problem will be breaking up fights without getting hurt, and without hurting the idiots who are fighting. At least, don't hurt them too seriously."

"You expect me to break up fights and not hurt the ones fighting?"

"Yes."

"With all due respect, Captain, that will guarantee that *I'll* get hurt. Where I grew up, a bar stool across the back of the head was a fair fight. If the guy tries to get up, you hit him harder with the stool. I'm not interested in being a referee, especially if the guys are on drugs. Guys on drugs do weird things and don't feel pain. If someone can't feel pain, the only way to stop him is to put him out cold."

The captain stared at me for a few seconds, rubbing his chin. "William, you're young and have reflexes. I'm old and my reflexes are shot. The only two ways I can break up a fight is by either putting my head in front of their fist and having them break their hand, or shooting them. Neither of those options are practical." He paused, rubbed his chin again. "Think about it. Recruit someone else to help you. Be innovative, but when we sail from Jacksonville, if you are still on the ship, you are my enforcer."

I sat in my cabin most of the morning, mulling over what the captain said. A major decision faced me. Figure out a way to break up fights with the least amount of damage to the participants and none to me, or sign off in Jacksonville and tell the captain to kiss my ass. Instinct told me to do the latter, but the captain had laid down a challenge.

I went looking for Greg. We had previously agreed that if one of us bailed out, so would the other. Decision time.

He was in his cabin, and I explained the situation.

"What is it about you that attracts these kinds of situations?" he said and laughed.

"Damned if I know. So, what are we going to do?"

"We? What's this 'we' stuff? No one's asking me to be a one-man army."

"C'mon, Greg, I'm asking for advice. You're the only one I trust."

"Thanks for the confidence, William, but I don't know what to tell you. Listening to you, I get the feeling you really want to do this, just to prove you can." Looking at me, he asked, "Do you?"

I stared at the deck and didn't answer.

He continued, "Yeah…you do."

"Dammit, Greg, I don't like to quit on anything. The captain needs help, that's obvious. I need to know if I can count on you if I need help."

Greg stared. "That's almost insulting, given what we've been through already. But I know how often your mouth moves before your brain engages, so I'll forgive you…and, yes, I'll help you."

"Thanks, Greg. That means a lot."

"There's one thing, though, before you run off and play hero."

"What's that?"

"Think about how you're going to minimize the fights to begin with, and remember that just about everyone aboard carries a knife. That will be the number one problem. How to get their knives away from them. Let me know what you come up with. We'll be in Jacksonville tomorrow morning."

By noon the temperature was 70 degrees, and the captain had all the vent cowlings open and facing the wind, balancing out the temperature in the holds. If I only had a method for evening out temperaments that was as simple.

When I got relieved at 1700 for supper, Greg was in the salon. He leaned over and whispered, "Any bright ideas yet?" but he smiled and that eased the tension.

I got off watch at 2000, then I sat in my cabin and doodled, drawing sketches. I had a few ideas on how to break up knife fights, and decided to run them by Greg in the morning.

CHAPTER 14

0630 on Thursday 1/26/67. Partly cloudy skies, sixty-five degrees, wind from the northwest at seven mph. Three- foot waves with a gentle counter-swell from the east. The ship, a little stiff, rolling four degrees on the swells.

We were approaching the St. John's River pilot station. The captain had reduced speed to half ahead at 0600 hours. I had smelled the pulp mills for the last hour when the wind switched from north to northwest.

There's no mistaking the stench of pulp mills. This is now the third time I've come to Jacksonville. Once on my training cruise aboard the *T.S. Bay State*, the second on my first trip to South America aboard the *Mormacpride*, and now. The smell never changed. Wet paper mixed with the sulfur smell of rotten eggs, all percolating under the cloud of a fart.

We picked up the pilot at 0700 hours and proceeded up the narrow, twisting channel at twelve knots. We drew 27 feet of water aft and 26 feet 2 inches forward. The channel depth was 34 feet, so we weren't sucking up any bottom silt. The pilot wanted to go faster, fifteen knots, but the captain said no. "It's an old ship, Mr. Pilot. Things break down on old ships, so if you don't mind, I prefer twelve knots."

The pilot, who didn't look any older than me, replied, "It's your command, Captain, I'm just an advisor."

Talleyrand Terminal is twenty-one nautical miles from the sea buoy at the approach to the river. It was 0900 before we were alongside berth #3. From the start of the voyage, the plan was for Jacksonville to be a short stop. We were to load toilet paper, beer, and soda. Since in Sunny Point, they filled out all the upper tweendeck wings, forward and aft; the only space left was in the hatch squares.

DeSantis and Gillies were signing off and leaving but their replacements hadn't shown up when the longshoremen started to work at 1300 hours. DeSantis told me where he wanted things to go, and I covered both hatches. #2 hatch carried cases of toilet paper forward and cases of Budweiser and Pabst Blue Ribbon beer aft. #5 hatch had toilet paper aft and cases of Coca-Cola forward.

Funny thing about the beer. Pop-tops had been around for a few years now, but all the beer was the old kind, where you needed a church key to open it. Another inane government rule, or just the usual inefficiency?

Payoff for those leaving and signing of articles started at 1500 hours. Seven men, including DeSantis and Gillies, signed off. I didn't know if the other five were the sober ones, as the captain had indicated, but he was dead right about the replacements.

Everyone had to sign the articles since this was a new trip. The entire crew trooped through the salon, where the captain, chief steward, and a U.S. Coast Guard ensign sat at a six-foot folding table, checking Z-cards, filling out allotment forms, and witnessing the signing. I was first in line, since I had to watch the loading operation, and neither the new first mate or third mate had arrived yet.

When I walked into the salon, there were three new men already there, waiting. An AB, a wiper, and an oiler. As I stepped past them, the strong reek of alcohol washed over me. The lead man, the oiler, grabbed my arm and slurred, "Hey, we been waitin. Get in line."

This was ballsy in itself, but the fact I was wearing my uniform with shoulder boards, showing my officer status, made it stupid. I grabbed the guy's wrist and twisted it, pulling it off my arm. He went down to one knee, more from the amount of alcohol in his system than the strength of my twisting.

"On this ship," I said, "you keep your hands to yourself."

The captain and the ensign, sitting four feet away, witnessed the entire scene.

"Ensign Drake," the captain said, "you have just witnessed this man assault my second mate, who was forced to defend himself. I refuse to sign him on as a crew member."

The ensign hesitated a few seconds, then said, "Yes, Captain, you're right. I'll report his conduct to my base commander." Turning to the oiler, still on one knee, he said, "Give me your Z-card."

I released the guy and stepped back. He stumbled to his feet and reached into his pocket. Instead of the Z-card, he pulled out a switch-blade knife, flicked it open, and lunged at the ensign, screaming, "Fuck you!"

The ensign fell over backwards from his chair and before the guy could do any damage, I jumped on his back, grabbing his knife hand. The table collapsed, and we both went down, him face-first. When his face hit the deck, he dropped the knife, and the ensign, scrambling to his feet, kicked it away.

I had him in a half-nelson face down and still had a grip on his right wrist. He was struggling, but feebly.

"Someone get some rope to tie him up," I yelled.

During all this, the captain had pushed his chair back, but otherwise hadn't moved. "Hold him," he said. "I have handcuffs in my cabin," and he got up and walked out. Two minutes later he returned and offered me the cuffs.

"I'm gonna put these cuffs on you, and if you fight me, I'll break both your arms, got it?" I rasped.

The oiler whimpered, but he went limp. I pulled his right arm behind him and got the cuffs on, then let go his neck and pulled his left arm back, securing the cuffs, still sitting astride him. I stood up, grabbed the cuffs and hauled him to his feet, making sure I hurt him. I walked him over to the far corner of the salon, pushed him down to sit on the deck, and whispered: "Don't! Fucking! Move!"

It was over.

The salon had filled during the scuffle, with more crew members standing outside in the passageway. The chief steward and ensign had set the table up again. One leg was bent, but it functioned.

"Mr. Connolly," the captain said, "I believe you were about to sign articles," and he handed me a pen.

After signing, I filled out the allotment forms for my pay to be sent home to my sister Betty, and signed them. As I handed them back to the chief steward, he smiled and whispered, "Nice moves, William."

I returned a rueful grin, feeling the pain in my knees where I banged them on the deck during the wrestling match. Turning, I said, "Captain, I'll be on deck watching the loading operations," and walked out.

CHAPTER 15

The longshore gangs knocked off at 1700 hours, due to return at 0800 hours the next day. During World War II, we would have worked around the clock to get the munitions to the fighting men on the front. Another effect of Vietnam being called a conflict rather than a war? When they left the ship, I went to my cabin and cleaned up, then went to the salon. Most of the officers were there eating, except Greg and the captain, and the conversation was subdued. The folding table I had knocked over leaned against the bulkhead, one broken leg poking up like a distress signal. Ensign Drake and the chief steward, Andrew Casano, sat at the captain's table, hands crossed in front of them like grammar school students.

"Andrew," I said, "What's going on? Aren't we finished with sign-on?"

"Not quite. We're waiting on the new first mate driving in from Tallahassee. The company waited until the last minute to hire a replacement for DeSantis."

I shook my head, sat at my usual seat, and looked at the menu. Salisbury steak or salmon. I sniffed, smelling nothing but this morning's coffee. Choosing the steak with red potatoes, green beans, and stewed tomatoes, I looked around for the pantryman.

"Sorry, William," Andrew called out. "Call it down yourself. Still no pantryman. Maybe in Panama."

Heading into the pantry, I called the order down. When I walked out, Greg came in the salon door. He following me to my table and sat opposite me, where the first mate would normally sit. "Heard you beat up my new oiler," he said and grinned. "The old one was an asshole, too, so you did me a favor. The wiper and I will get along fine with just the two of us. He doesn't drink."

Before I could respond, the new first mate strutted into the salon, all five feet zero inches of him. One hundred and twenty pounds soaking wet, his long black hair hung in a ponytail. Appearing to be maybe forty-five years old, he walked to the center of the room, put both hands on his hips and announced, "I'm Thomas Crozier, your first mate. Where's the captain?"

The chief steward responded, "Probably in his cabin. We need to sign you on so we can finish things here."

"Who are you?" Crozier demanded.

"Andrew Casano, chief steward. This is Ensign Drake, and he has to get back to his post. We've been waiting for you. You're the last to sign articles."

"Then you should have given me more notice, and I would have been here earlier," Crozier replied, exuding hostility.

"Mate," Andrew said, "this isn't my doing, nor is it Ensign Drake's doing. Get as pissed off at the company headquarters as you want, but don't take it out on us." Ensign Drake visibly cringed but didn't say anything.

Crozier didn't reply, but pivoted slowly, looking around the room, both hands still planted on his hips, then walked to the table in front of Ensign Drake and said with total insincerity, "My apologies. Where do I sign?"

After signing articles, he didn't make out an allotment form, a legal document that allows you to name a designated person to receive as much of your pay as you decide. He walked out in search of the captain. He wasn't five seconds out the door when the chief engineer pronounced, "Boys, it looks like Napoleon traded in his big white horse for this rust bucket and is sailing with us." It drew a few chuckles.

Greg said, "Well, William, it looks like you're hanging in here. You did sign the articles, didn't you?"

"Yeah, I did. Hell of a way to start. The captain got rid of the oiler, but the other guys didn't look any better, and they all stunk of booze."

"Have you seen the replacement third mate yet?" Greg asked.

"Nope, been on deck all afternoon. Don't even know if we're on sea watches or port watches. DeSantis never said anything, just left. Normally, in a U.S. port we'd break sea watches and get night mates from the union. I'll check with the new first mate after supper. How's your end? Any changes in the engineers?"

"Just the unlicensed guys. Too soon to tell how they'll behave, but you did me a favor by dumping the replacement oiler. We're already short a fireman, but my wiper is a quiet guy, a good worker, and has both an oiler and fireman rating. He'll get double pay as wiper and oiler, unless the chief engineer makes him split it with someone. He's also black, so he adds class to the group," and he gave me that "gotcha" smile.

"What about the missing fireman?" I asked.

"The two firemen are splitting the watch, six on and six off, so they're happy."

After supper, I went looking for the first mate and found him with the captain. Knocking on the open door, I waited for the captain's "Come in" before entering.

"Excuse me Captain, have we broken sea watches? DeSantis didn't say anything before leaving."

"William, meet our replacement first mate, Thomas Crozier."

Extending my hand, I said, "I'm William Connolly. Pleased to meet you."

He hesitated a second before shaking hands, and just nodded.

"I was explaining to Thomas about our crew shortage problem," the captain continued, "and how he would have to stand a watch at sea." He continued, "We'll stay on sea watches, since the union can't supply night mates. We'll be sailing tomorrow evening. Give Mr. Crozier the night to get organized. Bring him up to speed on the cargo operations, since you're the only one who's paid attention to it today."

"Yes sir, Captain," I answered.

"Do you want to go over it now, mate?"

"No. I'll find you in the morning."

Nodding to both, I went to the bridge to check on the charts for tomorrow's sailing.

Standing on the inshore bridge wing, dragging on a Marlboro, I saw a small delivery van pull up to the foot of the gangway. The driver got out, looked up, and waved to someone at the top. Three men started down the gangway. Leading the way was OS Highstone, the guy AB Winkler had made fun of, saying he was high and stoned all the time. Both were on my watch. I didn't recognize the other two, so they must have been replacements.

At the bottom, Highstone talked to the driver, then handed him an envelope. The driver opened it, looked inside, and riffled through the contents. I figured it was cash. He then opened the rear door of the van, and the two crew members each picked up two cases, each the size of a whiskey case. Highstone carried one case and also took a bulging manila clasp envelope from the driver. They never saw me watching as they climbed back aboard, but then, they didn't seem be hiding anything.

At 1940 hours my AB, Winkler, came in to the bridge and said, "We don't know who to call for the next watch."

"Neither do I, the new first mate never told me what watch he was standing. I'll find out." Going below, I knocked on the captain's door. After a minute, he opened the door. "William, something wrong?"

"No one has relieved me, Captain. I don't know who has the eight-to-twelve watch, the new third mate or the first mate."

"Me either," he replied and stepped into the passageway. "Come with me." I followed him to the first mate's room, where he knocked on the door and called out, "Mr. Crozier." When the first mate opened the door, clad in only his boxer shorts, the captain said, "You were supposed to inform the other mates who was standing what watch. No one has informed Mr. Connolly, and no one has relieved him."

"I'm taking the twelve-to-four watch," he replied. "Wake up the third mate."

"I'll get him," I said and left the captain and first mate staring at each other, a real Mutt and Jeff scenario. Returning to the bridge, I told Winkler to call out the third mate and tell him to report to the bridge. It was already 2000 hours.

At 2010 hours, the new third mate came rushing on to the bridge. "Sorry I'm late, I was asleep, and no one woke me up."

"That's okay. Did you even know you had the eight-to-twelve watch?"

"Yeah, the first mate banged on my door around 1830 and told me. I'm George Cavers," and reached out his hand.

"William Connolly, George, welcome aboard."

Cavers stood five-foot-nine, weighed maybe one-seventy, with brown, shaggy hair that looked as if it had been hacked with a dull knife. He had a large, curved scar on his right cheek, and an indentation on his cheek bone that looked like a crushing injury. I filled him in on what cargo we were carrying and when we expected to finish cargo operations and sail.

He gave me a short version of his background. He came up through the hawsepipe, meaning he worked his way up from an ordinary seaman and never attended any of the maritime schools. Been sailing since he was eighteen, got his third mate's license five years ago. Now forty-five, he was single and had no desire to sail anything except third mate. "Too much responsibility," he said.

I left him at 2045, went below, and turned in, feeling less than confident I had made the right decision by signing on for the voyage.

I woke and sat up just before the OS knocked on my door to call me for the watch. At sea, my inner clock did that a lot. In port, not so much. I stretched, did a few touch-your-toes to get the kinks out, cleaned up, and went to the salon for coffee. The new first mate, Crozier, sat there drinking coffee and smoking. So tempted to say, "Smoking will stunt your growth," I had to stifle a smile.

"Good morning, Mr. Mate," I said.

"Good morning. It's William, right?"

"Yes, sir."

"I got off on the wrong foot yesterday, what with the late call-out. Came in a little grumpy. Call me Tom." He offered his hand. Unlike yesterday, this was a real handshake. "So," he continued, "I looked at the cargo plan. Tell me what's happening when the longshoremen show up this morning."

"Simple. They're just filling out the squares in the upper tweendecks of #2 and #5 hatch. Should finish by noon. Don't know if anyone has ordered carpenters to secure the cargo. We should check on that first thing. Most of the stow is tight, but the toilet paper cases are cardboard. I think we should erect a wall between them and the beer and soda."

"Okay, sounds good. Call me at 0600 and I'll reach out for the agent and make sure we get carpenters." He stood, picked up the pack from the table, crushed out his cigarette—an unfiltered Old Gold, the same kind my mother smoked—and left.

0730, I stood at the top of the gangway talking to George Cavers, the third mate. "The first mate called for carpenters this morning, but it's too late for the morning shift." I told him. "They won't show until 1300 hours. The longshoremen should be done loading by then."

"Okay, anything in particular I need to keep an eye on?"

"Make sure they leave at least six inches space between the beer and soda cases and the toilet paper cases. The mate wants to drop a wall between them. The toilet paper can't go anywhere, but the beer or soda could fall and the TP cartons won't take the pressure."

I slept through lunch and woke at 1500 hours. Grabbing a coffee and two chocolate chip cookies left over from lunch, I wolfed them down, chugged the coffee, and knocked on the captain's door. I thought I heard something but wasn't sure, so I knocked a second time.

"I'm coming, hold your water." Thirty seconds later, the captain opened the door. "Mr. Connolly, I never mind being woken up, but when I am on the toilet, I am constrained by Mother Nature. What is so urgent that you had to pound on my door twice?"

"I'm sorry, Captain, I didn't hear anything, so I knocked again."

Waving his hand in a dismissive gesture, he said, "So what's the problem?"

"You said you wanted me to be your enforcer. I believe in the adage, 'An ounce of prevention is worth a pound of cure.'"

He waited, raising an eyebrow, so I continued. "Last night from the bridge wing I saw my OS Highstone, and two other guys I didn't recognize, carry five cases of what looked like whiskey aboard. He also had a manila envelope of other stuff, probably drugs. I suggest we raid his cabin, confiscate the booze, and deep-six the drugs."

The captain pursed his lips, scratched his chin, and said, "You're probably right. The problem is, the crew are entitled to have liquor and beer aboard. They can't drink while on duty, so, until they act up, I don't have a valid reason for taking it away. Drugs, however, we can act on any time."

"Can't we confiscate their booze and parcel it out to them, limiting their intake?"

"We could, but that's more headaches for us. I'd rather wait until they give us a reason to dump it overboard." He smiled. "Do you have any more prime suspects?"

"Everyone on board other than you, me, and Greg, the third engineer."

"Your instincts are good, William. Ask your friend Greg to keep an eye out in the engine department for troublemakers and let you know. In the meantime, stay alert."

"Yes, sir." I left, closing the door behind me.

It was 1530 hours. I walked out on deck and found the third mate, Cavers, standing on the offshore side at # 2 hatch, watching the longshoremen still at it. "How's it going, George?" I asked.

"Slow, William. They dragged their feet all morning. I think they'll finish up here in an hour. #5 hatch will take a little longer. The stevedore supervisor told me they set back the carpenters until 1700 hours."

"Okay, let me find the first mate and check with him, then I'll come back and relieve you."

"He just went forward looking for the bosun. Take your time," he replied. "I'm not going anywhere."

The first mate stood outside the bosun's locker, talking into the shadows. As I approached, the odor of paint and fish oil assaulted my nose. I saw Boat's frame filling the doorway. Boats looked up when I neared, and the first mate turned. "Mr. Connolly?" he said.

"Just checking on the work tonight. I understand the carpenters will arrive at 1700 hours."

"That's right. They'll work until they finish. The captain set the sailing board for 0600 tomorrow morning."

"Any special instructions on the securing?"

"Nope, your suggestion of erecting a wall between the heavy cases and the toilet paper is the right thing, that's all we should need. The cargo is tight against the hull on both sides." With that, he walked aft, toward the house.

Turning to Boats, I stepped to the doorway and said, "They'll need cargo lights. Have the crew break some out."

"Sure thing, mate." The reek of stale beer washed over me. I looked closer. His eyes were blood shot.

It's now or never, I figured. "Boats, you're on duty, and you stink of booze. You're bleeding to death through your eyes. Is this what I'm going to see and smell every time I see you?"

An instant hardening of his features. "Nah, mate. It was a rough night last night, and I had a little hair-of-the-dog. I'll be fine."

Holding his gaze, I said, "Good. Glad to hear it." I then walked back and relieved Cavers, the third mate.

Both gangs finished loading and were off the ship by 1700 hours, the carpenters passing them, coming aboard. The carpenters started at #5 hatch and made ten-foot wide and eight-foot tall sections of fencing using 4' x 4' hardwood posts and 1' x 6' boards nailed across them. They slid each completed section down into the narrow space between the two types of case, creating a solid fence. When they completed the wall, they dug down a few cases on each side so they could reach the ship's steel frames and attached shackles to the lightening holes in them. Then they looped one-inch diameter steel cable between the shackles and attached a turnbuckle at one end. They had to dig out a few more cases of toilet paper to make room for them to tighten the turnbuckle. I told them to leave the loose cases on top of the stow, in the square of the hatch, in case we had to tighten the turnbuckle during the voyage. When finished with #5, they repeated the process in #2 hatch, then covered up both hatches.

They worked fast. With a minimum guarantee of six hours pay, they were on their own time. When Cavers relieved me at 1950 hours, they were laying the final pontoons on the hatch. Reminding Cavers to tell the bosun to have the crew secure and batten down the hatch tarps when the carpenters finished, I went to my cabin, washed up, and went to the salon to see what might be available to eat. I had slept through lunch and skipped supper and was hungry.

All the engineers except Greg were in there, watching television. The chief engineer and the captain sat at the captain's table. There were papers on the table, but neither one looked at them. The captain looked intense and stared at the chief, talking in a low voice. When I walked in, the captain glanced at me, a look of consternation on his face.

I went to the sideboard and got a coffee. The mid-meal for the late watch wasn't out yet, so I made three pieces of toast and slathered them with grape jelly. Not a gourmet meal, but it worked. As I stood to get a refill for my coffee, I heard the captain growl, "I'm serious, Wesley. Fall off the wagon again and you're off my ship!" Everyone in the room heard it.

The chief engineer mumbled something, stood, and tottered out the door. No one spoke. The captain stood, and as he walked past me, signaled with his eyes and a nod to follow him. I took my coffee and followed him to his cabin.

"Sit down William," he said, sounding tired and frustrated. "Sorry that had to be in front of everyone, but the chief didn't give me any choice. The chief is a recovering alcoholic, like me, but has a harder time staying on the wagon. He'll go for a week or two and then get drunk—usually not more than a day, but he can be a real asshole when he's drunk. If he's not sober in the morning, his cabin will be the first one you raid."

CHAPTER 16

0530 hours, Saturday, 1/28/67. Pilot aboard, two tugs alongside, fore and aft. Cloudless sky, wind from the northwest at fifteen MPH, temperature 57 degrees. Our sailing draft is 27' 9" aft and 26' 11" forward.

At 0555, the captain gave the order to single up the mooring lines. We had docked the ship starboard side to the pier, so had to turn around before proceeding down-river. Letting go the aft spring line, the pilot ordered "dead slow ahead" to pivot on the forward spring line and bring the stern away from the dock. The wind was on our starboard quarter so that helped push us off. At the same time, the pilot ordered the aft tug to take a strain and start pulling us off the dock. As soon as the ship moved, he ordered "stop engine." When the stern was fifty feet off the dock, he ordered the forward tug to take a strain, pulling the entire ship off the pier at an angle.

When the bow was two hundred feet clear of the berth, the pilot ordered the forward tug to push against the bow. With the aft tug pulling and the forward one pushing, we were spinning in our own length in the middle of the channel. Once aligned in the channel, the pilot ordered "slow ahead," and the ship gained headway. He released the forward tug but told the aft tug to stay tethered loosely and follow the ship down the channel. When we reached Blount Island about halfway down, he released the second tug. We were on our own.

At 0800 hours, we were in open water, getting close to the drop-off point for the pilot. The third mate relieved me. The captain, who had been on the bridge for the entire transit down the river, asked me to stop in and see him after I had breakfast. Nodding, I said, "Aye, aye Captain," and went below.

In the salon, the chief engineer, Wesley Gibson, sat at the captain's table with his head propped up, both fists lodged under his chin, looking rough. Greg was at the engineer table along with the second engineer, studiously avoiding one another. The first mate, Crozier, occupied the mate's table. After ordering coffee, scrambled eggs, bacon, and toast, I joined him.

"Not a happy group," he said when I sat down.

I looked around. "Doesn't seem to be."

"Was it this way before I came aboard?" he said, showing a wry smile.

Shrugging, I replied, "Some of it was, yeah. The thing with the chief engineer—that's new."

"And by 'the thing' do you mean he's drunk?"

"Last night, yeah."

"Look again, William—he's stinko!"

I turned and looked as the chief's head slipped off his fists and he thunked his head on the table, letting out a loud "What the fug?" He rubbed his forehead and peered around the room, focusing on the first mate. "What the fug's the matter?" he asked the room in general. No one responded, but the first mate kept staring at him. The chief pushed himself erect, weaving, pointed at the first mate and yelled, "You got a fuggin problem, Napoleon?"

The captain walked in as "Napoleon" hung in the air. "Wesley," the captain said. The chief continued to glare at the mate. "Chief Gibson," louder now, "I am talking to you."

The chief looked at the captain and barked, "What?"

The look on the captain's face turned to steel. "Chief Gibson, go to my cabin, now. We can talk privately there."

After ten seconds of glaring, the chief stumbled out of the room.

Addressing the rest of us, the captain said, "Gentlemen, go on about your business and put this bit of unpleasantness behind you. William, come with me." Then he turned and left. I followed.

Outside the salon door, he handed me a key.

"This is a master key. Go toss the chief's room now. Any booze or drugs you find, bring to my cabin."

He left, and I went to the chief's cabin, which was unlocked. The chief had a small office as well as a bedroom. I didn't try to be neat. Fifteen minutes later, I had found a case of Cutty Sark Scotch, less two bottles, and about three pounds of marijuana. The marijuana was stuffed into socks in his clothes drawer.

I didn't knock. Walking in, I put the booze and marijuana on the captain's settee. "This is all I found, Captain."

The chief sprawled in a chair. When he saw the Scotch, he said, "Hey, that's mine," and tried to stand. I stepped between him and the settee as the captain said, "Sit your ass down, Wesley, and shut the fuck up!"

I shot the captain a surprised look.

The chief wavered, then collapsed into the chair.

"I warned you last night. You didn't pay heed." Looking at me: "William, what's in the socks?"

"Marijuana, Captain."

He reached both hands up and rubbed the bridge of his nose and forehead. "Wesley, William here is going to pour all of your Scotch down the sink. Then he is going to throw your marijuana overboard. If you so much as whimper, I'll have him put you in handcuffs, and I'll leave you attached to a rail on the flying bridge until you sober up. Then I will enter the entire incident in the ship's log." He paused and took a deep breath. "If you sit there and behave, and if you are not drunk again tomorrow, this incident will be forgotten. Your choice. Decide."

The chief squirmed for a few seconds, and muttered, "Okay. Can I go to my cabin?"

"Yes, you may, but nowhere else until you're sober."

The chief tottered out the door. The captain waved his hand, and I dumped all the Scotch down his sink drain. As I picked up the marijuana, he said, "Throw the case and bottles away. I don't want the smell here." As I picked them up, he said, "My language to the chief was not the king's English." He paused. "It's really a matter of timing and effectiveness."

My dumb look spurred him on.

"For example, if a large crate were falling into the hold onto the longshoremen and I said, 'Excuse me, gentlemen, but you might want to consider moving, since that crate will most likely injure or kill you,' they would all be dead by the time I finished my sentence. A simple 'Get the fuck out of the way!' is more effective."

I smiled and said, "Yes, Captain, it sure is," and left.

I threw the case into the trash barrel in the salon pantry. As I walked past the first mate's office, he called out, "Hey, William, whatcha doing?"

"Throwing stuff overboard, captain's orders."

He walked into the companionway. "What is it?"

Holding up the socks, I said, "Marijuana."

His eyes bulged. Shaking his head, he retreated to his office. I walked out, heaved the socks into the sea, and went back to the salon to salvage breakfast.

Sitting, sipping coffee, I was the only one left.

I recalled having my one and only marijuana joint in the Blue Star Bar in Santos, Brazil. One of the B girls working there offered it. After a couple of drags, I thought, this tastes like shit. Never had enough of a hit to feel it, and never tried again. Not being in the trade, I had no idea of the value of what I had just deep-sixed, but thought about it now. If the captain uses me as the trash collector, instead of tossing the junk overboard, maybe I can make a few bucks, selling it back to them after they sober up. Something to keep in mind.

That afternoon, I relieved the first mate at 1550 hours. We were steaming south along the coast of Florida, the sun was shining, temperature up to 73 degrees, and a light wind from the west. The captain's plan was to transit the Bahamas, ensuring we cleared west of the lighthouse at the eastern point of San Salvador with ample room. Such was not always the case, as I learned from a story told by a classmate of mine. A new third mate he sailed with had plotted a course two miles to the east of the light, which would have landed them square on the beach. His captain was not happy. Once clear of San Salvador, we would track down through the Crooked Island Passage and the Windward Passage, then on to the entrance to the Panama Canal at Colon. So far, so good.

When the AB relieved the helmsman at the wheel, the first mate and I walked onto the starboard bridge wing.

"William, this morning, after I saw you tossing the Mary Jane, I walked through the crew quarters. The unlicensed quarters reeked of booze, and at the engine room fiddly casing, I smelled marijuana." The fiddley casing is the structure surrounding the upper engine room that leads to the smokestack.

Pausing, he added, "I like a little toke myself, but never on duty. Judging by the captain's reaction today, he's going to be strict about keeping everyone sober. That's good."

I didn't say anything.

"Yeah, thash good," he continued, suddenly slurring.

I looked at him. He was sweating and squinting. "You okay?" I asked.

"Head hurts. Feel funny." He took a step, shivered, and crashed head-first into the steel windbreak.

Kneeling beside him, I saw that the right side of his face looked slack, and he twitched.

I called out to the helmsman and ordered him to put the ship on autopilot and to notify the captain. Thinking Crozier was having a seizure, I rolled him onto his side and cleared his mouth. He wasn't trying to bite his tongue as an epileptic would. Conscious, he tried to talk but couldn't get the words out—only drooled and gasped like a fish. I kept repeating, "You're gonna be okay," until the captain showed up.

I explained what happened. All the time, Crozier stared at us with beseeching eyes.

The captain squatted. "Mr. Crozier, I think you are experiencing a stroke. We'll get you to your room, and I'll contact the Coast Guard and get medical advice. You understand?"

Crozier just gurgled, but looked more ashen.

The captain went into the bridge while I sat on the deck and cradled Crozier's head in my lap. In a few minutes, the chief steward and the bosun arrived. Boats stooped, picked up Crozier as he would a child, and carried him to his room, following the chief steward.

"Get Sparky and have him come to my cabin," the captain ordered. Sparky is the radio operator. All of them are nicknamed "Sparky," a carryover from the early days of radio transmission when telegraph keys could actually spark during use.

Banging on Sparky's door, I barged in. He lay stretched out on his bunk, reading a technical manual. "Captain needs you in his cabin, right now. Something's wrong with the first mate."

Unlike the two predecessor "Sparkys" I had known on the *Mormacpride*, this one reacted in a friendly manner. "Right away," he said. He got up, slipped on sneakers, and went to the captain's cabin while I returned to the bridge.

When the third mate relieved me for supper, I asked the captain how Crozier was doing.

"It's a stroke. He can barely speak. The right side of his face is drooping, and he's semi-paralyzed in his right arm and leg. He has a severe headache. The chief steward is communicating with him by asking him questions and having him raise one finger for a yes and two for a no. Even that's a strain for him."

"Did you get in touch with the Coast Guard?"

"Uh huh," he answered, nodding his head. "They got a doctor and debated having us divert to Miami, but decided since he's breathing okay, to continue to Panama where they'll take him ashore."

As I stood to return to the bridge, I asked, "What about watches? How do you want to split them up? Crozier sure can't stand a watch."

He thought a minute. "Split it between you and the third mate—six on, six off, at least until we reach Panama."

"Aye, aye, Captain," I responded, and returned to the bridge.

A drunk chief engineer, crazy chief cook, belligerent first engineer, dumping perfectly good booze down the drain and tossing marijuana into the drink, first mate down for the count—all only two days out of Jacksonville. What else could go wrong?

Not getting off in Jacksonville was looking pretty dumb.

"Hey, George," I greeted Cavers, the third mate. "The captain wants us to stand six on, six off until we get to Panama. I'll keep the watch until midnight, then we can start the rotation. The unlicensed crew will stay on their regular watches."

"How's Napoleon doing?" he asked, without rancor.

"Good enough so they won't divert us to Miami to put him ashore."

At 2100 hours, the captain came up and called me out to the bridge wing. His Ichabod Crane frame, bowed, bore a pall of weariness.

"Yes, sir?" I queried.

"Instruct your ordinary seaman to stand his watch in Crozier's cabin. If he sees any problems, have him call the chief steward."

"Yes, sir, but what kind of problems? Crozier's pretty screwed up as it is."

"If he stops breathing. That kind of problem."

"You think it's that bad?"

"I don't know. I don't know enough about strokes."

"You talked to the Coast Guard, didn't you?" I asked.

"I did, and they passed the buck to some doctor who said, and I quote, 'It doesn't sound critical to me. The patient is breathing normally. To divert the ship to Miami is costly. He should be okay until you reach Panama. But, of course, it's your choice, Captain.'"

The captain continued, "What kind of doctor talks about the cost of diverting a ship when asked for a medical opinion? A fucking company doctor—that kind. I never even got his name."

"Why didn't the Coast Guard tell you to divert?" I asked.

"Mr. Connolly, you got a lot to learn about the Coast Guard. It's there to enforce its rules, most of which were made by steamship line owners through their

Washington, D.C. contacts. Those rules determine who can get a license or seamen's papers. Those rules control the crews for the shipping line owners."

He sighed, rubbed his nose and shook his head in a slow, exaggerated way. "Every captain is pressured to keep the schedule. Time is money. Our time, company money. That's the message the 'doctor' sent me." Shaking his head again, he said, "What I do know is, if we made the wrong decision not to divert to Miami, it's on me, not the asshole doctor who gave the advice. I don't like playing God with someone's life."

I wanted to sympathize with him, but thought: If that were me in Crozier's place, I'd want a doctor, ASAP.

The captain went below, and I had the helmsman go down and tell the ordinary seaman to babysit Crozier and pass it on to the other watches. Then I entered it into the log as a standing order until otherwise rescinded.

At midnight, the third mate relieved me.

"You look tired, William. Better get some sleep."

"It's been a long day, George. See you at 0600."

On the way down, I checked on Crozier. The ordinary sat on the settee in the office and the bedroom door was closed. "What the hell are you doing out here?" I growled. "You got x-ray vision? You can see through doors and bulkheads?"

"Easy, mate," he said. "They told me to wait out here."

"Who's 'they?'"

"The steward and the captain."

Turning, I tapped on the bedroom door, then opened it. The stink of shit hit me. Crozier was naked on the bed and the steward was cleaning him up. With little or no control of his bowels, he had shit the bed.

"William," the steward said, "put the blanket on the chair. When I lift Mr. Crozier, pull the entire mattress off the bed." The soiled sheet lay bundled beside Crozier.

I nodded and complied. He lifted him, then placed him in the chair, but held him upright by the shoulders and wrapped the blanket around him.

"There are spare mattresses in the storeroom next to the galley," he said. "Throw this one overboard. We'll never get it clean." He handed me his key ring. "It's one of them."

During this entire time, the captain hovered, silent, in the corner.

Calling in the ordinary, I said, "Grab the back corners of the mattress. We're gonna carry it below. Don't let the sheet roll off."

I grabbed the front corners and led him out, down past the galley and out the after door, to the deck at #4 hatch. "Drop it," I said. "Leave it here."

I went to the storage locker, and the ordinary followed me. I fumbled through four keys before finding the right one. We pulled a new mattress and two sheets out into the passageway, and I locked the door.

157

"Damn," I said, as a thought occurred to me. "We gotta wake up Boats. I need some plastic to put on the mattress under the sheets, or we're gonna make this run again."

"No need to wake Boats," he said. "I can get the plastic."

"Good. Help me carry the mattress back up, then bring the plastic," and we set off.

Crozier still sat in the chair, head bobbing, drool running down his chin, the steward holding his shoulder, dabbing at his chin with a face cloth. I straightened the mattress onto the bed and told the steward we were waiting for plastic to put under the sheets. The steward nodded, strain showing on his face.

When the ordinary returned, we stretched the plastic over the mattress and made the bed with the clean sheets. Together, the steward and I carried Crozier back to the bed and lay him on it. With his cheek next to mine, I heard him mumble, "Thanksh." He was crying. It was hard not to cry with him.

"Need anything else?" I asked of no one in particular.

Both the captain and steward shook their heads, so I left, closing the door behind me. The ordinary sat on the settee in the office.

"Thanks for your help," I said. "Sorry about yelling at you when I first got here."

"No problem, Mr. Mate. If they leave, I'll go sit in there with him."

I patted his shoulder and went after the mattress full of shit. I had plans for it.

CHAPTER 17

Wound up tight, I was feeling sorry for the first mate and anxious for myself because of the longer watch hours forced on me due to his condition. In that frame of mind, I conceived my mattress plan.

For days, I had been wondering how to minimize the odds of my getting hurt breaking up a knife fight, or, God forbid, an ax fight. Fire axes were at every fire station, and accessible. My solution: Sew canvas straps on one side of the mattress to use as handles. That way, another person and I could push the knife wielder in front of us down the narrow passageways, until we reached the bulkhead. We could pin him there and, hopefully, disarm him. The mattress protected us and I wouldn't have to shoot the guy. Now all I needed was a sap, for whacking him on the head after we had him pinned. A sap would stun him but wouldn't break the skin. The less blood the better; especially mine.

Stretching out on my bunk, I flexed my neck, trying to rid myself of the tension. Around 0200, I fell asleep.

The ordinary seamen woke me at 0530. Rolling out of bed, I peered into the mirror above the sink. Tired, strained, blood-shot eyes peered back. Rinsing my face twice, I dried off, and stretching, took a deep breath. The aroma of bread baking, mixed with a hint of bananas, perked me up.

After hitting the head, I went to the salon for coffee. On a whim, I went down a deck to the galley and saw the chief cook, Joselito, taking banana bread out of the oven. He wore pants hacked down to shorts, ragged edges showing his boxer shorts underneath, and a tee shirt showing at least four meals on it. Both shorts and tee shirt used to be white. With a ragged, sweat-crusted red bandana on his forehead, he wasn't antiseptic. I'm not squeamish, but we were averaging one complaint per meal about dirty dishes, cutlery, or hair in the food.

"How you doing, Joselito," I said, and he jumped, almost dropping the bread.

"Jesus, you scared me!" he said, eyeing me warily.

"Just smelled the banana bread. Thought I might get a piece to take on watch."

He didn't say anything, just put the bread on the counter.

"Doing the baker job now, too?" I asked.

Nodding, he sliced two pieces of bread, put them on a dish, and handed it to me, avoiding eye contact.

"Thanks," I said. Returning to the salon, I picked up my coffee and climbed to the bridge to relieve the watch.

"Morning, George," I called as I entered the bridge, balancing the coffee and dish of banana bread.

"Hey, William. What you got there?" pointing at the dish.

"Banana bread. Hot out of the oven."

"Any good?"

"Don't know, haven't tasted it yet. Smells good."

George gave me the details of course and speed. There was one ship on our starboard quarter that was almost pacing us, dropping astern as the lateral gap between the ships closed. I relieved him, checked with the helmsman, then carried my coffee and banana bread to the port bridge wing. The banana bread was great. Joselito had talent other than fighting with his cousin. As I savored it, the sunrise, and salt air, the tension seeped away.

Sunday morning, a day of reflection and faith.

In grammar school at Gate of Heaven Catholic Church in Southie, we had to attend eight a.m. Mass on Sundays. In the eighth grade, near the end of the school year, my family went to a memorial Mass for my grandparents in Roslindale, so I was absent for the head count at Gate of Heaven. On Monday morning, all the heretical miscreants, five of us, who had missed the eight a.m. Mass were lined up in front of the office of the principal, a very tough monsignor known for his lack of tolerance.

I was first in line. I was also bigger than the monsignor. Five-foot-ten and 230 pounds, most of it blubber and little muscle. Maybe he felt he needed to make an example.

Motioning me to step up to his desk he rasped, "Did you go to the eight a.m. Mass?"

"No, Monsignor," I replied, and before I could offer an explanation, he leaned over and punched me in the nose, knocking me through the door of his office and into the kids lined up behind me. With a broken nose and blood spattered all over my face, I did what most eighth graders would do: I sat and blubbered.

"Get out of my sight!" he yelled, and I scrambled to my feet and went to the boys' room, where I cleaned up as best I could, then returned to class. Not a murmur from the nuns I passed or my teacher.

As I reflected all day on this hypocritical behavior—preaching peace and practicing violence— I determined that Catholicism wasn't where I wanted to place my faith, and vowed to never go back to church once I escaped grammar school. I didn't.

Despite that, I said a prayer for Crozier, just in case. You never can be sure.

The captain interrupted my day dream. "William."

Blinking and turning, I answered, "Yes, Captain?"

"I've been in touch with the New York office. There's a good chance we won't get a replacement for Mr. Crozier in Panama. They're hoping we can get someone by the time we reach Hawaii. We're not scheduled to stop there, but will if they can find a replacement."

I nodded, not sure if he wanted me to comment. What could I say? It was out of my hands.

"Go get breakfast," he said. "I'll relieve you and the third mate for meals, save a little wear and tear on you guys."

"Yes, sir." I gave him the course and speed, reported the ship following us, noted the time for the log as 0750 hours, and went below.

As I walked through the door of the salon, I saw that the chief engineer, Wesley Gibson, and the first engineer, Frank Harrison, sat together. The chief stared at me but said nothing. The first eyed me with daggers. I had now pissed off the top two engineers by punching one, then pouring the other's booze down the sink and tossing his marijuana overboard. Greg sat at their table, ignoring them, eyes buried in a technical manual.

Glancing at the menu on the table, I went into the pantry and called down for hotcakes and bacon. I grabbed a cup of coffee, inhaling its rich aroma. I laced it with sugar and cream, and returned to my table. The first engineer hadn't yet relieved the second engineer, and it was already 0800. He was too busy giving me the evil-eye. "Hey, Greg," I said, "how's it going?"

"Morning, William. It's going just fine. How about you?"

Knowing I should shut up, but irritated by the juvenile behavior of the chief and first engineer, I couldn't resist. Looking past Greg at the other two, I said, "Not busy now. The captain hasn't given me any extra jobs to do, and no one's tried to take my cigarette away lately."

The first engineer said, "Fuck you, asshole," and started to rise. Grabbing his forearm, the chief said, "Go relieve the second."

The first pulled his arm away, but walked out without another word.

"Mr. Connolly," the chief said, "it's clear that tact isn't your forte." Pausing, he added, "But don't push it."

Nodding, I rose as the bell rang, announcing the dumbwaiter, and retrieved my breakfast from the pantry.

The chief stood as I returned and faced me. In a low voice, he said, "You're right, but rubbing salt in the wound isn't smart. I took you for a smart guy; don't prove me wrong"—and he walked out.

When I sat down, Greg said, "I heard that."

"So did I. Kind of surprised. The chief sounded almost friendly, as if he gave a shit." My cynicism was showing.

Greg tapped me on the forearm. "Stranger things have happened. Don't presume one stupid mistake defines the person," then turned back to his manual. Lifting his head, he said, "By the way, thanks."

"What are you talking about?"

"The first engineer used to dislike me. Now he hates you and ignores me. So, thanks." And he smiled.

Finishing my breakfast, I returned to the bridge and relieved the captain. Now I had something else to ponder during the rest of the watch.

After watch, I skipped lunch. I hadn't exercised and felt I was gaining weight. Instead, I got paint rags, bleach, and a piece of canvas from the bosun's locker, making sure I cleared it with Boats. No one touches Boats' things without permission. Going aft to where we had dumped the shit-stained mattress, I found it still lying there at # 4 hatch. I put on my leather work gloves and used a couple of paint rags to wipe the shit stain, then poured bleach on it and wiped it again. Using my four-inch-long seaman's knife, I cut four two-foot-long strips of canvas. Folding them over, I used my well-worn sail needle and palm to hand sew them to the mattress, on the opposite side of the shit stain, each about one foot in from each corner.

Hefting the mattress by the top handles, I found I could maneuver it by kicking the bottom as I moved, screening me for the whole width of the passageway. Better if I had someone else helping me, but doable on my own. I decided the best place to store the mattress was outside my cabin door, one deck above the crew level, with a ladder leading down just outside the watertight door. I hung one strap over the top of the CO_2 fire extinguisher on the bulkhead. Coming from forward, you could still see the fire extinguisher. From aft, the mattress hid the extinguisher. No big deal except all fire-fighting equipment is supposed to be in plain view at all times.

My main defensive shield in place, I changed into gym shorts and tee shirt, put on my sneakers, and headed for the salon to get a cup of water before running the ladders. As I entered, I heard shouting echoing up the passageway from the crew's quarters. Remembering the captain's view of me as the enforcer, I turned and jogged down the stairs, moving faster as the shouting increased.

As I stepped into the passageway from the stairwell, I got bumped, hard, by a small black crew member running by me, followed by a skinny white guy in his skivvies. He was small, around five-foot-three, and one-hundred and thirty pounds, with wispy brown hair and a wild look in his eye. What got my attention, however, was the machete he had in his left hand.

I stepped back into the doorway as he viciously swung the machete, backhand, and it clanged off the door frame, hitting just under my right hand. I heard and felt the shock. Inches higher and I would have been missing fingers. Taking another half-step back as he came forward into the opening, I swung a left hook as hard as I could in the general direction of his head. It connected on his cheekbone and nose, staggering him, but he didn't go down, and he didn't drop the machete. Letting out a roar, he drew the machete back for another swing.

Instinctively, I held my position, head sticking out the doorway, until he started his forward motion. Being left-handed, his swing carried the machete past and away from me. I leaped out into the corridor, grabbing at his left wrist with my left hand and, using my right arm, clubbed him in the back of the head, driving his head into the steel bulkhead. Not waiting to see if he could react, I grabbed the back of his neck and slammed his head three more times into the bulkhead, finishing what I had started with his nose, until he collapsed to the deck. He still held the machete. He was out cold, but wouldn't let go.

Standing up, panting, I saw three other crew members at the end of the passageway, gawking at us. I heard a noise and spun around. The small black guy who had been chased stood there, holding up his hands in supplication, saying, "Easy, mate, easy!"

I reached down to get the machete and couldn't pull it loose so, muttering "Motherfucker," I stomped on the guy's hand, twice, before his grip relaxed. Wearing sneakers, I wished I had work boots on.

I pointed at the black guy, and said, "Go get the captain. Bring him here," and he took off. As I finished, the chief steward rounded the corner.

"Jesus, William, what's going on?"

"This asshole was chasing the black guy with a machete when I came through the door and he attacked me." I wasn't panting any more, but I was getting more pissed off. When the guy on the deck stirred, I said, "Don't move," and knee-dropped with both knees onto his back to ensure he didn't. I didn't need to, but it felt good.

The captain arrived, carrying his .45 Colt in his hand and trailed by the black guy. I explained what had happened. Pulling a pair of handcuffs from his rear pocket, the captain tossed them to me and said, "Cuff him, hands behind his back." It was when I cuffed him, I realized the back of my right hand was bleeding. The machete must have scraped me as it bounced off the door frame. The captain asked the black guy, "Why was he chasing you?"

"He crazy, Cap'n. He high on coke, but he crazy."

"Andrew," the captain said, "clean him up and bring him up to the bridge."

"Moses," Andrew said to the black guy, "help me pick him up," and the three of us got him to his feet. With my hand on the cuffs, I steered him into the crew mess where Andrew cleaned up his face. There wasn't much he could do for his nose. I had spread it all over his face. He had severe acne scars. Not a pretty sight.

While Andrew tended to him, I probed Moses further. "Moses? What's your full name?"

"Moses Delight, mate," and he stood tall, all five-foot-two inches of him, and broke out a huge grin when I smiled.

"What's your job?"

"I the crew BR." BR is bedroom steward, the equivalent of a maid.

"What started it, Moses?"

"He a mean man when sober. He worse when he get high on coke."

"Sure you didn't do or say anything to set him off?"

"No sir, Mister Mate. That boy don't need no pushing. He just mean."

I nodded and asked Andrew, "Is he okay to move?"

"Yeah, but before we go, let me fix your hand." He swapped it with iodine, which stung. It was a scrape with a small patch of skin peeled back. He pressed the skin down and taped a gauze pad over it.

"Thanks, Andrew," I said, then reached down and pulled machete-man up by the arm. "Let's go," I said, and we walked out of the crew mess and up to the bridge.

The captain met us at the door to the bridge and said, "Flying bridge." We led everyone there.

Staring at the guy, Andrew identified him as Bobby Punser, a wiper. The captain said, "Turn around and sit down on the deck by the railing."

Punser didn't react, just stared at his feet.

"He's still out of it," the captain said. "Cuff him to the bottom rail. He can sit here until he's sober."

I jerked Punser around, facing aft and said, "Sit down or I'll knock you down." That registered, and he slumped to the deck. I unhooked one side of the cuffs, looped it around the lower railing, and refastened it to his hand, cinching them tight. He had about ten inches of vertical play in the cuffs so he couldn't stand up.

The captain thanked Andrew and me, and we left Punser there to stew.

I got a drink of water from the salon. My adrenaline was sky-high and I needed to burn it off., so I ran the exterior ladders for thirty minutes. Squinting as I ran, blotting out the vision of the machete coming at me, I replaced it with memories of Meg's ass twitching in front of me when she ran the ladders with me on the 'Pride. The images were so real, I reached out to touch her at the top of the ladder. Nothing there but heartache, and an instant, useless hard-on. Feeling sorry for myself, I wanted to kick Punser, vent my frustration over Meg. Instead, I walked around on the flying bridge, cooling off for a few minutes, ignoring Punser, who ignored me.

I leaned against the forward, starboard railing and stretched. The salt crust coated my hands, a regular occurrence in the tropics or when in heavy weather. I licked my palm, remembering Meg had once done that when I told her about the salt rime on the rails. That flick of her tongue on my palm had been erotic. I shivered as I recalled it. Would I ever get the chance to see her again?

"William, you up there?" a voice called out.

I looked down onto the bridge wing. George stood there, staring up at me. "The captain's looking for you."

I nodded, said "Okay," and went below to the captain's cabin. Knocking on his closed door, I called, "Captain. It's William."

"Come in, William."

I entered. He sat there at his desk, his .45 Colt disassembled, lying on a cloth in front of him. He was cleaning it. Sitting across from him sat the chief steward, Andrew.

"Sit down," the captain ordered, pointing at his settee. I sat. "Andrew tells me the chief cook complained to him that you invaded his galley and intimidated him, demanding he bake you some banana bread."

"What?" I yelled—then noticed the captain's smirk. I looked at Andrew and he smiled, too.

"He did complain," Andrew said, "but since I had put banana bread on the menu, I knew it was bullshit. He did say, though, you told him the next time you saw him, you'd have a gun. That sounded serious."

I looked at the captain. He raised his eyebrows.

"Captain, this is bullshit." I related what happened back in Sunny Point when the chief cook and the baker were fighting, and when I told the chief cook if it happened again, the next time it would be my gun pointing at his head, and not the Army sentry's.

The captain sat silent for a few seconds, then asked, "How was the banana bread?"

I smiled. "Pretty good."

"Well, at least the son of a bitch can bake." Turning to Andrew, he asked, "You okay, Andrew?"

"I'm good, Captain, at least with the cook. I smell a lot of booze and marijuana throughout the crew's quarters, but other than Punser, no one is acting up yet, at least not in my department."

"Any other departments?" the captain asked.

"An ordinary and Punser seem to argue a lot with everybody. Nothing physical, though, until today."

"Which one?"

"The ordinary is Highstone."

"Okay, Andrew, thanks. If you hear or see anyone acting up, let me know right away."

"Yes, sir." He nodded at me and left.

After the door closed, I said, "Highstone. He's the guy who led the parade when they brought all the booze aboard. My AB, Winkler, says he fits the name because he's high and stoned all the time. He's on the four-to-eight watch."

The captain nodded. Reaching into a lower drawer of his desk, he placed a Smith & Wesson .38 Police Special with a holster next to the Colt .45 parts.

"I know you're proficient with small-bore pistols. Ever shoot a .38?"

"Yes, sir, a few times. I've shot a .45 caliber also a couple of times."

"If you're going to tell someone, 'next time it'll be my gun,' then you need to have a gun." Pointing at the .38 S & W, he said, "Carry this whenever you're on duty. It's a belt holster and I want everyone to see it—a deterrent for semi-sober people. Sober people don't fight a gun with a knife. This should at least lower the odds of anyone getting violent."

"I've been working on my own deterrent, Captain." And I explained about the shit-stained mattress.

He laughed. "Waste not, want not, eh, William? Excellent idea." He handed me the revolver and a box of Remington ammo. "I pray to God you don't have to use it."

CHAPTER 18

The captain left Punser cuffed to the rail for twenty-four hours. During that time, he cried, screamed, pissed, and shit himself. Every two hours, either I or George gave him a cup of water. We didn't let the crew members up there, for fear they would give him more drugs. On Monday, at 1800 hours when I got off watch, I uncuffed him and told him to go clean up. I had him lean away from me to get at his cuffs, but the stench of shit still made me hold my breath. He rolled onto his hands and knees, grabbed the rail and pulled himself up, the entire backside of his skivvies putrid brown.

"Mate," he mumbled, mouth-breathing because of his smashed nose.

"Yeah."

"What did I do?"

Incredulous, I asked, "You don't remember?"

"No."

"You tried to kill Moses and then attacked me with a machete."

His eyes widened, and he leaned back against the rail. "Jeez!" After a minute, "I'm sorry, mate."

"Tell that to Moses."

Nodding, he moved aft, stepping like a man with a load of shit in his pants, and went below.

I went to my cabin and washed my hands, feeling dirty after touching him, then went to the salon. All the off-duty officers sat there chatting, and the chief engineer and captain were talking. When I walked in, all conversation stopped.

"What shape was he in?" the captain asked.

"Punser's okay, other than stinking of shit. Andrew should see if he can do anything about his nose. It's a mess."

Andrew emerged from the pantry. "I think it'll take more than I can do. He should see a doctor in Panama."

"I'll have Sparky call ahead and request it," the captain replied.

Tonight's special was meatloaf. The salon reeked of onions, so I looked at the chief engineer's plate. Onions smothered the meatloaf. I called down for meatloaf-no-onions, mashed potatoes, peas and carrots, with gravy on the side, then grabbed a cup of coffee and sat down. I had to adjust the holster on my right hip as I slid into the seat. That caused Greg to lean over and whisper, "How ya doin', Wyatt Earp?"

I smiled and replied, "No one's attacked me with a machete in the last twenty-four hours, so I guess it's working."

He gave me that wry, sympathetic smile and said, "It's good to be the sheriff."

With the exception of keeping an eye on the first mate, monitoring his condition, the next two days were boring.

The lower deck still reeked of booze and marijuana, but Punser's experience had minimized any overt displays of hostility. At 1500 hours, we anchored in the area reserved for ships carrying explosives, on the western edge of the general anchorage area off of Colon, Panama. The captain had received word we had to wait twenty-four hours for a window of passage. There were seven other ships at the anchorage, waiting their turn to transit, but we were the only ship with explosives on board.

The captain had requested launch service to take the first mate ashore to the hospital, and had arranged for Punser to go, as well, to fix his nose. At 1700 hours, I stood at the gangway as the launch showed up with medics, along with a Seamen's Union representative sporting a Stan Laurel type derby. The union rep demanded to see the first mate. I pointed out the stretcher being carried onto the launch. "There he is. He had a stroke, and they're taking him to the hospital."

The union rep stammered, then demanded to see the captain. He also asked to see Wiper Punser, and I pointed him out. "He's going to the hospital, too. Broke his nose."

"That's why I'm here," the rep said. Calling to Punser, he cornered him and spoke for a minute. "He can go later," the rep said. "I want to see the captain now."

"Follow me," I said and led him to the captain's cabin.

The union rep started to walk through the open door of the captain's office when I grabbed his arm. "You knock before entering the captain's office," I said. He glared at me, then knocked on the door frame.

"Come in," the captain called out, and the rep walked in with Punser and me on his heels.

"Captain, I'm here because I got a notice of an assault on Mr. Punser here," nodding in his direction, "and cruel punishment—locking him up on the flying bridge."

The captain stared at him. "Would you like to remove your hat? It's considered common courtesy to remove one's hat when in the captain's office."

Yanking his derby off, he muttered, "Sorry, Captain."

"Do you have a name?"

"Mike Amesbury, Captain. I'm the shop steward for this local union."

The captain nodded and continued. "You said you received a notice. How?"

"A message came in to the union hall."

"How? Who sent it? No one is allowed to communicate via the ship's radio without my permission, so how did the message get out?" Looking at Punser, he demanded, "Did you send the message, Mr. Punser?"

"No, Captain, I didn't send nothin'." Every word puffy with nasal overtones.

The captain tapped his fingers on the desk, then said, "We'll get to that later. Let me explain a few things, Mr. Amesbury," and he related the events of the machete attack and what followed.

"Now," he continued, "you have a choice to make. I can make the official entry into the ship's log, which I have not done so far, in the hope that Mr. Punser could redeem himself. If I do that, we can all go to a Coast Guard hearing and watch Mr. Punser lose his seamen's papers, and Mr. Connolly get exonerated for defending himself and another crew member. Or, you can accompany Mr. Punser to the hospital where he can get treatment for his broken nose, which has already been delayed due to your actions, not ours. Once there, you can forget about this so-called assault ... What will it be?"

"Could I talk to Punser?" the rep asked.

"Of course. Why don't you step into the passageway."

Amesbury nodded his head toward the door and Punser followed him out. The voices were harsh but subdued. The only word I understood was "cokehead." Thirty seconds later, after knocking, they were back.

"Mr. Punser says it was all a misunderstanding and wants it all to go away. I agree. Thanks for your courtesy, Captain. At the hospital, I will also introduce Mr. Punser to the narcotics abuse counsellor."

"Excellent idea, Mr. Amesbury," the captain said, standing and coming around his desk. "As soon as the launch returns, you can go." Shaking hands, he said affably, "In the meantime, would you like a drink?"

"Coffee would be fine. I'm a recovering alcoholic."

"So am I, Mr. Amesbury. Follow me to the salon, and I'll get you your coffee."

The launch returned at 1800 hours just as George, the third mate, relieved me on watch. Amesbury nodded as he escorted Punser down the gangway, but didn't offer to shake hands.

I entered the salon and Sparky, the radio operator, was talking with the captain, standing in front of his table at attention. "No one sent any message out other than the ones you directed me to, Captain. I keep my place locked when I'm not there." He paused. "There are two guys on board who are hams and have their own rigs."

"Who are they?"

"The second engineer, Swenson, and Highstone, the ordinary. I let them run their antennas up the mast. Didn't see any harm in it."

"Okay, Sparky. Thank you."

"Want me to pull their antennas down?"

"No, not necessary, thanks."

Sparky nodded and left.

During their exchange, I stood at the sideboard, playing with my coffee cup, eavesdropping. When Sparky passed me, I went to the table and looked at the menu. Pork chops, fried, French fries, and cauliflower. I hate cauliflower and settled for the pork chops and French fries, a full ration of grease. The dessert was already on the sideboard, apple pie.

Only Greg, the captain, and chief engineer were there, and I ate in silence. They had finished. Greg, as usual, had his head in a manual; the chief stared into space; and the captain tap-tapped away with his fingers at the table. When I got up to bring my dishes to the pantry and get a slice of pie, the captain said, "I told Mr. Amesbury he had my permission to hold Punser ashore if he thought he needed to get help for his addiction. Being a recovering alcoholic, he understood."

The chief looked up when he heard "recovering alcoholic," but said nothing.

Since we were at anchor, and grateful that boredom had returned, I stood watch that night on the bridge, checking the bearings every hour to ensure we weren't drifting. Three of the seven ships at anchor had gone in transit through the canal. At 0400 hours, as I smoked another Marlboro on the bridge wing, I watched a fourth, a big tanker near Panamax size, weigh anchor and move to the canal entrance.

Thoughts of Meg kept invading my solitude— disturbing, erotic thoughts. To stop them, I dug out my dictionary, a scuffed Webster unabridged, and resumed my word training. Starting at "A" I'd thumb through until I found a word I didn't know, then do the drill. I was at the end of the "G's" and the first word I came across was "gwyniad." It's a fresh water white fish found in Lake Bala in Wales. I went through a couple more, but couldn't concentrate and slammed the dictionary shut, slid it roughly across the chart table, went out to the bridge wing, and lit another Marlboro.

At 0550, George stepped onto the bridge to relieve me. Sunrise wasn't until 0639, but the clear skies, uncluttered except for a few thin cumulus clouds, showed dawn approaching. It had been a long, tedious night. I never thought fighting memories could be so exhausting. I gave George the particulars, told him the anchor held fast, and went below. I collapsed into my bunk and, to my surprise, fell asleep.

CHAPTER 19

The knock at my door woke me. This time it was the captain.

"We're going to raid the crew's quarters," he said. He stood at my door while I rinsed my face with cold water to wake up. Already dressed—I hadn't even taken off my shoes—I followed him out.

In the salon, me, Greg, Andrew, and Wesley Gibson, the chief engineer, listened while the captain explained.

"We'll hit every cabin, but the first ones are Highstone's and Punser's. Chief, you and Greg will take the engine side. William, Andrew, and I will cover the deck and steward cabins." Everyone nodded. "Good, let's go," and we followed the captain out and down to the crew quarters, where Greg and the chief went to port. The captain, Andrew, and I went to starboard.

Highstone's cabin, which he shared with the two ABs on his watch, Winkler and Preen, was the third one aft. Knocking on the door, with a nod from the captain, I turned the knob. Locked. The captain pulled out his master key and unlocked it, then stepped back. As I opened the door, a wave of marijuana smoke washed out, overshadowing the unkempt drabness of the room.

Highstone slumped on the deck, leaning against the bottom of the bunk beds, head hung down, out cold. He wore dirty khaki pants and a stained, gray sweatshirt with the sleeves cut off. A stain covering the front of his pants showed he had pissed himself. Since it was only 0830, and he had the four-to-eight watch, he had to have been in this condition while still on watch.

"Is he breathing?" the captain asked.

Kneeling, I leaned in and heard the rasp of his breath. He reeked of sour booze. I looked over my shoulder at the captain and nodded. "He's alive."

"See what's here," the captain said and stepped back into the passageway.

Andrew and I pulled open drawers. Nothing. Not in his drawers, nor in Winkler's or Preen's. Nothing under the mattresses. Kneeling again, I pulled a Lucky Strike cigarette pack from his shirt pocket and tossed it on the bunk. Only a lighter in his pants pockets, and I threw that on the bunk. As I straightened, Winkler's voice came from outside the doorway. "What's going on?" He stood peeking around the captain, since he couldn't see over him.

"What's it look like?" Andrew answered.

Winkler just shook his head.

"Your roommate is passed out, stinks of booze and marijuana, and we're looking for his stash," Andrew continued.

Winkler looked over his shoulder, then back at Highstone, and whispered, "You're lookin' in the wrong place. We don't let him keep any of that shit here. This is our cabin, too."

"Where should we be looking?"

Winkler shuffled his feet, rubbed both palms on the front of his dungarees, and whispered, "Boats' locker."

As we turned to leave, Winkler called out, "Hey."

Pointing at the pack of Lucky Strikes on the bed, he said, "He don't smoke…cigarettes."

Stepping back in, I picked up the Lucky Strikes pack and shook one out. Marijuana. Nodding at Winkler, I pocketed the pack and went looking for the captain, who had disappeared.

We found him standing out in the passageway on the port side, next to Punser, who was squatting on the deck and leaning against the bulkhead. Next to them stood a black man. He was about five feet ten inches tall, weighing at least 230 pounds, and all muscle—massive shoulders, trim waist, his tee shirt bulging at the seams. The big guy was silent, hands behind his back in a military at-ease position, just watching.

As I approached, Greg came out of the room and said, "Nothing, Captain." The captain nodded and pointed at the next cabin. Greg patted the black man on the shoulder as he walked past—a reassuring pat, much like he's done to me at times, and said, "Thanks, Isaiah." The man smiled at Greg and walked into the room. Punser stood and followed, closing the door. His nose didn't look any better after his doctor visit.

"When did Punser get back?" I asked no one in particular.

Greg answered. "The launch brought him around 0730. Isaiah is my oiler. He told me."

"Captain," I said, "it seems that Highstone is stowing his stuff in Boats's locker. I don't know if Boats knows. I can't imagine Boats not knowing if anyone uses his locker, or what his reaction will be when he finds out."

"Damn. I was counting on Boats." He paused, then said to me, "Go get Boats and meet us at his locker. Greg, Andrew, Chief, come with me." Striding forward, he went out the port-side watertight door.

I went to starboard and knocked on Boats's door. When it opened, he stood there in his skivvies, scratching his crotch. "Boats," I said, "the captain wants to see you...at your stores locker."

He looked puzzled. "Okay. Let me get dressed," and he emerged two minutes later in pants, tee shirt, and boots.

At the locker in the forepeak, the captain faced Boats and said, "I was told some crew members are using your stores locker to hide their booze and drugs. Know anything about that?"

Boats face turned crimson, and he balled his fists. I took a step back and looked around for a weapon other than my gun, thinking he would erupt. Instead, he took a few deep breaths, his fists relaxed, and he said, "No, Captain, I don't know nothin' about that, but if someone is using my space to hide their shit, they're gonna be one sorry motherfucker!"

185

The captain stared at him for five seconds, a long time in that situation, then nodded and said, "Good. Let's find out if someone is messing with your space," and he pointed at the door of the locker.

Boats stepped forward, opened the door, and stepped over the raised threshold. I followed, turning on the lights. The locker is as wide as the hull, tapering sharply as you go forward. About twenty-five-feet deep, it ends at a four-foot-wide bulkhead and is crammed with gear. It smelled of rope, paint, tar, and fish oil. Fish oil is used as a rust retardant on deck plating—effective, but it stinks.

"Which side you want to look?" he said.

Feeling this was a test of trust I said, "Your choice, Boats."

He started on the starboard side and I moved to port. Between us we moved every coil of rope and wire, bucket of paint, turnbuckle, shackle, and sheet of canvas. I stood on stacked paint buckets and peered along the steel scantlings in the overhead. Standing side-by-side at the forepeak with nothing but sweating steel bulkheads in front of us, Boats said, "Wait a minute." He turned and stared at the five-gallon paint buckets. Then he started to heft them, one at a time.

I understood and did the same for the ones on my side, until I came across one that was lighter…much lighter. I didn't notice it the first time I moved it, because I was only looking for things hidden behind it.

"Boats," I said, and handed him the bucket.

He peeled off the top. I would have needed a pry-bar. There were bags of marijuana and other plastic bags, maybe cocaine, filling two-thirds of the five-gallon bucket.

Walking to the doorway where the captain waited, he said, "Here's your shit. Who put it there?" —a menace in his voice that the captain didn't miss.

"Thank you, Boats. I'll tell you who put it there, but I want your word you won't kill him."

Boats said nothing, just clenched and unclenched his massive fists, and I thought, strange choice of words, "kill" him and not "hurt" him. What did the captain know about Boats that I didn't?

"I'm waiting, Boats. This piece of trash isn't worth losing your seaman's papers over, much less going to jail for."

Boats stood there another fifteen seconds before saying, "Okay."

The captain breathed an audible sigh. "It was Highstone. I'm locking him up on the flying bridge, same as we did for Punser, until he sobers up, then we'll deal with him. William, bring the bucket"— and he turned on his heel and walked aft, those long Ichabod Crane legs and arms flapping as he strode away, followed by Greg, Andrew, and the chief.

I left the bucket in the captain's bedroom. He locked the interior door, then said, "Bring Highstone to the bridge." He had dismissed the three other searchers when we reached the doorway of the house, telling them, "That's enough for one day. Thank you, gentlemen."

At Highstone's cabin, he was still out cold. Neither Winkler nor Preen were anywhere to be found. Rather than wrestle Highstone to the bridge myself, I knocked on Boats's door again and asked him to help me carry the man to the flying bridge. His eyebrows went up, at least the one without the scar, then he grinned.

"Sure thing, Mate. Be glad to help."

Boats hefted Highstone and threw him over his right shoulder like a gunnysack, feet forward. I counted at least six solid thuds as Highstone's head bounced off the bulkheads and door frames on the way to the bridge. One ear, his left one, had a gash in it that bled profusely. That must have caught on a door jamb.

I pointed at the deck in front of the forward railing, the same spot we had cuffed Punser, and Boats dumped Highstone there, head first, giving him another cut on the scalp. Not deep, but a scalp cut bleeds easy.

"Thanks Boats, I'll take it from here."

He grabbed my right hand in his huge paw and said, "Thanks for letting me help ya, Mate. I feel better now," and he smiled an evil grin.

I smiled back, less evil, more conspiratorial. "We have to watch out for our shipmates," I said.

Pointing at Highstone on the deck, he said, "I'm a man of my word. He ain't dead!"

Propping up Highstone, I remembered wrestling with Punser when I locked him here, and I was glad Boats had handled the heavy work. I was also glad Highstone wasn't covered in shit like Punser. That would have pissed off Boats even more.

As I cuffed him to the railing, I thought, Boats deserved his revenge. I checked the bleeding at Highstone's ear and forehead. Neither one seemed serious, but I opted for prudence and found Andrew. He bandaged him up.

CHAPTER 20

1500 hours, a gentle westerly breeze off the land, seas under two feet, the canal pilot is aboard and we weigh anchor.

Off duty, I leaned against the railing on the flying bridge, determined to enjoy the ride. My only previous Canal transit was on the training ship, *Bay State* and I spent the west-bound transit in the engine room. The east-bound transit was at night, and lights out was 2200, so I still didn't get to see much.

Starting at the Atlantic side of the Canal, we entered the first of three locks, known as Gatun Locks, named after Lake Gatun, the first of two lakes in the transit. The locks are a gravity feed system. The ship enters the lock; they close the lock gates behind; open valves; and gravity lets the water in the upper lock flow down into the lower lock. When the water levels are even, they open the forward lock gates and the ship proceeds into the next lock where the process repeats itself. Simple stuff, but you're riding a 560-foot ship in narrow channels, so paying attention is a priority.

The Pacific Ocean side of Panama is nine and one-quarter inches higher sea level than the Atlantic side. The highest point inland is the middle of Lake Gatun, at eighty-five feet above sea level, with some fluctuation, depending on the season and the amount of rainfall. Both the locks and the main channel have a controlling depth of thirty-four feet. Plenty for us, since our draft sailing from Jacksonville was 27' 9" aft and 26' 11" forward, a ten-inch aft trim.

As we approached the locks, small railroad engines, called mules—two on each side, one forward and one aft—each took a mooring line from the ship and guided us along. They also controlled forward speed, and slowed you down to minimize propeller wash in the lock.

Different from the locks in the Great Lakes. There, we had to lower a crewman in a bosun chair onto the lock apron using a man-killer boom to handle the ship's mooring lines as we worked our way along the lock. The crewman, after letting go the last line, had to make a pier-head jump to get in the bosun chair and get lifted back aboard, while the ship moved out of the lock. It could get exciting and was always dangerous.

The locks are in pairs, one for each direction. Going in, the first lock isn't impressive, just a channel with steel walls. The higher you go with each lock, the more fascinating it becomes, because the ship is now floating above sea level, and looking aft is an eerie feeling. At the top of the third lock, entering Gatun Lake proper, the view aft is intimidating. You can't help but think, what if the lock gates broke? Not a good feeling.

As we were going up, another ship, a small tanker, was going down, in the other direction. In the middle locks, we wave at each other from the bridge wing—elevator riders passing each other. Most of the transit is on Gatun Lake, about twenty and one-half miles, dodging islands that once were hilltops. They created Gatun Lake when they dammed the north end of the Chagres River, the main feeder into the lake. On an average year, the Chagres River empties into it the equivalent of the entire capacity of the lake.

At the end of the lake, after passing through Gaillard Cut—a man-made slice in the hills—the ship reached Miraflores Locks. A two-lock step-down to Miraflores Lake, a short transit across the lake, then the Pedro Miguel Locks—the final step-down into the Pacific Ocean.

Clearing the last of the Miraflores Locks, the canal pilot had asked what all the yelling on the flying bridge was about. It was Highstone, awake and hurting and pissed off. The captain told the pilot, "There's a crew member high on drugs, and we're waiting for him to sober up. Ignore him."

The pilot gave the captain a strange look, but never said another word.

A normal transit takes eight to ten hours. Except for Highstone shouting on the flying bridge, this one was normal. I came on watch at 1750. The sun, already low in the sky, would set at 1825. We were already well into the Lake Gatun passage. The Miraflores Locks and Pedro Miguel Locks would be in darkness, except for the lights on shore. The captain never left the bridge except to relieve his bladder. Not nervous, just watchful.

At midnight, we cleared the Pedro Miguel Locks and disembarked the pilot thirty minutes later. The Pacific side smelled different; less jungle influence, more salt air.

Warm and humid, clear night, western stars more prominent now that we were away from the wash of the shore lights, we came up to sea speed and set course onto the great circle route that would take us close to Guam, on the way to the Philippines. The captain said goodnight and went below, reminding me to give Highstone a cup of water every two hours.

Clearing Colon, I looked to settle into a nice groove—six hours on, six hours off. If we got word of a replacement first mate at Hawaii, we could alter course and go get him. Fourteen days sailing to Hawaii, twenty-three-and-a-half days if we went straight to Guam.

The captain had freed Highstone an hour after George, the third mate, relieved me. I skipped breakfast, went right to bed, and slept until 1130 hours. Sitting in the salon, sipping coffee, chewing on a stale biscuit, I hoped for a peaceful passage. No such luck. The bosun stuck his head in the door and said, "Hey mate, Highstone's fucked up. Wants to kill himself."

Rising, I asked, "Where is he?"

"In the crew mess. One of the guys is keeping an eye on him."

"Let's go," I said and trooped out.

In the crew mess, four of the crew stood in a loose circle around Highstone, wary, not looking sympathetic, and parting when I approached. Highstone sat on the deck, leaning against the sideboard, shaking and sniveling.

"What's the problem?" I asked.

He didn't look up. Shivering, he stammered, "I wanna die."

Figuring he was suffering withdrawal, I almost felt sorry for him. "You aren't going to die. You're coming down from all the drugs you were on. It'll pass. Might take a day or two, but it'll pass."

He looked at me. Instead of a pitiful face, other than the red eyes, I saw a sly look. This asshole was playing me, but I didn't know what the game was. "Leave me alone," he said. "I just wanna die."

Turning to the bosun, I said, "Boats, take him to his cabin. Keep him there until I tell you different, okay?"

"Aye, aye, Mate. Let's go, Highstone," and he stepped toward him. I touched Boats's arm and nodded at him. He got the message. Back off a little.

Reaching down, he helped Highstone to his feet and guided him out the door. Highstone didn't have any reason to be apprehensive of the bosun, since he didn't know who had caused all the damage to his head on the way to the flying bridge. He had been out cold the whole time.

Finding the captain in his office, I explained what happened.

"I don't trust him, Captain. He may be suffering withdrawal, but the look in his eye tells me he's trying to connive his way out of something."

Stroking his chin, the captain said, "So he wants to die? Maybe we should let him."

My face must have given me away. He continued, "Don't worry, if he really wants to go, we won't be able to stop him. Besides, there's too much paperwork involved."

I nodded my agreement.

"I'll give him the benefit of the doubt for the rest of the day." the captain concluded. "Let's see how he is on the morning watch."

"Aye, aye, Captain."

The afternoon watch went by, nothing but coffee and cigarettes. Little appetite, I sat in the salon at supper, pushing around on my plate something vaguely similar to Salisbury steak, and stewed about Highstone and the games he was playing. I had Winkler check on him at 2000 hours when he went off watch. He came back in ten minutes and said, "The asshole is faking it. There's nothing wrong with him. He's sleeping like a baby."

I put my hand on his shoulder. "Thanks, Winkler. I appreciate your doing both jobs. I'll check out Highstone in the morning.

Back on watch at midnight, I paced the bridge, starboard wing to port wing and back, Marlboro smoke trailing behind me like a steam engine. The twelve-to-four watch ABs stayed at the helm, avoiding crossing my path. When

Preen came on watch at 0400, I heard the AB whisper to him, "He ain't stopped moving all night."

We were in typical Pacific weather, eighty-two degrees, scattered cumulus clouds, sun trying to peek above the horizon behind us, tendrils of light reaching through the clouds to announce its arrival. The prevailing winds were still from the northeast and blowing at twelve miles per hour.

They were predicting this as a "La Nina" year, and the water surface temperature should drop a couple of degrees colder than normal. "El Nino" is the opposite. The water temperature rises one or two degrees.

In the states, weathermen worry about El Nino more than La Nina because it has a more dramatic effect on the jet stream winds and weather patterns across the U S. I think they exaggerate, but there are more El Ninos than La Ninas, so they'll be right more than wrong. Weathermen generalize as much as possible, but still only have a fifty-fifty average of being correct. The only thing other than forecasting that keeps you employed if you're right only half the time is baseball. If you batted even .400 in baseball, you'd be a superstar. Here, at sea, we get the basic data on barometric pressures over the radio and plot the isobars, creating our own weather maps. It's a tedious process, and we're always behind the curve, timewise.

Weathermen on TV are becoming like rock stars instead of forecasters. One guy in Boston I used to race sail boats against, became an unofficial spokesman for catamarans when they came on the scene in the late

1950s, and he switched from one-tens to Tiger cats. His forecasting was better than his sailing.

Leaning against the starboard bridge wing bulkhead, enjoying the rushing sound of the ship's bow wave, I looked aft and, in the pre-dawn light, saw Highstone standing on the top of the rail on the main deck, holding on with one hand and staring at me. When Winkler arrived on the bridge at 0545, I told Preen, the AB going off as helmsman, to tell Highstone to report to the bridge.

As I stared back at Highstone, Preen came running out on the wing, no easy task since he was sixty-four years old and had smoker's lungs.

"Says he's gonna kill himself," he gasped.

Without taking my eyes off Highstone, I ordered Preen to get the captain, fast.

Highstone was smiling at me when the captain arrived. The instant the captain's head appeared over the windbreak, the smile disappeared and he used both hands to balance himself against the bulkhead.

"What's he doing?" the captain asked.

"Playing a stupid game, I think."

"I'm going down there," the captain said. "Don't take your eyes off him. If he jumps, do a 'Williamson,'" he instructed, referring to an emergency procedure for man-overboard.

"Aye, aye, Captain."

On the way down, the captain called the engine room and told them to drop to maneuvering speed, just in case. I peeked into the bridge and Winkler was at the helm. He had taken it off autopilot.

I stared at Highstone, feeling the reduction in engine revolutions about the third minute. Then he changed his position, looking backward and talking to someone. I kept staring. About four or five minutes went by, then he jumped off the rail, onto the ship.

George, the third mate, relieved me at 0600, but I waited around to see what would happen. It was a half-hour before the captain returned to the bridge. I stood there; eyebrows raised but silent.

He motioned me out to the bridge wing, apparently reluctant to say anything in front of George.

"He's a crafty piece of shit, I'll give him that," the captain said. "Told me he's afraid of you. Wants to stand another watch where you can't hurt him."

"Me hurt him? He's lucky Boats or his roommates don't kick his ass."

"I pointed out to him he had pissed off more than a few of his fellow crew members by his drug-addled behavior, but he had nothing to worry about from you or anyone else, provided he behaved himself."

"What did he say to that?"

"He whined how everybody was picking on him, so I gave him a choice. Stand his regular watch, or I'll lock him in his cabin until we reach port, where I'll turn him over to the military authorities for a psychiatric evaluation." The captain smiled. "He didn't like that last part and agreed to stand his watch."

"Do you want to return to sea speed?" I asked.

"Damn, I forgot. Do it now."

Walking inside, I told George, and he called the engine room. Whoever was on the phone was loud, because George held the phone away from his ear. I stepped in and motioned to George to give me the phone, which he did, readily.

"Who is this?" I asked.

The first engineer growled. "What the fuck is going on?"

"Little problem with a potential 'man overboard.' Everything's fine now. Bring her back up to sea speed," I ordered and hung up, cutting off any retort.

The captain came in and said to George, "I'll be back at 0800 so you can get breakfast," and went below.

"Okay to put her back on autopilot?" Winkler asked.

I looked at George and said, "Yeah, good thinking," and walked out to the starboard wing and lit another Marlboro. I was up to two-and-a-half packs a day, now.

When I went down for breakfast, Greg was the only one in the salon. "Heard you had a little excitement this morning," he ventured.

"Yeah," and I explained what happened. "I think the asshole is playing a game, but you never know. Drugs do weird things to people."

Greg nodded.

"By the way," I continued, "how did you get Punser on your watch? I thought it would be just you and your wiper."

"It was. I must have looked too happy. The first engineer gave me Punser and is letting his oiler get all the double pay. At least he has to pay Isaiah oiler wages. The first engineer doesn't like me, but I think he mostly didn't want to put up with Punser."

"Too bad. Isaiah seems like a nice guy, and big."

"Isaiah? Yeah, he is, both. He pumps iron a couple hours a day, but he's a gentle soul. He and Punser still room together. That's a pain in the ass—both getting woken up when they call the watch. I know Isaiah doesn't approve of Punser, especially his drinking, but he tolerates it."

"Well, I wouldn't want Isaiah to get mad at me. He'd break Punser like a twig."

"No," Greg replied, "I wouldn't want him mad at me either."

CHAPTER 21

Back on the bridge, early afternoon, boredom set in. No ship traffic, the helm on autopilot, I had sent both ABs to work with Boats and the OS. They were forward, using chippers to scale rust off the deck. I stood leaning against the port-side windbreak, watching them, telling myself I should cut back on smoking as I lit a fresh Marlboro from the last one. At this rate, I'd be able to smoke all day off one match.

I stretched, then leaned against the bulkhead and did fifty semi-pushups, trying to unkink the knots in my neck and shoulders. Perfect time to daydream about Meg, but even half a world away, it was too painful. I wondered what she'd think of my role as the captain's enforcer. I wasn't sure what I thought of it. It seems to bring out the darker side of me, the side I've been pushing down, trying to repress. I spent the whole afternoon stewing about it, until relieved at 1800 hours.

Even though off-watch, I came back up to take star sights to check our position. Sunset is at 1831 hours, and thirty minutes after sunset is the perfect time for star sights. There are a lot of options, depending on what hemisphere you're in and what season of the year it is. Tonight, I shot Rigel, in Orion's belt; Kaus Australis in Sagittarius, low on the southern horizon; and Aldebaran, in the Taurus constellation. Aldebaran is easy to notice due to its orange color, and is referred to as the red eye of the bull. A clear sky and hard horizon gave me a good position. George shot the same stars, but his hand shakes. My intersection of the three lines is within a half mile. George has a four-mile triangle.

When you shoot a celestial line, whether star, moon, or sun, the height above the horizon is subject to fluctuation depending on the steadiness of your hand and the clarity of the horizon. Since the ship is moving, the quicker you shoot all three lines, the closer in time they will be. Time is critical. Until they invented a reliable chronometer, finding your longitude was pure guesswork. Where the three lines intersect is your position in the ocean. Rarely is it an exact intersection, most often a small triangle.

I came on watch at midnight, starting to get used to the six-hour shifts. Later, when the four-to-eight watch came on, I sent Winkler down to tell Highstone to report to the bridge. Winkler returned right away. Highstone came up the outside ladder, and he took twenty minutes to make the two-minute trip. Stumbling over the bridge wing door threshold, he stood in the dim light and said, "Whaddaya want?"

He was scruffy-looking, as usual. Knowing he was looking for an excuse to goldbrick, I kept my cool and said, "I want you to do your job. Go up to the bow and stand lookout."

"What for?" Belligerence oozing off each syllable.

I walked to within a foot of him, smelled the air but didn't detect alcohol, and hissed at him: "I gave you an order. You're on watch. When I tell you to stand lookout, you say, 'Yes, sir,' and go do it…That's 'What for.'"

He turned and walked out the door. A few minutes later, I saw the light from the WT door shine on the deck, then saw him working his way forward by flashlight.

Turning to Winkler, leaning against the forward bulkhead and staring out the porthole, I asked, "Jason, did you see me threaten or hit Highstone just now?"

"No, Mate. You didn't do nothing."

"Thank you, Jason. He may try to invent some story and complain to the captain tomorrow. I wanted to make sure you and I have our story straight."

"You betcha, Mate. Highstone's the only thing that ain't straight around here," and he snickered.

Beautiful Sunday morning, sunrise still forty-five minutes away, and glimmers of light stealing their way into the sky over my shoulder. George had relieved me at 0550 hours, but I hung around for the morning star lines. Different stars in the morning than at night, but same concept. The horizon was fuzzier, so my triangle is a mile wide. George's is three miles wide.

I told George I had posted Highstone as a lookout. Normally, when a lookout is posted, the ordinary and AB not steering take turns—one hour on, one off. When Winkler got relieved at the helm, I told him not to relieve Highstone yet. The third mate, George, would decide if he needed to keep a lookout or not.

After laying down the star-line plot on the chart, I said goodbye to George and looked forward through the port hole. Highstone wasn't on the bow.

"Hey, George," I asked, "did you tell Highstone to go below?"

"Nope," he replied, shaking his head. "Never told him nothing."

"Do you need him as look out?"

"Nah, nothing around, and I can see for miles."

"Okay, George, see you later."

Heading down to the salon, I was pissed off. Highstone decided on his own to leave his duty station without being relieved. That's serious shit.

In the salon, the captain sat drinking coffee and munching on a piece of toast. I walked up to his table.

"Excuse me, Captain. I have a situation with Highstone, and I'd like your advice."

"How refreshing," he said. "Someone actually gives a shit what I think," but he smiled as he said it. "Sit down. What's the problem, William?"

I explained what I had done with Highstone, and how he had walked off his station without approval or being relieved.

"And, of course, it was a very dark night, and in your opinion, it was prudent to have a lookout on duty, right?" he said, and he raised an eyebrow.

"Yes, sir, absolutely."

"Good. That's what I thought." He rubbed his chin with both hands, apparently not aware of doing it, then said, "After breakfast, bring Highstone to my office. Don't say anything to him ahead of time."

I nodded, said, "Yes sir," then ordered breakfast.

I was finishing my last bites when the captain walked out. At the door, he turned and said, "William, ask Boats to come along, as well." And left before I could finish swallowing.

I took a minute to brush my teeth, then collected Boats and Highstone and marched to the captain's cabin. Inside his office, Highstone stood in front of the captain, seated at his desk. Boats and I flanked him.

"Mr. Highstone," the captain began, "why did you leave your duty station this morning without being relieved?"

Highstone's complexion was yellow. He had a stricken look. He turned and glared at me and stammered, "I didn't leave my station. What's he telling you?" He jerked his thumb in my direction.

Boats growled, "Watch your hands, boy." Highstone jerked his hand back to his side.

The captain continued. "Were you ordered to stand lookout in the bow by Mr. Connolly?"

"Yeah, but he didn't say how long I had to stay there."

The captain paused. "How long have you had your seamen's papers?"

"About ten years."

"And you have been ordered to stand lookout before, haven't you?"

He nodded, which prompted a not-so-gentle poke from Boats. "Yes, sir," Highstone said.

"Have you ever before walked off the job without the mate in charge giving you permission to do so, or without being relieved by one of the crew?"

He shuffled his feet and mumbled, "No, sir."

The captain slammed his hand down on the desk, startling all three of us, and roared, "Then what the hell makes you think you can do it now, on my ship?"

Highstone stood there, trembling, shaking his head, but didn't answer.

"This will go in the log as an act of insubordination. If you pull another stunt like this, I will call it attempted mutiny. Do...you...understand?"

"Yes, Captain."

"Good, you're dismissed," and Highstone ran out of the office.

"Sorry if I startled you, Boats," the captain said, smiling. "I had to get his undivided attention."

"Mission accomplished, Captain," Boats replied, also smiling.

"I think I hurt my hand," the captain said. "That will be all, gentlemen."

In the passageway, Boats said, "The captain scared the bejesus outta him. Maybe the asshole will wake up now."

"We can always hope, Boats. Thanks for your help."

He nodded and walked away.

CHAPTER 22

Highstone behaved himself for three days. We were well out in the Pacific Ocean, and the only other problem had been a minor scuffle between the chief cook and the crew bedroom steward over a piece of cornbread.

I had gotten into the habit of walking through the crew's quarters at odd times. An ounce-of-prevention habit, since I always wore my S & W .38. At 1030, I heard "Motherfucker!" and hurried into the crew mess, just as Moses Delight, the crew BR, heaved a piece of cornbread at the chief cook. It would have been laughable if he hadn't included the plate in the throw, hitting the cook square in the corner of the eye and splitting him wide open. Moses looked at me with my hand on my gun, and his eyes bugged out. Putting his hands up, he backed away.

"I'm sorry, I'm sorry."

"Sit down and shut up," I ordered. Turning to the cook, I said, "Joselito, let me look at that," and I gently pulled his hand away. There was a lot of blood. The edge of the plate had sliced the skin at the left edge of the eyebrow through to the bone. The eye itself didn't look bad. Grabbing a wad of paper towels, I pressed it to the wound. "Keep pressure on it," I said.

Turning to Moses, I said, "Stay here until I come back and tell you otherwise. Understand?"

"Yes, Mate," his head bobbing, "I'm staying."

I steered Joselito, who was muttering curses at Moses, to the chief steward's cabin and banged on the door. When he opened it, I said, "Got another patient for you who needs stitching."

"Come in, let's see what we got here."

Joselito entered. I said, "I'll be back. I need to take care of the asshole who did this."

In the crew mess, Moses hadn't moved. When I walked in, he tried to stand, then collapsed back down. Looking closely at him, I saw his pupils were dilated, and he kept licking his tongue over his lips. Even though it was warm, he wore a long-sleeve shirt. This isn't the happy-go-lucky guy I met earlier in the trip. I suspected he was high on something. Two other crew members stood by the sideboard, watching.

Addressing them I said, "Did you see any of what happened?"

"Uh, uh."

"Not me."

"Okay, thanks." Pointing at Moses, I ordered, "Come with me, we're going to see the captain." He managed to wobble to his feet, and I followed him out. At the captain's cabin, I knocked on the open office door and announced myself.

The captain peeked, looked at us, and said, "What?"

"We've had an incident, Captain. The BR threw a dish at the chief cook and cut his head."

"Give me a minute." He retreated. Half a minute later I heard the toilet flush and he reappeared, tightening his belt, and sat at his desk. Looking at the BR, he asked, "What's the story, Moses?"

"Cap'n," he began, licking his lips and scratching his left forearm. He hesitated, then said, "The cornbread's hard."

The captains' eyes opened a little wider. "What do you mean, hard?"

"Hard…old…stale."

"That's it? The cornbread's stale?"

"Uh huh."

"Bullshit!" bellowed the captain, leaning forward on those bony hands. "You don't hit someone with a dish because the cornbread's stale."

Moses cringed, scratching harder. "Didn't mean to throw the dish, just the cornbread."

The captain shook his head, tone softer. "Why, Moses?"

"Dunno, just threw it."

"Captain," I interjected, "I think Moses is on something." Tapping him on the shoulder I said, "Roll up your sleeves, Moses."

Moses seemed to shrivel, hard to do for someone who's only five-foot-two to begin with.

"Roll them up," I repeated.

Undoing his button, he rolled his right sleeve up two turns. I pulled it all the way up and saw the needle tracks. Rolling up his left sleeve, I found more tracks. Except for one, they all looked old. Moses started to cry.

"William," the captain said. "Go search his cabin."

Twenty minutes later, I returned with one new syringe and one used one, a piece of surgical tubing he used as a tourniquet, a burnt spoon, and twenty packets of tin foil.

When I walked in to the office, I smelled puke. Moses was on his knees, head hung over the captain's trash bucket. I showed the evidence to the captain.

"Open one," the captain said, indicating the tin foil packs, so I did. It contained what looked to be heroin.

I expected him to read the riot act to Moses. Instead, he was calm, almost gentle.

"Moses, where did you get the drugs?"

No answer.

"Moses, how long have you had the drugs on board?"

"I ain't, Cap'n. Ain't had no drugs."

"But you did shoot up today, right?"

"Been trying to be clean, Cap'n," he continued, tears flowing and nose running. "He talked me in to it."

"He? Who's he?"

"Highstone, Cap'n. He sold me the horse."

I watched the captain flex his fingers, open and close them into a fist.

"Moses, you go to your cabin and stay there. Do not leave. You understand?"

Moses nodded and mumbled, "Yes, Cap'n."

After he left, I said, "This is a surprise, Captain. Up until now, Moses didn't look and act like a junkie, and I haven't heard any stories about him."

"I think we heard the truth, William. Moses is a junkie trying to stay clean." The captain paused. "Get Highstone here. Bring Boats along as a witness."

I took twenty minutes to track Boats down in the forward locker and explain what happened. He did the same thing the captain did, slowly flexed his fingers, probably envisioning them around Highstone's neck.

We found him in his bunk, asleep. Boats grabbed the front of his shirt and lifted him off the bunk, yelling, "Wake up, asshole," then steered him out the door, following me. In the captain's cabin, Boats never let go of Highstone's upper arm, holding him immobile in front of the captain.

"My patience is at an end with you," the captain began. "Tell me where you got the heroin to sell to him."

Highstone tried to back away, raising his forearms in protest, but the bulk of the bosun stopped him. As he twisted, he kicked the trash can and it tipped, spilling Moses's puke onto the deck. I heard Boats's intake of breath and Highstone's squeal of pain at the same time. Boats squeezed his arm like a vise.

"You're gonna clean that up, asshole, but first answer the captain's question," Boats growled.

Panting, whether from fear or pain or both, he gasped, "I don't know what you're talking about. You threw my stash overboard."

"You sold him some heroin. He's in trouble because you talked him into shooting up." The tension was palpable, with Highstone's body odor battling the stink of puke for top spot.

"Now, where is the rest of your 'stash?'" the captain demanded.

Boats must have been close to breaking his arm because Highstone was ashen.

The captain said, "Boats, let him go."

Boats did, and Highstone fell to his knees, landing in the pool of puke.

"I'll get a swab," Boats said, and left the cabin.

Highstone stood up, shaky, and pointed a finger at me. "He tossed my stash overboard. Maybe he kept some for himself. Maybe he sold it to Moses. He hates me."

I was about to hit him when I realized what he said. The captain caught it at the same time.

I didn't move. The captain stared at Highstone. No one spoke until Boats returned with the swab and thrust it at Highstone. "Clean it up."

Fumbling with the swab and trash can for a few minutes, he mopped up most of the puke. Holding the swab, he looked slyly at the captain, thinking he had conned him.

"I don't know why I am being so lenient," the captain started, shaking his head, "but I will give you a choice. You can spend the next ten or more days in irons on the flying bridge, living on bread and water, or you can tell me, now, no bullshit, no excuses, where the rest of your stash is." Raising his hand, he added, "Before you answer, there is no second chance. I won't ask you again. I won't ask you to clarify. I won't ask you diddley-squat. One chance...By the way, we never said it was Moses, you did....What's your answer?"

His face turned ashen again, and he shivered. He must have remembered sitting in a pile of shit, being miserable, because he said, "It's in the lifeboat."

Boats and I led Highstone to the boat deck. "Which one?" I asked.

"Number four."

That made sense. We carried four lifeboats, two on each side. Numbers one and three on the starboard side, and two and four on the port side. The two forward boats are called Rescue Boats, propelled by oars, and the two aft boats are motor boats, propelled by small gas engines. They had to be powerful enough to do six knots in calm seas with a full load, and have fuel capacity to run for at least twenty-four hours. There were more hiding places in a motor boat.

Laying a ladder alongside, I loosened the boat-cover clews enough to pull the cover up a couple of feet. Crawling inside, I motioned to Highstone, and he climbed the ladder.

"Where is it?" I demanded.

"Under the engine hatch. Off-shore side."

I undogged the hatch and struggled to lift it. It wasn't so much the weight as the fact the edges were set into the waterproof seal on the bottom. Finally, the suction broke, and the hatch pivoted up on its forward hinge until it hit the cover. I had brought a flashlight and shone it into the engine space. Two items, each the size of a shoebox, lay wrapped in canvas. I dragged them both out.

"Get down," I told Highstone, and he climbed down the ladder. At the gunnel, I tossed both packages to Boats, then went back, re-secured the engine cover and climbed out. I reached for the cover to pull it into place and Boats called up, "I'll get that mate." So I climbed down, and we all went back to the captain's cabin.

"Well," the captain asked, "what is it?"

I unwrapped the canvas. One pack was heroin, about one hundred packs of tinfoil. The other was cocaine, wrapped in pieces of Saran Wrap. I didn't count them, but the box was full.

Highstone shifted, foot to foot, smelling even worse with the odor of puke diffused. He looked down at the deck, quiet, until the captain said, "Boats, take him to the flying bridge and handcuff him to the rail." Then he screamed.

"You said if I told ya, ya wouldn't tie me up!"

"Did I? I thought I said I'd leave you there for ten days or so. I won't do that, but looking at all this shit, I'm thinking of how much trouble you could have caused me. So, for the next twenty-four hours, you'll have time to ponder on your wicked ways while enjoying the fresh air. Boats, take him away." He paused, "Oh, and Boats—a cup of water every two hours, nothing else."

The smile on Boats's face was evil but contagious. "Aye, aye, Captain." He pulled Highstone by the arm out the door.

Sitting at his desk, tapping his fingers, the captain said, "Well William, at least we haven't had to shoot anyone yet."

CHAPTER 23

Thursday 2/9/67, another beautiful day, cumulus clouds, bright sunshine, temperature 82 degrees.

A sailor's paradise, if we didn't have a collection of nuts, goofballs, alcoholics, and drug addicts as a crew.

True to his word, the captain released Highstone from the flying bridge at noon, twenty-four hours after Boats locked him there. Less than an hour later, looking aft over the starboard side, I saw him perched on the top rail at the main deck looking up at me…smiling. Here we go again.

Calling down to the captain, I told him what was happening.

"That sonofabitch. Okay, I'll go aft, you stay there and watch."

"Should I alert the engine room?" I asked.

"Yeah, I guess you better," he said, and hung up.

I told the AB at the helm to take it off autopilot and stand by for orders, then called the engine room. When I lifted the phone, I knew that Cavers had been on the phone: The receiver reeked of raw onions, a daily staple with him.

"Greg, drop down to maneuvering speed and stand by for orders."

"What's going on?" he yelled, the high-pitched whine of the turbine shrouding other sounds.

"Highstone's at it again, standing on the rail back aft. I presume he's threatening to jump overboard."

"Geez," he said, and he hung up.

Walking back out to the bridge wing, I looked aft. Highstone was talking to someone, looking inboard. I couldn't hear him, but heard others shouting. He shook his head vehemently and said something else. Finally, he looked in my direction, leaned forward so whoever he was with couldn't see his offshore arm, and gave me the finger. Then he either jumped or got pulled onto the main deck.

I ordered the AB to put it back on autopilot and called down to Greg. "Rev it back up again, Greg. The asshole backed off and didn't jump."

"Too bad," was all he said. That was unlike Greg. Things must be getting on his nerves, as well.

The captain walked onto the bridge as I hung up, and motioned for me to join him on the bridge wing.

"It looked like he was arguing with you, Captain."

"He was. Insisted it was all your fault."

"Well, he gave me the finger just before he jumped back on deck. Made sure no one but me could see it."

"He didn't jump back. When he leaned forward, I thought he would really jump, so I had Boats grab him and pull him in. Now he's got another lump on his head to whine about."

"Who was doing all the yelling?" I asked. "There was a lot of noise."

"Yeah, that's another thing. Five of the crew were there, and they all looked drunk or high. They were goading him to jump. I want you and Boats to search the rest of the lifeboats. That shit has to be hidden somewhere, and that's as likely a spot as any."

"When, Captain?"

"As soon as Boats gets here. I'll stand the watch while you're searching."

Feeling the nervous pangs in my stomach, I lit a Marlboro. I had two drags and stubbed it out. It doesn't taste good, it never did, but satisfies a craving. When Boats arrived, we started at rescue boat #1.

Loosening the clews on the boat cover, we undid enough so we could pull the cover all the way offshore, opening the whole boat up. Other than the containers of food and water strapped down, there was nothing. Noticing one container was loose, I climbed in and tightened the strap, sitting on the floor boards to do so. As I arose, I saw a lump under one of the seats and called out to Boats. "Hey, Boats. Is there supposed to be anything attached to the underside of the seats?"

He shook his leonine head. "Nothing I know about, Mate."

I had been using the fold-out awl on my knife to clean my nails when this all started, and had left it on the chart table, so I said, "Give me your knife. Let's see what we got here."

He passed me his knife, and I lay on my back on the floorboards. There were two packets attached to each seat bottom. Long and narrow, they each stretched half the length of the seat, about two inches thick, held in place by duct tape. On the third seat, one pack was missing, the tape marks obvious. No doubt, the one the crew partied with earlier today. All the packs were of heavy-duty plastic, a total of five packs.

I handed them to Boats, and he dropped them onto the boat deck. Then we secured the cover and moved the portable ladder back to #3 motorboat. After setting up the ladder, I gathered the packs and piled them aft, up against the bulkhead next to the accommodation ladder. Boats went into the boat this time, and I leaned over the gunwale watching when I heard a noise.

Looking aft, I saw that Punser lay face down on the deck, struggling to get up. "Boats," I whispered. "We got a situation here." I climbed down the ladder, walked over and stood at a distance between Punser and the ladder as he pulled himself up the bulkhead, clearly stoned. I watched as he stood, leaned over, and tried to lift one of the packs, banging his head against the bulkhead. He was determined, though, and didn't drop the pack. Turning, he took two tottering steps toward the accommodation ladder when he saw me.

His jaw dropped, but it was obvious his brain wasn't processing right. Staring at me, he continued to totter toward the ladder when I said, "Where you going, Punser?"

Slack-jawed, drooling, and squinting, he said, "Huh?"

"I said, where you going?"

"Below," he managed to get out.

"What are you carrying?"

He looked down, looked at me, and said, "Nothin'."

That's when "You motherfucker," preceded all two hundred and forty pounds of Boats hitting Punser in the back with the hardest shoulder block I've ever seen. I jumped out of the way as the pack went flying through the railing down to the next deck. Punser would have followed the pack but the rail stopped him. It saved his life. In his condition, that ten-foot drop would have killed him. As he lay wheezing on the deck, Boats threw another "motherfucker" at him, grabbed him by the left arm and dragged him down the ladder, knees and elbows hitting every rung.

"I'll be right back, Mate," Boats called.

I trailed him down the ladder and retrieved the pack Punser had dropped, adding it back on the stack. Leaning against the bulkhead, I lit up a Marlboro, slid down and sat on the deck, thinking, "Holy shit."

Boats returned five minutes later. "What did you do with him, Boats?" I asked.

"He's in his room."

"How is he?"

"He'll live."

"Okay," I said, not wanting to push it any further. "Let's bring this stuff to the captain, then we'll finish searching the other boats."

Nodding, he picked up the stack and followed me to the bridge.

"You were right, Captain, we found these in #1 boat. While we were in the boat, Punser came up on deck and tried to take one of the packs. He was stoned."

"Where's Punser now?"

Looking at Boats, standing stone-faced, I said, "Boats escorted him to his room."

I saw a glimmer of a smile from the captain. "Escorted, Boats?"

"Yes, Captain. He went along peaceful-like."

The captain leaned back in his chair. "All right," he said. "Did you check the other boats?"

"Not yet, sir. I wanted to bring this stuff here, out of sight first, so we don't have any other Punser incidents from other crew members."

"Good thinking. Go finish checking the other life boats."

An hour later, I released Boats and reported back.

"Nothing else, Captain. What do you want to do with Punser?"

"How rough was Boats with him?"

I hesitated. "He'll live, but he got what he deserved."

"Okay. Have Boats lock him up on the flying bridge." As I turned to leave, he added, "William, toss this shit overboard, first," pointing at the five packs we had left on the bridge wing.

"Aren't you going to check what's in them?"

Leaning back against the windscreen, he stretched his hands behind his neck and replied, "Nope. Don't care. It's contraband, so over it goes."

"Aye, aye, Captain." I picked up the five packs, walked down through the crew quarters, making sure they saw me, and out to the fantail, where I tossed them, one by one, into the wake. When I turned to go back in, four members of the crew, including Joselito, the chief cook, were watching me, none of them happy. I walked directly toward them and they moved apart, Joselito glaring at me. I stopped and faced him. "You got a problem, Joselito? Any of that shit belong to you?"

He continued to glare but shook his head.

I went to Punser's room, where I found Boats standing outside. Looking inside, I saw Punser unconscious on the deck, bleeding from the nose. "This your handiwork, Boats?" Curious more than angry.

"Nah. He pissed off his roommate, who gave him a poke. Didn't hit him hard, just enough."

"Isaiah? Punser must have pushed his button hard. He's such an easy-going guy."

"Assholes like this"— he jerked his thumb at him— "can push anybody too far. He's too stupid to live."

223

"Anyway, the captain wants him locked up on the flying bridge again. Would you do the honors?"

Boats stepped in, hoisted Punser onto his shoulder, and followed me up the ladders to the flying bridge. I didn't hear any head knocking sounds, but I also didn't look to check.

Boats dumped Punser on the deck, and I secured the handcuffs on his wrists to the rail. As I stood, he came to, looked around wildly and screamed. No words, just sounds, awful gargling noises.

I didn't need to exercise as much to keep the weight off. My nerves had killed my appetite. Every loud sound had me jumping out of my skin. Leaning into the windbreak, I stretched and decompressed, easing the tension in my neck and shoulders. The overnight light salt crust lay on the metal and I touched my nose to it, thinking of Meg again.

Once again, I wondered why I was here among a bunch of wackos on a rust-bucket in the middle of the Pacific Ocean, instead of in the arms of the woman I loved, halfway around the world.

CHAPTER 24

I listened to Punser's whining for the whole watch. There was no place on the bridge to avoid his noise. The captain relented and let him go to the head, so he didn't shit himself. At the watch change at 0400 hours, I woke up Boats and asked him to escort Punser. When Boats brought him back to the bridge, I thanked him and took Punser to the flying bridge. He behaved until Boats left, then started to argue as I led him up to the flying bridge, saying I was picking on him.

There was nothing to argue about, so, dangling the cuffs in front of him, I said, "Just shut up, turn around, and sit down on the deck."

He tried to move away, and I grabbed his arm. That's when he made a big mistake, grabbing for my pistol.

There wasn't any thinking on my part, just pure reaction. Clamping down on his hand, I head-butted him, smashing his already mangled nose. Still holding his hand, I kicked his legs out from under him, and he went down hard on his back, smacking his head on the deck. Rolling him onto his stomach, I locked one cuff on his right wrist, grabbed his left wrist, pulled him backward to the rail, and secured his left wrist. Conscious but dazed, he didn't resist. I left him and went down to the bridge.

Winkler stood next to the helm, smoking when I came in. The chart room door was open, and the glow from the red night light cast an eerie glow on us.

"Hey, Mate, what's that on your forehead?"

Reaching up, I wiped my forehead. It was blood. Punser's.

"Be right back," I said. "Gotta hit the head." After checking the radar and looking around the horizon and seeing no traffic, I went to my room and washed the blood out of my hair.

When I returned to the bridge, I had second thoughts about leaving Punser unattended. I sent Winkler down to wake up the chief steward, Andrew, and ask him to come up and bring his first aid kit with him. Andrew arrived five minutes after Winkler returned. Motioning Andrew to follow me, I went up to the flying bridge and shined my flashlight on Punser.

Bending down Andrew asked, "What happened?"

I told him and he grunted. "His nose is getting to be a habit with you."

I returned to the bridge, and fifteen minutes later Andrew came in.

"Don't think anyone's going to be able to fix that nose. Two thumpings in four days. He'll need a Roto-Rooter to breathe through it again."

"Thanks for your help, Andrew. I'll be sure to mention it when I tell the captain, when he wakes up in the morning."

When I got relieved at 0600, I knocked on the captain's door. No response, so I checked the salon. The captain sat there with the chief engineer, drinking coffee.

"Excuse me," I said to both, mindful of the chief's last conversation with me. "Captain, I had a problem with Punser this morning."

"What kind of problem?"

I explained.

The chief said, "Captain, he assaulted an officer. What would he have done with the gun if he got hold of it?"

Appreciating the chief coming to my defense, I stood there, silent.

"William," the captain said. "Write this up. Be as accurate as possible. I'll have Andrew write a report, as well." Shaking his head, he muttered, "This is getting out of hand."

The next four days were filled with tension and bitterness. The crew members who were high when we found their second stash of drugs came down from their highs, and were pissed-off at me. Even though it was the captain who ordered the search, Highstone convinced several of the crew it was all my idea. The last go-round with Punser only added fuel to the fire. They wouldn't dare take on the captain, but a second mate—especially a temporary one—is an easier target. I'd been trying hard to keep a neutral attitude, but after talking to Boats, it was clear that things had now become personal. I took it to the captain.

Sitting in front of him at his desk, I said "Captain, I need your advice."

"What is it, William?"

"I feel like I'm back in the streets of Southie, in the wrong neighborhood."

"How so?"

"Every second, I'm looking over my shoulder, waiting for someone to jump me. Highstone has the crew revved up, telling them I'm goading you into busting their balls by raiding their stashes. They've made it personal. This morning, Boats told me one of the ABs, he wouldn't say who, told him he'd heard Highstone and the chief cook talking about putting something into my food."

Tapping his fingers on the desk, the captain said, "That's not good. Not good at all."

"No, it isn't. I'm not eating much anyway, because my stomach is in knots. But now, I can't trust anything coming up from the galley."

"I'll handle this, William."

Nodding, I went to my cabin, shut and locked the door, and dozed off, with visions of Joselito, the chief cook, spitting in my food, and worse.

Later, the captain told me of his conversation with Andrew.

"I told Andrew about the threat. He said, 'It's easy to do, Captain. The cook can slip anything into the food, and you wouldn't notice, unless you watched him the entire time.'

"I asked him what he could do and he said 'I can warn him. If anyone gets sick, we have a record of his threat.'"

"Warn him?" I interjected.

The captain held his hands up. "Take it easy William. Andrew assured me it will be a very strong warning. One he'll take to heart."

I left the captain and went looking for Andrew.

In his office, I said, "What the hell kind of warning can you give that will make these clowns behave?"

"I'll tell you what, William. Come along with me. But promise me you won't interrupt. This is my show. Okay?"

"Okay."

Andrew waited until 1430 hours, the slowest time in the galley, before calling me on the bridge. "Now's the time, William."

"I'll be there in five minutes."

With me trailing, Andrew approached Joselito, who stood at the main work table, slicing and dicing vegetables for the soup he was making.

"Joselito, you have a problem."

"What problem?" oozing hostility and eyeing me.

"It's one thing to get high on drugs, it's a whole different thing to threaten to poison a ship's officer."

Joselito stepped back, gripping his knife. "Wh…what you talking about? I ain't poisoned no one."

Wary of the knife, Andrew continued. "I know you haven't, but you threatened to, and that's just as bad. You lose your seamen's papers and go to jail for stupid shit like that."

Still stammering, Joselito protested, "I didn't threaten nobody," staring past Andrew at me.

"Yes, you did. We have witnesses."

"Who?"

"You'll find out at the Coast Guard hearing at the end of the trip." He paused, "But in the meantime, if nothing else happens and no one…no one…gets sick from food poisoning, maybe I can talk the captain into forgetting the whole thing. I already saved your ass once when I kicked your cousin off the ship. Maybe I should have fired both of you. This is your second chance. You won't get another chance from me, you understand?" Andrew leaned in, almost touching nose to nose. Gritting his teeth, he repeated, "Do…you…fucking…understand?"

Joselito's eyes were wide when he said, "Yeah, I understand."

Leaning back, Andrew hitched up his pants, said "Good," and left with me behind him.

It took two and a half days for the simmering fuse inside Joselito to set off the dynamite. Two and a half days, where I ate nothing but cold cuts, peanut butter and jelly sandwiches, and coffee. Two and a half days, where I carried a homemade sap and handcuffs and the pistol everywhere I went. Two and a half days, where I cautiously opened doors before stepping out.

Sitting at breakfast, I stuck with coffee and toast I made myself. Then I heard yelling from below, someone shouting, "Knife fight!" I jumped up and looked at Greg. He got up and followed me.

I ran down the stairs, then turned toward my cabin.

"Where you going?" Greg called, still behind me.

Grabbing from the bulkhead the mattress I had rigged, I said, "Secret weapon." I dragged it behind me down one more deck to the crew quarters.

"Make way!" I yelled at the crew in the corridor outside the galley and they scattered.

Inside, I could see Joselito circling the work table with a butcher knife in one hand and a meat cleaver in the other, alternating between English and Tagalog as he cursed at his intended victim on the other side of the table, AB Harvey Preen.

"We gotta get him out here into the corridor," I said to Greg. "He's got too much room to swing in there. I'll try to get his attention to let Preen out. Hopefully, he'll follow him or me out the door, so be ready to pin him with the mattress when I come out."

"You know, you're nuts," Greg said.

"Yeah, I think you're right."

I stepped through the door.

I moved toward Preen's side of the table and Joselito screamed and started after me. As we rounded the table, I pushed Preen toward the corridor door but kept circling the table, wanting to give him time to get clear.

Glancing at the doorway, I saw Greg peeking in, but Joselito noticed and moved toward the door, hoping to cut me off—literally. When I stopped, Joselito edged back. Sidling toward the end of the table away from the door, I let Joselito get closer to my end—then faked slipping and falling to the deck. He took the bait and rushed around the end of the table, but I was already scrambling along the floor heading for the door.

Greg held the mattress slanted by the upper strap, peeking from behind it at the bulkhead. I slipped by it, turned and grabbed the bottom strap.

"Now!" Greg shouted, and we both pushed in concert, filling the width of the corridor with the mattress and pushing Joselito with it. He couldn't swing the cleaver, but stabbed at the mattress with the butcher knife, penetrating it four inches from my nose. After three steps, he fell, and we landed on top of him, the knife still embedded in the mattress and the cleaver skittering down the deck toward the WT door.

I leaped over the mattress. He lay dazed, face down, no longer a threat. "Greg, drag the mattress," I said. As Joselito appeared from beneath it, I straddled him and put the cuffs on him.

Leading him away, followed by Greg dragging the mattress, I heard one of the crew say, "Geez, fuckin' Batman and Robin."

Greg and I brought Joselito back to the salon. The entire incident only took twenty minutes, but Greg and I aged a lot in that time. The captain and chief engineer still sat there, chatting, as if nothing had happened. I explained what had occurred, and they both shook their heads. Not sure if they were doing it because of my actions or Joselito's, I stood holding one of Joselito's elbows and Greg held the other.

"Joselito," the captain asked, "Why did you attack Mr. Preen?"

Silence as Joselito stared at the deck, refusing to meet the captain's eye.

"Did he do something to you?" the captain pressed. "There has to be a reason. No one starts swinging a knife and meat cleaver at someone else just for the hell of it."

"That fucker say I poison him," jerking his head in my direction. "I no poison anyone. He lie!"

"So instead of poisoning Mr. Connolly," he said, pointing at me and his voice rising, "you try to kill Mr. Preen with a meat cleaver?" He stood and leaned on the table, his voice louder, now. "What in hell makes you think either one of those stunts is okay?" His voice went up yet another notch. "You think you're God, deciding who lives and dies?"

I felt Joselito cringe and I clung tighter to him.

"Well, you're not God!" he said, now in a full-throated roar. He slammed his fist on the table. "This is my ship, and here I am God, not you! I decide who lives and dies, not you! My ship, my rules!"

Joselito was shaking. I looked at Greg and the chief, and both were wide-eyed. If the captain were putting on a show to intimidate someone, it was working.

Pulling himself to his full height, he took a deep breath and in a normal tone he pronounced sentence.

"Mr. Bautista"—I had forgotten Joselito's last name— "I am placing you under arrest. When we reach port, I will turn you over to the authorities and charge you with attempted murder of Mr. Preen, Mr. Connolly, and Mr. Russell." Looking at me, he continued. "Lock him in the pilot's cabin and leave the handcuffs on. He has already shown what he is capable of doing, so if he resists you in any way, I will interpret that to mean he is again trying to kill you. Therefore, you not only have my permission to shoot him, I am ordering you to do so, before he can harm another member of this crew."

Joselito sagged, crying.

"Mr. Connolly, do you understand your orders?"

"Yes sir, Captain, I do." I was straining to hold Joselito upright.

"Take him away."

Greg and I dragged him out and up a deck to the pilot's cabin, where I gave him a chance to use the head before locking him up. I didn't feel sorry for him; I just didn't want to smell him if he pissed or shit himself. He shook uncontrollably the whole time. As we walked back to the salon, Greg gave a nervous laugh. "You got to hand it to the captain, that was a Shakespearean performance he put on."

"What makes you think he was acting?" I asked.

CHAPTER 25

Saturday 2/18/67. Midnight, clear skies, trade winds a little stiff, about fifteen MPH. We'd been steaming steadily at sixteen knots. This was as close to Hawaii as we would get.

The captain had received word from the main office that no first mate was available, so we continued on course for Guam.

I checked out the midnight meal Andrew had left for the night watch. Cold cuts and pound cake. I passed on the cold cuts, but took a cup of coffee and two slices of pound cake up to the bridge. After checking the chart and radar, I asked Cavers if Joselito, occupying the pilot's cabin behind the bridge, had behaved himself or acted up.

"Nah. He's been behaving himself. Asks permission to take a piss. The captain must have put the fear of God in him."

I laughed, and he said, "What's funny?"

I told him about the "God" sequence during the captain's rant at Joselito, and he chuckled.

"It's true. The captain is God on board ship."

I relieved him and he went below. Taking my coffee and pound cake to the starboard bridge wing, I relaxed in the warm breeze. The moon was in the first quarter, bouncing sparkles off the wave tops, therapeutic in its serenity. I could use a little therapy: Meg—the heartache didn't go away, just felt distant.

The next two days were calm. With the chief cook locked up, Andrew had taken over the duties of cook, so I felt safe to order and eat food from the galley. Not a lot—my stomach was still in knots—but eggs and soup kept me going. He was a good cook, and the captain made sure to compliment him every meal. If he resisted, or worse, refused, we would have a sizeable problem, but he was a trouper and didn't complain about the extra workload.

The hours passed, and the four-to-eight watch came on and changed helmsmen. AB Preen had the first shift. We were on autopilot, and he leaned on the binnacle and smoked. I'd been making Highstone stand a lookout post every time, rather than let him sit on his lazy ass in the crew mess. I looked toward the bow and didn't see him there.

"Preen," I called from the bridge wing. "Did you remind Highstone to go on lookout?"

"Yes, Mr. Mate. So did Winkler."

"Why did Winkler have to remind him if you did?"

He paused. "The baby was fussy this morning."

"Fussy? What's that mean?"

Another pause. "Bitchin' more than usual."

"Well, I don't see him on lookout, so go check on him."

Sighing, he replied, "Sure thing, Mr. Mate," and he went below.

Ten minutes later, he returned. "He ain't there. I walked to the bow. He ain't there, either, and he ain't in our room."

Immediately, I walked to the starboard wing and looked aft. Sure enough, there was Highstone, standing on his favorite perch on the rail. My blood pressure rose. I was getting tired of this shit.

Walking back inside, I called the captain and got a sleepy, "What?"

"Sorry to bother you, Captain, but it's Highstone again. He wouldn't post lookout and is standing on the rail again back aft."

"Damn him." Then silence. "All right, William, I'll go back and talk him down."

"Yes, sir," I answered, and hung up. I didn't bother to take the ship off auto-pilot, and didn't call down to the engine room to reduce speed.

The captain and Boats walked in, and the captain told Preen to get himself a cup of coffee. Preen disappeared.

"Same crap, Captain?" I asked.

Sighing, "The same." Going to the forward port he looked out. "He's up there now.

"I got Boats and took him with me. When we stepped through the WT door, Highstone shrieked, 'He's trying to get rid of me. He wants me to kill myself. No one else has to stand lookout. Why do I?'

"Boats was less than tactful. When he approached the rail, Highstone yelled, 'Stay back! I'll jump!'

"Boats stopped but said, 'I wish the fuck you would.'"

"What happened?" I asked.

"I told him the story of the boy who cried wolf, and warned him no one would believe him anymore if he kept this crap up. Then I told him to get his ass down from the rail and go on lookout."

"Captain?"

"Yes, William."

"As long as he gets you to react, he thinks he's winning. He isn't going to kill himself. It's all a show. If he does it again, let me and Boats handle it. Once he sees you aren't there, he'll stop playing the game."

Looking at Boats, the captain said, "That okay with you, Boats?"

"Yessir. I agree with Mr. Connolly. He's playing a stupid game. Hey, what's the worst thing that can happen, he jumps?" A smile crept over his face.

The captain blew out a big breath, then said, "Okay. If it happens again, you deal with it. I'm going back to bed."

After he left, I said, "What do you think, Boats?"

"I think if he climbs on that rail again, we leave him there until he gets tired or, if we get lucky, he falls in."

"Sounds like a plan. Thanks, Boats."

He gave a tired smile and left. Five minutes later, Preen returned, lit up a cigarette and stared out the forward port. An old-timer who knew when to say nothing.

CHAPTER 26

It was Washington's Birthday. I wondered how he would have reacted if his crew rowing him across the Delaware were drunk and obnoxious? The painting has them working at odds with each other, fighting the ice floes. With three people standing in the boat, one of them holding the flag, and George in a tenuous position with his right foot on the gunwale, it didn't look stable. But he made it across, so there was hope for us on the *SS West Way III*.

It was not your usual balmy day. Squalls had been passing through, and the wind gusts in them reached fifty miles per hour. Boats had the crew checking the battens on the hatch covers, just in case.

At 1330, Joselito banged on the locked door of the pilot cabin. Yesterday, the captain had relented and removed his handcuffs, so when I went to the cabin, I told him to stand away from the door before I opened it. He stood with his butt against the bunk.

"What are you making all the noise for?" I asked.

"I gotta pee."

"So what? You been peeing for six days, and all you had to do was call. Why are you banging on the door, now?" A little hostility in my demeanor. After all, this is the asshole who wanted to poison me.

"I wanna talk to the captain. It's no right he keep me lock up." Softening his tone, he said, "I know I fuck up before, but I no on drugs. Please tell captain. I no cause trouble."

"Okay, I'll tell him, but you gotta pee or not?"

He nodded, and I followed him to the head, waited while he peed, then locked him back in the cabin.

The captain had relieved Cavers for breakfast, and when he returned to the salon, I told him what Joselito had said and done earlier.

"Do you believe him?" the captain asked.

"Right now, maybe, because he's sober, and he's had time to think about what will happen when we get back to the States. Maybe he's hoping he can talk himself out of trouble by promising to be a good boy. But…he was sober when he threatened to poison me, and he was sober when he tried to kill Preen. Pissed off, but sober. Yeah, I believe him—but I still don't trust him."

The captain did his two-hands-rubbing-his-face thing and said, "I'll think about it."

That afternoon, when Joselito asked to pee, I told him I had talked to the captain about releasing him, and the captain said he would think about it. Tensing, he glared at me, and I took a step back. Then he relaxed, said "thanks," and went into the cabin. When I locked the door, I heard a muttered "Fuck."

The man was still dangerous, so lying about his intentions didn't mean much. Lying was a way of life with him, Punser, Highstone, and others like them. I find it ironic that today, George Washington's birthday—the man who supposedly couldn't tell a lie—all I'm dealing with is liars.

After supper, the captain and chief engineer sat at the captain's table, drinking coffee and talking. Everyone else but me had left the salon. The chief steward walked in and stood beside the captain.

"Captain, you wanted to see me?"

"Yes," the captain replied. "Andrew, I have a question for you. William, listen in."

I faced them.

"The chief cook is trying to talk me in to letting him out and going back on duty. Says he'll behave himself. William has already told me what he thinks," he said, looking at me. "What do you think?"

"Captain," I interrupted. "In case I wasn't clear when we talked, I prefer he stay locked up. I wouldn't want to have to reload my gun."

Andrew and the chief stared at me but this was the captain's show, so I sat there and stared back, silent.

"Captain," Andrew offered, "when this trip began, and we had the problem with Joselito and his cousin, the baker, I didn't think Joselito was capable of hurting anyone except his cousin. I no longer feel that way. Joselito's proven he's dangerous. He may or may not behave himself, but I just don't know."

"Having him locked up adds a lot of work to your day."

"Captain, I don't like working sixteen-hour days, but I'd rather do that than be responsible for Joselito poisoning or stabbing anyone."

The captain nodded for a few seconds, then said, "Okay, he stays locked up. I've already called and asked for a replacement for him in Guam, but I wouldn't hold my breath waiting for one."

"Should I tell him what your decision is, Captain?" I asked.

"Not unless he asks."

At midnight, when I relieved the watch, I asked Cavers when was the last time he let Joselito out to visit the head. He said at 2300 hours, so I would get through the night without having to confront him.

We still had an occasional squall pass through, but they were thinning out and were less violent. Squalls at sea interrupt the wave pattern and create choppy seas. Not necessarily large waves, but they disrupt the pattern caused by the trade winds, and the ship gets slammed a lot with shorter, misdirected waves. In between squalls, I stayed on the bridge wing and chain-smoked my Marlboros, once again second-guessing myself for coming on this trip, and drowning in memories of Meg. I still loved her. The details of her smile, the sparkle of her eyes, the sensuousness of her body, were still achingly vivid.

When I got relieved, sunrise was still forty minutes away and the sky heavy with clouds. There would be no star sights this morning. Another day of dead-reckoning navigation. I was restless and decided to run the ladders and work off stress. When I changed into my jogging shorts and tee shirt, I debated leaving the revolver in my cabin, but at the last second strapped it on. It was cumbersome when exercising, but had become second nature, so I wore it.

Running and stretching for thirty minutes, I was on the flying bridge, cooling off, when I heard shouting from the bridge: "Joselito, come back!" Not knowing if it was Cavers or one of the ABs, I ran down the rear ladder and into the bridge. Cavers stood there.

"That crazy bastard just took off when I tried to put him back in the pilot cabin."

Turning, I ran below. As I turned the corner from the starboard side, I saw Joselito run into the salon and I went after him, pulling my revolver as I ran, worried he would confront either the captain or the chief steward.

It wasn't either. It was both.

He stood five feet inside the door, a butcher knife in his right hand. The captain sat at his usual seat. The chief steward stood with his back to the pantry pass-through opening. The chief engineer, first engineer, and Greg sat at their table. No one spoke. Everyone's eyes riveted on Joselito.

The captain glanced at me, then said, "Joselito, you said you would behave if I let you out. Is this behaving?" He pointed at the knife.

245

"You no let me out," Joselito rasped, and took a step toward the captain.

"Joselito!" I yelled, and he spun, facing me.

"Drop the knife," I said, keeping the gun down by my side in my right hand.

He took a step forward, and I raised the gun and pointed it at him. Realizing the captain was directly behind him and in the line of fire, I said, "Captain…move."

The captain stared at me blankly for a second, then realized the danger he was in and scrabbled to his left, toward the pantry.

Joselito had stopped when I pointed the gun. I could see rage fighting with reason in his eyes. He wanted to stick that knife in me so bad, but there was enough common sense or survival instinct in him to realize my bullet would move faster than his knife. He stood there, shaking. I stood, resolute and amazingly calm, my hand steady, the gun pointed at the center of his chest.

"Joselito," I said, my voice soft, now. The only other sound was the shuffle of someone's shoes. "Please put the knife down. Don't make a bad situation worse."

After a few seconds, he lowered his hand, but didn't drop the knife. Watching his eyes the entire time, I saw the rage blaze in them. He was six feet from me, and I had a bad feeling. When his hand was all the way down to his side, I lowered the gun but stepped back at the same time. That step saved me. Lunging at me, he brought the knife up in a crossing motion toward my neck.

Raising the gun, I brought up my left arm at the same time. His knife sliced my left forearm when I pulled the trigger.

His motion carried him forward, and I moved to my left, pivoting and pushing him as he slid past. Staggering a step, he turned, facing me, still holding the knife hanging at his side. I sensed he was no longer a threat, but kept the gun aimed at him. His left hand came up and touched the bloody stain on the right side of his chest. Looking at me, stunned, he dropped the knife, brought his right hand up and covered his left hand, then collapsed to the deck.

The chief steward grabbed a handful of napkins and knelt next to Joselito, ripping his shirt open and pressing the napkins into the bloody hole. He turned him over to reveal an exit wound. The bullet had entered the right side of the chest and had angled downward and outward. "Give me some more napkins!" he shouted, and Greg grabbed some and knelt down beside him.

"Hold these in place while I get my medical kit," he told Greg and ran out of the salon.

I stood, watching, ears ringing from the blast in closed quarters, smelling the cordite, gun still in hand until the captain came up and said, "Sit down, William."

Looking at him, I nodded, holstered the gun, and looked at my left arm. Blood poured from the six-inch slice, and I got dizzy. I can take looking at someone else's blood but not my own. Leaning on the table, I pivoted into a seat.

The chief engineer handed me a wad of napkins, and I pressed it on the wound, trying hard to not pass out. By the time the chief steward returned, I was steady.

He knelt again over Joselito, who was panting rapidly, sweating profusely, and obviously in great pain.

"Captain," he said, "I think the lung is punctured. The exit wound is sucking air." Turning to Greg, he ordered, "Go to my office and get two thimbles out of my desk top drawer. The metal ones, not rubber. And get a roll of Saran Wrap from the galley," he shouted after him as Greg ran out the door.

We sat there, waiting for him to return, no one speaking, Joselito's rasping the only sounds.

Greg returned and handed the thimbles to Andrew, who said, "Rinse them and your hands in the alcohol in the blue bottle." When Greg did so, he instructed him to insert one thimble into the rear exit wound. Greg did it, causing a deep gasp from Joselito. Rinsing his own hands in alcohol, Andrew inserted the second thimble into the entry wound, eliciting another, louder gasp.

"Greg, sit him up," Andrew ordered.

Greg moved to Joselito's head and slid his hands under his shoulders, lifting him to a sitting position.

Andrew put a square of gauze over each hole then wrapped the thin plastic sheet around Joselito's chest, four layers, cinching it tight. He put pressure pads on the wounds and finally wrapped the entire chest with bandages. "You know," he said, "in basic training, they teach you to use a poncho to wrap a sucking chest wound. God bless Saran Wrap. "Okay," he said, "let's get a litter and take him to the pilot's cabin."

While Greg and the chief engineer did that, Andrew inspected my arm, muttered, "Damn," and sewed me up. It took twenty-five of Andrew's stitches. I felt every one of them.

CHAPTER 27

The captain had asked me to stop by his cabin when I got off watch. Inside, the captain and chief steward both looked worried. I had interrupted their conversation.

"What do you think, Andrew?" the captain asked. "Is he going to make it?"

"It doesn't look good, Captain. The Saran Wrap is working, insofar as keeping air from leaking out of his chest, and the thimbles help. But he's got to be torn up inside, and I don't know how to treat that. I've got him on an intravenous saline solution, and I gave him a shot of penicillin, just in case. God knows what type of infection he can get."

"We're smack in the middle of no-return," the captain said. "Six days from both Guam and Hawaii. We have to keep going. I've alerted the ship's agent in Guam, and I'm waiting to hear from a doctor—hopefully a military doctor familiar with gunshot wounds."

Just then, Sparky ran through the open door and yelled, "The doc's on the line," and the three of us followed him back to the radio room. Sparky sat at his seat, donned his headphones, and said, "The voice is bad, but Morse code is clear. What do you want me to send?"

The captain looked at Andrew and nodded. "Tell him there's an entry and exit wound, and I've plugged both," Andrew said. Sparky held up his left hand with one finger extended, indicating wait, while his right hand tapped away in code on the telegraph key. Pausing to listen, he wrote on his pad when they answered.

Andrew leaned over Sparky's shoulder and read the message. When Sparky raised his head, Andrew continued. "Tell him I've started an I.V. and gave him a shot of penicillin. Ask him what I can do now."

Sparky did his magic with the key, rattling away, then wrote again.

The message read, *How is his breathing?*

"Tell him it's labored, but steady. I've got him propped up with pillows, and that seems to help. Ask him—" Sparky's hand shot up, cutting him off. After thirty seconds, Sparky waggled his fingers, and Andrew continued. "Ask him if there's anything else I can do."

When Sparky finished tapping, there was a pause. Then he scribbled furiously on the pad.

"Shit," Andrew said, reading Sparky's scrawl. "We don't have any blood…Tell him I have I.V. needles and bags for drawing blood. Ask him if we can give him blood direct from a donor."

More clicking and scribbling.

"We have to know their blood types. Correct matching is critical," Andrew read.

Sparky scribbled again, then clicked a few times, sat back, and spoke. "The doc said put him on oxygen if you have any, then he signed off."

"Thanks, Sparky," the captain said.

Andrew spoke. "We have two oxygen bottles, Captain. Don't know how long they'll last, but I'll check."

"Do that, Andrew. How do we find out what Joselito's blood type is?"

"A lot of the crew have medical cards they carry with them that has that information. Let me check his locker and see if I can find one. We'd still have to find a matching volunteer."

Sitting on my bunk, leaning against the bulkhead, I cradled my arm. It stung like hell. Every few minutes, I would shake and get a chill, nerves catching up with me. I had had the shakes before and after a fight, but this was different.

I had shot a man. Once the fight-or-flight decision is made, consciously or unconsciously, punching or kicking someone who is doing the same to you is a natural reaction. Now, with time to think about it, I wondered why I had been so calm, knowing I would shoot him, knowing it could be fatal. Why didn't it bother me about pulling the trigger? I still didn't feel bad about shooting him, but thoughts crept in of what faced me if he died.

It was 1130 hours. I had washed down with a facecloth, not wanting to get my arm wet. The arm had changed from a sting to a dull throb. I preferred the sting. Walking into the salon, I felt days had passed, but it was only five hours. Greg and the chief engineer were there.

"How you feeling, William?" the chief asked.

"Sore. Apart from that, I'm okay."

The chief nodded and walked in to the pantry.

Greg, a concerned look on his face, whispered, "You sure you're okay? You been stabbed, and you shot a guy. That's serious shit, man."

I nodded twice. "Yeah, I know," I sighed, wondering why I was not more upset. I fetched a cup of coffee, and the captain and Andrew came in as I walked to the table.

The captain said, "How's the arm?"

"Pretty sore, Captain."

Andrew said, "You need a sling. Keep your arm from hanging down. Won't throb so much."

I asked, "How's Joselito doing?"

"I don't know," Andrew answered. "I don't know what's good or bad. Nothing seems to have changed in the last few hours, so I guess that's good."

"By the way," the captain said, addressing everyone, "do any of you have type 'A' or type 'O' blood?"

Greg caught on immediately. "He needs a transfusion, doesn't he?"

"Yes. The doctor we talked to in Guam recommended it. Unless we get a donor, it won't happen."

"I'm type 'O' positive," I said. "I'll donate the blood," not knowing why I said it. Hidden guilt? Thinking ahead to my possible trial. Looking to score brownie points? Who knows, but I offered.

Andrew said, "No way. You've lost a lot of blood yourself."

"I don't hear anyone else offering. If you find another volunteer, I'll step back. Let me know."

A minute of silence, then Greg said, "I'm type 'B.' I don't match his blood."

The chief engineer said, "I'm type 'AB'. I don't match either.

"What about you, Captain?" the chief asked.

"I'm 'O' positive, like William, but if you think I'm going to donate my blood to the son-of-a-bitch who tried to kill me, think again."

It struck me: *The captain had me do his dirty work and now is washing his hands of it. Captain Pontius Pilate. Sonofabitch!*

"I'll ask the crew and see if I can get a volunteer, Captain," Andrew said. "If not, I'll take William up on his offer."

The captain walked to his seat, paused, then bent over, peering at the back of it. He reached into his pocket, came up empty-handed and muttered, "Fuck!" Walking to the sideboard, he got a knife and returned to the seat, probing the back of it.

He extracted the spent bullet. If I hadn't warned him to move, that bullet would have hit him in the stomach. I would have shot two men.

CHAPTER 28

Andrew had given me a sling. Now I paced the bridge wing, the throbbing in my arm reduced, but the pounding in my head twice as bad. Pain, fueled by anger. I was pissed at the captain's attitude, knowing I couldn't do anything about it. He had led me down this path, but I had followed willingly, a self-righteous dupe.

"William," Andrew's voice interrupted my self-pity trance. He stood in the bridge's doorway.

"Something wrong?" I said, immediately realizing the incongruity of my question. Right now, everything was wrong.

"What isn't?" he replied, echoing my thought. "I've asked everyone in the crew to donate blood. The only one willing to do it is Isaiah Smithfield, but he's type 'B'"

"That's Greg's oiler, the big black guy?"

"Yes, a gentle man, but strong as hell. When I asked him, he grasped my hand and told me it's his obligation to help. I mean, what is he, a born-again Christian? Who today feels obliged to help anyone? My hand still hurts. I don't think he knows his own strength."

"Well, I guess I'm the official donor. When do you want to do it?"

"We'll wait until you get off watch. Give you a few more hours to build up your blood level. Not much, but every little bit helps. Every half-hour I've been checking on Joselito, and nothing seems to change. A couple of times he was awake but looked disoriented. I told him to not talk. Didn't want to strain his lungs any more than necessary."

"Okay, I'll see you when I get relieved."

"Make sure you eat something and drink a lot of water between now and then."

I continued pacing the bridge wing until the four-to-eight watch came on duty and the helmsmen switched off. Winkler, the AB, took over. The ship was on autopilot. After checking the course, he stepped out on the wing and lit a cigarette, offering me one.

"No thanks, Jason."

We stood there, silent for five minutes, then he offered, "Mr. Connolly, the good guys in the crew are behind you. We know how crazy Joselito could get."

"Thanks, Jason, I appreciate your support." Then I snickered, and he looked at me strangely. I explained, "How many of the crew are good guys, and how many are drunks and druggies?"

He laughed. "That's a good question. We're outnumbered," and we both laughed.

Turning to go into the bridge, I looked at the bow. No lookout. My standing orders for Highstone to stand lookout hadn't changed, and he wasn't there. "Jason, was Highstone in the crew mess when you came up?"

"Come to think of it, I didn't see him."

"Go check on him. Tell him to get up on lookout where he belongs."

He went into the bridge and down the inside companionway, returning in ten minutes.

"He's on his way up there."

Lifting an eyebrow, I asked, "Did he say why he wasn't already there?"

"He forgot."

"Where was he when you found him?"

"Asleep in his room."

I nodded. No sense arguing with Jason over the idiocy of Highstone.

In the captain's office, I listened to him and Andrew briefly debate where I would give blood. The captain thought it should be right next to Joselito, but Andrew said if Joselito woke up, it could scare him, and he didn't need any more stress. Laughing, I interjected, "He's the one who caused all the stress."

We did it in my cabin, with the I.V. plastic bag receiving the blood in a big bowl of ice on the floor. "What's the ice for?" I asked.

"Keep the blood cool," Andrew answered.

"That doesn't make sense. You're going to give it to Joselito right away, aren't you?"

"Yes."

"Won't cold blood cause some kind of shock to his system?"

"You're right," he said. "I was thinking in terms of storing the blood." He poured the ice into my sink and replaced the bag into the bowl.

Andrew cleaned and swabbed my left arm with alcohol, then had me squeeze my fist several times to raise the vein in my arm. Deftly he inserted the needle, then opened a little valve on the end of the gadget attached to the needle. Gravity took care of the rest.

Every couple of minutes, Andrew would stoop down and rock the bag.

"What are you doing?" I asked.

"Keeping the blood moving. Don't want it to clot."

"How do you know to do that?"

"I'm pretty sure there's an anticoagulant in the bag, but seems like common sense. If blood doesn't flow, it will clot up."

It took ten minutes to fill the bag, or at least fill it to Andrew's satisfaction. Shutting the little valve, he unhooked me and put a gauze pad and band-aid on the needle hole. He handed me a bottle of ginger ale and instructed, "Drink this and stay in your bunk until I come back." Picking up the bowl and tubing, he walked out.

Curious as to how the transfusion would work, I opened the ginger ale, took a swig, then rose and followed Andrew up to the bridge. I had donated blood a lot when

258

I was younger, to the Red Cross and also direct to hospitals (they paid two dollars for a pint of blood). I had plenty of experience in giving, but never saw anyone getting blood. I peeked in through the door of the pilot cabin while he worked on Joselito.

The room stunk of piss and shit. Andrew had previously screwed an eye-hook into the overhead to hold the I. V. bag. Now he shut off the flow of saline solution and disconnected the tube. Hanging the blood bag on the hook, he cracked the valve until the blood started to drip, then shut it and inserted it into the I.V. in Joselito's arm. Opening the valve, he saw the blood was flowing and breathed a sigh of relief.

Joselito hadn't stirred during the transfer.

"That looked easy," I said.

Andrew jumped. "Jesus, don't you ever do what you're told? You should be lying down."

Showing him the bottle of ginger ale and taking a sip I responded, "I'm doing what you said, drinking ginger ale. How's he doing?"

Andrew motioned me out of the room, and I preceded him to the bridge. "I never know whether he can hear me, and I don't want to scare him any more than he is."

Nodding, I asked, "So, how is he? The room smells like a sewer."

"He seems to be breathing better, not as labored. Woke up this morning and asked for water. I gave him a few sips, and he went back to sleep. If he's not bleeding too bad internally, this transfusion should help. As for the stink, I did my best to help him use a bedpan, but there's no escaping the smell. I'd like to change the sheets and his underwear, but I'm afraid to move him."

"You've saved his life, Andrew. No one else aboard could have. Feel good about that."

And then I went back to my cabin and fell asleep.

During daylight hours, Andrew continued to check on Joselito every half hour. After 2200 hours, the mate on watch, me or Cavers, would check him with the understanding if something looked wrong, call Andrew. At 0200 hours, I looked in and Joselito was awake.

"You feeling okay?" I asked, a dumb question under the circumstances, but to my surprise, he smiled—sick and anemic, but a smile, and nodded.

"Thirsty," he croaked.

"You can only have a sip, to help your dry throat. Andrew says you're getting enough water from the I. V."

Nodding, he sipped from the cup I held to his lips. When I turned away, he rasped, "Thanks."

We looked at each other, my eyes accusatory, his questioning. "Steward say you give me blood." A whisper.

I nodded. "That's right."

"Why?"

"Damned if I know." And I walked out.

False dawn was showing in the sky to the east. False dawn, also referred to as zodiacal light, is a lightening of the sky about an hour before sunrise. It's caused by sunlight reflecting off tiny space particles. The sky was clear, and I planned on getting a few star sights when the horizon got light enough. Looking forward, I could make out the form of a man walking aft from the bow. Stopping twenty feet in front of the house, he looked up at the bridge. . . looked at me. I couldn't see well enough to recognize him, but it had to be Highstone. No one else stood lookout in clear weather. He did, because I forced him to. He was the asshole, and I was the prick.

As I watched, he raised both arms and gave me the Italian salute, slamming his left hand onto the elbow juncture of his right arm, then walked into the house.

I wanted to ream his ass, but realized only he and I had witnessed his actions. His word against mine. Instead, I told Winkler to go below at 0600 and ask the bosun to stop up and see me. Boats always woke up by 0600.

"Morning, Mate," Boats said as he walked onto the bridge. "Lookin' for me?"

"Morning, Boats. Thanks for coming by."

He looked at me a little strangely, still not used to an officer being polite and asking him to do something, instead of ordering him to do it. Same outcome—he'd do it, but being old-school, it threw him off-stride.

I had already been relieved and finished my star lines, so I motioned Boats out to the starboard bridge wing, out of earshot of the third mate and helmsman. "I think

Highstone is getting ready to act up again, Boats." As I told him what happened earlier, his face hardened.

"Yeah, he's been mouthing off in the crew mess. Shuts up when I come in. Whining about being picked on."

"Boats, if he climbs the rail again, let me know, but don't let the crew congregate there. Keep them inside. I don't want anyone egging him on to jump, but I also don't want any witnesses to his line of bullshit. The captain wants you and me to handle it, and we will. Okay?"

"Sure thing, Mate. No problem."

Stopping in on Joselito on the way down to breakfast, I found him awake, and Andrew was there. "How's the patient?" I asked.

"Better. The transfusion seemed to help. His color is better, and he wants to eat."

"Good," and I headed out. As I reached the door, Andrew said, "I'm going to clean him up and could use some help to move him."

"Got just the guy for you," I said over my shoulder. "I'll send him up."

In the crew mess, Boats, Highstone, and five others sat there, eating, drinking coffee, and smoking.

"Good morning, Boats. The chief steward could use help getting Joselito cleaned up. Got any volunteers?" I asked, staring at Highstone the whole time.

Boats smiled. "I'm sure someone will volunteer. When does he need him?"

"Right away. Thanks, Boats."

As I walked away, I heard Highstone shout, "Why me?" And Boats replied, "Cuz of all your experience with puke and shit."

I smiled.

Skipping breakfast, I exercised, then slept until 1130, when they called me for the watch. In the salon, Andrew regaled us with the story of how Highstone had helped him clean up Joselito.

"Boats stood in the doorway watching the entire time, but never said a word. I handled Joselito. Got him standing while I held him under the armpits, and Highstone changed the sheets and washed and dried Joselito's ass. It was quite a show. Boats helped me put Joselito back in the bed."

I was surprised when the captain chimed in, "That's probably the only nice thing that jerk has ever done for anyone." I'd thought he was talking about Boats, then realized he was referring to Highstone. Then he announced, "I contacted the doctor in Guam and described Joselito's condition. He said to keep giving him antibiotics. Infection is the biggest risk now." He turned to Andrew. "You saved his life, Andrew. Good work."

It was two days to go to reach Guam. Joselito was holding on. The weather had turned, and it had been raining for twenty-four hours. A ship showed on the radar, eighteen miles west of us and approaching. This was our first sighting of another ship since passing Hawaii. It was on a reciprocal course. I ordered the helmsman to switch back to manual steering and notified the captain. My plot showed it would pass within one mile, and that's too close when you're in the middle of the ocean.

"Any change?" the captain asked when he walked onto the bridge, cigarette smoke trailing him.

"No, sir. Looks like it will pass to port within a mile of us. It's moving slow, about ten knots."

"Anything going that slow is old. Old ships might not have modern radar, and visibility is under a mile." He paused. "Too close. Alter course ten degrees to starboard."

I relayed the order, and the helmsman repeated it, coming ten degrees to starboard. The captain stared at the radar through the hood, while I calculated that at a combined speed of twenty-six knots, we were closing at a rate of about half-a-mile per minute.

After ten minutes the captain said, "Ten more degrees to starboard. I think he's turning to port."

An oncoming ship on a reciprocal course needs to either stay on course or turn the same way you turn. If you turn to starboard, so should he. That guarantees separation of space between ships. By turning to port, he was closing the gap between us instead of widening it. Stupid and dangerous.

Ten more minutes of the captain staring at the radar screen and me peering ahead into the rain and the captain said, "Mother-fucker! What is wrong with this clown?" Raising his head, he called out, "Right twenty degrees rudder. Come to course 350 degrees."

We were turning almost due north, ninety degrees from our original course. By my mental dead-reckoning, from the time I plotted it at eighteen miles out, the oncoming ship was now only five miles away. The captain stood by the radar so I couldn't plot anything, but with our drastic change in course, it should be obvious on the screen we were now pulling apart.

"Okay, William," the captain said. "He's turning to starboard. Run ten more minutes and come back onto the original course."

"Aye, aye, Captain."

The ship passed us two-and-a-half miles to our port side, and we never saw any of her lights in the rain. That's when I realized Highstone wasn't up on the bow standing lookout. Instant rage. The bastard was getting under my skin and I wanted to stomp him.

Winkler was on the helm. I took a few deep breaths to calm down and told him to put the ship back on autopilot and then go down and get Highstone and bring him up to the bridge. Winkler had a pained expression, knowing he would have to listen to Highstone's whining, but he did as he was ordered. Ten minutes later he was back.

"Mate, he ain't coming."

"What?"

Winkler looked defensive. "He said he ain't coming to the bridge, and he ain't going on lookout…He's whining again about being picked on."

"Okay, Winkler. Go down and wake up Boats"—before I could finish, Winkler's eyes widened; no one woke up Boats unless he wanted to be woken up—"and ask him to come to the bridge and see me. Don't go near Highstone. Okay?"

"Sure, Mate." He left again.

I went out to the bridge wing and looked aft to see if Highstone was on the rail again. Visibility was bad, but good enough for me to see he wasn't there. When Boats arrived ten minutes later, I told him what had happened.

He shook his head. "There's no cure for that asshole."

"Boats, go down and tell him he either does his job, or I'll lock him up on the flying bridge."

As Boats turned, Preen—the other, older AB on watch—ran onto the bridge and gasped, "That crazy bastard is saying he's gonna kill hisself."

"Is he in the crew mess?" I asked.

"He went running aft, just like the last time."

"Boats, we're not waking up the captain. You want to handle it, or me?

Boats smiled that semi-evil grin and said, "My turn, Mate. I got it." Turning to Preen, he said, "Go down to the crew mess and stay there. If any one comes in and asks what's going on, tell them to go back to their cabin. No one comes out on the fan tail. Got that?"

"I got it, Boats," he said, and he did his old-man version of running back out the door, Boats following him.

From the bridge wing, I could see Highstone on the rail. After a few minutes, he was obviously talking to someone, but I couldn't hear anything other than his initial yell, "He hates me."

After about ten minutes, Boats walked up behind me.

"Well?" I said.

"I told him he had fifteen minutes to jump or get down off the rail. If he don't, I'll throw him overboard." He paused, "I might of told him you'd shoot him, just so he'd bleed a lot and attract the sharks."

I looked back aft and Highstone was gone. "Sounds like a reasonable solution, Boats. He's down from the rail."

CHAPTER 29

Talking with Greg at breakfast, chiding him about having part of yesterday's eggs on his coveralls, I asked him how things were going in the engine room.

"Well, the engines are still turning over, but the engineers are getting wackier by the day."

"All of them?"

"No, just the first engineer and the chief. The first has gotten into the habit of showing up and walking around in the middle of my watch. The guy's getting on my nerves and making Isaiah nervous, too. He'll sneak up behind me and lean over my shoulder. Scared the shit out of me a couple of times. He never says anything to me, but he'll give Isaiah that bug-eyed look and bark at him about not tending the boilers, or some such bullshit."

"Sounds like he's bullying Isaiah. Dumb. I'd pick a smaller target, if I was him."

"That's what I'm worried about. Isaiah is slow to get mad, but lately he looks like he's ready to pop his cork. Besides the first engineer, Punser has been bugging him."

"What's Punser doing now?"

"Stupid crap. Leaving his stuff on Isaiah's bunk, accusing Isaiah of taking his candy bars. And he stinks. Doesn't take showers. Everyone's got a breaking point, I hope they don't push Isaiah past his."

"What has the chief done to irritate you?"

"Took away my maintenance overtime, giving it all to the second engineer, Swenson. We used to split it, though I always got the shit jobs."

"Well, Gibson is the chief engineer, the boss. That's the chief's right, isn't it?"

"Oh yeah, he's the boss. I want the money, but that's not the problem. The problem is, the second engineer is a decent guy, but dumb as a rock when it comes to steam engines. He's okay with diesels, but can't find his ass with both hands with steam. I don't know how Swenson passed his exams for third engineer, much less second."

"Does the chief know how dumb the second is?"

"Yeah, I think he does. That's what's so scary. Gibson's doing it for spite, but doesn't check anything the second repairs." Greg paused. "I think the chief's been drinking again."

"What makes you think that? The captain threatened to fire him if he got drunk again. You were there. You heard it."

"Yeah, I heard him, but I smell too much mouthwash. The chief reeks of it, and it can only be to cover up the booze smell."

Pausing to take a bite of eggs and toast, I gulped, coughed, and almost decorated the front of my shirt to match Greg's coverall. I took a swig of coffee to clear my throat. "Really, Greg? The chief is cutting you out of overtime for spite? What's he got against you?"

Greg laughed. "The freaking ice maker."

Blinking, I shook my head. "The ice cube machine?"

"That's right. I made the mistake of telling him it wasn't working. Looked at me and said, 'You're a fucking engineer, fix it.'"

"Did you?"

"No, I told him the second engineer already fixed it once, that's why it doesn't work. Factual but not diplomatic." He smirked. "Ever since then, he's given all the overtime to the second. I'm waiting for something to blow up or fall apart."

"That's not funny, Greg."

"No, it isn't. It's dangerous."

Later that day the weather was acting up. We had passing squalls, nothing dangerous, just inconvenient. The four-to-eight watch had come on, and Winkler was on the helm. I was in the chart room when I heard feet pounding on the interior ladder, coming up to the bridge. Punser ran in, wide-eyed.

"He's trying to kill me," he gasped, out of breath.

"Who is?"

"Smithfield." He was looking over his shoulder at the door.

It took me a few seconds to register that Smithfield was Isaiah, Greg's oiler. "Why would he do that?"

"I dunno...He's crazy...You gotta hide me...He's got an ax!"

That woke me up. Isaiah with his bare hands would be trouble; with an ax, he'd be lethal. Grabbing Punser's arm, I pulled him toward the pilot's cabin. "Get in there and don't make a sound. Latch the door…and don't bother Joselito."

He leaped through the door and I heard the latch. It wouldn't stop a fire ax, but hopefully, it wouldn't have to.

I walked back into the bridge just as Isaiah came in through the exterior door. Knocking on the bulkhead, he said, "Excuse me, Mister Mate, I'm looking for Punser, my roommate." Frighteningly calm, even without the ax held in his right hand, and the tone of voice scared me, like a recording, not live. His voice was calm, but his eyes blazed.

Turning to my right so my body shielded my movement, I drew the .38 S & W Police Special and slid it down beside my leg, never taking my eyes off the ax. Now I had five chances at success, one for each shell. One ax, five shots. That's the way I liked it.

I looked at Winkler at the helm, and his eyes were bugging out. Slowly, I shook my head, hoping he wouldn't make any quick movement.

"Haven't seen him, Isaiah. Why are you looking for him?"

"Need to find him, Mister Mate."

"Any particular reason, Isaiah? Maybe he's in his room."

"Nope. Ran away. Ax got stuck, and he ran away."

"Ax got stuck?" My grip on the .38 S & W tightened.

"Yeah."

Desperate, not knowing where this was going, I asked him, "Why do you need the ax?"

Looking at the ax, then at me, he said, "Need to kill him."

I sensed, rather than saw, Winkler sidle away from the helm and move toward the port-side bridge wing door. Isaiah fixated on me, and the ax rose and fell as he twitched his wrist, like it was a toothpick.

"Isaiah, that's kind of scary, saying you're going to kill him. Why do you want to do that?"

"Got to do it. Punser's no good. Bad man. Got to do it."

"How about if I help you look for him, huh?"

Pondering this a few seconds he said, "No. Thank you, Mister Mate, I'll find him," and he turned and went out the way he came in, moving slow and sure.

Turning to Winkler, all the way over by the bridge wing door, I said, "Get the captain and tell him what happened. I'm gonna follow Isaiah." And I inched my way out into the passageway, pistol still in hand.

Following his steps retreating down the ladder, I hurried to the door and peeked down. Isaiah stepped out of the ladderway and disappeared into the passageway below. I tiptoed down the ladder and listened for a few seconds before looking into the passageway. Empty. Flipping a mental coin, I went to port and looked down the aisle.

Nothing. Reversing, I went to starboard and looked again. Nothing, so I went down one more deck to the crew quarters and repeated the process.

Isaiah stood at the entrance to the galley, still calm, still holding the ax, peering in.

I relaxed, easing my grip on the revolver. "Any luck finding him, Isaiah?" I asked, prepared for a strong reaction.

He turned slowly. "No sir, Mister Mate. Nobody's seen him, but I'll find him. He's gotta be somewhere," he said, and he stepped into the galley.

Rushing to the door, I saw two BRs edging away from him, keeping the big, stainless steel work table between them and him. He did a full circuit of the galley, and so did they. Instead of exiting when they reached the door, they kept circling, always keeping the table between them. Maybe they felt safer there than in the passageway. When they passed me, I smelt the acrid odor of fear. Some of it had to be me. The cook's array of knives hung on the bulkhead, and the BR looked as if he contemplated taking one.

"Hey," I whispered. His head snapped around toward me and I shook my head, afraid that taking the knife would trigger Isaiah. He got the message and kept backing away from Isaiah, herding the other BR behind him as he went.

As Isaiah came full circle, I eased back out the door giving him room. Stepping into the passageway, his massive wrist twitched, causing the ax to jump up and down. He looked over my shoulder. I sensed someone, but didn't take my eyes off him—just gripped the revolver tighter, my trigger finger straining to stay straight and off the trigger. He turned to his right and walked aft, same slow measured pace, the executioner seeking his victim.

As he walked away, I turned, careful not to raise the revolver. The captain stood there, his .45 colt on his hip.

"What's going on, William?"

"He's flipped, Captain. Greg told me earlier Punser and the first engineer had been picking on him, and he's gone over the edge. Says he wants to kill Punser. I believe him."

"Has he threatened anyone else?"

"Not that I know of. Just walks around like a zombie, twitching that ax. Pretty scary guy."

"Follow him, William. I'll get you a walkie-talkie and we can communicate. And William..."

"Yes, sir?"

"Don't get hurt."

"That's my plan," I said, not exuding confidence. "By the way, Punser is hiding in the pilot's cabin. I hope he stays quiet and doesn't agitate Joselito."

The captain nodded and left.

Following Isaiah forward, I passed the starboard WT door on the way to the forepeak, and Winkler handed me a walkie-talkie. I called the captain.

"Captain, I've got the volume set low. Don't want to attract his attention any more than I have to. We're heading forward. He doesn't seem to mind if I follow him, but I'm not getting close."

"Okay. Let me know if he settles down anywhere."

"Will do, Captain." I signed off, resuming my bizarre ship's tour.

Isaiah moved around for two hours—aft around the fantail, forward through the bosun's locker, onto the foredeck, around the anchor windlass, back through the house, down into the engine room, then into the crew mess. All the time, I'm thinking, what can I do to stop him? Where can we trap him? But mostly, I thought, don't get him pissed off at you. He's a big, dangerous guy.

In the crew mess, he stood in the middle of the room and stared at the portholes, ax no longer twitching, but hanging at his side. Sensing his indecision, I ventured, "Isaiah, can I help?"

He didn't look at me, but hung his head. Then shaking his head, he said, "It ain't right, Mister Mate."

"What's not right, Isaiah?"

"People like Punser. Nothing but mean in him. Ain't right." He stood there another thirty seconds, then put the ax on the table, walked to the sink, poured a cup of water, and chugged it.

Tempted to grab the ax, I knew if he wanted to take it back, it wouldn't be much of a battle. I'd lose unless I shot him, and I couldn't bring myself to do that unless he attacked me. Isaiah was a good guy, and my sympathies were all with him.

Putting the cup in the sink, he walked back, picked up the ax, and walked into the passageway. I followed him to his cabin, where he went inside, latched the door open on the hook, and sat on Punser's lower bunk. That's when I saw the gash in the edge of the bunk above. Isaiah must have swung the ax while Punser was in his bunk, and it stuck in the metal sheathing long enough for Punser to run out of the room. Lucky bastard.

I went to the end of the passageway and keyed the walkie-talkie. "Captain," I whispered, "he's sitting in his cabin. He's still got the ax."

"Any ideas?" was his comeback.

"I wouldn't try anything in the cabin unless he falls asleep. Let's get my mattress down here, along with Greg and at least one other guy. We can lock the exit door aft and wait at the forward end. When he comes out, we can rush him and push him all the way back to the door and pin him there. He can't get the ax past the mattress—it's the full width of the passageway—but we gotta push him fast enough so he can't get too many swings at the mattress. Strong as he is, he'll bust through."

"Stay there. Watch him. I'll get things moving."

"Aye, aye, Captain."

I knew my plan was the only practical way to subdue him, but the odds of someone getting hurt were still high.

Within ten minutes, Second Engineer Swenson—a big guy, six-feet-four and well over two hundred pounds—along with Greg, the captain, and the chief engineer, were all around the corner at the forward end of the passageway.

"The bosun is chaining a couple of the securing dogs on the door aft," the captain whispered. "Tell the boys here what you intend to do."

He stepped back. I was in charge.

I explained my plan, and they agreed we would have to move fast to minimize injury, ours and Isaiah's.

"Greg," I said, "he trusts you. Should we try to talk to him first before rushing him?"

Greg raised his eyebrows twice and rubbed his right cheek— not his usual cool, calm self.

"I don't know. He's been weird for a couple of days, not talking at all on watch. I can try, but if he reacts badly, we won't have much maneuvering room." Shaking his head, he said, "Besides, anything I say might get him mad, and then I'm the meat on the chopping block."

We stood there, falling silent. It was clear the captain was leaving this to me, so I decided.

"No talking. Too risky. Here's how it will go down," and I explained what I wanted. "I've already shot one crewman. I don't want to add to the headcount, so let's get this right."

Gathered forward of Isaiah's cabin door, we tucked the left edge of the mattress against the left side bulkhead, angled so there was room at the right side, with the second engineer holding the strap handles. Greg stood behind him and I stood at the right side in the exposed space. Greg and I each had a pair of handcuffs. We were ready. At the last second, I decided to not wear the gun, and I handed it to the captain. I reminded myself Isaiah wasn't a bad guy, just someone pushed too far by assholes.

I squeezed past the mattress edge, walked forward and peeked in the door. Isaiah still sat on the edge of the lower bunk, the ax head resting on the floor, the handle leaning against the bunk. "Isaiah," I called. "Could I talk to you?"

He looked up, puzzled.

Again. "Isaiah, could we talk?"

"Sure, Mister Mate," and he rose.

Please don't pick up the ax. Just walk out.

He started forward, paused, turned, and picked up the ax.

Fuck!

Backing away, I turned aft, away from the mattress and toward the locked door. Isaiah stepped out, never looking at anything except me. I kept backing up, giving Greg and the second a chance to get past the cabin door and cut off any escape for Isaiah. Focusing on his face, I willed myself to not look at the mattress looming behind him, hoping he wouldn't see it until they ran into him.

He didn't, and they did. He roared, turning, and I leaped onto his back, grabbing the handle of the ax just below the head with my right hand and hanging on for dear life to his neck with my left arm in a choke hold.

Still flailing at the mattress with the ax, he couldn't do much damage. If he hit flesh, it would be a different story. I heard Greg yelling, "Push!" and we kept going backwards until my back hit the WT door.

I yelled, "Back up!" while pulling back hard on the ax head; then I dropped lower, wrapped my legs around Isaiah's and pushed forward off the door just as Greg eased the pressure. It worked. Isaiah crashed to the deck, face first, and I landed on top of him. It stunned him enough for Greg and the second to get around the mattress and jump on him.

I still had a death grip on the ax, but Isaiah let it go. He deflated, mentally and physically, letting us handcuff him. Not a word. No emotion. He just lay there.

CHAPTER 30

The captain had been in radio contact with the doctor in Guam every day. During his last transmission the previous afternoon, the doctor said they would send medics on a boat to the ship to collect Joselito. A second boat would come for Isaiah.

The captain had kept Isaiah restrained in his cabin, both leg irons and handcuffs. To my surprise, he called me to his office and asked my opinion on keeping Isaiah locked up.

"Captain, he's not the same guy. He snapped. A week ago, I'd have said locking him up is crazy, but now…I don't think we have a choice."

The captain shook his head, perplexed.

"No one was closer to him than Greg," I said, "but he was afraid to talk to him before we rushed him. Besides, there's no guarantee we'd be able to corral him again if he does go wild. What then? Do you or I shoot him?"

"Yes. You're right. Keep him in handcuffs…leg irons too."

We had to take the cuffs off when he took a crap, so we had set up a routine. Boats and the second engineer, the big guys, walked him to the head. I waited in his cabin. We were there at 0700 hours for that reason. Isaiah hadn't said a word after the incident and robotically followed directions—until Punser showed up at the door of the head while Isaiah was sitting on the toilet, and yelled, "You crazy motherfucker!"

Isaiah roared and shot off the toilet, bowling over Swenson in his rush to get to Punser, then tripped on the leg irons, coming down hard on top of Swenson. It took all of Boats's and the second engineer's strength to calm Isaiah down.

At Punser's shout, I got off the bunk and ran out the door in time to see him fly out the aft, WT door onto the fantail. I ran toward the door and stopped short, looking at a strange sight. Isaiah and the second sat on the deck of the head; Isaiah's pants were around his ankles; and he was crying while Swenson cradled his head, saying, "It's gonna be okay, Isaiah. It's gonna be okay." Boats loomed over them, handcuffs dangling from his fist, shaking his head. "Punser," is all he said when he saw me.

"Did he finish his business?" I asked, pointing at Isaiah.

"Don't think so," Boats replied.

"Put him back on the throne."

They lifted Isaiah and sat him back on the toilet. I went looking for the captain.

I explained to the captain what Punser had done. "Come on," he said, and I followed him to the chief engineer's cabin.

"Chief," the captain said, "Punser's acting up again. I'd like to throw him off the ship, but I know you're already short-handed. Any ideas?"

"Punser's a pain in everyone's ass," Gibson responded, "but I'm already short an oiler and a wiper, and you're sending Isaiah ashore—that makes me two oilers short. That's one man per watch when there should be two. Take away Punser, and I'm screwed."

The captain shook his head and left, with me trailing him.

I went back to the officers' salon, and despite my stomach being in a knot, had an egg sandwich and a cup of coffee. I was sitting there when Boats tapped on the door frame. "Come in, Boats. What can I do for you?"

"I been thinkin'. I know you'd like to fire Punser, but the engine room is short-handed. One of the ABs on the eight-to-twelve watch has sailed as an oiler. I don't know if his certificate is up to date, but he knows his shit. If the chief would okay it, I can talk him into standing an oiler watch, at least until we can get a replacement."

"Boats, you're a life saver! Let me talk to the captain and let him talk to the chief. I'll let you know." And I rushed out the door to find the captain.

An hour later, the deal was done. The AB would stand his regular eight-to-twelve AB watches and the twelve-to-four daytime oiler watch. He'd get paid overtime for the oiler work. The twelve-to-four nighttime oiler watch would be unfilled. Greg stood the twelve-to-four watches and agreed to do it because the chief engineer agreed to stop being an asshole and let him work overtime again. No one told Punser. He'd continue as normal until we reached port. The chief would tell him when we arrived at Guam.

On a great circle route from Panama, we had tip-toed through the northern islands of Micronesia and now approached Guam. Rounding the southern tip, we stayed three miles off Cocos Island, then turned onto course 351 degrees, heading for Apra Harbor, where there is a U.S. naval base. The water depth was in excess of 350 feet all the way up the coast.

Two-thirds of Guam, the northern and central parts, consists of raised limestone with two volcanic formations, Mount Santa Rosa and Mount Mataguak, rising to 870 and 630 feet respectively. In the southern and western areas, extinct volcanoes form ridges rising as high as 1274 feet.

Apra Harbor is formed by Cabras Island to the north and Orote Peninsula to the south, and like many harbors seen from the air, it looks like a giant jaw biting the sea. The volcanic ridges backdrop the harbor.

Guam has a rich maritime history as a fishing port and stopover for whalers. "Apra" comes from the Chamorro word "low," and is the original name of Cabras Island. Controlled by the Japanese from 1941-1944, when liberated in 1944, we did tremendous damage to the coral reefs while clearing channels for ships. It is slowly recovering.

0639, Wednesday 3/1/67, sunrise, fair weather cumulus clouds and a westerly trade wind. With the bulk of the island blocking the rising sun, we approached the Apra Harbor channel, and a U.S. Navy pilot came aboard.

There are civilian pilots, but since we were chartered to MSTS and carrying munitions, the Navy controlled all movements. The captain greeted the Navy pilot and asked, "Why can't we put Joselito on the pilot boat and get him ashore?"

"Sorry, Captain, the boat stays on station out here. Besides, it would be hard to transfer someone in a stretcher in these seas."

At "slow ahead," we crept into the harbor. To the north is a commercial port, and all the south belonged to the Navy. We passed Glass Breakwater to port, named after U.S. Navy Captain Henry Glass, who claimed Guam as U.S. territory on June 20, 1898. Half a mile later, at 0810 hours, we dropped anchor in the center of the area marked "explosives" at the anchorage.

I was off watch, but was called out by the captain to anchor, along with Boats and an AB. Boats and the AB loosened the safety lanyards and removed the chain-hooks, which acted as safety stops to prevent the anchor from being accidently let go. We were in fifty feet of water, and the captain rounded the ship into the wind and came to a stop.

Letting go the anchor, we let out four shots of chain as the captain let the ship drift back for a scope of six to one. It was a sandy bottom, so the captain opted for a longer lead. "Scope" is the ratio of the length of deployed anchor rode to the height of the anchor hawsepipe above the seabed. The longer the scope, the more horizontal the pull on the anchor, the better it will hold.

Our anchor chain was marked so we could read how much chain was let out. At fifteen fathoms (one shot) it was painted red; thirty fathoms (2 shots) painted white; and forty-five fathoms (3 shots) painted blue. The pattern then repeated itself for each additional shot of chain.

After securing the anchor windlass and attaching the safety lanyards, Boats sent the AB to hoist the anchor ball, required under the International Rules of the Road to signify a ship is at anchor. At night, it is a single white light visible 360 degrees.

On the bridge, sipping coffee and peering aft through the binoculars to study the island, I saw a Navy launch emerge from the inner harbor and turn left toward us, passing between a dry-dock that stuck out from the land, and a shoal spot immediately offshore of it. December through June is the dry season here, but the prevailing westerly trade winds keep it pleasant most of the year. Those same westerly winds were buffeting the launch head-on as she approached.

I told George, the third mate, and he notified the captain, who ordered him to lower the starboard gangway to make it easier for them to board.

The coxswain of the launch—it looked to be an old captain's gig—laid it alongside the bottom of the gangway deftly, and two hospital corpsmen jumped on to the gangway. Both were E-5, wearing the blue patch denoting HM Second Class with two red chevrons, and the white eagle perched above a white caduceus. Each carried a medical kit over his shoulder.

Andrew had been waiting for them, and led them up to the pilot cabin.

The captain and I were there when they arrived. I opened the door and stepped aside.

"Hi, I'm HM Second Class Keating, and this is my partner, HM Second Class Johnson. We're going to take care of you. What's your name?"

"Joselito," he answered, stronger than I expected.

Keating checked the I.V. insert and put a blood pressure sleeve on Joselito, as Johnson listened to his heart and lungs through a stethoscope. Turning to the captain, Keating said, "He seems to be stable, so we won't open the dressing here. Do you have a stretcher, or do we need to get the one from the boat?"

"We have a safety basket, wire mesh type."

"That's clumsy. Call to the boat and ask the coxswain to send up our litter."

The captain looked at me and I nodded, ran to the gangway, and hailed the coxswain, telling him what they wanted. I then went down the gangway and waited. A crew member brought a wood-and-canvas litter to the gangway, and I grabbed it. When I got back to the pilot's cabin, they had Joselito hooked up to their own I. V. and had an oxygen mask on him. They got him on the litter by pulling him to one side of the bunk, rolling him onto his side, laying the litter down and rolling him back onto it. Then they strapped him down.

I offered to help carry the litter, but they declined and let me carry their medical kits instead. We used the outside ladders to avoid tight turns in the stairwells, and got to the top of the gangway.

Keating said to me, "Carry our kits down and put them on the boat. You go aboard and help Jonesy when we hand him the litter."

I nodded, descended the gangway, and jumped aboard as the coxswain maneuvered the stern of the boat to the foot of the gangway. As soon as I landed, he pulled the boat away from the gangway and waited.

"Are you Jonesy?" I asked the crewman who had grabbed the medical kits.

"Yes, sir." He was a seaman (SN) wearing the three diagonal white stripes on a blue patch.

"Keating said for me to give you a hand when they pass the litter aboard. Okay?"

"Yes, sir." He paused. "You ever do this before, sir?"

"No."

"They'll be moving fast. Once you grab the end of the litter rod, step back lively, and whoever is on the other end will come right with you. Don't hesitate."

"Got it, Jonesy. I'll keep pace with you."

He nodded.

There were four-foot waves, and the coxswain, a petty officer first class, did a remarkable job of keeping the launch stationed ten feet off the gangway. When the two HMs had the litter with Joselito on it at the bottom of the gangway, Keating, standing at the lower end, lifted his end up over his head and crouched. The coxswain backed the launch toward the gangway, and at the last second, gunned the motor, stopping the launch dead in the water at the top of a wave.

Jonesy and I reached out and grabbed the end poles of the litter as Keating ducked and Johnson ran down the last two steps. He stepped on the railing of the launch and hopped aboard just as the launch dropped into the wave trough. Keating then jumped aboard and the coxswain pulled away. It was a superb bit of boat handling and alacrity by Johnson and Keating.

The launch was one hundred feet away before Keating said, "Do you want to go back aboard?"

"No, I'll get a ride back. He's waited long enough for help," I said, pointing at Joselito.

There was an ambulance waiting at the dock. As we were docking, Keating asked me, "He said you shot him. Is that true?"

"Yeah…he was trying to kill the captain and decided to stab me first…so I shot him."

"He also said you donated the blood for his transfusion."

"Yeah, I did."

"Helluva a trip you guys are having." As he walked toward the ambulance he called back, "The launch will be returning to the ship in about an hour. You can catch a ride back then."

CHAPTER 31

After the ambulance left, I sat on a bollard on the dock and waited. Twenty minutes later, two MPs drove up in a Jeep, got out, and approached me. Each wore the Shore Patrol arm band, but one of them was a chief petty officer and wore a gold Duty Master at Arms badge. I stood, and he faced me while the other stood to my right. Both had their holsters unsnapped and their hands on the butts of their weapons. "Sir, are you from the *West Way?*" he asked.

"Yes, Chief, I am. I'm the second mate."

"No one is allowed ashore on base without permission, sir."

"I didn't know that, Chief, but I didn't have any choice. I helped the HMs bring one of our injured crew members onto the launch, and they left with me aboard. The HM told me to wait here and take the launch back to the ship. That's what I've been doing, waiting here."

"Sir, is there any particular reason you're armed?"

That's when I realized I still wore my S & W .38 in my holster. I froze, hands out to my sides, knowing an unanticipated move might cause them to draw their guns.

"Chief, I was ordered by the captain to always wear this on duty. We've had some serious crew problems. Drugs and alcohol."

"So I've heard. I'll have to ask you to surrender your weapon while ashore. We'll return it when you go back aboard."

"Sure thing, Chief. Do you want me to hand it to you, or do you want to take it?" I asked, still keeping my hands away from my sides.

"I'll take it, if you don't mind," and he stepped in and removed my gun from the holster, then stepped back. Unloading the weapon, he handed the gun and bullets to his partner, who stuck them in a small knapsack.

"When is the launch going back to the ship?" I asked.

"1300 hours—soon as the coxswain finishes his lunch. We'll be going with him. We understand you have a crewman under restraint, and we'll be taking him to the brig."

"Sorry to hear that, Chief. He really needs to see a doctor, a shrink. He's a decent guy who flipped out because of being hassled by his asshole roommate and a few other jerks." And I told them the story of what happened with Isaiah.

"That's some story. When I talk to the brig OD, I'll tell him. It's a civilian matter, so this will be turned over to the State Department once we have custody of him."

Nodding, I said, "The good news is, you'll be taking the guy who started it all back with you, too. The captain fired him. He just doesn't know it yet. The name's Punser, and he's a drunk, druggie, and all-around asshole.

I wouldn't trust him as far as I could throw him. The ship's agent is supposed to make arrangements to send him back to the States."

"Thanks for the heads-up. We like to know what we're dealing with."

"Okay if I smoke?"

"Sure, no problem."

Lighting up a Marlboro, I took a deep drag and sat down on the bollard, waiting for the coxswain to show up.

Twenty minutes later, fifty yards away, the coxswain stepped out of a shed, followed by Jonesy, his crewman, and walked toward the launch. Stopping in front of the chief, he said, "You ready?"

The chief nodded, and we all got aboard.

Another twenty minutes and the coxswain did his stern-wagging routine at the foot of the gangway. The three of us boarded the ship and they followed me to the captain's office, where I introduced them to the captain and Andrew, who was there.

Both saluted the captain, then shook hands.

"Gentlemen," the captain said, "you'll be taking two crewmen ashore with you. One, Isaiah Smithfield, is in restraints. The other, Robert Punser, I fired for insubordination, drug use, inciting a riot, and endangering the ship. He is not restrained. Feel free to clap the cuffs on him if you want to, or you feel he is a risk."

The chief pointed at me and said, "Your second mate filled us in. We'll take good care of both of them." He instructed his partner to return my revolver and he did, bullets first, then the gun. I stuck the bullets in my pocket and holstered the gun.

"If you'll lead me to them, we'll get going."

I led them to Isaiah's cabin and explained to Isaiah what was happening. Isaiah nodded but said nothing. The chief stepped up and faced Isaiah. In a solemn, but not harsh voice, he said, "At the top of the gangway, we'll remove the leg-irons. Once we're aboard the launch, we'll put them back on. Follow my instructions and there won't be any problems. Understand?"

Isaiah nodded.

Everything went without a hitch getting Isaiah on the launch. Punser was a different story.

Boats appeared at the top of the gangway dragging Punser by the arm. Winkler, the AB, followed, carrying two duffle-bags, Punser's personal effects.

"Why do I hafta get off?" Punser yelled. "I didn't do nuthin'."

Standing aft of the head of the gangway watching the show, I tried hard to not smile.

Winkler brought the bags down and tossed them in to the launch, then climbed back to the main deck. Boats walked Punser down the gangway, belly-bumping him every other step. At the bottom, Punser held both handrails and appeared to resist Boats as the launch pulled alongside. Boats leaned in close and said something to Punser, and the next thing I saw was Punser flying through the air and landing in a sprawl on the launch. As they pulled away, I saw the chief point at Punser and point at a seat in the stern.

It was over.

Or so I thought at the time. Only later, when I had a chance to read the full incident report from the witnesses, did I learn what happened next.

From the launch, the chief watched the scene as the bosun pushed Punser down the gangway. Telling his assistant to keep an eye on the big guy, he talked to the latest arrival, now lying on the deck in front of him.

"You," pointing a finger at Punser. "You're not my problem, so make sure you don't become my problem. Drag your ass over there"—he pointed to a seat aft— "and sit. Don't move an inch. Got it?"

Punser nodded and crawled aft to the seat, hanging his head and staring at the deck. Five minutes passed. That's when he apparently saw Isaiah in the cuddy cabin and shouted, "He's crazy! Don't let him near me!"

Both the shore patrol men looked at Punser, and the chief took a few steps aft toward him.

Isaiah had been oblivious until he heard Punser's voice over the throbbing of the engine. It seemed he was ejected from his seat, bowling over the shore patrol man as he ran toward the stern, doing a hop-shuffle with the leg-irons.

The shore patrol man   yelled, and the chief turned as Isaiah reached him, knocking him to the deck as well. Isaiah never slowed down. Grabbing Punser by his belt, he lifted him, then stepped forward, hit his knees on the gunnel, and they both tumbled overboard.

"Man overboard!" the chief shouted, and the coxswain whipped his head around and pulled the throttle back to neutral.

In the water, Isaiah's heft, the weight of the leg irons, and their momentum carried them deep. Punser's struggle was futile. Staring into the wild eyes of Isaiah, inches from his, his final scream was silenced by salt water filling his mouth.

Above, there wasn't a trace of either man. Not a bubble. Jonesy stood at the railing, balancing himself in the four-foot swells, holding a life preserver but with no target to throw to.

The chief stood there, looking at the sea.

I'm fucked. There's no explaining this away. One guy in irons and a skinny little shit, and the two of us couldn't corral them. I'm gonna get hand cramps from the paperwork.

Aboard ship, two hours later, the captain received a message from the agent informing him the Navy had started an inquiry and we were to stay at anchor until further notice. The crew was restricted to the ship. No one allowed ashore. They ordered the captain to come ashore for an informal hearing tomorrow morning. He was to bring me with him.

That's when they told him Smithfield and Punser had gone overboard and drowned.

CHAPTER 32

The captain had communicated with the agent and requested a lawyer be present, since this was an official inquiry and two deaths were involved. We were told there would be a civilian lawyer representing the company, but he wouldn't be allowed to participate, only observe. He also told us, since we were both Navy Reserve officers, if we wanted a lawyer, the Judge Advocate General's (JAG) office would appoint someone to defend us, either jointly or singly. The captain called me to his office and explained it all.

"What do you think, William? Want a JAG attorney?"

"Why do we need an attorney at all? They were off the ship, in the custody of the Navy. We shouldn't be involved at all."

"They were off the ship and in the custody of the Navy because I asked the Navy to take them off. Like it or not, it all started here, aboard ship, and remember: They have another crew member in their hospital that you shot."

That registered. *Why should I worry about defending myself because of what happened to these two guys? Isaiah was a nut-case, likeable but loony. Punser was an asshole. Growing up, anyone who had an attorney was usually in trouble.*

"I guess we better have an attorney," I said, adding sarcastically, "Truth, Justice, the American Way."

"I believe that would be prudent. Since we have the same story to tell, I think one attorney for the both of us will do, but that's your choice. If you want your own attorney, you can get one."

Is he trying to get cute here? Set me up? I better stay close to him. "No, we're in this together. One will do."

The captain relayed that message to the ship's agent.

The captain and I rode the same launch ashore, accompanied by Lieutenant JG Grady, who rode the boat out to greet us. He had been assigned by the JAG's office to represent us. He made a big deal of letting us know he wasn't there to "defend" us, since we weren't charged with anything. He was polite and quiet.

The captain and I were nervous. The sweat dripping from my armpits was the combined product of heat, humidity, and nerves. A car met us at the dock and drove us half a mile to a two-story, faded-green office building. Inside, everything smelled slightly musty. There was no air-conditioning, and all the windows were open.

The room we were shown into didn't look like a courtroom, but rather a spartan board room. I had been expecting pomp and propriety. Lieutenant JG Grady reviewed the details of what happened on the launch. Then he gave us a two-minute drill on listening carefully to the questions asked, answering accurately, not guessing, and above all, telling the truth.

There was a yeoman acting as Clerk of the Court, and a shore patrol chief petty officer as bailiff. He called "All rise" and announced the presiding officer, a Navy commander. We stood, then sat when the commander told us to.

"We are here today for the purpose of determining the facts surrounding the incident where Mr."—he glanced at a sheet of paper in front of him— "Isaiah Smithfield and Mr. Robert Punser, traveling aboard a Navy launch between the *SS West Way III* and the dock, fell overboard and were drowned.

"This is not a trial. It is an inquiry." He wore Ben Franklin style half-glasses, and he peered at us over them after glancing at the paper again. "Captain Johnston, the incident aboard the launch is entirely a U.S. Navy affair. However, you and Second Mate Connolly were asked to be here to give us background information on what led up to the removal of the two persons from your ship being necessary. Not incidentally, the fact that another member of your crew is now in our hospital, recovering from a gunshot wound inflicted while aboard your ship, lends gravity to this situation. I see you are represented by counsel."

The JAG attorney leaped to his feet. "Good morning, Commander. Lieutenant JG Sean Grady, representing both Captain Malcolm Johnston and Second Mate William Connolly." Then he sat.

"Captain," the commander said, "normally, fact witnesses are kept sequestered and not allowed to hear another witness's testimony. In light of the fact your ship is being delayed while we are conducting this inquiry, and

299

since we do not suspect foul play on either of your parts, but are merely looking for corroboration and detail on background, Second Mate Connolly may stay during your testimony, and vice versa. Do you have any objections?"

"No, Commander. That's fine with me."

"Mr. Connolly, do you have any objections."

I leaped to my feet. "No, sir," I barked, and sat down, eliciting a smile from the commander.

"There is no need to stand when responding."

"Yes, sir," I replied, feeling sheepish.

We were both sworn in, and the commander asked the captain to relate what caused Smithfield to be put in restraints and sent ashore, and why Punser was sent ashore. The captain took half an hour to sum up Punser's wild activities and why he fired him. He then took ten more minutes to talk about Smithfield. The commander made an occasional note on the pad of paper in front of him.

"Thank you, Captain," the commander said. Looking at me: "Mr. Connolly, is there anything you wish to add to the captain's account?"

Grady leaned over and whispered, "You don't have to say anything, if you don't want to."

Despite the warning, I stood. "Commander, the only thing I want to add is that Isaiah Smithfield was a good man who got pushed too far by a mean-spirited jerk. He may have had some mental problems, but the one who pulled the trigger on him was Punser." I deliberately did not mention the first engineer also harassing him in the engine room. I figured that would open a whole new problem, and neither the captain nor I needed that right now.

"Thank you, Mr. Connolly. Please sit down." I sat. "I have a few questions for you concerning," and he looked at the paper again, "Mr. Joselito Bautista."

I sat up straighter and waited.

"Please tell me the circumstances in which you shot him."

I related the entire scenario, emphasizing that I was convinced Joselito was going to attack the captain until I intervened, and then that he attacked me, despite the fact I had a gun pointed at him.

The commander then asked the captain if he wished to add anything, and the captain said, "Yes, Commander, I do." He cleared his throat and scratched his nose. "I believe there is a better than even chance I, and maybe others, would be dead right now, if not for the actions of Mr. Connolly. He carried the gun only because I ordered him to. He did only what he had to do, and no more. Furthermore, despite being attacked and stabbed by Mr. Bautista, it was Mr. Connolly who donated his blood to give Mr. Bautista a transfusion, one that, in my opinion, saved his life."

There was silence for thirty seconds, only the whirr of the three, tired ceiling fans straining to push the humid air. Despite the open windows, it was hot.

The commander spoke. "These were sad and difficult circumstances for the both of you. Command of a ship is always a difficult responsibility. In your case, it was almost mutinous circumstances. Under those circumstances, I think that you and Mr. Connolly behaved in the most reasonable manner you could have. Thank you for your testimony. I will send my report to the Head of Investigations and recommend to the base commander that your ship be allowed to sail."

I raised my hand.

"Yes, Mr. Connolly?"

"Sir, I was told when we got here today how Isaiah grabbed Punser and jumped overboard. If I may, I want to say I don't believe the chief and his partner could have physically stopped Isaiah, short of shooting him. The captain told you what we had to do to stop him. That took three of us, and that was under much better, closed-in conditions. I hope the chief doesn't get in trouble for this."

The Commander smiled. "Mr. Connolly, whether the chief gets in trouble or not will be decided at another level, but I will pass on your message to the appropriate party." The bailiff yelled, "All rise," we stood, and the commander walked out.

Standing outside the building, I lit a Marlboro and inhaled deeply. We were waiting for a car to take us back to the dock when a Jeep pulled up. The shore patrol chief leaned out and said, "Can I buy you guys a beer?"

Word traveled fast.

The captain and I looked at each other. He said, "Sure, but for me it's a Coke. No alcohol." And we climbed in.

"Mind taking the shoulder boards off? We're going to the NCO club."

The captain and I both shucked our shoulder boards as the chief pulled into a parking spot, and we followed him inside.

I wasn't two steps inside the door when I heard, "Son-of-a-bitch Connolly, what are you doing here?" My eyes were still adjusting to the low light when a slap on the back nearly knocked me over.

It was a classmate, Bruce Fisher, and he had a good head start on us with the drinking. I introduced him to the captain and the chief, and the bullshit began. His ship was docked and working at the commercial piers. He regaled us with tales of a recent trip to Vung Ro in Vietnam, where his ship got chased out of the harbor by Viet Cong shellfire. It was good to see him, an ally in a hostile world.

An hour into it, the captain got my eye, pointed at his wristwatch, and nodded toward the door. We thanked the chief and wished him well, said goodbye to Bruce, and went to the Jeep where the chief had a seaman waiting to drive us back to the dock. An hour later, we were back aboard ship.

CHAPTER 33

0700, Saturday, 3/4/67, clear skies, west winds at fifteen MPH. Sunrise at 0641, so the island still blocked the sun but plenty of light. We weighed anchor and locked it in place, then secured from anchor detail. Bound for Subic Bay, Philippine Islands.

We dropped the Navy pilot off before clearing Glass Breakwater. The westerly wind had a good chop going, and the pilot launch was bouncing six to eight feet in the waves. We had picked up and stowed the gangway as soon as we boarded the pilot, and rigged a Jacob's ladder on the starboard side for the pilot to disembark. He was nimble. As the bow of the launch rose on the crest of a wave, he hopped off the ladder, dropping a foot before landing on the deck of the launch. Turning, he waved at the bridge, then went into the cuddy cabin of the launch to get out of the spray.

The captain ordered full ahead, and we went to our sea speed of sixteen-and-a-half knots. Two miles clear of the harbor, the captain ordered a course of 285 degrees, which would take us to the northern tip of Luzon Island in the Philippines. It was a stretch of 585 miles, and for most of the leg a half-knot current flowing west aided us. The depth of the water ranged from 14,700 to 17,000 feet.

We were headed for Subic Bay because the ship's agent had relayed a message from the owners saying they were sending a replacement first mate and a cook. Subic Bay was a convenient port for that purpose. Since the ship was time-chartered to MSTS, the owners didn't worry about lost days. Uncle Sam was footing the bill.

Within one hundred miles of the coast of Luzon, the current changed to northeast at 0.7 knots, and we made a slight adjustment in course to offset the northeast drift. From due north of the tip of Luzon, we steered 228 degrees for eighty-eight miles until abeam of and thirty miles offshore of Cape Bajeador. The weather continued fair with northwesterly winds. We then steered 189 degrees for seventy-five miles, until abeam of Cape Balinao, now only ten miles offshore.

I had been in a funk since sailing from Guam, avoiding talking to anyone. Despite being cleared by the Navy inquiry, being the center of the inquiry bugged me. When the AB Winkler came on duty as helmsman at midwatch, I asked him how the crew reacted to the news of Smithfield and Punser. He was his usual reluctant self, but after prodding again, he responded.

"A couple of the BRs are talking trash, blaming the captain for firing them and sending them ashore."

"That's bullshit," I interjected.

"I know, and so do the sober guys, but the druggies are too screwed up to figure it out. A couple of guys friendly with Smithfield are pissed at Punser...they're pissed at the first engineer, Harrison, too."

"I wondered when he would come into this. I know he sold them drugs, so you're not giving away any secrets."

"Ain't no one happy in the crew's quarters right now, but Boats is keeping them in line."

"Thanks, Winkler. I appreciate you telling me."

At Cape Balinao, we changed course again to due south for another fifty-one miles, keeping in deep water. Then we changed course to 135 degrees for the last thirty-seven miles, which brought us to the harbor approaches of Subic Bay.

At Subic, a local pilot and a U.S. Navy "advisor" boarded the ship together. Unlike Guam, where the Navy controlled everything, the cooperation between the local pilot and the Navy advisor was tangible. They were friendly and joking, and when the captain gave the Navy advisor a querying look, he pointed at the pilot and said, "He's your man, I'm only here because you're carrying munitions. I'm just along for the ride." The pilot smiled, ordered half-ahead on the engines, and took us into the harbor to the anchorage.

At the anchorage, we were welcomed by a quasi-jungle odor, a rotting vegetation smell that seems to be on most Pacific islands, mixed in with the aromas of diesel oil, stack emissions, and something rancid, source unknown. Boats, the AB, and I went to anchor stations and repeated the steps we had taken in Guam. The bottom here was rocky, sixty feet deep, so the captain had us let out four-and-a-half shots of rode before snugging up and securing the anchor clamps.

Releasing Boats and the AB, I got a cup of coffee and went to the flying bridge, enjoying the tranquility. I logged in the official arrival time as 1600 hours on Wednesday 3/8/67. For the past four days, there was nobody on oxygen or bleeding; no one irritating their roommate to the point of murder; nobody threatening to jump overboard; and I didn't have to wrestle with someone twice as strong as me. Taking a gulp of coffee, I set the cup on the deck and lit a Marlboro. Coffee, cigarette, gentle breeze, warm weather, and no trouble. All was good with the world.

Subic Bay has a long and colorful history as a naval station. The sheltered anchorages and deep water came to the attention of the King of Spain when explorer Juan de Salcedo reported its existence. The Spanish already had a Philippine home for its fleet in Cavite, but the port had shallow water, poor shelter, and unhealthy living conditions. In 1868, a military expedition explored all of Subic Bay and reported back it was a much better place to home-port the fleet. High command politics prevented the moving of the fleet from Manila to the relative isolation of Subic Bay until 1884, when a Royal Decree declared Subic Bay to be a naval port.

Olongapo, the principal town on Subic Bay, became an island when the Spanish navy created a drainage canal separating Olongapo from the mainland. They dredged the harbor, built seawalls and causeways and a short railroad, creating the *Arsenal de Alongo*.

During the Philippine-American War, Subic Bay and Alongopo played a minor role, but later President Theodore Roosevelt concurred with Admiral George Dewey and Admiral Henry C. Taylor that Subic Bay was the best place to build a naval base, and he issued an executive order creating the Subic Bay Naval Reservation.

Later, during World War I, the shipyards at Subic Bay became famous for their conversions and repairs, especially their work on destroyers. Between the wars, the Washington Naval Treaty of 1922 was signed. This treaty, also known as the Four-Power, Five-Power, and Nine-Power Treaty, was negotiated between November 1921 and February 1922. It limited the construction of battle cruisers, battle ships, and aircraft carriers. Other type warships—destroyers, submarines, cruisers, etc.—weren't limited in numbers, but in size. The maximum size allowed was 10,000 tons displacement. The purpose was to prevent an arms race. The treaty was signed by the United States, Italy, France, United Kingdom, and Japan.

As I sat on my ship carrying bombs and munitions to Vietnam and Thailand, the irony of this hit me.

During the 1930s, the naval station added a golf course and became a tropical paradise, with streets lined with hibiscus, gardenias, and palm trees.

In December 1941, faced with a Japanese Army advance, the U.S. abandoned the naval station and destroyed all equipment and supplies. It wouldn't be until October 1944 that the U.S. returned to the Philippines. The Japanese burned the town of Olongapo and the U.S. rebuilt it.

Construction of the naval air base at Cubi Point, just across the harbor from Olongapo, was completed during the Korean War. In building it, the small town of Banicain was demolished and its residents relocated to Olongapo.

Now, February 1967, Subic Bay was the forward base for repair and replenishment for the U.S. Seventh Fleet, with over two hundred ships per month calling on the port and utilizing its facilities. They brought food, ammunition, fuel oil, jet fuel, aviation gasoline, spare parts, and sailors. Lots of sailors.

The captain had called ahead and requested a military guard for the entire time we were in port. He felt their presence would force more rational thoughts into the heads of the crew members. The Navy assigned two shore patrol members: a chief (red hash marks, not gold) and a petty officer third class. The PO-3rd stood watch at the gangway while the chief roamed the ship. Each carried an over-sized billy club, more of a Louisville Slugger, and a Colt .45 1911.

The captain had refused to allow Highstone to go ashore because of the previous problems with him. He didn't want to give him a chance to restock his drugs or booze. In the end, it made no difference, because the other crew members brought back enough drugs and booze for everyone. Business was brisk after they returned to the ship.

We had warned the shore patrol to watch out for drugs and booze, but they obviously turned a blind eye, because when I went raiding the next morning, I thought I was shopping at a pharmacy.

The first one I looked at was Highstone, and he was high and couldn't even stand. I didn't find anything in his room, and I figured he wouldn't have the balls to try to store anything in Boats's locker, not after Boats's reaction the first time. Leaving him in his room, I walked into the crew mess, where four of the crew were in various states of weirdness. One of the BRs was doing lines of cocaine off the stainless-steel sink top. Another BR leaned against the bulkhead, eyes closed, a smile fixed on his face, humming "Somewhere Over the Rainbow." An AB lay on top of the table, out cold, and an OS sat on the bench with his head on the ABs chest, also out cold.

I frisked both the AB and OS cuddled together and came up with handfuls of pills and capsules—green, red, yellow, and blue. Later I identified them as "uppers" and "downers," something I knew nothing about. I frisked the BR against the bulkhead and found cardboard sheets with little tabs of what looked like sugar. It was LSD. While I went through his clothes, he kept on humming, oblivious to my presence.

The BR doing lines of cocaine finally realized I wasn't there to party with him, snorted a line, fumbled putting plastic bags into his pants pockets, then tried to leave. I stood in his way and said, "Empty your pockets."

He shook his head, muttering "no, no, no" in a low tone.

"You aren't going anywhere until you empty your pockets," I demanded, and I reached out and grabbed him by the front of his belt—in hindsight, a stupid move.

He threw a punch at the left side of my face, but was too close. All I got was a whiff of gag-inducing armpit odor. Ducking, I spun around behind him and undid his belt, de-pantsing him, then shoved him forward. He fell to the deck, tripping over his pants. I finished the maneuver by pulling his pants all the way off. Then I wrapped all the pills and LSD in them and kept them as evidence.

When I turned to leave, the first engineer came in, and the BR on the deck said, "Hey man, he took all my stuff," pointing at me. "I want it back."

The first's eyes gave him away, guilt stamped in them. "I don't know what you're talking about," he growled, and backed out the door.

"Hey, man," the BR called after him. "I need some shit. Get me some more."

"He the guy who gets you the shit?" I asked, nodding toward the retreating engineer.

The BR was sober enough to realize he shouldn't say any more other than, "Fuck you. Get your own shit."

I found the captain in his cabin and he got hold of the shore patrol chief. After I explained to the chief what I found in the crew mess, I asked him, "Isn't part of your job stopping this stuff from coming aboard?"

311

"No." Blunt and harsh. "It isn't. Look, I know you guys have a problem, but three-quarters of the sailors and soldiers passing through here are trying drugs of some kind. It's a frickin' epidemic. So, no, I'm not trying to search them for drugs or anything else. I'm here to make sure they don't kill you or themselves while you're here in port."

Stunned, all I could say was, "Jesus, it's that bad?"

"Yeah, it is."

"Okay, Chief," the captain said, "At least we now understand what we're up against."

After the chief left, I said, "We got another problem, Captain. The first engineer came into the crew mess while this was going on, and it's clear from what the BR said, the first is supplying some crew with drugs."

"That's two strikes on him. He had as much to do with Isaiah going nutso on us as did Punser. Now this," he sighed, shaking his head. "Ask the chief engineer to come and see me. I'll call you if I need you."

"Aye, aye, Captain."

After letting the chief know, I went to my cabin and flopped on the bunk. Last night, after four days of peace, I felt good. Now, fifteen hours later, my shoulders were tight, stomach acidic, and the low-grade headache was back. Nothing had changed, just a lull in the fireworks. I lay there, shrugging and stretching, trying to ease the tension. Inevitably, thoughts of Meg intruded, enough to give me a hard-on. I got up and went to the flying bridge,

my mental escape chamber, and stared at the harbor
entrance.

CHAPTER 34

That night, I went ashore.

The other crew members riding the launch avoided eye contact and scrambled ashore when we docked. I wore civvies, since this was a Navy town and our Merchant Marine insignia would have confused everybody.

Walking out the main gate, I crossed over the bridge that spanned the Shit River. If it had a real name, no one used it. Filled with raw sewage and stinking like shit, to everyone there it was the Shit River. There were young Philippine boys standing on the bank at the end of the bridge and a few on the bridge itself. Five or six sailors and three Marines stood there, and I watched as a sailor flipped a quarter high into the air, toward the river. Two of the boys on the bank dove into the water, trying to catch the quarter. The two boys on the bridge climbed onto the walkway rail and called to the sailor to toss another one. When he did, they dove. The quicker one snatched the quarter in mid-air before it hit the water. I was impressed with their agility, but disgusted by the conditions. These were kids jumping in to a cesspool.

One of the Marines, a private, dug into his pocket for a coin and leaned over the rail close to where I stood. Before he tossed it, I heard a loud, raspy growl from behind us.

"Marine! Don't even think about it."

All three of the Marines froze, and I turned and watched a Marine gunnery sergeant walk up beside them.

Glaring at them, he continued in a deep-South drawl, "You boys want to give these kids a quarter, you hand it to them. If you make them jump in that shithole, I will make damn-sure you hit the water before they do."

"Yes, Sergeant," they yelled together.

"Good. Glad you see you boys are quick learners."

Turning, they walked toward the bar area just past the bridge when the growl came again.

"You forgettin' something, Marines?"

They froze, then faced the sergeant, who hadn't moved.

"You were gonna give those boys a quarter."

All three dug into their pockets and came up with coins and signaled the boys on the river bank, who came running. The Marines handed over their coins, looked at the sergeant for permission, and walked away fast.

As the boys jostled for position in front of the remaining sailors, expecting them to hand over coins also, all but one sailor edged toward the street. The one sailor, only five feet away from the sergeant and standing at the rail, yelled at the boys, "I ain't no fuckin' Marine. You want my money, jump for it," and held his hand over the rail, leaning dangerously.

Watching, I couldn't believe how fast that sergeant moved. He stepped in, enveloped the sailor's hand in a huge fist, bent the arm behind his back, and shoved. The money dropped onto the bridge decking and the sailor went over the rail, too surprised even to shout as he tumbled into the Shit River.

No one moved until the sergeant pointed at the coins and said, "Hey boys, I think that's yours." As the boys ran to the coins, he looked over the railing at the sailor in the river, smiled, and walked up the street.

Intrigued, I followed him.

The odor of motor oil, diesel fuel, and gasoline pervaded—not strong enough to overcome the smell of the Shit River, but ever present. Most of the traffic comprised Jeeps, interspersed with the occasional pickup or sedan, all military. Halfway up the block, the sergeant turned into a bar, and I stayed on his tail. At the door I looked up at the sign, "Lulu's," and walked in, the sergeant a few steps ahead—an obvious regular, because the bartender knew him and most of the ladies waved at him, earning a nod in return. He took a stool—not to be confused with the contents of Shit River—at the end of the bar, and a Budweiser in a can appeared before him. A lady, skimpily clad, came up and said something to him, earning her a smile.

I stepped up and said, "Excuse me, Sergeant, can I buy you a beer?"

He glared at me. "Why?"

Not the answer I expected, but I continued. "I saw what you did at the bridge for those kids."

He stared for a few more seconds, then smiled and said, "Sure, pull up a stool and have one with me."

I introduced myself, and he did the same. "Call me Gunny, everyone else does."

"Okay, Gunny," and I offered my hand, which he discreetly crushed. I told him I was on a ship carrying munitions and other stuff heading for Vietnam and Thailand. Not worried about the old "loose lips sink ships," since he was an obvious Marine lifer and no one else paid any attention to us. For the next two hours, I got a year's worth of life lessons in how to survive in a hostile environment, the most important lesson being, know when you are in a hostile environment.

I mentioned the stink of the place and Gunny snorted. "This ain't nothin'. The worst is body rot. In-country, we carry Vicks," he said, referring to the vapo-rub product. "A dab under your nose works good."

I also learned other valuable basic facts, such as, all the beer from the tap was 3.2% panther-piss, no matter what label it bore. Never let the bartender or waitress open the bottled beer. They recycled the bottles, not cleaning them, just refilling them and pressing on old bottle caps you could pop off with your fingers. They refilled the bottles with the same panther-piss, and sold it as brand-name beer.

The girls in the bar were beautiful, sexy, territorial, possessive, and dangerous. A short-time was two dollars. An all-nighter cost seven dollars. All this I learned from the sergeant's girlfriend, Maya, who flitted around him liked a protective mother hen.

317

A few times, different girls approached me, but the sergeant politely waved them away. An hour into it, after an especially beautiful redhead approached me—the red hair bringing forth visions of Meg—he tapped me on my forearm, pointed at the girls, and said, "I ain't keepin' you pure, William, just keepin' you safe. Every gal here is a professional, and they like to keep steady company. Once you get attached to a gal, you belong to her. If you hit on another gal, you're gonna get nicked." Turning to Maya, he said, "Show William your butterfly trimmer."

She stepped around the sergeant, reached down, and pulled out a small, razor-sharp knife, which she twirled in her hand. I don't know where it came from, since she only wore a bikini bottom and bra, but the next thing I knew, she had the knife against my jugular.

"Standard procedure against any sailors who mess with these ladies."

"What do you mean, 'mess' with them, Sarge?"

"Mess with them. Do something they think is unfair. If they think you cheated on them."

"How do you know what's unfair?"

"Ah," holding up his index finger, "that's the interesting part. It ain't what I think or I mean. It's what's in their heads. Don't pay them what you owe. Get too familiar with a different gal than the one thinks she owns you," and he gave the thumb-across-the-throat motion. "They'll cut each other up, too. Depends on their mood that night."

"Jesus," I said.

"Jesus ain't got nothin' to do with it. Most of these gals are Catholic and go to church on Sunday."

Slapping me on the back, he barked, "Don't worry. You're riding a ship filled with bombs and bullets, and you're heading for 'Nam. You're safer with these ladies than where you're going. Enjoy yourself."

I asked him what else there was to do here, besides drinking and girls. He gave me a look. "Well, there are a lot of scams run by the locals, the most notorious is, 'feed the duck to the crocodile.'"

"What's that?" I asked, and he regaled me with his run-in with "Papa Duck," the guy who ran the scam.

"Up the road is a small, saltwater pond with crocodile living in it. Papa Duck, that's what he calls himself, sells baby ducklings to the sailors for fifty cents, and tells them to throw the duckling in the pond to feed the crocodile. He called it a Buwaya. If the duck dies, Papa Duck will pay the sailor a dollar."

Pausing, he scratched his armpit, burped, and continued. "What the sumbitch doesn't tell the sailors is there's a small tunnel leading from the edge of the pond, so the ducks can escape. It's too small for the croc to get through. Old Papa Duck made a lot of money. But I made a mistake one day." He turned, looked at me, and smiled. "There was alcohol involved." Turning back to the bar, he went on. "I decided to outsmart Papa Duck, so I paid fifty cents, got the duck and bit the head off it, and threw it in the pond."

Despite the vision of the duck's head in his mouth making me want to gag, I asked, "Why was that a mistake?"

"Cuz Papa Duck came out swinging a machete. I'd a had to shoot him if the shore patrol hadn't been right there."

"What did they do?"

"They saved my ass. Calmed Papa Duck down, told me to pay him ten dollars for the duck, which I did, and everything was okay. A lot of those shore patrol boys are pussies but a few..." He shook his head. "If I'd a shot Papa Duck, my ass was grass, and those few...they can be the biggest lawn mower you ever did see. Their billy clubs are the size of baseball bats, and they know how to use them. When they come in a bar and say 'Hit the deck,' anyone who doesn't lay down gets knocked down. But that night, they were in a good mood." He shook his head again. "I threw the dead duck right at the gator and it didn't twitch. Papa Duck musta fed the croc. It wasn't biting nothin'. Should a known."

"Sergeant," I said, reaching into my pocket for my wallet, "I'm going to walk around a little, see what's out there. Given your advice about being unfair, is there a standard amount you tip the bartender?"

"I give him a buck for every hour I been here. How much money you spend, don't mean nothin' to him. The bar is his personal space. He lets you sit here, kinda like rent."

I paid the tab and left four dollars for the bartender, a dollar each for the sergeant and me, for the two hours I had spent there. It seemed exorbitant, but I wasn't going against Sarge's advice.

I shook hands with the sergeant, said goodbye to Maya, and walked out. At the doorway, the Shit River stink hit me. I turned left and walked a block up the street and stepped into another bar, to escape the stink. If it had a name, I didn't notice. I ordered a beer. A Budweiser in a can.

CHAPTER 35

Despite the promises of the ship owners, the first mate never showed up. The cook was easier. Coming from Manila, he joined us the morning after my night out with Sergeant Gunny.

At 1130 hours, we were gathered in the salon, enjoying a different aroma, something spicy, tangy. Andrew walked in and the captain asked, "Andrew, what's that delightful aroma?"—an unknowing and unintended slight of Andrew's prior culinary efforts.

"The new cook is hard at work. He calls it Afritada—chicken stew, but spiced up. Smells great. We'll see how it tastes."

"Well, I'm glad you can get a break, now." Looking at me, the captain said, "No such luck for you, William. It seems the replacement first mate got on a plane in San Francisco that stopped in Hawaii. When the plane arrived in Manila, he wasn't aboard. No explanation, just not there."

"Not surprised, Captain," I responded, shaking my head. "The way everything else has been going, one more screw-up is par for the course."

The captain snorted, "Par for the course, all right, and we got the worst golfers playing the toughest course as crew. We'll be sailing tomorrow morning at 0700. If he shows up between now and then, fine; if not, the watches stay the same."

Around 1500 hours, Boats came to the bridge, where I lolled, leaning against the forward windbreak.

"Hey, Boats. What's up?"

"Thought I'd give you a heads-up."

Given what we'd been through on this trip, I stiffened, apprehensive. "Why do I need a heads-up?"

"The new cook's name is Bayani Bautista. He's a cousin of Joselito Bautisa—you know, the guy with the bullet hole in him."

"Holy shit. Does he know what happened?"

"If he don't, it won't take long for someone to tell him."

I thumped my forehead against the bulkhead. "It never ends." Standing straight, I stretched my back and craned my neck. "Okay, Boats. Thanks for letting me know."

"Sure thing, Mate," and he went below.

Inside the bridge, Winkler had been putzing the brass, make-work with nothing else to do.

"Winkler," I called in. "I'm going below for a minute. Keep an eye out."

"Aye, aye, Mate" trailed behind me as I went down the outside ladder, looking for the chief steward.

In his office, Andrew said, "It didn't register with me at first, since I deal with a lot of Filipinos and Bautista's a common name. Standing in the galley, it struck me, and I asked him if he was related. All he did was laugh and say, 'Everyone's related in the Philippines.' Turns out he's a cousin of Joselito."

"Does he know what happened to Joselito?"

"Don't think so. Told me he didn't know who he replaced. I told him it was Joselito, he got injured on the job, and we put him ashore in Guam. 'Hope he's okay' was all he said."

"Okay Andrew, thanks."

As I turned, he said, "His first name is Bayani. In Tagalog it means 'Hero.'"

Back on the bridge, smoking my Marlboro, I wondered if he would live up to the name, or be a loser like his cousin, Joselito. What's the word for "loser" in Tagalog?

That evening after supper, the excellent chicken stew and its lingering aroma relaxed me. I sat with Greg in the salon, alone except for the cloud of my cigarette smoke and the subtle scent of his jasmine tea, an irregular habit he'd acquired. It would be coffee for two weeks, water for two weeks, and jasmine tea for two weeks. No rhyme or reason, other than he liked to change things. The jasmine tea helped soothe muscle tension, or so he claimed.

"Greg, something's been bugging me. Do you think Punser and the first engineer picked on Isaiah because he's black?"

Greg arched an eyebrow and gave me that sardonic grin. "White boy getting a touch of conscience?"

"Come on, Greg, I'm serious."

"Still, way too sensitive, William. You'd never last as a black man." He laughed. "Okay, okay. I think Punser did it because he was an ignorant little shit, white trash, and there's nothing more openly prejudiced than ignorant white trash." He paused and shook his head. "I don't think the first did it because of Isaiah's color. The first seems to be miserable with all the crew, regardless of color. No, he picked on Isaiah because he couldn't get to me. The jerk knew I wouldn't put up with his bullshit. Isaiah made an easier target."

"You're black and he tried to pick on you."

"Man, you're a genius. You figured out I'm black," and he burst out laughing. "The operative word is 'tried' to pick on me. No, the first is a miserable person and a bully. If Isaiah and I were white and didn't play his stupid game the way I won't now, he still would've picked on us. He saw us as a threat to his authority. Me, really, but I protected Isaiah, so in the first's warped mind, we were one and the same."

"Greg, you know the first engineer is selling drugs to the crew."

"I didn't know, but I heard stories. How do you know?"

"He came in and gave it away in the crew mess, when I was rousting some of them."

"Once an asshole, always an asshole. Does the captain know?"

"Yeah, said he'd talk to the chief engineer. Don't know if he did or not."

Another arched eyebrow. "I'm not gonna hold my breath waiting for the chief to do anything. He's having too many 'breath mint' days lately."

Leaning back and stretching, I said, "You know, when the captain and I went to the hearing at the Navy base, I never said anything about the first engineer picking on Isaiah, only Punser. Thought it would open Pandora's box if I did. Do you think I should have said something?"

Greg pursed his lips and took a sip of tea. "Don't know. I wouldn't want to get in a pissing 'he said/he said' contest on something so serious. Was the hearing officer white?"

"Yes, he was."

"Nope. I think you were right to stay mum. What happened with Isaiah and Punser happened, and it was mainly between the two of them. Can't see how dragging the first engineer into it would have helped, and I sure don't want to get dragged into anything in a military kangaroo court. As you so ingeniously noticed, I'm black. Things are different when you're black. You've seen a taste of it when we were in South Africa, enough to be aware of, but you haven't lived it. You can't." He laughed, brittle and harsh. "At least you're trying, William. Give you a lot of credit for trying."

"It doesn't seem right the first should get off scot-free."

"Something else you learn young when you're black."

I looked at him, silent.

"Sometimes, there are things you just gotta leave alone."

I sat for half an hour after he left, wondering how hard I was trying.

CHAPTER 36

Saturday, 3/11/67, 0700 hours, warm, squally weather, intermittent rain, westerly wind at twelve MPH, we weighed anchor.

The same pilot and Navy advisor that guided us in, now took us out of the harbor. After dropping them off, making a slight turn to starboard to create a lee for them to disembark, the captain ordered the ship up to sea speed and on course 255 degrees. It was a straight shot of 340 miles across the South China Sea to Cam Ranh Bay.

At breakfast the next morning, Andrew tapped my shoulder. "Can we talk a minute…privately?"

Standing, I followed him out to the passageway. "What's up?"

"The new cook would like to talk to you."

"What about?" I said, hostility rising.

"What the crew are telling him about Joselito."

"You know what they're telling him. I shot him!"

Holding a hand up, he said, "Easy, relax. I don't think he's a threat. I think he's trying to warn us."

"Of what?"

"Not sure. Maybe that's why you oughta talk to him."

Leaning against the bulkhead, I pressed my head back against it. "Only if the captain is there."

"Okay. I'll talk to the captain and set a time."

"And Andrew…"

"Yes?"

"I will have my pistol."

He went to find the captain, and I returned to the salon to add coffee to my already acidic stomach.

An hour later, in the captain's office, I leaned against the forward bulkhead; the cook stood directly in front of the captain; and Andrew stood beside him.

"Mr. Bautista, you wished to speak to Mr. Connolly," the captain began, pointing at me. "Go ahead."

"Yes, Captain. Thank you." He seemed calm but was pouring sweat. "The crew, they tell me Mr. Connolly shoot my cousin, Joselito, for no reason but he no like him. I no argue with crew. I here on ship one day. No want trouble." He reached into his back pocket. The captain stiffened and my hand went to the butt of my pistol, but he pulled out a large red handkerchief and wiped his brow.

"I know Joselito. He always fight with people. If Mr. Connolly shoot him, I think good reason for it." He spread both hands in front of him. "Joselito no my problem. No want problems," he concluded, wiping his brow again.

The captain nodded. "I understand, Mr. Bautista. So you have a clear understanding, I want Mr. Connolly to tell you exactly what happened when Joselito got shot."

Waving his hands in front of him. "Not necessary. You no have to tell me. Not my business."

"Yes, it is necessary, so you will understand the motives of the crew members telling you these things."

The captain waved at me, and I related the entire story to Bautista. The captain finished by telling him how none of the crew telling him these stories would donate blood, but I did, saving Joselito's life.

I felt better with the captain stressing my "good guy" side. I needed an ally, even if only a mental sop for my angst.

At the end, Bautista said, "Joselito crazy." Until then, other than the sweat, he seemed relaxed, matter-of-fact.

We stood in silence for a few seconds, then I said, "Mr. Bautista, I have one question for you. Is any one crew member pushing this?"

He shuffled from one foot to the other, reluctant to answer.

"Has anyone threatened you?"

Now he looked down, avoiding eye contact, still shuffling.

"I'll tell you what, Mr. Bautista. Don't answer my question, that's okay. But I have another question. Can you read?"

He nodded yes.

Stepping to the captain's desk, I said, "May I?" I tore a piece of paper from his notebook. Picking up a pen, I printed a name on the paper. Returning the captain's pen,

I walked around the desk and showed Bautista the paper. The next twenty seconds were tense.

His eyes bugged wide. I looked at him and lifted my eyebrows, questioning without words. He nodded, slowly and deliberately, three times.

"Thank you, Mr. Bautista. If anyone asks, you can tell them the truth. You never answered any of the questions I asked you."

He looked at the captain, who nodded toward the door, and Bautista left, wiping his brow.

I laid the paper on the desk so Andrew and the captain could clearly read, "Highstone."

CHAPTER 37

After Bautista left the office, Andrew and I stayed to talk with the captain. "That son-of-a-bitch has been nothing but trouble since he showed his ugly face," the captain railed, referring to Highstone.

"He's not so obvious with his antics now," I replied. "Hasn't threatened to throw himself overboard since Boats had a talk with him."

"Yeah, I know. Too bad!" Seeing the startled look on Andrew's face, he added, "I don't really want the idiot to jump overboard...but I wish he'd jump ship in port and go bother some other captain."

Andrew laughed. "It's not my natural inclination to wish bad things on people, but if he tried jumping again, I might throw him a brick."

Smiling, the captain, said, "Nah, too much damn paperwork."

I joined in. "You saw how Bautista reacted when I asked if he had been threatened. Maybe Andrew should stop in the galley on a regular basis, for the next few days at least. Let the crew see we're watching them. I'll drop by, too. That's the least we can do. Maybe give Bautista a little breathing room."

The captain nodded, "I may show up there on occasion too."

Andrew said, "Sure, no problem."

Beginning at one hundred miles off the coast of Vietnam, there is a northeast current ranging from one-half to one-and-one-half knots. Inside of forty miles from the coast, the current reverses itself to run in a southerly direction, and increases speed ranging from one to three knots. That's a potential five knot shift in speed and complete reverse of direction, so you have to stay alert and watch the shore lights, beacons, and markers or you can get in trouble.

Luckily, we were going straight in and would have the use of beacons and markers at night. Ships traveling the coast did so blacked out, under Navy orders. Something else to be nervous about, the Navy had warned us of to be leery of motorized sampans taking a shot at us in the dark. I thought of my classmate's story, of his ship being chased out of the port of Vung Ro by artillery fire, and hoped we wouldn't suffer the same fate, or worse.

The captain had received a wire telling him we were to go to anchor outside Cam Ranh Bay and await further orders. Originally scheduled to arrive Monday morning, since there was no longer a fixed arrival schedule, he dropped speed down to eight knots to save fuel. That would get us there early morning on Tuesday. A prudent move, and one that the owners always approve of since it saves money. Helps score him brownie points, something every captain needs to do to retain his job. A never-ending balancing act for the captain: keep the ship operating safely and on schedule, and keep the owners happy. Many times, these three things are mutually exclusive.

When I got relieved at 0600 on Monday morning, instead of hitting my rack, I went down to the galley to check on Bautista. Hearing voices, I waited outside the door and listened. Bautista was talking.

"This my work place. You no belong here. Get out."

Highstone's whiny, nasal voice answered. "I'll go wherever the fuck I want, and there's nothin' you can do about it."

"Get out."

"Or what? Ya gonna call your mommy, the steward?" A taunting sneer.

Sensing someone behind me, I whirled, hand going to my holster. It was Andrew. "You hearing this?" I whispered.

He nodded. "What should I do?"

"Your call. I'll be here."

Nodding again, he stepped around me and went in.

"Mr. Highstone, you have something to say about me?" he asked.

A momentary pause and a muttered snarl, "I got nothing to say to you."

"You seem to have a lot to say when I'm not here."

The direction of voices changed so they must have moved around the galley. I peeked through the hinge crack.

Highstone snapped. "Hey, fuck you! You're just a fuckin' waiter wearing stripes. I don't hafta listen to you. Give me any more shit and I'll kick your ass."

"You threatening me, Highstone?"

"Goddam right, you and your gook buddy"—he pointed at Bautista. "Now, back the fuck off."

That was enough for me. I stepped in. Andrew had gone to stand beside Bautista, so Highstone had his back to me. When I tapped him on the shoulder, he jumped, leaping to his left.

"What the fuck?" he yelled.

"Gotcha, asshole." I felt a snide smile on my face. "Three witnesses to you threatening an officer and a crew member. Turn around, lean your head against the bulkhead, and put your hands behind you."

"What for?" All sulk and petulance, braggadocio gone.

"So I can put the handcuffs on you. You're going to the flying bridge. You remember the flying bridge, don't you?"

Andrew had stepped around and came up on the other side of him. Faced with two of us, he turned and put his hands behind him.

Cuffing him, I marched him to the flying bridge where I secured him to the upper rail.

"Hey, I can't siddown, hooked up like this."

"We'll be in port tomorrow. You can stand for a day."

"What if I gotta take a piss?

I walked away, smiling. He already knew the uncomfortable answer.

Stopping in the bridge on the way down, I told the third mate about Highstone and told him to ignore him. George gave a big smile and said, "No problem." I heard the helmsman chuckle.

By the time I arrived at the salon, Andrew was sitting with the captain and had already told him what happened.

"Give me a written report, both of you. I'm going to nail the coffin shut on this clown. See if you can get Bautista to sign one, too, but don't push him. He's had enough shit for only two days on board."

Andrew said, "I'll ask him." Looking at me: "Sorry, but you scare him."

"I seem to be scaring the wrong guys."

"No," the captain interjected. "You're scaring everybody, and that's the way I want it."

The OS woke me at 1130 for the watch change. I had skipped breakfast, my stomach in a knot after the Highstone incident, and that same stomach rumbled now, reminding me it needed to be fed. I brushed my teeth, hit the head, then the salon. The hot meal was meatloaf. Calling down, I asked Andrew—he still helped at meal times—to make me two meatloaf sandwiches. The dumbwaiter rang within four minutes. Grabbing both sandwiches and a couple of sugar cookies off the sideboard, I hustled to the bridge.

"Hi, George, sorry I'm late." It was 1500 hours. Normal relief time is ten minutes early.

"Okay, William. I ain't going nowhere."

"Any problem with the guy upstairs?" I nodded to the overhead.

"Nah. He whined for a while when you first locked him up, but I ain't heard him since then." He related the course and speed and I relieved him.

I greeted the new helmsman, Winkler, and went into the chartroom, setting my dish on the chart table. Then I walked to the starboard bridge wing and checked for traffic. Seeing nothing, I went to the port side and did the same. Again nothing, so I ate lunch.

The wind had freshened to eighteen miles per hour and shifted to north-northwest. The seas were up to ten feet, and we rolled five or six degrees regularly, getting an occasional wave slam on the starboard bow, causing the old girl to shudder. Going to the port-side aft ladder, I climbed halfway up and peeked onto the flying bridge. Highstone stood slumped forward over the top rail. Retreating, I called the captain on the phone. "Captain, I'm going to give Highstone something to eat and some water. Want me to let him go to the head?"

"You put him there, William. I don't give a damn if you feed him or not, so long as he doesn't die on us. You decide," and he hung up.

"Winkler," I called through the open door.

"Yeah, Mate." He stuck his head inside; the ship was on auto-pilot.

"Go to the galley and get a meatloaf sandwich for Highstone. A cup of water too."

"Okay."

"Wait. Take this plate down with you, too." And I handed it to him. "Thanks, Winkler."

"Welcome, Mate," and he left.

On the flying bridge, Highstone trembled as he balanced himself against the motion of the ship. He needed a fix and knew it wasn't gonna happen.

I walked up behind him, noticing his shaking and trance-like state.

"You want to eat?"

"I don't feel good," was his reply.

Standing downwind from him, the reek of piss stung my nose. "Don't look or smell so good, either. That's what happens when drugs and booze control your life. Here, drink some water," I offered, handing him a cup.

Half of it splashed out, but he got enough down to slake his thirst.

Taking the cup back, I said, "Last chance. You want this?" holding out the sandwich wrapped in wax paper.

He nodded and I put it in his hand, turned, and walked aft.

CHAPTER 38

Twenty-five miles off the coast, we ran into the monsoon. There are two monsoon seasons in Vietnam. From April to October, the southwest winds blow, and from December to late March, the northeast winds blow. We were at the end of the northeast wind monsoon season, with frequent forty-five-to-fifty-knot gusts.

Due to the severe weather, the captain relented and moved Highstone from the flying bridge to the pilot cabin, still in cuffs. I prevailed upon him to at least make Highstone take a shower and put on clean clothes. He smelled like a sewer. While he did that, I ran the handcuffs under hot water in the sink.

Saigon was the location in Vietnam heard most often on the news at home, but Cam Ranh Bay is where most of the cargo moves through. One hundred and eighty miles northeast of Saigon, its main asset is deep water. Currently, it's the main port of discharge for military cargo supporting our "conflict" efforts there. I'm a patriot, and this "conflict" is all about stopping the spread of communism, so I support it, but it amazes me why neither the president nor congress has the gumption to call it a war. When you are killing people en masse, it's a war!

Take away the grim aspect of war, and it's a beautiful port. The long peninsula protected both the outer and inner harbor.

The bay has long been significant to the military. It was used as a staging area for the forty-ship Imperial Russian fleet prior to the battle of Tsushima in 1905. Located between Tsushima and Iki islands, off the northwest corner of Japan, it is a channel of the Korea Strait connecting the Sea of Japan, Yellow Sea, and East China Sea.

Admiral Zinovy Rozhestvensky, commanding the Russian Second Pacific Squadron, suffered a crushing defeat by the Japanese Combined Fleet under the command of Admiral Togo Heihachiro. The unique feature of this battle is it was the only decisive engagement of battleship fleets in modern times.

The Japanese followed the Russians using Cam Ranh Bay as a preparation point for the invasion of Malaysia in 1942. In 1945, the U.S. Navy Task Force 38 destroyed twenty Japanese sea planes and most of the Japanese facilities, and the bay was abandoned.

From 1954 through 1956, the French used Cam Ranh Bay as an evacuation point for their troops.

In 1963, Admiral Harry D. Felt, U.S. CINCPAC, foresaw the need for additional facilities, and ordered the construction of a pier and causeway, 350 feet long. In 1966, four DeLong piers were added, the first of which was used for munitions transfer, enhancing the efficiency of loading/discharging operations, although they continued to use the original stone pier for munitions discharge.

The DeLong pier was invented by Colonel L. B. DeLong, an Army engineer. It consists of a floating barge with circular holes along the edges, into which they insert steel tubular caissons. The caissons are pile-driven into the harbor bed, then a special air jack is lowered onto them. Acting like a kid shinnying up a tree, the air jack alternately grasps and releases, lifting the barge out of the water in the process. The final product is a sturdy pier, ninety feet wide and as long as the number of sections of barge used. Prior to the building of these DeLong piers, with only one stone pier available for berthing, the backlog of ships waiting at anchor to be unloaded was very high.

The port was actually run by the Army, with the 124th Transportation Command running both the port and trucking activities. Naval activity was growing and, while the port facilities served the purpose, the shore facilities were limited. It wasn't until mid-1966 the shore installations could take over the task of feeding and quartering support personnel from APL-55, a barracks ship anchored in the harbor. During our short stay there, the entire northern half of the eastern peninsula containing the air field hummed with activity.

We anchored at the outer bay anchorage in sixty feet of water in howling northeast winds, the rain driving sideways in sheets. The depth ranges from fifty-two to one hundred and four feet throughout the harbor. Due to the high wind, the captain ordered five rodes of chain, and we snugged up well at that length.

As a civilian ship, we were assigned Army security, three privates and a corporal. Unlike in Guam, where we got a sergeant, there were a lot of ships requiring security, hence the lower ranks, but they were good at their job. This was solely due to the ship being in the zone, making us a potential target for mines and rocket attacks. The fact we carried bombs and munitions was incidental, other than making the explosion bigger if we were hit.

I greeted the soldiers when they came aboard. The corporal explained why they were there, and said they have their own rations, but would use ship water and latrine facilities.

"No problem, Corporal. I'll show you where the crew heads are located. There is drinking water at any tap in the galley, and you are welcome to eat in our mess, as well. The food's pretty good aboard, and it sure-as-shit is better than those MCI-rations you guys lug around."

He smiled, and in a west Texas drawl said, "Cat food's better'n this crap. Thanks for the invite. The guys will appreciate it, and we'll stay out of your way."

I toured them through the lower deck and offered them the use of Smithfield's and Punser's cabin during their off-hours. I showed them how to find my cabin and the captain's office, then left them.

During the day, the soldiers took turns walking the deck, alert to anything approaching the ship, especially local fishing vessels. At night, they did the same, but with an added effect. At irregular intervals, and at different locations along the ship, they would drop hand grenades over the side, close to the ship's hull, but not close enough to damage it. This deterred potential divers from attaching mines to the hull, since the concussive effect would kill a diver. That night, at the first detonation—a dull thud that vibrated the ship—I bounded out of bed, grabbed my pistol, and ran outside in my skivvies, thinking we were under attack. The soldier eyed the pistol in my hand and explained the process. I went back to my cabin, on edge but less so. The second "whump" woke me, but I rolled over and went back to sleep. It's amazing how quick we can adapt to strange circumstances. We sat at anchor for three days, the last of which was St. Patrick's Day.

At supper, the captain announced we would dock in the morning at the old ammo pier to discharge the munitions, but would then switch to another pier to discharge the rest of the cargo. He also announced tonight was his annual sobriety test.

"I am originally of Scottish ancestry, but most of the family decamped to Ireland, so I regard myself as Irish. I am an alcoholic and have been sober for seven years. Every year on Saint Patrick's Day, when most of my Irish brethren and much of the non-Irish world get stinking drunk, I drink one beer, a Guinness. This satisfies my craving for the world's best beer, and tests my resolve to stay sober."

With that, he popped the top on the bottle and poured it into a mug at a 45-degree angle, as tradition requires. Unlike pouring from the tap, he didn't let it sit, but leveled the glass at the end to get the traditional foamy head.

All eyes were on him during the process, silent, until he took the first sip. The chief engineer clapped and the rest of us joined in.

"No, Chief. Bad timing. Clap when I finish the bottle and don't open another."

The crew drifted out of the salon over the next ten minutes. When it was just me and the captain, I said, "Captain, how do you stop at one drink?"

He smiled. "I only carry one bottle of Guinness with me. I don't replace it until six months after Saint Patrick's Day."

The pilot, an Army lieutenant they refer to as Marine Pilot, boarded the ship, and we heaved anchor, heading for the ammo pier. The approach to the pier is a narrow channel that is tricky in heavy winds. This day, there was a fine drizzle, with a steady twenty-knot wind.

There are six tugboats in the port. Languages were an issue, since the tugboats had mixed crews of GIs, Koreans, Filipinos, and the largest tug, one hundred feet long, was Vietnamese. We had two small tugs assigned to us, with only four hundred and fifty horsepower each, according to the pilot. That's no more than the average Indy race car. The pilot carried two walkie-talkies, one connecting him to the harbor master and one to the tugboats.

At the ammo pier, it was mandatory that all ships dock facing out to sea. In case of attack, they could leave quickly. To accomplish this, we had to spin-ship far off

345

the pier, then back all the way in. For the same reason, none of the mooring lines were dead-ended on the bollards. They were looped, and the head of the line brought back to the ship's bitts. That way, we could slip the lines without the aid of line handlers and not have to cut them.

The pilot did a good job of backing, and stuck the stern against the pier at about a ten-degree angle. Once we had a spring line landed, he leveraged against that and, with both tugs pushing on the bow, got her secured. Our military security detail went ashore as soon as the gangway lowered.

The stevedores were Army. Untrained, raw recruits who weren't familiar with our type ship. The superintendent was a second lieutenant who didn't know a thing about stevedoring. A college grad (ROTC), he relied on a staff sergeant and a corporal who were seasoned longshore foremen, doing their stint here. They managed to keep the other workers reasonably straight. It was slow but steady.

All our cargo booms were five-ton capacity. Hatches #2, #3, and #4 had double sets of booms, one set forward and one set aft. Hatch #1 had a single set on the forward end, and hatch #5 had a single set on the after end. Unlike the *Mormacpride*, my former ship, there was no heavy-lift boom. Given the lack of experience of the longshoremen, it was just as well.

The main deck hatch cover consisted of six to eight steel pontoons, each five feet wide and one foot thick.

Their length depended on the width of the hatch. They set on a ridge along the hatch coaming, and you lifted them out with wire bridles and stacked them at a convenient spot on the deck alongside the hatch. Painstaking work if you knew what you were doing. Dangerous, if you didn't.

Below decks, the hatch covers were wooden, three feet by five feet sections. Each section comprised three boards, butted side by side with bronze strapping on the ends to hold them together as a unit. There was a handhold at diagonal opposite ends for lifting the boards.

The boards sat on a series of steel latticework beams set into notches in the hatch coaming at regular intervals. They only had single tarpaulins on the below-decks hatch covers. This was to protect the cargo from rain when the upper hatch cover was open.

With a normal stevedore gang, it took about thirty minutes to open any hatch cover. With the Army longshoremen, it took an hour.

Our first problem came when we showed them the stow plan. Unlike in the States, they hadn't received a copy of it ahead of our arrival. Their philosophy was "If it's there, unload it." The stumbling block was the Army rule that restricted the ammo pier to munitions operations only. In #2 and #5 hatches, where we had the munitions stowed, we had cartons of beer, Coca-Cola, and toilet paper filling the tweendeck squares. They had to discharge that before they could get at the munitions. The second lieutenant and sergeant argued for ten minutes with someone at the other end of their walkie-talkie, then the decision was made: Discharge the dry cargoes here, though they wouldn't remain dry in this weather. Unlike the DeLong piers that had transit sheds at the inland end, the ammo pier was wide open. All the munitions were stored outside, at least initially.

Boats and our crew stripped the tarps off #2 hatch and #5 hatch, and the longshoremen went to work uncovering. At the start of work, the rain had slowed to a mist. Within an hour, it was pelting again, and every cardboard carton was getting soaked. Slinging the full pallets in the hatch worked okay, but when they had to place the loose cartons on to a pallet, things went south in a hurry. Cans of beer and coke were rolling everywhere. The toilet paper would probably have to be used with one swipe to a roll. I don't know how they would separate the clogged sheets.

On the pier, they landed the pallets on the dock, and small forklifts lifted them on to flatbed trucks that had backed all the way down the narrow pier. I got hold of the sergeant and stopped the operation.

"Sarge, there's an easier way to do this. We have nets lined with tarps the guys can dump the broken cartons into. If you get a few six-by trucks here with the tops uncovered, you can dump the nets right in to the back of them and pull them loose. What you do with the mess after the trucks leave the pier is another problem, but at least we'll get the hook moving and get to the munitions faster."

"Gimme a minute. I gotta convince the second louie it's a good idea, and it's his idea."

I laughed and said, "Good luck. In the meantime, I'll break out the nets."

He wandered off. I found Boats and told him what to do, then headed to the salon to get out of the miserable rain for coffee and a cigarette. There was no smoking allowed at the ammo pier, and the captain didn't allow it on deck with open hatches, either. Even if I wanted to stay outside and get soaked, I doubt if I could light one in the wind and rain.

In the salon I looked out the forward porthole and saw the gang switching to the nets. Sarge must have convinced the second lieutenant to follow his advice.

CHAPTER 39

The work in #2 hatch took five days to complete. A day to unload the M2 shells from the upper tweendeck. A day and a half for the 105 mm shells in the lower tweendeck. And two-and-a-half days for the 198 mm shells in the lower hold. Hatch #5, with one-fourth the amount of cargo—comprising .30 caliber, 5.56 caliber, and .45 caliber ammunition—took two-and-a-half days, the difference being the men in #5 were lazy, stupid, recalcitrant, or all three.

Twice, the crane operator at #5 hatch ran the cargo hook all the way to the top of the block and jammed it. We had to lower the boom to the deck to get at the area and clear it. Three times, he bounced a load of bullets off the hatch coaming. On the third try, two boxes shattered and a shower of 5.56 mm bullets rained down on the men below. I was walking by on the offshore side when it happened.

"What the hell are you doing?" I yelled. "Get off the controls."

The operator stared at me, eyes wide, not saying a word. A chorus of "mother-fuckers" rose from the men in the hatch as I ordered him to come down from the winch control platform. He reached the deck as the sergeant ran from the top of the gangway. We all got there at the same time.

"What the fuck are you doing?" the sergeant shouted into his face. "You're gonna kill someone."

"Sarge"—the sergeant's roar had the odd effect of calming me down—"just get him off the ship. I'll shut the power off if he gets on the controls again."

The sergeant knew I was right, but it was clear, at least to me, he didn't like me threatening to shut everything down. That was a challenge to his authority and would reflect badly on him if it got reported to his CO. If we were in the States, the union would file a grievance for removing the winch operator; but, in the States, the longshoremen are professionals and good at what they do. I wouldn't have had to call for his removal.

In a softer voice: "Sarge, you know I'm right. That guy"—flinging a glare at the crane operator—"is a menace, and the guys he'll kill are your men. Let's do this the easy way: Just get him out of here."

He nodded, still staring at the operator. "Get your ass down the gangway and stay at the bottom until I tell you different," he said, venom dripping from every word. The sergeant didn't like being embarrassed. Leaning over the coaming, he yelled, "Anyone hurt down there?" Satisfied with the response, he turned and strode forward, calling over his shoulder, "I'll send another guy here." Five minutes later, a man from the gang working in #2 hatch climbed up to the control platform, looked down into the hold, and yelled, "You guys ready?"—then lowered the cargo hook and slinging wires into the hold.

I watched him for ten minutes. He was slow but sure at what he did, so I went for coffee.

Using Sparky's radio set, the captain had been communicating with the harbor master's office about getting Highstone removed from the ship. When I went in for coffee, he sat at his table, drumming his fingers on the table top, a habit that had gotten annoying. "Do you know what they told me?" he said, a little too loud.

Without waiting for my response—we were alone— he continued: "'Civilians aren't our problem.' Imagine that—not their problem."

Figuring I should say something, I asked, "Why not, Captain?"

Snorting, he rubbed his nose, another annoying habit, then barked out a short "Hah! The lieutenant in charge says, and I quote, 'We got too many loonies of our own to deal with.'"

Hesitant to push it, not wanting the captain to take out his wrath on me, I stood there, silent.

The captain bowed his head almost to the table top and came up laughing. "What the hell. We're stuck with him, at least until Sattahip."

"You want to keep him locked up?"

"Hell, no. Put the sonofabitch to work. Let him earn his keep."

"Right now?"

"Is there a better time?"—giving me an "I thought you were smarter than that" look.

"Aye, aye, Captain." Setting my coffee cup in the sink, I went to find Boats. There was no way I would set Highstone loose without Boats being aware of it.

He was in the forward locker, straightening things out. Stepping through the door, the smell of paint and fish oil, a staple on every ship, enveloped me—strangely reassuring, giving me a sense of normalcy.

"Got bad news, Boats. The Army won't let us dump Highstone ashore here, so the captain wants him to work until we can get rid of him. I'm going to uncuff him. Where do you want him?"

Boats reached a huge hand and scratched the back of his head. "Send him up here. We'll have a little talk, make sure he knows how lucky he is to still be breathing."

We exchanged conspiratorial grins. "He'll be right along," and I went back out into the rain.

In the pilot cabin, before uncuffing him, I talked to Highstone. "This is real simple. We can't put you ashore here, so the captain wants you working. I'm handing you over to Boats. You'll work for him the rest of the time you're aboard. No watch standing, since we can't trust you to do it right. If you fuck up, if you get stoned or drunk or even piss off Boats, for any reason, you're back in irons and on the flying bridge. I don't care if it's a hurricane, you won't come down." Pausing, I took a deep breath. "You understand?"

He nodded.

"I can't hear anything rattling in that empty head of yours, and I don't read sign language. Answer me."

"Yeah, Mate," reluctant but docile, "I unnerstand."

"Turn around." Unlocking the cuffs, I said, "Boats is in the forward storage locker. Go find him. Don't stop to talk or take a piss or anything." I stepped aside, and he went past, careful not to bump me.

Returning to the salon, I poured a cup of coffee, sat in my seat, and pondered my role as tough guy. Lifting the cup, my hands shook. If they only knew how scared I got. For my sake, they better never find out.

Tuesday, March 21, 1967 at 1800 hours, we shifted from the stone ammo pier and moved to the #2 DeLong pier. By 2100 hours, we were secure alongside, again facing outward. Work would begin at 0700 tomorrow.

The DeLong pier had a better, wider work surface than the stone ammo pier, but the flatbed trucks still had to back down. The six-bys drove down and did a U-turn.

We started gangs at #1 hatch discharging pallets of MCI-rations; at #3 hatch discharging pallets of MCI-rations and crates of parts; and at #4 hatch discharging pallets of burlap bags, crated helicopter blades, ambulances, Jeeps, and small trailers. A different sergeant was in charge, but just as skilled and efficient as the one at the ammo pier. The gangs here worked in the same manner, slow but steady. Once things were moving, the stevedore sergeant and I discussed working the shore crane, since we had to use one to lift the heavy APCs and Commandos. The Army had a Linkbelt 100-ton crane, a dependable and durable piece of machinery. Adequate working space on the pier was the problem. The weight of the crane alone was a strain on the pier, but with steel plates under the outrigger shoes, it was doable.

The body of the truck crane is about forty feet long and had to be positioned far enough away from the side of the ship so it could fully extend its outriggers—which meant it had to be almost at right angles to the ship. That would allow for a safe operation. We calculated the length of boom needed to reach the mid-point of the hatch, then calculated the working range radius with the maximum load, which was the 27,000-pound Commando. None of this was the ship's responsibility, but the sergeant seemed a little unsure, and I didn't want the crane to come crashing down on the ship, so we worked it out together. We would set up the crane tomorrow at #3 hatch. The gang working at #1 could continue work, since they were using six-bys to move the cargo down the pier. A six-by could squeeze past the crane in the space left over. The heavy lifts would be a daytime-only operation, and that controlled the length of stay at the berth, so everything else would be daytime-only.

That night, I went to the bridge and watched the distant activity at the airfield through binoculars. I also watched the far end of the bay, where a tender for a small fleet of P-5 Marlin seaplanes lay at anchor. Three of them had flown in during the day. Even with the high winds, the end of the bay where they landed was accessible.

On the initial approach to the anchorage, I spotted a small Swift Boat base at the south end of the peninsula.

They were used to patrol the Delta. Swift Boats—officially, Patrol Craft Fast (PCF)— are the PT boats of this era, though smaller and slower. The PT boats had wooden hulls and the Swifts are aluminum hulls. One thing they have in common: courageous crews going into nasty places with mayhem on their minds.

The next morning, while it was still raining, they positioned the shore crane at #3 hatch and started discharging the Commandos from the lower tweendeck. They used two signalmen: one at the rail of the ship in line-of-sight of the crane operator, the other over the hatch, watching what happened there. The first two units discharged were slow. The space was tight. Once they got elbow room, they moved right along. A driver in the hatch would position a Commando in the square, jump out, and go get the next one, while they hooked up the one in the square. Once the load was clear of the hatch, he'd drive the next one into place.

In the meantime, the gang at #1 hatch kept discharging the pallets of MCI-rations onto the open backs of six-bys, squeezing by the truck crane and getting off-loaded at the transit sheds at the end of the pier. The gang at #4 hatch, using ship's gear, discharged the ambulances, Jeeps, and small trailers, half of which had to be jump-started. A few of the Jeeps had to be towed away.

Twice during the day, I spotted a Swift Boat idling past, crew on stations but relaxed. I waved at them. On the second boat, a crew member waved back. I thought of President Kennedy, killed a little over three years ago, and his time on a PT boat. I wished these guys luck, hoping they'd all make it home.

Greg had a cribbage board, and we played a few times, in between breaking up fights and trying to sleep. During one of our conversations in the middle of the Pacific, the topic of card games arose.

"The only game I play is cribbage," he said. "My dad taught me when I was a kid. Said it was the only civilized card game. Bridge was for snobs and poker for idiots."

I laughed. "I went from 'Go Fish' right to cribbage. My father played poker with the Democratic Ward 7 guys once a week, but cribbage was his favorite. I think I was five or six when I started playing."

After dinner that night, letting the beef stew the cook called Mechado settle in our bellies, Greg and I played cribbage, smoked, and drank coffee. While we played, I told him about seeing the Swift Boats and my concern for the crews.

He put the cards down, took a sip of coffee, and said, "We're pretty lucky, William. We're in a war zone getting paid bonus money for the risk of being here, but our risk is nothing compared to the guys in-country. We sleep in comfortable bunks, not the mud and rain. We eat good food, not the MCI-ration crap, and nobody's shooting at us or shelling us." He slowly shook his head. "I honestly don't know why we're here. I'm damn skeptical of the 'save the world from commies' line we get from Washington."

I had forgotten the entire crew got paid a war-zone bonus. Normally, the first mate would keep track of deck department overtime hours and time in the zone, but since we were shorthanded, the captain did all that. "You're right, Greg, we are lucky. A lot of guys I knew in Southie volunteered, and they're over here somewhere, if they're still alive. I gotta believe we're doing this for the right reasons, but I have doubts. Look at what happened in Korea. My brother was over there. That never ended.

"Yes, it did."

"No. It didn't. They signed an armistice agreement in July of 1953, three years after it started, but every day they stand and face each other at the DMZ straddling the 38th parallel, and anything could trigger it again. In Korea, we went to help South Korea when the North Korean army invaded. Here we are, fourteen years later, and no resolution. Here in Vietnam, no one invaded. This is a philosophical war, Capitalism against Communism. Vietnam is beginning to look like it's another Korea. No end and no way out."

"Sounds like you're as skeptical as me."

"No one's as skeptical as you." Smiling a rueful grin, I went on. "I want to believe what we're doing here is right. There's too many lives at stake for this to be a political stunt."

"Amen, William...Amen."

CHAPTER 40

Slow and steady, through incessant rain, sometimes in sheets, sometimes a mist with winds varying from ten to forty miles per hour, we slogged on, finishing unloading on Monday, March 27, 1967, at 1600 hours. The Army wanted us out of the berth. They had ten ships waiting at anchor, so the captain agreed to sail that night at 2000 hours.

The captain gave me a bottle of Scotch, Dewar's Black Label, to give to the sergeant. I don't know how he knew that Sarge was a Scotch drinker, but he hit it on the head. The sergeant's eyes lit up when I handed it to him.

"Thanks, Mate. This is hard to come by over here," he said, shaking my hand vigorously.

"Good working with you, Sarge. Stay safe."

Standing at the head of the gangway, I watched as he walked down, cradling his gift. He looked up and waved as he climbed into the waiting Jeep.

At 2000 hours, we stowed the gangway, singled up the mooring lines, and secured the hatches. Everything down below was soaked and would stay wet until we got out of the monsoon area.

Despite the rain, I was hot. Coming out of the harbor, we dropped the pilot and steered a course of 140 degrees, until we were abeam of and five miles off Mui Da Vach, relying on the radar all the way. We turned to course 193 degrees and steamed seventy-seven miles, reaching the island of Dau Phu Qui, keeping it five miles to starboard. The rain was easing, but the wind remained strong, fifteen miles per hour with gusts to twenty-five miles per hour. The quartering seas had us cork-screwing occasionally. The captain had pumped sea water into the ballast tanks of #1 and #2 hatches to bring the bow down. With the exception of the bombs in #5 hatch, we were empty.

A normal run would be just under two days. But the NavRep liaison in Cam Ranh Bay had notified the captain a berth wouldn't be available until Friday; so once again, the captain ordered us to creep along at eight knots, which would get us there at 0400 hours on Friday.

From Dau Phu Qui, we steered 214 degrees for one hundred and eighty-five miles down to latitude eight degrees north, and turned due west, following the latitude line for another two hundred and fifty-one miles. The rain had let up, and we got an occasional glimpse of the sun. The captain ordered all the cowl vents trimmed to windward, to start the drying out process.

Our target was a point in the middle of the Gulf of Thailand, which would keep us clear of the shoals and wrecks. We picked up the faint glimmer of the light at Hon Khoai, twenty-six miles away to starboard as we passed it. The final leg of three hundred and ten miles on course 330 degrees brought us to the turn-in point to Sattahip, seventeen miles south-southwest of Sattahip light. As we worked our way closer to shore, the incoming tidal current increased, as strong as three knots.

A ship occupied the berth, but, because of the extreme tidal currents running north and south, the captain didn't anchor. He cruised up and down offshore of Ko Khram island, twenty miles north, then south. Around 1400 hours, we were abreast of the pier when something exploded there. I reported it to the captain, and he came up and looked but couldn't figure it out. This pier was used exclusively for discharging bombs, but bombs don't explode if they have no fuze inserted, and it was forbidden to carry bombs with fuzes intact. What should have been an eight-hour delay in berthing became a twenty-four-hour delay. The captain lengthened our shuttle run to thirty miles.

When we picked up the pilot, it was close to high tide, and the current was less than one knot. The captain asked him what had happened yesterday with the explosion. His answer: "Bomb blow up!" No other explanation.

By the time we had docked, the tide was outgoing for an hour and was up to three knots. We were on the northern, inland side, so we were pressed against the pier. On the advice of the pilot, we doubled up the bow and stern lines. It was good advice.

The main port is to the south and around the corner from our pier, which is another DeLong pier jutting out perpendicular to the shore. Built for the purpose of handling munitions ships, it was far away from the other docks. The docks at the main port paralleled the shoreline, so the tide wasn't as big a factor when working there. The DeLong pier stuck out like the proverbial sore thumb, and the tide is brutal.

A lieutenant and a sergeant came aboard, the former green as grass and the latter a lifer. After introductions, the lieutenant was smart enough to let the sergeant do the talking. His name was Huey Long, and like his namesake, the politician, he hailed from Louisiana. There was one striking difference. The sergeant was black.

At that stage of my life, I ignored politics. I had never heard of Huey P. Long, Jr. Neither had I heard of his son, Russell Long, sitting U.S. senator from Louisiana, but I got an earful about both at lunch. The captain always invited the head stevedore to stay for lunch. This time both the lieutenant, whose name I never learned, and the sergeant whose I will never forget, took him up on his offer. When I led them in to the salon, Sergeant Long stopped, pointed at Greg sitting there, and asked, "You an officer?"

A little nonplussed, Greg warily responded, "Yes. I'm an engineer. Why?"

"Glad to see a brother getting ahead in the world, that's all."

Greg smiled. "Well, 'brother,' are you staying for lunch?"

"That I am."

Pointing to the seat across from him, Greg introduced himself and said, "Have a seat." Sergeant Long sat.

I took my usual seat, at the table next to Greg, and told the lieutenant to sit opposite me, next to Sergeant Long. I took their orders and called them down to the galley. Greg asked Sergeant Long, "How did you get such an infamous name?"

"Infamous? That depends on your point of view. Senator Huey Pierce Long, Jr. was a hell-raiser, but he fought for the poor folks, and my daddy was poor. Daddy told me he was a good man, so he was a good man."

Greg snorted, "He was a white, southern senator from Louisiana, a state not known for lending a helping hand to black people."

"That's where you're wrong, Mr. Engineer. Most southern politicians, yeah, I'll agree with you; but not Huey P. Long, Jr.," and he related how, as governor and U.S. senator, Huey P. Long, Jr. pushed for the rights of the little guy, the poor folks, and how his son—the current sitting U.S. senator, Russell Long—was following in his daddy's footsteps.

I sat there, fascinated, while this sergeant gave us a history lesson. Even Greg's cynicism got pared back a touch when Sergeant Long exposed Greg's stereotyping of the southern politician.

By the end of lunch, we had been tutored on the "rightness" of wealth distribution and how "wrong" it was for the upper levels of society to control all the wealth. An ideological point of view at odds with mine.

Greg and I sat talking after the sergeant and lieutenant left. "He's an interesting guy," I said. "I never heard of Huey P. Long, Jr., or his son until today."

"He is interesting, that's for sure. I knew who the Longs were, but I don't buy his 'distribute the wealth' theory. No one's entitled to take what someone else earned."

"I agree. I might be guilty of envy, but I want to get what 'they' have by working for it. Nobody owes me anything. I just want a chance to earn it."

Greg chuckled. "I'm not sure he really believes everything he's saying, but he tells a good story."

"I knew your cynicism would resurrect itself."

"It's justified. There's still a difference between you and me. We both want a chance to earn it, but doors open faster and easier for those white hands"—he reached out and tapped my right hand— "than it does for these," he finished, holding out both of his hands.

With no defense to his statement and no inclination to create one, I nodded.

Standing on the offshore, forward end of #5 hatch, I watched them manhandle the packaged bombs, slinging the belly wires and hoisting them to the pier, where they landed them on six-bys modified into flat-beds. Sergeant Long walked aft from the gangway, and I went inshore to join him.

"Sergeant, no one yet has told us what blew up the other day. I see a piece of cap-log missing on the pier, and the caisson has a few good size dents in it. Care to explain?"

"Well, Mate, it's like this. Someone fucked up big time, but no one knows who, or if they do, they ain't saying."

I waited for him to continue, not knowing where the story was going.

"Two-hundred-and-fifty-pound bombs don't explode all by themselves. They need help. It's called a fuze. It's damn obvious when a bomb has a fuze in it, and when it don't. There's no way that bomb got loaded, carried all this way, and discharged without someone seeing it was different from all the other bombs. By my reckoning, some ignorant dipshit in the ground crew here thought it would be funny to stick a fuze in a bomb— maybe make some of his buddies nervous."

"You think someone did it as a joke?"

"I do. Can't prove nothin'. The only reason no one got hurt is because it rolled off the flatbed where no gangs were working. It blew the back end of the truck to hell, damaged the pier some, and the driver needed new skivvies after he shit himself, but that's all the damage." He shook his head and murmured, "Hmmmm, mmmm! Kinda makes you believe in fate. If it ain't your time to die, it ain't your time."

The tide had turned and was pulling the ship off the pier. When the distance between the ship and pier reached three feet, every mooring line was taut and humming. The sergeant called for the tugs to stand by and halted the off-loading operation. "They're already too many bombs sitting on the bottom here; don't want to drop no more." The tugs arrived within twenty minutes, lay their bows against the side of the ship, and pushed.

With the ship almost empty, it was easier for the tugs to push against the tide. Unfortunately, the wind from the south, same direction as the tide, pushed against the freeboard, like a mainsail. The tugs stayed there and pushed for the next eight hours. The captain was convinced we would have snapped the mooring lines if it weren't for the tugs.

When we first arrived, the captain went ashore and, via telephone, queried the NavRep liaison, who was in Bangkok, to see if he could get rid of Highstone. No such luck. Apparently, if we were in Bangkok, they could take him off our hands; but we had no way of getting him to Bangkok, so we were stuck with him.

The last day—overcast sky, eighty-eight degrees, 99% humidity—and the sergeant, having lunch with us, was relating a story he heard, maybe rumor, about a possible mutiny. "It's those Navy pukes. They gotta guard the pipeline, and they're getting bit by snakes."

"Snakes?" Greg said and shuddered. He hates snakes.

"They got over thirty kinds of poison snakes here, and a whole bunch of other kinds. It seems the snakes were biting the swabbies who were watching over the pipeline."

"What pipeline?" I asked.

"There's a pipeline, carrying mainly jet fuel, that runs from the port to U-Tapao Royal Thai Navy Airfield. Runs through the middle of nowhere. The southern section is patrolled by a detachment stationed at the naval base.

They been expanding that airfield for over a year now. The Air Force flies KC-135 tankers out of there, refueling the flyboys. Anyhow, rumor has it the swabbies refused to go out in the jungle. Regular mutiny. Ain't heard nothin' beyond the rumors." Before he went back out on deck, he said, "Too bad you boys ain't gonna be in town longer. Coulda got you set up for a couple days in Bangkok. Good looking women, cheap booze, a good time all around. Maybe next trip."

We finished cargo operations at 2000 hours that night, too late to make the slack tide so we waited until 0500 hours the next morning.

CHAPTER 41

Completely overcast. No rain but with 84 degrees temperature and humidity at 98%. The wind at 9 mph from the south. Gentle four-foot rollers from the south.

We sailed at slack tide. The pilot wouldn't do it any other time. After seeing how hard the tugboats had to work to hold us on the pier at the midpoint of the tidal run, the captain wasn't about to argue. Both tugboats pushed us hard against the pier while we let go the lines. As the last line let go, with less than one knot current, they backed down and pulled us off the pier.

As soon as the tugs backed down, the pilot put engines at half astern, and we glided into the stream. The aft tug stopped pulling and the forward tug started pushing, straightening the ship on a southerly heading. Once we had headway, both tugs released. The after tug approached where we had the Jacob's ladder set up. Ten minutes later, the pilot climbed down the Jacob's ladder to the tugboat.

Sitting high in the water, with just enough ballast to keep most of the propeller under water, we reversed our course and headed for the northern tip of Luzon. From there, we'd head for the Panama Canal.

We were heading home.

Even though none of the crew had gotten ashore in Sattahip, the captain wanted to do a raid for drugs. In his cabin, three hours after dropping off the pilot, we discussed it.

"Everyone seems to be calmed down, Captain. Even Highstone's been behaving himself. Won't this just rile the crew up?"

"There's something you're missing, William."

"What's that, sir?"

"They're only quiet because they don't have drugs to stir them up."

"Isn't that what I just said?"

"Yes, but why don't they have drugs? Because the first engineer wouldn't sell them any. Have you forgotten who the worm in the apple is?"

"Yeah, I had, but more of a snake than a worm…He won't keep the stuff in his cabin. The man isn't stupid. Maybe he has it hidden somewhere in the engine room. That's the only place he can go without anyone questioning why he's there."

"Maybe I should talk to the chief."

"I thought you already had talked to him?" My accusatory tone was obvious by the captain's arched eyebrow. Knowing I'd gone a step too far, I kept going. "The chief may not be too reliable, right now. Have you noticed how many breath mints he takes?"

Expecting a bite, I didn't even get a bark from him. He smiled. "I'm an alcoholic. I know all about breath mints."

"Sorry, Captain, I'm a little frustrated."

"Go ask the chief to come and see me. You come back, too."

Fifteen minutes later, sitting in the captain's cabin with the door closed, he didn't waste any time.

"Chief, I need to know if I can count on you. If you remember, I told you before that if you got drunk, I'd fire you. Heard you've been having halitosis problems lately. Bad teeth or alcohol?"

Wesley Gibson looked at the captain, but he was smiling. I expected him to be pissed off. "Breath mints kill the taste of Listerine. I've had a gum infection that comes and goes. Listerine controls it." He nodded at the captain and gave me a sideways, "Any smart-ass questions?" look.

"Good, that's settled, because I need your help. Your first engineer"—stressing the "your"—has been selling drugs to the crew. You have any inkling of this?"

The chief pursed his lips. "You asking me for help, or implying I'm in on it?"

"Asking for help, Chief."

"Okay. I have no proof, but I suspected he was up to no good when our happy-go-lucky Swede, the second engineer, asked me what the first was selling. The second is a likeable square-head, too gullible for his own good. Apparently, he saw the first dealing with one of the crew.

370

When he asked what he was doing, the first told him he was selling candy. When he asked to buy some, the first said he just ran out. Upon reflection, Ingvar, that's his name, decided it didn't look like candy, so he came to see me."

"When was that?" The captain asked.

The chief rubbed his chin, cogitating. "When we were at Subic Bay."

"William," the captain ordered, "tell the chief what you witnessed."

Relating the incident in the crew mess, I said, "It was obvious to me, the first is the primary supplier to the crew." The chief didn't say anything, so I continued. "I think he's stashed his stuff somewhere in the engine room. Any suggestions as to where that might be? No one knows the engine room better than you."

More rubbing of his chin. "I can't think of anyplace off the top of my head, but maybe we can flush him out."

I leaned forward, "Flush him out, how?"

"It'll have to be during the twelve-to-four watch, when Greg is on duty." Looking at the captain, he said, "I know you trust Greg as back-up to your boy-wonder here, so I presume he'll cooperate."

Not appreciating the "boy-wonder" remark nor the smirk that accompanied it, I let it pass.

The chief continued, nodding at me. "Let it be known you're going to search the crew quarters, then the engine room. He won't care about his cabin, but he may try to move it out of the engine room…if it's there. Greg will be on watch and can keep an eye on the control areas, and I'll hide in the upper reaches of the boiler, where I can see down into a few areas without being seen. It's a long shot, but what the hell."

I waited for the captain to react. When he nodded his head, I said, "Why not? I'll get the word out at lunch tomorrow, just before noon."

A bit later, I asked Greg to come and see me on the bridge when he got off watch. He stepped inside just as the clock sounded eight bells. Leading him to the port bridge wing, I explained what would happen tomorrow. He smiled, a cold smile. "I'd love to see that jerk get what's coming to him. See you tomorrow."

"By the way, the chief says he takes the breath mints to take away the bad taste of Listerine. He takes that for a gum infection."

"And you believed him?" he scoffed, as he walked away.

It turned out to be easier than anyone thought. The captain was covering my watch on the bridge. I used Boats as the prop for the message. Standing outside the crew mess, knowing Highstone sat just inside the door, I told Boats, in a stage whisper, we'd be raiding the crew quarters starting at noon, and then searching the engine room.

Walking aft, I leaned against the bulkhead on the aft cross passageway, just behind the engine room door, my walkie-talkie in hand. Both Greg and the chief had walkie-talkies, too. Now we waited.

I heard the door open and peeked around the corner, in time to see Highstone going into the engine room.

On the inside of the fiddly casing, six feet above the door, a metal walkway ran along for twenty feet, providing work access to the upper parts of the boilers. Plywood sheets lay on the walkways so anyone below couldn't see if someone stood directly above them. The chief, Gibson, reported over his walkie-talkie that he had seen Greg go down to relieve the first a few minutes ago. Now he watched Highstone work his way down the ladders. At the bottom, Highstone ran into the first coming up and leaned in, yelling something to him. It was impossible to hear with all the noise. The first responded and pointed up the ladder. Highstone climbed up and exited the engine room.

The first watched until the door shut behind Highstone, then looked over his shoulder in the direction of the control board. Satisfied Greg didn't see him, he went forward a few steps then bent over and lifted one of the diamond-plate floorboards from the walkway. Sliding it forward, he rested it on the abutting section of diamond-plate, then jumped down into the bilge. When he jumped, the chief, eyeballing him the whole time, climbed down from his perch. Keying the walkie-talkie, he asked, "You hear me?"

Nothing from Greg, but I responded. "I hear you."

"He went into the bilges. I'm going down there."

"I'm right behind you," I said and ran up the passageway.

There was no easy way to get to the forward end of the boilers, so the chief positioned himself aft of the walkway opening and behind the evaporator casing, peering between two insulated pipes. Looking up, he saw me come down the ladder from the entrance door and waved at me to stop, pointing at the opening to the bilge. I nodded and stepped back from the ladder, partly hidden by ten-inch insulated steam pipes. Together we waited.

The first's head popped up, scanning the area, then dropped again. When he emerged, he carried an oil-stained knapsack and tossed it onto the deck plating before climbing out. Replacing the diamond-plate, he turned to get the knapsack. The chief stood there, holding it.

Surprise, fear, anger, and cunning—all flitted across the first's face while he stood there. "Hey, Chief," he shouted, doing his best to look innocent, "what are you doing here?"

The chief lifted the bag and yelled, "This yours?"

Momentarily stumped, not knowing to admit it or bluff his way through, he said, "Yeah, thanks," and reached for the knapsack.

The chief jerked his hand back, shaking his head. That's when the first lunged at him. The first is six feet tall, two hundred solid pounds. The chief is five foot six inches, twenty pounds lighter, and over twenty years older. It was no contest. The first threw a roundhouse left and caught Gibson on the temple. The chief stumbled

374

back and fell, banging his head on the pipes. The walkie-talkie flew out of his hand along the deck plate toward the control platform. The knapsack dropped onto the deck plate.

Bending over, the first looked at the chief, then picked up the knapsack and straightened just as Greg hit him with a flying headbutt, flattening the nose I had flattened a month ago. He went down hard with Greg on top, flailing away. By the time I pulled Greg off him, he was out cold, his face a bloody pulp.

I turned my attention to the chief and helped him sit up. He was dazed but functioning. Greg had a lump on his forehead, and both hands had knuckle cuts.

"You okay? I asked him.

"Better than that motherfucker," he said, pointing at the inert first engineer.

"I'm going to get the steward and Boats to help here. Keep an eye on the chief," and I ran up the ladder.

Ten minutes later, Andrew had checked the chief for a concussion and decided he was okay. He told Greg to put ice on his forehead and knuckles, then tended to the first, who was sitting on the deck, leaning against the railing, blood covering his shirt front. Boats stood guard over the first, but there was no fight left in him.

"I didn't know what was happening until I saw the walkie-talkie skitter along the deck plate," Greg said. "When I looked up and saw the chief down, I kinda flipped out."

"I'm glad you did," I said. "Now there's someone else they can call 'the enforcer,' take the attention off me."

Andrew waved at me, needing help with the first. Boats stood him up, and I preceded him backwards up the ladder with Boats pushing from behind. He was conscious, but really out of it. We got him to his cabin and into his bunk, sitting up against the bulkhead. Andrew didn't want him lying down. Too much blood clogging his nose. I thanked Boats and told him to take the rest of the day off.

He laughed. "Ain't got nothin' to do right now, anyway."

I explained everything to the captain in his office. The chief came in and repeated his version of the story.

"This complicates things," the captain said. "I was only going to toss his stuff overboard so he couldn't sell it. With him assaulting you," looking at Gibson, "I've got no choice but to write this up."

"What's to write about?" the chief said. "It's not the first time I've been punched, but I hope it's the last. I'll survive. He's the one who got the shit kicked out of him. His face looks like a strawberry marshmallow. You got his bag of drugs. Sounds like a win-win to me."

The captain gave him an astonished look, then smiled. "You sly old dog. You don't want to have to stand his watches if I lock him up, do you?"

"Let me talk to him, tomorrow, when he can think straight. Okay?"

The captain stood, walked around his desk, and shook the chief's hand. "He's all yours, Chief."

CHAPTER 42

At noon on Thursday we were running north along the coast of Luzon, approaching the top end of the island, where we would turn east. We had not done any weather-mapping since initially entering the South China Sea inbound to Subic Bay. The captain had relied on local weather reports that Sparky picked up. The plan was to start downloading the weather data once we were clear of Luzon and headed into the Pacific. Most of the information we received came from ships at sea and routed through the National Weather Service. It was raw data—atmospheric pressure, wind direction and speed, cloud cover, temperature, humidity, and precipitation. We also got isobar details and could create our own charts, a boring process. Since we didn't plan on starting our tracking until clear of Luzon, Sparky didn't pass along anything other than the local weather reports.

Turning the corner at the top of Luzon, the clouds were increasing and the barometer dropping. The wind shifted inexorably from the east, backing to the northeast. Sixty miles out from Luzon—with the wind at thirty-five miles per hour and gusting higher, seas up to fifteen feet, supplemented by slightly higher rollers, and rain coming in irregular bands—the captain was nervous. He ordered Boats to check all the hatch tarps and secure any loose gear.

Too late to download the daily weather data—which was always twenty-four hours behind actual conditions, anyway—the captain asked Sparky to raise the weather station in Luzon. Six hours later—with the wind from the north at seventy miles per hour, seas up to twenty-five feet and cresting, we got the local report.

We were in the teeth of Typhoon Violet.

Typhoons in the North Pacific rotate counter-clockwise. If you face the wind, the center of the storm will be to your right. That meant we were heading straight into the eye of the storm.

On the bridge, the captain stood forward, peering through the rotating rain screen, holding onto the rail. The rain blotted out everything, and visibility was such that he couldn't see the bow at times. I came out of the chart room after marking our dead reckoning position and stood beside the captain, while the ship rolled a constant twenty to twenty-five degrees. The helmsman, Winkler, worked the wheel hard, keeping us on course. The ship pitched, but only about ten feet.

"William, we're going to have to turn into the wind if the seas get any higher. The problem is, with the ship so high in the water, when we do go head on the screw will be popping out of the water." The captain had maxed out the usable ballast tanks, and we couldn't get any deeper.

He leaned his head against the windscreen frame. "Call the engine room. Drop speed to seventy-five revolutions. Warn them about the possibility of the propeller catching air."

I timed the roll, leaped to the bulkhead, braced myself, and called down. The chief engineer answered.

"Chief," I shouted—the roar of the wind and crashing seas making it difficult to hear, so instinctively I raised my voice. "Drop the speed down to seventy-five revolutions. If we have to turn into the wind, she's going to slam a lot and the prop may come out of the water."

"Gotcha," Gibson shouted back. "Gimme a heads-up when you're turning."

"Will do." I hung up. Again, timing the roll, I slithered across the deck and grabbed the rail. "The chief is down there."

The captain nodded. "Figured he would be."

For an hour, we stood there, clinging to the rail, listening to the groans of the ship as the metal strained and twisted. The ship rolled, and a heavy wind gust hung her on her side for what seemed forever. I couldn't see the inclinometer, but I was sure it was more than thirty-five degrees. When the ship shuddered and started to return upright, the captain said, "That's enough. Let the chief know we're turning."

When I reached the phone, the captain ordered Winkler to bring her up into the wind. Now it was a waiting game. At first, the captain tried to make headway, working northward to get away from the oncoming eye, but the pitching got too violent and he was forced to slow down. The bow would rise, sniffing the air, then plunge into the next wave, lifting the stern out of the water, propeller biting nothing but salt air, emitting a '*whhhm, whhhm, whhhm*' sound that scratched at our nerves like fingers on a chalkboard.

For ten hours we danced on the wave tops, slamming the bow into the waves and feeling the shudders and vibrations every time as the stern lifted. Each time we dipped into the sea, a solid wall of spray would join the already thick salt spume and smack into the bridge. Giving up on making forward headway, the captain dropped the revolutions down to fifty. We couldn't maintain steerage way at any less. The chief's biggest worry was the engine speeding up when the prop was out of the water. Fifty revolutions seemed to be the optimal speed, but I suspect the chief had his hand on the throttle all the time.

We changed the watch. The captain had instructed the chief steward to secure the galley, so no hot food was available. The cook had made sandwiches and managed to brew a pot of coffee. At the captain's request, he delivered sandwiches to the bridge, wrapped in napkins—a tricky feat considering you needed both hands to hang on.

When I came back on watch—after spending five hours wide awake, spread-eagled on my bunk, grabbing at the rail—the wind had shifted, moving to the north-northeast. This was good news. Using the "face-it-and-look-right rule," it meant we were in the northwest quadrant of the storm and the eye was dropping back and to our right. Whether we were moving away from the eye, or it was moving away from us, it was good news.

We maintained headway making about one knot, barely more than steerageway, for the next fourteen hours, following the wind and waves as they worked around to the east. The captain put us back on our original course thirty hours after heaving to.

The highest gust we recorded was ninety miles per hour. The highest sea, purely an estimate, was forty feet, and the lowest barometer reading was 935 millibars. Everyone had bruised elbows, shoulders, and knees from banging into bulkheads and railings, but we were afloat and alive to tell about it.

With the first engineer's stash of drugs ditched over the side, there was no artificial stimulation to cause the crew members to act up. Now they relied solely on their oddball personalities and quirks, and again, Highstone stirred the pot.

After having his "talk" with the chief engineer, the first engineer agreed to do and say nothing, in exchange for the captain not recording the incident in the ship's log. His conversations with Greg, when they changed the watch, were short, barely civil. Greg didn't care. He took the high road, knowing what he had done was justified. Word got back to me through Boats that the first engineer blamed Highstone, thinking he had set him up when he warned him about the engine room search. He had, just not knowingly.

Since rounding Luzon, we had been slogging our way back for five days. Uneventful days, except for the growing sense I had made a mistake leaving Meg the way I did back in South Africa. With no distractions, she hovered in my mind constantly...red hair, infectious smile.

One recurring image of her—hovering over me, hair hanging down, eyes closed, beatific smile on her face as we made love—was like a poster. Everywhere I turned, I saw her—tantalizing, alluring, painful.

Boredom reigned. Inactivity gave me too much time to think and brood. Every night I dreamt of Meg, waking up with a hard-on or wet underwear. What was she doing? Did she have any regrets or second thoughts? Had she moved on and found another guy? Being on a ship in the middle of the Pacific reduced my options to nothing. On land, I could call her and test the water, or jump on a plane and surprise her. It was frustrating to have so many damn questions and no answers, and I realized I desperately needed answers.

One night, I dreamt Highstone was trying to throw Meg overboard, and I couldn't get to her. He made her stand on the railing. I grabbed for my gun. As he reached to push Meg, in desperation I aimed and pulled the trigger. Highstone turned and laughed as the blood spread over Meg's chest. Reaching out her arms for me, she fell, and I woke up screaming, in a sweat.

I ran to the head and threw up. On my knees, I sobbed. It was a nightmare, but the pain of killing Meg clawed at me, visceral and real.

I rinsed my face and went back to bed, sitting up, afraid to fall asleep.

Twenty-one more nights faced me until Panama. Those nights were interminable. The days, when the sun shone, were bearable, and I was barely civil. When it rained, my mood soured even more and people avoided me—even Greg. The captain still insisted I carry the gun, and I admitted I felt naked without it. My paranoia was rising. I'm sure it would be cured when I found that everyone really did dislike or fear me.

CHAPTER 43

Two days out from the Panama Canal the captain called me, Greg, and the chief engineer to his cabin.

"Gentlemen, we need to get our stories straight. I don't know if the Coast Guard will come aboard in Panama, or wait until we arrive in New York, but we need to be prepared."

"Other than about the first engineer, I don't have anything to tell," the chief said. "He slipped on oil and smashed his face into the casing when changing burner tips. It's simple and no one can dispute it." Looking at Greg, he lifted his eyebrows, looking for assent.

"That's the story we agreed on. I found him that way when I came down to change the watch."

"What about the oiler or wiper on his watch?" the captain asked.

"They weren't there. All they know is what we told them."

"Okay. William and I have to deal with the Smithfield and Punser situation." Looking at the chief, he said, "Luckily, William had the presence of mind to not tell the Navy inquiry officer that the first engineer had contributed to Smithfield's mental state by bugging the shit out of him."

The look on Gibson's face caused Greg to interject, "It's true, Chief. He hounded Smithfield. He'd come down when I was on watch and follow Smithfield, bitching about everything he did."

"Sonofabitch…maybe we should reconsider letting him off the hook."

The captain stared at him. "Ultimately, that's your call, Chief, but we've had the story out there for a month. Changing it could open up other issues." I knew he was thinking of the problems of doctoring the ship's log if the story changed.

"Nah, let it go."

"So," I asked, "the only one we're pressing on is Highstone?"

"He's been logged for his behavior. I see no reason to give him a break," replied the captain.

We sat silent for a minute, each contemplating what had to be done and, equally important, not done.

"Of course," the captain said, looking at me, "*you* also have the Joselito shooting to deal with."

I didn't like the *you.*

"You mean *we* have to deal with it. All three of you were witnesses to what happened. The steward, too."

"Yes, of course," the captain said. "We all have to deal with it."

I learned later that, at the same time, in the crew mess, Highstone was whining to Boats.

"I'm the only one chipping decks. Why can't the other guys do it?"

"Because I told you to do it. When we get to New York, your days of chipping paint will be over. You're gonna lose your seamen's ticket for the shit you've pulled."

"Yeah, well I won't be the only one. I'll tell them you and that asshole Connolly took Punser's stash for yourselves. The same way you took the first engineer's stash, after you beat him up."

Boats wanted to smash him against the bulkhead, but opted for, "Get back to work."

That afternoon, he came to the bridge and told me what Highstone had threatened to do.

"It's our word against his, Boats, so I wouldn't worry about it. The captain can vouch for the fact we turned over the drugs to him, and then tossed them overboard."

"Yeah, he can, but will he? He didn't look in the lifeboat, we did. He didn't toss the shit overboard, you did. If he gets cold feet, we get screwed."

"He won't get cold feet, he'll tell it right," I insisted, not feeling as sure as I hoped I sounded.

"It woulda been easier if that little shit had jumped overboard, like he promised."

That thought stuck with me.

The next afternoon, a day out from the Canal, the weather was perfect, only a slight breeze and two- foot waves. Walking around, stretching my legs, I looked aft and saw Boats and Highstone on the fantail. Boats was pointing up to the top of the flagstaff where we would fly the flag when in port. Highstone seemed to be arguing with Boats. Finally, Highstone climbed up on the top railing, holding onto the flagstaff with one hand while reaching and pulling on the halyard with his free hand. It must have been stuck.

I saw Boats reach up to Highstone and I lowered my gaze. When I looked again, Highstone was gone. Boats was looking over the stern to the ship's wake. He stood there for thirty seconds and I stood where I was, not moving, for the same thirty seconds.

Then Boats turned. He looked up and saw me watching him. He took a few hurried steps toward me and waved his arms, shouting, "Man overboard."

I walked into the bridge, and said, "Get on the wheel," to the helmsman. The ship was on autopilot. Calling down to the engine room, I told them to go to maneuvering speed, we had a man overboard, then ordered a Williamson Turn and called the captain.

We followed our own wake back for three miles, with lookouts posted on the bow and bridge wings. There was no sign of Highstone. The captain radioed to the Canal and informed them we were searching for a crew member. They, in turn, sent a notice to mariners requesting any ships in the area join in the search. At dusk, a Greek freighter appeared, following our original track. They contacted us by radio and said they'd been looking ever since they got notice, and hadn't seen anyone.

By 1930, it was full dark, and the Greek called and asked us if we wanted them to stay. The captain thanked them and told them we were calling off the search for the night. We would continue in the morning, but they were free to leave. The Greek wished us luck, and we watched his stern light fade into the distance.

By 0600 we had enough light to begin the search again. The captain calculated the current drift, and we moved a little north, tracking back and forth over a four-mile stretch. At noon, he gave up.

"William, set course for the Canal. I'll have Sparky let them know we're calling off the search."

The captain called me down to his cabin at 1000 hours, sending George, the third mate to cover for me. When I walked in, Boats stood in front of the captain's desk.

"Okay, Boats, for the record: Tell me what happened."

"We were doing odds and ends stuff, and the halyard was stuck in the flagstaff. I told Highstone to climb up on the rail and free it up. He was pulling on it when he slipped and fell into the wake. I never saw him come up."

"That's it?"

"Yes, Captain, there ain't no more to tell."

"William, you have anything to add?"

"No, sir. I looked back aft as Boats was running and calling "man overboard." Then I called the engine room and you, and performed a Williamson Turn. You know the rest."

"Okay, thank you. Both of you. That will be all."

I followed Boats down the passageway. "Just one thing, Boats. The flagstaff is hinged at the bottom. You could have pulled the pin and lowered it, instead of having him climb on the rail."

He stopped, turned, smiled, and said, "Never thought of that." Then walked away.

Boats pushed Highstone, I know it, but no one cares—so why should I rock the boat? The bosun and I are in the same boat, literally and figuratively. Will it sink?

What now? What will I face in the hearings when we return? There has to be hearings. Too much shit happened for the Coast Guard to sweep this under the rug. Only trustworthy guy on board is Greg. Will the captain stand-up for me or let me be the scapegoat?

If I get through the hearings, do I look for another ship? Do I go to Africa to salvage my relationship? Do I even care?

YES! That's one answer I'm sure of. I still care. For Meg, for my career, for my future.

But...have I changed so much because of this trip that Meg won't see me as the same person? And have I really changed...or just exposed the real me?

CHAPTER 44

We never heard a word from the Coast Guard in Panama, so I presumed we would get word when we hit the first U.S. port.

The transit through the Canal was uneventful, except for the mail drop. We were still on charter to the MSTS, so they gathered any mail for the crew and dumped it on the ship at a time and place convenient to the FPO, Fleet Post Office. The Canal Zone was a convenient spot, and a mail bag was delivered, coming aboard at the first lock.

Three letters. Two from Ma—and one from Meg. Delivered to Ma's address, she had forwarded it along with her second letter.

Holding it gingerly, apprehensive, I carried it to lunch, unopened.

Greg said, "What's the matter?"

"Why?"

"You look like you've seen a ghost."

Holding up the letter, I announced, "It's from Meg."

"I'll be damned. What does she have to say?"

"Don't know," I said quietly. "I haven't opened it."

"Well, what the hell are you waiting for? It can't be too bad. You already got the bad news leaving South Africa. Open it."

Fumbling with the envelope, I tore it open, and unfolded the letter.

A single sheet, light green, smelling faintly of num-num's, the plum bush at her mother's place outside of Durban. That was the smell I remember when we had made love with the windows open. Now, shivering while thinking of it, I started to read.

It was dated a month after I last saw her.

Dearest William:

I miss you so much. I long for you to hold me, kiss me, make love to me, laugh with me. I have never been so happy as when you were with me and so miserable with you gone.

I made a terrible mistake when I left you in Cape Town. You said you would return, but remembering my last words, I feel I've made the gap too wide to cross…

She had said, "We'll have to see how it goes"— diffident at best.

You made it clear that I would have to choose between Mum and you…

I had said, "Your mother is your problem, not mine."

I've chosen. Please come back to me.

I love my Mum but now realize I can't let her control my life. She's happy here with her new husband Mark while I have nothing but memories. As much as I love it here on the farm, it's her life and not mine. I want to come to the States with you, marry you and raise our child there.

All my love,

Meg

"I haven't seen that big a smile in a long time," Greg said. "Must be good news."

"Yeah, it is." I tried to speak calmly, while my heart pounded. "She wants me to come back."

"To live in South Africa? With apartheid?"

"Nope. She'll come to the States."

"Yeah!" Greg yelled. "That's more like it! I'm happy for you, William."

Throughout this, the captain sat at his table, listening, saying nothing. Now he chimed in.

"She must be quite a lady, the way you two are excited."

Greg replied, "Yessir, Captain, she really is quite a lady. William is a lucky man."

I leaned back in the seat, took a deep breath, then read the letter again…

I can't believe it. She wants to come to the States, and get married and raise our kids here. . . Wait. She didn't say children, she said "child." I love her, but is she asking me to come back because she's pregnant? Why did she say child instead of children? In Cape Town, she told me she'd thought about not using the IUD but couldn't bring herself to do it.

Did she?

As we approached the pilot station at Jacksonville on Saturday, May 6, 1967, one hundred and six days after sailing from New York., I breathed a sigh of relief. It had seemed a lifetime.

Twenty miles away from the station, the captain received orders from the company to divert to New York. We would go to anchor there pending further instructions. The ship owner didn't care, since they get paid every day on charter to MSTS.

Who was ordering the ship to wait? Were we waiting for a berth to open up, or was the Coast Guard putting us on hold?

Now I had decisions to make. Get off in New York and find another ship? Any tramp steamer going to Vietnam would most likely have crew problems similar to what we faced. I had no desire to repeat this trip from hell.

Could I get a ship running to Africa? Would MorMac take me back after all that happened on the 'Pride? Did I really want to go to South Africa?

Did I really want to get on another ship, at all? I had to, because of my service obligation. I had to sail a minimum of nine months out of twelve, for three consecutive years, to avoid being called up in the draft—

or I could go active duty, since I have a U.S. Naval Reserve commission. But the allure was gone. Now that I'd seen Vietnam, even from the safety of the ship, I didn't want to go in-country, for any reason.

An hour later we received another message, informing us there would be a formal Coast Guard hearing convened when we arrived in New York. We knew it was inevitable, but hearing it officially announced sent a shiver down my back.

A door that was shut had been reopened with Meg's letter. Should I walk through it, or slam it shut again? Would I have a choice? Would the hearing now shut other doors on me, permanently?

Three days later, on Tuesday, May 9, at 0800 hours we anchored in New York, awaiting a berth at Bayonne. After clearing Customs and Immigration, a Coast Guard lieutenant came aboard and met with the captain. Four hours later, they emerged from the captain's office and gathered the entire crew in the salon for an announcement.

"Gentlemen," the lieutenant began. "There will be an inquiry held next Monday, May 15 at 0900 hours in the Coast Guard headquarters building, pertaining to the events that occurred during your last voyage. The following persons are hereby commanded to attend: Captain Johnston, Chief Engineer Gibson, First Engineer Harrison, Second Mate Connolly, Third Engineer Russell, Bosun Gaithers, and Chief Steward Casano. You are not and will not be released from Articles and will remain on board until further notice, except to attend the inquiry." Turning to the captain, he continued. "The ship owners have been notified, and the ship will remain at anchor until further notice."

The captain nodded, then said, "Starting at 1600 hours, a launch service will provide shuttle service every four hours until midnight for those crew members who are permitted to go ashore. It will start again at 0800 hours tomorrow morning. That will be all."

CHAPTER 45

Monday, May 15, 1967.

The presiding officer, a U.S. Coast Guard commander, had explained the process to the group assembled. He was the only U.S. Coast Guard officer there, unlike a trial, where a panel of at least three officers acting as judges are necessary.

Outside, waiting in the corridor for it to begin, the captain had explained this wasn't a "Perry Mason" trial. No jury, no prosecutor, no showboat, last-minute theatrics, just the hearing officer.

The commander called the captain to the witness stand. The clerk, a yeoman, swore in the captain, and the commander began.

"Captain Johnston, this hearing is for the sole purpose of determining if any of your actions or inactions, or those of the other attendees, during the voyage on the *SS West Way III* during the period January 25, 1967, through May 9, 1967, were detrimental to the welfare of the crew and/or endangered the safety of the crew and ship. Do you understand you are entitled to have an attorney present?"

"Yes, Commander, I do. I choose to not use an attorney."

"Very well. I have a number of questions for you. Since the captain is the only one allowed access to firearms on Merchant Marine ships, did you authorize

Temporary Second Mate Connolly to carry a gun at all times, and if so, why did you do so?"

"Yes, Commander, I did," and he explained the problems with drugs and drinking and the behavior and fighting of many of the crew. Then he added, "I supplied the gun."

"Did you authorize, at various times, locking crew members Highstone and Punser to the railing of the flying bridge, being exposed to the weather, and denying them food and water and bathroom privileges?"

"I authorized locking them on the flying bridge because of their dangerous and disruptive behavior. We were in the middle of the Pacific Ocean in warm weather. My other order was they be given water every two hours. When they sobered up enough to eat food and utilize the bathroom, they were allowed to do so."

Close enough to the truth, I thought, and the only witnesses were dead.

"Did you fail to follow standard rescue procedures when a crew member, Mr. Highstone, fell overboard?"

"No, Commander. The mate on watch at the time, Mr. Connolly, immediately executed a Williamson Turn, notified the engine room to reduce to maneuvering speed, and notified me. I set lookouts and notified the Canal authority, then coordinated the search with a Greek vessel that was in the area. We did everything we could to find our missing crew member."

"While the captain's authority is paramount, crew members are still entitled to privacy. Did you authorize

Mr. Connolly and others to participate in a search of crew members' quarters, and in so doing, did you confiscate personal belongings of any crew members?"

The captain hesitated and rubbed his nose before answering. "On a number of occasions, I authorized searches by Mr. Connolly, Chief Engineer Gibson, and Third Engineer Russell. In every instance, the search was for drugs and alcohol, and only drugs and alcohol were removed from the crew quarters or persons. Furthermore, in anticipation of your next question, all the drugs and alcohol that were taken was delivered to my cabin and then tossed overboard. Nothing was retained."

"That *was* my next question, Captain," eliciting a smile from the commander and a noticeable lessening of tension in the room. "Did you keep a record of what you confiscated, who did the confiscating, and under whose control it was until you jettisoned it overboard?"

"No, Commander, I didn't log any of it. The drugs stayed in my cabin for a short time until I ordered Mr. Connolly to toss it overboard."

"I have received and reviewed a copy of the U.S. Navy report on the deaths of crew members Smithfield and Punser in Apra Harbor, Guam, in which you testified. Do you have anything you wish to add to that report?"

"No, sir, except to say it's a damn shame what drugs and alcohol can do to someone to make them behave in such a terrible way."

"You confiscated a lot of drugs and alcohol from individuals' quarters and from individuals. Why are you not pressing charges against those individuals, since their behavior constituted a danger to the safety of the ship?"

Again, the captain hesitated. "In the case of alcohol, it isn't illegal to have alcohol on the ship, or in one's possession. When the behavior of a person got out of hand, I took away their alcohol. There was no reason to go beyond that." Drawing himself up, he took a deep breath and continued. "In the case of finding drugs in the quarters, everyone had at least one roommate so, absent a confession, and there weren't any confessions, there was no way to determine who was the actual owner of the drugs. As for the individuals who we found drugs on their persons, they are both dead. That is a high enough price to pay."

The commander shuffled his papers, appearing to be thrown off by the captain's answer. "My final question for you, Captain. Is there any one of your crew who you believe deserves to lose their license, either temporarily or permanently, because of their actions on this past voyage?"

The captain looked over at First Engineer Harrison, who had fidgeted and scratched continually, and then shook his head, still staring at him. "No, Commander, there's been enough suffering, and three crew members have paid the ultimate price for their actions. If anyone contributed to that tragedy, I have no proof, but I would hope it preys on their conscience for a long, long time."

The commander, moved by the captain's testimony, said, "Off the record, please." The clerk stopped the recorder and sat up from hunching over the stenotype machine. "Captain, is there anyone you would not let serve with you on another voyage?"

The captain again looked at the first engineer, then answered, "I'd rather not say, Commander."

The commander watched the first engineer bow his head while the captain responded, then said, "Back on the record. Thank you, Captain; you may stand down."

While the captain returned to his seat next to me, the commander beckoned the bailiff and whispered something. The bailiff nodded and left the hearing room.

"Mr. Connolly," the commander announced, "please take the witness stand."

I went to the stand and got sworn in by the clerk. My armpits were swimming. While the captain had made it clear I hadn't acted on my own, my future was at stake, and to say I was nervous is a huge understatement.

The commander repeated his opening statement about the purpose of the hearing, then asked, "Mr. Connolly, you too have the right to have an attorney present. Do you wish to retain one?"

"No, sir, I don't need an attorney."

He looked skeptical, and the hoses in my armpits went into high gear.

"You have a permanent Third Mate's License and a Temporary Second Mate's license, correct?"

"Yes, sir."

"How much sea time do you have?"

"A little over a year, sir."

"Don't you think the captain's asking you to carry a gun was a little extraordinary for someone with such little experience?"

Now it was my turn. The captain had stood up for me. "He's the captain. It's his job to control what happens on his ship. I had no reason to question him."

"But why you, the least experienced officer aboard?"

"That's a question for the captain, but he saw me handle myself in an awkward situation during sign-on, and he asked me if I knew how to handle a gun, so I guess that had something to do with him choosing me." I paused, seeming pensive but giving myself time to think what to say next. "Was I surprised? Yes, but there was no denying the problems with the crew we signed in Jacksonville, so I wasn't going to refuse."

"How many times did you have to use the gun?"

"Just once, sir, and I had no choice." I avoided telling him when I had drawn the gun but didn't have to shoot. "The cook was threatening the captain and other officers with a knife. I confronted him, told him to put the knife down, then he lunged at me and cut me, so I shot him."

The commander opened a file on his desk and said, "Was that Mr. Joselito Bautista?" butchering the pronunciation of his name.

"Yes, sir."

"I understand criminal charges are pending against him when he is well enough to travel."

"I don't know, sir, but he stabbed me and threatened to stab others."

"Mr. Connolly, you were on watch when Mr. Highstone fell overboard, is that correct?"

Wondering how to respond while ensuring Boats came out looking good, despite knowing what he did, I said, "I was on watch, but I'm not sure he fell overboard."

"What do you mean?"

I felt everyone in the room listening closely.

"On at least three other occasions, Highstone threatened to commit suicide by jumping overboard. The captain and the bosun each talked him down. So, I don't know if he fell, or carried out his threat to kill himself. When I looked aft and saw Boats running toward the bridge and waving his arms, yelling 'man overboard,' that's when I did the Williamson Turn, as the captain explained."

The bailiff returned and went to the commander and said something. The commander nodded.

"How many other times did the captain call upon you to keep the peace?".

"It wasn't always at the captain's direct request. Once he designated me his"—I hesitated; the word "enforcer" would sound too Mafia-like, so opted for the commander's word— "peacekeeper, when a situation presented itself, I intervened. Half a dozen times, maybe.

For example, I followed Mr. Smithfield for hours before we could tackle him and take the fire ax away. We used the mattress for that."

"Mattress?"

"Yes, sir," and I explained the mattress to him, without the shit-stain part, which caused him to shake his head and state, "You are innovative. We are going to take a short recess. Please be back here in twenty minutes."

We all stood as he left. The first engineer left the room, still scratching and twitching. Everyone else stood or stretched. I leaned over to the captain and said, "What do you think?"

"You're doing okay. Don't get too creative, you might bite yourself in the ass."

After fifteen minutes, I heard a commotion in the corridor. As I stood to go look, the commander returned, so I stayed. As he took his seat, the bailiff and two Coast Guard MPs came in from the corridor, hauling the first engineer in handcuffs.

Standing him before the commander, the bailiff said, "As you suspected, sir. We caught him shooting up in the bathroom. Heroin."

The commander shook his head. "Get him out of here. Turn him over to the NYPD, along with the evidence."

The first collapsed, and they dragged him out.

"Mr. Connolly," the commander said, "please get back on the stand."

When I sat down, he reminded me, "You are still under oath." He cleared his throat, twice, then asked, "Did you ever discover who was supplying the drugs to the crew?"

It was clear he suspected the first, from the way the captain and I had stared at him, and the first being stupid enough to get high at the hearing. But the captain had already given the first a pass. If I accused him, that would make the captain out to be a liar. Looking at the captain, I saw him give a perceptible nod.

"Yes, sir, I suspected the first engineer from things the other crew members were saying, then caught him with a stash of drugs in the engine room."

"What did you do with those drugs?"

"I turned them over to the captain, then, upon his instructions, threw them overboard, like the other drugs we found."

"The captain previously said he didn't have direct proof of any individuals, except for the two deceased crew members. Did you tell him where you got the drugs?"

This was it. Who goes off the cliff, me or the captain?

"Yes, sir. I told him I found them in the engine room. But I didn't tell him they belonged to the first engineer."

"Why not?"

"I didn't think he'd care, as long as we got rid of the drugs."

"When did you find the first engineer's drugs?"

I thought for a few seconds then responded, "The day after sailing from Sattahip. I knew he wouldn't be able to replace them until we reached home, and the trip was over. The risk to the crew disappeared when I tossed the drugs overboard." Pausing, I did my best to look contrite. "I can see now that was a bad decision on my part. I should have told the captain."

The commander nodded, "Yes, it was a bad decision. But considering all you were going through, and the fact the drugs were no longer available to the crew, I don't think it did any harm."

He shuffled his papers, then said, "That will be all, Mr. Connolly. You may step down."

The only other person called to testify was the chief engineer, and he played dumb to any probing questions, backing up my and the captain's version of the shooting incident.

When he sat down, the commander tapped the gavel once and said, "This is a sad and tragic series of events. Three seamen have lost their lives, and a fourth will undoubtedly lose his license. What is clear is that Captain Johnston and Temporary Second Mate Connolly, while forced to take extraordinary measures to ensure the safety of the crew and ship, did so in a rational and, given the circumstances, reasonable manner. I see no reason to take disciplinary action against any of the crew members here today. The first engineer will get a separate hearing on his activities. There is a possibility some of you may be called upon to testify in that hearing." He looked up and said, "This hearing is concluded. The clerk will notify the Coast Guard Operations Office that all restrictions are lifted, and the ship is free to proceed." He then banged the gavel.

We rose, the commander left, and the captain and I turned to each other.

"We both know what we got away with," he said, "and we both know we were right in doing what we did. I think the commander understands what crewing problems everyone is having, and decided accordingly." He reached out, and we shook hands.

"Good luck to you, William. I'd love to see you stay aboard the *West Way*, but I imagine you're heading in another direction."

"Thank you, Captain. I have a feeling I may be heading back to Africa."

From behind me a hand rested on my shoulder, and Greg's voice boomed: "You're a damn fool if you aren't."

I walked out of the room feeling physically free, but not entirely guilt free.

At the end of the corridor, I stepped into the phone booth, dug the phone number out of my wallet, and dialed.

The phone rang and my heart soared as I heard, "Hello?"

"Meg, it's me."

MARITIME GLOSSARY

1MC	A loud speaker communication system used on ships in the 1960's.
Abeam	Direction that is at right angles to the fore and aft line of a ship.
Able Bodied Seaman (AB)	Member of the deck department. Stands watches as a helmsman. Performs maintenance.
Bight	A loop or slack curve in a rope or wire.
Bitt	Either of a pair of posts on a ship's deck used for fastening ropes or cables, usually mooring lines.
Boatswain/Bosun/Bos'n	Highest ranking unlicensed person in the deck department of a ship. Equivalent to a Chief Petty Officer in the Navy. Usually a day worker, not a watch-stander.

Brow gangway	A short flat portable gangway used to span short distances.
Burthen / Athwartship	Interchangeable terms meaning side to side rather than fore and aft on a ship.
Captain	Person in charge of the entire ship. Highest ranking member of the crew.
Chief Engineer	Highest ranking licensed officer in the Engine Department. Usually a day worker, not a watch-stander.
Coaming	The raised edging or border around a hatch for keeping out water.
Cowl ventilator	A metal hood that provides ventilation to cargo spaces and engine rooms. It rotates in order to face into or away from the wind as weather circumstances dictate.

Deadweight Tonnage	The weight in tons of all the cargo, fuel, dry provisions, supplies, etc. carried on board the ship. Also known as "displacement tonnage" (When something floats, it "displaces" water equal to the weight of whatever is floating), It is a relatively good indicator to ship owners of how much revenue the ship may generate.
Deckie	Anyone working in the Deck Department of a ship, either Merchant Marine or Navy. A term used derogatorily by members of the Engine Department.
Fid	A conical pin or spike used in splicing rope.
Fiddley	Vertical space directly above the engine room extending up the stack.
First Engineer	Second-highest ranking licensed officer in the Engine Department.

Usually a day worker, not a watch-stander.

First Mate	Highest ranking licensed officer of the Deck Department. In charge of cargo operations and ship maintenance. Usually a day worker, not a watch-stander.
Gross Tons	The measure of the ships total interior volume. It is calculated by taking the interior volume of the ship (V) in cubic meters and multiplying it by a variable known as (K).
Hawsepipe	Opening in a ship's bow where the anchor cable passes through.
Hold	That part of a ship where cargo is stowed. The lowest level of the ship.
Jacob's Ladder	Portable ladder made of rope and/or metal primarily used to board ships.

Junior Third Engineer	Fifth-highest ranking licensed officer in the Engine Department. Stands the eight-to-twelve sea watch.
Junior Third Mate	Fourth-highest ranking licensed officer of the Deck Department. Stands the eight-to-twelve sea watch.
Notices to Mariners	A publication issued regularly by the USCG advising mariners of important matters affecting navigational safety including new hydrographic information, changes in channels and aids to navigation and other important data.
Oiler	Member of the engine department. Stands sea watches and performs maintenance.
Ordinary Seaman (Ordinary)	Member of the deck department. Stands watches as a lookout. Performs maintenance.

Pelorus	A device used in navigation for measuring the bearing of an object relative to the direction in which the ship is traveling.
Putzing	Nautical slang for polishing, usually brass fixtures.
Second Engineer	Third-highest ranking licensed officer in the Engine Department. Stands the four-to-eight sea watch.
Second Mate	Second-highest ranking licensed officer of the deck department. Responsible for the navigation of the ship. Stands the four to eight sea watch.
Snipe	Anyone working in the Engine Department of a ship. A term used derogatorily by members of the Deck Department.
Sounding tubes	Tubes extending from the main deck down into the

lowest parts of the holds
and tanks for taking
soundings (reading the
levels of liquids).

Swage fitting

A fitting compressed onto
the end of a wire. Could
be an eye or hook.

Third Engineer

Fourth-highest ranking
licensed officer in the
Engine Department.
Stands the twelve-to-four
sea watch.

Third Mate

Third-highest ranking
licensed officer in the deck
department. Stands the
twelve-to-four sea watch.

Tweendeck

That part of a ship below
the main deck and above
the hold where cargo is
stowed. There may be
upper tweendecks and
lower tweendecks
depending on the
configuration of the ship.
Each deck is separated by
a hatch cover.

Williamson Turn	A nautical maneuver created for the purpose of turning a ship one-hundred and eighty degrees and have it end up exactly where it started the turn. Devised for rescue in a man-overboard situation.
Wiper	Member of the Engine Department. Stands sea watches and performs maintenance.
W T Door	A watertight door especially designed for ships.

AUTHOR'S NOTE

Thanks to all of you who have read and enjoyed this and my other books. My entire life has been oriented towards maritime activities, providing me boundless stories and memories, which gives me the opportunity to weave them into coming of age adventure novels for your enjoyment.

I would greatly appreciate you taking the time to write and post a review. In today's book world, reviews are critical to authors. Reviews help other readers who may consider reading my books and also play a role in how Amazon, Goodreads and other outlets present and promote books.

The review can be any length. It doesn't have to be a literary masterpiece, simply say what you enjoyed about the story. "Great read. Loved the book!" will suffice. Read the existing reviews for ideas.

I would love to hear from you on this or any of my books. You can contact me at the addresses below:

Website: http://www.walterfcurran.com
Email: walter@walterfcurran.com

Amazon Authorpage;
www.amazon.com/author/walterfcurran

If you do write a review, please email me and let me know and I will respond to thank you.

To post a review, use the following guidelines.

AMAZON

Type in my facebook author page www.amazon.com/author/walterfcurran.

Click on the book you wish to write a review about. When it appears, near the top of the screen you will see five stars and the words "customer reviews."

Click on "customer reviews" and a box appears "Write a customer review."

Click on that box then **Click** on the number of stars you wish to rate the book. A box appears in which you can write the actual review. After you write, it will prompt you to write a short header.

GOODREADS

On google search for GOODREADS.COM.
When it opens, find the "search books" link and **type** in the name of the book.

When the book screen opens, **click** on the "want to read/read" window under the book cover and then **click** "read" and a window opens in which you can write a review.

After you write the review, at the bottom of the page are two checkboxes, "Facebook" and "Twitter." **Check** Facebook and/or twitter if you use them, then **check** "save" on the review.

My book titles:

Young Mariner-Novel
On to Africa-Novel
Bombs Aweigh-On to Vietnam-Novel
Slices of Life-Cerebral spasms of the soul-Poetry

Walter F. Curran is a retired maritime executive living in Ocean View, DE with his wife. He has sailed on merchant ships and worked on and around the docks in Boston, Philadelphia, Baltimore, Jacksonville and San Juan, Puerto Rico. A member of the Rehoboth Beach Writer's Guild, the Eastern Shore Writer's Association and Maryland Writer's Association, in addition to "Bombs Aweigh-On to Vietnam" he has published "Young Mariner" and "On to Africa" the first two of the Young Mariner series.

He has also published a book of poetry, "Slices of life-Cerebral spasms of the soul."

When not writing, he does maritime consulting, plays golf and is the Mayor of Ocean View, DE.

Readers may contact Walt via his website http://www.walterfcurran.com or his Amazon Authorpage http://www.amazon.com/author/walterfcurran

Made in the USA
Middletown, DE
04 July 2019